MEMORY HUNTERS

ALSO BY TONY MOYLE

'The Circuit' Series
MEMORY CLOUDS
MEMORY HUNTERS

'Ally Oldfield' Series
THE END OF THE WORLD IS NIGH
LAST OF THE MOUNTAIN MEN

'How to Survive the Afterlife' Series
THE LIMPET SYNDROME
SOUL CATCHERS
DEAD ENDS

MEMORY HUNTERS

THE CIRCUIT BOOK 2

TONY MOYLE

LIMBO PUBLISHING

First published: Nov 2020

ISBN - 9798564425117

Limbo Publishing, a brand of In-Sell Ltd

www.tonymoyle.com

Cover design by Damonza

In Memory of…

Nita Brown, Alan Parker and Ian Evans.

"There are only two days in the year that nothing can be done. One is called yesterday and the other is called tomorrow. Today is the right day to love, believe, do and mostly live."

Dalai Lama

WELCOME TO THE REALM...

ONE

THE PROCLAMATION OF DISTRUST

The carbon rods were the world's respirator. Wherever humans congregated in large urban areas, from Santiago to Sofia, Cardiff to Cairo and everywhere in between, they were always there. Sometimes organised in vast plantations that stretched as far as the eye could see, sometimes in small, neat clusters like a niche craft beer trying to compete with a global behemoth. The bigger the size of the estate, the greater the number of individual rods. In North Africa the rods were a hundred metres tall and had trunks thicker than giant redwoods. Whether large, small, tall or short, the rods served the same purpose.

To help humans to breathe.

In the year twenty fifty-four carbon rods were more important than trees, mostly because they outnumbered them many times over. When they were smaller, Jake and Tyra Montana challenged each other to see who spotted one first during family outings. They both pronounced themselves the winner when the first one came into view, often within minutes of leaving home. Unless you lived in the middle of a city with looming skyscrapers and coverage of thick smog, they were easy to spot because they dwarfed other structures.

Like the wind turbines that preceded them at the end of the last century they weren't universally popular, at least not to begin with. Homeowners who lived nearby complained that the farms were an eyesore which devalued their properties and disrupted their everyday life. Most dropped their opposition when they were told it was either accept the carbon rods or take up a new hobby of holding your breath for sustained periods of time. A couple of days should do it. Even with these threats a small portion of the community continued to protest. Their concerns remained until the Circuit sent the utility drones around and they experienced a miraculous change in attitude.

Like most of life's challenges, change always felt worse before it occurred. More often than not, people's anxieties evaporated when they realised it wasn't as bad as they first imagined. Fifteen years after their introduction most people barely noticed the carbon rods were even there, no more noteworthy than seeing a real tree. Look, it's a tree! How many people walked around excitedly pointing one of those out? Unless of course you happened to be a dendrologist or a three-year-old, not very many. Humans eventually became blind to the beautiful and unapprecia-tive of the ordinary. The Memory Cloud didn't make it any better. It soon distracted people from their real-life concerns by dragging them back into the safety of the virtual world.

There were thirty-two carbon rods that extended out of the soil in this particular field. She knew because she'd counted them many times before. Shiny, dormant cylin-ders, at least three times taller than her own height, standing to attention about a metre or so apart from each other. They were active day and night but the only evidence was the gentle hum from the base. If you lay flat on your back, on one of the rare sunny days, sometimes you could see the oxygen gas seeping out like haze, distorting any objects that lay in the background. This was where Tyra always came when she wanted to hide from the grim reality of her life. It wasn't a particularly safe place to hide. Their importance in sustaining life, and the health risks associated with anyone lingering there too long, meant the carbon rod farms were under constant surveillance.

Which was partly why Tyra came here. If you avoided the attention of the estate's employees and their guard dogs it was a good place to get high.

Tyra lay back on the grass and watched the dense clouds suffocate the night sky. Her jet black-dyed hair blended in perfectly with her jacket, torn denim trousers and clumpy boots. Not even the eagle-eyed rod farmers would spot her dressed like this, although they weren't the only ones watching. Dark clothing and the cover of night wouldn't keep her hidden from the Circuit. They'd spot her eventually. How quickly it took was dependent on two factors: how busy the Memory Hunters were at the moment and whether anyone had reported her missing. Only one person would. The only person left in her life. But even then she knew from experience that the hunters always sent a warning message to move on before they lost patience and issued a formal violation.

She really couldn't afford any more of those this year.

Tonight she'd managed to escape the Memory Hunters' attention for an hour, more than enough time for the oxygen-rich air to sufficiently adapt to her mood. Scientists and teachers had warned her that it wasn't wise to remain amongst the rods for longer because an overexposure to pure oxygen had long-lasting effects on health and had proven to be fatal in rare cases. She didn't care very much what other people thought or said these days. The oxygen had rejuvenating properties and that's all that mattered. It wasn't the only way she abused chemicals to enhance her outlook, but it certainly was the cheapest.

Recreational drugs had all but disappeared since the Circuit rose to dominance in the West some forty years ago. While the use of medicinal drugs had increased exponentially, most of them controlled and regulated by the very same organisation, other less accepted forms of stimulation weren't tolerated. Most drugs weren't of much interest to Tyra anyway. Smoking dope was about the limit for her, not that she enjoyed the taste very much. It wasn't really about how the drug affected her, it was more about rebellion. In a strict totalitarian world where your every action was scrutinised, determined and controlled, doing the opposite was the only way to express individuality. Whether the rules came from her grandfather, her teachers or the system, she strived to break them at every opportunity. Avoiding the Circuit's rules was the most challenging form of rebellion and required both skill and a surplus of bravery. Smoking dope was an easy way to do so without getting a violation.

The Circuit saw everything, heard everything and knew everything, but crucially they couldn't smell everything. The hunters might break into her memories and witness her smoking a thin cigarette, but as long as she imagined it was just a normal roll-up then that memory would be logged in her cloud. The Circuit couldn't prove otherwise unless she got caught in the act. Generally fourteen-year-olds weren't under the microscope the way adults were anyway, so she'd decided to smoke grass while the sun didn't shine. The biggest problem was supply. Tricking the Circuit by imagining a lie was one thing, but receiving a package from a dodgy dealer was a much harder memory to forge.

That's why she came here instead.

Like most fourteen-year-olds, Tyra's ability to manipulate the Memory Cloud bordered on genius. There was nothing she couldn't do in the virtual world and it certainly beat spending time in the real one. In the last few months she'd lost interest in engaging with what other people called life. Her parents had been extradited to the Source and even with her exceptional talents they were beyond her reach. After their convictions her grandfather had been granted custody over her welfare. They disagreed intensely about what this meant. She certainly didn't feel well and the world under his rules was anything but fair. He didn't understand what she was going through – how could he? He rarely spent any time in his own cloud and had no appreciation for how hard life was for someone her age. Unlike her parents' relatively light-touch parenting, his authoritarian rules were almost as oppressive as the Circuit's. Life sucked. She had no parents, no freedom, too many rules and no one's empathy.

These were all minor considerations in the context of Tyra's annoyance at the world.

The biggest factor was Jake.

All of life's pain and misery was his fault.

If he'd been more compliant and less selfish none of the disasters that affected her would have happened. Until recently she'd always followed the rules and where had that got her? Nowhere, that's where. In contrast, Jake always got his own way whether he followed them or not. In her opinion older siblings always did. Not anymore. She was doing things her own way from now on. But that change of attitude wouldn't be enough to heal her wounds. The agonising hurt she'd been subjected to because of his selfish behaviour would be a permanent scar until Jake repented or she forced him to.

A memory seeped into her cloud feed and obscured the view of the broody, dark skies above her. It appeared automatically without her needing to search for it. Past memories would often launch like this when the hormones surging through her body interacted with her Memory Cloud like two separated strands of DNA combining as one. Tyra was a third-generation implant wearer whose physiology had developed so it no longer felt like they wore the technology, rather that the devices were entrenched organs no less crucial than the lungs or kidneys.

This particular memory happened about six months ago. She knew that because she replayed it regularly. It was one of those rare days when the sun was uninhibited by clouds and its rays basked their small backyard in glorious autumnal warmth. In the real world it was almost nine o'clock in the evening, but the projected memory consumed the vista of the carbon rod farm and placed her in the middle of the afternoon sun, triggering all the sense that went with it. The warmth spread across her skin, birds chirped joyfully in the hedge and the smell of burning charcoal wafted up her nostrils. Then the other actors in the memory broke her tranquillity.

"He's late," announced Deborah with an uncomfortable balance of annoyance and concern.

"He'll be alright," replied Kyle, feeling rather more relaxed about it. "The world's a safe place."

"Safe but sinister," added Paddy grumpily. "A hundred years ago people used to leave their doors unlocked all day. I don't see you doing that very often, Kyle!"

Although Paddy was right, it wasn't a great argument. A hundred years ago most people didn't own anything worth stealing, and what they did was so massive potential burglars had to weigh up the risks of giving themselves a hernia in return for stealing a radio the size of a small car.

Kyle ignored his father-in-law, something he did routinely.

"It's not just about safety," said Deborah. "A promise is a promise."

"He probably just got caught up in his own bubble, that's all. You know what he's like when he's with Christie, everything else seems to lose focus. Give the lad a break," replied Kyle.

"You never give me a break," huffed Tyra from the other side of the table's rotating hotplate. A robotic arm was constantly darting in and out to adjust the position of the sausages and chicken squares so they were perfectly cooked on every side.

"You're fourteen," snapped Kyle. "Different rules."

"Why?"

"I just said, because you're younger."

"It's not about age," she argued. "It's favouritism."

"One more word out of you, Tyra, and I'll be forced to restrict your access."

Tyra knew what that meant. It was the only parenting tactic that worked on her. The fear of losing some of her Memory Cloud's functionality quickly reduced her urge to argue.

"Send him a notification," said Kyle. "If you're really worried."

"I've sent him three. He's not replied to any of them and the last time I looked his proximity sensor indicated he was on the beach."

"There you go, then, he's safe," said Paddy. "The poor lad can't even get up to some harmless hanky-panky without someone watching him. I think it's disgusting you're always spying on him. Wouldn't have happened in my day. I was always sneaking around behind bike sheds or down in the woods with my girlfriends to see how many bases I could manage!"

Tyra gagged and immediately placed the memory in quarantine along with other toxic remarks she'd heard from Paddy down the years.

"I asked him to be back by now and he doesn't respect my wishes," added Deborah. "I bet he's never late when he's meeting Christie."

"That's because he's in love!" said Paddy, slamming his fists down on the table and displacing a chicken square. The robotic BBQ arm tried desperately to retrieve it from the ground but it just didn't have the reach. After several attempts and aware that no one seemed bothered, it returned to the ones still on the grill.

Jake strolled casually around the side gate, leaving it open to sway in the wind and clang against the frame as he always did to the annoyance of his parents.

"What have you got to say for yourself?" huffed Deborah angrily.

Jake looked a little confused. What had he done this time? Instantly he rewound his memories from the last few hours to double-check the evidence before inadvertently making it worse with some ill-judged or defensive remark. Nope, looked like a clean bill of health as far as he was concerned. They were just being parents, it's what they did. They didn't need a reason to be annoyed, it was just natural in adults after experiencing childbirth. Maybe they were just deflecting another marital disagreement because he was an easy target.

"I'm not sure what you mean?"

"You promised me you'd be back by two o'clock!"

Jake checked the clock in his cloud feed. "I'm only fifteen minutes late!"

"But you're still late," Tyra chimed in.

"Stay out of this please," added Kyle.

"It's the principle," said Deborah.

"What's the problem? Christie and I found a lost dog so we had to take a detour to return it to its owner."

"Rubbish!" blurted Tyra.

"Check if you like," said Jake with a smirk, pelting Tyra's feed with a virtual pack of dogs that snapped and snarled viciously until she dispatched them without moving.

"Give him a break, Deborah," replied Paddy with an assertive tone and a look that suggested there was an unspoken understanding between them.

Deborah's demeanour transformed. Her scowl evaporated to be replaced by an expression of personal guilt. She had to lighten up. She couldn't keep him on a leash forever. One day he'd have to survive on his own without her protection. It wouldn't be that long. His Ascension Day was only months away, and when it arrived she'd have no control over his actions.

"That was a kind thing to do," said Deborah, having checked Jake's story through her connection with his feed. "I'm sorry, I just worry about you."

"What?!" whined Tyra. "That's not fair. He broke the rules AGAIN and you're letting him off scot-free?!"

"That's it. I'm removing cloud privileges," said Kyle angrily.

The memory faded from view and was replaced by a menagerie of other stimuli. Tyra was well equipped to deal with multiple sources in her cloud feed at the same time. She'd often be watching a movie in one corner, be on-cloud shopping in another, while chatting with several friends simultaneously. Even then she still had the band-

width to engage with a string of adverts and announcements without the slightest sign of distraction.

The faded memory was one of a string of repeats she'd
replayed over the past few weeks. Every one of them had
the same outcome. Jake broke the rules and she got
punished for pointing it out. Yet on the rare occasions
when she stepped out of line it had resulted in a reprimand
that was always longer and more severe than his. She'd put
up with it for years in the hope that when Jake's Ascension
Day finally arrived her relationship with her parents might
improve. She'd receive the approval and attention that he'd
monopolised for most of her life. Then in one final act of
brotherly cruelty he'd even taken that away from her. She
didn't blame her parents for the way they constantly
admonished Jake, she blamed him for exploiting their blind
spot.

An alert entered her feed and killed all other inputs.

The euphoria from the oxygen gas in her lungs clashed
as a different hormone washed through her body. It was
adrenaline but it was dispelled almost as quickly as it
arrived. The hunters hadn't located her position as her
initial reaction had suggested. The alert was merely to
notify her that the 'Proclamation of Distrust' was about to
begin. The Circuit's primary announcement now played
out daily, and while it was on nothing else in the cloud
worked. It was compulsory viewing for all and she knew its
contents by heart.

"Danger!" she mimicked dramatically, anticipating the
opening line. "The people of the East are the greatest
threat to peace and harmony. They will stop at nothing to
destroy our way of life! See for yourself."

Tyra closed her eyes and visualised the scenes that
would follow the opening statement. For fourteen years the
same message had been broadcast every other day. Like an

irritating ear worm that gets stuck in your head, the Circuit's message was hard to shift. The 'Proclamation of Distrust' always featured the same unnamed city where shops and buildings were boarded up with sheets of plywood and the streets were swamped by litter and filth. Shabby-looking citizens of all ages stumbled around like hunchbacks wrapped in sackcloth garments and wearing dirty, loose-fitting shoes. Violent squabbles broke out over nothing more than a stranger's glance or the discovery of a discarded credit under a pile of rubbish.

Then the camera zoomed in on their angry, warped faces or highlighted their vicious, primitive weapons which they used against each other with a complete disregard for life. In the centre of a market square that no longer served as a place of retail therapy a poor-quality representation of the Circuit logo had been daubed on a crumbling, blood-stained wall. Men, women and children paid a daily visit to attack or spit or urinate on it in a symbolic act of almost religious-level hatred for those that lived under its protection.

Rarely did anyone in the West question the validity of this desecration. Most had passive brain chemistry and struggled to reasonably decipher between what was in the real world and what was in the virtual one. Passive minds had nothing to do with your importance factor either. It didn't matter if you were vital or superfluous: if your brain was passive you believed everything the Circuit showed you. If you were one of the rare few in the population who demonstrated active brain function then you might just question it, even if you kept those doubts to yourself. There was one simple question those people in particular might have considered more than once: how were these scenes of barbarism being filmed if no one from the West was allowed in the East?

Tyra had never been subjected to the pain and disorientation that accompanied an upgrade. Her implants were the same ones she'd received when she was three months old. Jake's had been changed almost as many times as she'd had birthdays. Another factor that marked him as different and redirected attention away from her like a suction pump. She didn't know what the significance of it was, and like ninety percent of people didn't have the desire to challenge it either. That was just how passive brains worked. Her daydreaming was abruptly cut off by a clock counting down from five to signal the start of tonight's announcement.

"Danger! Jake Montana is the greatest threat to peace and harmony. He will stop at nothing to destroy our way of life."

Tyra couldn't believe her ears. Was there no safe place to escape the spectre of her brother? At no point in her short life had the 'Proclamation of Distrust' changed and now he was right in the middle of it. Why was he there at all? Was he so keen to show the world he was better than her? She tried to focus on the message in case it was a one-off and she missed the detail.

"The people of the East are no longer a threat," announced the narrator whose voice was the same as it always was.

No one knew who he was, but he had an unmistakeable voice that was gruff yet assertive. Tyra imagined it was how you'd speak if you'd taken elocution lessons at an expensive university. Every word was delivered with precision, every inflection placed to have the maximum effect on the listener. If the broadcast was aimed at highlighting whom you shouldn't trust, the voice offered an essential balance. Everyone trusted what he said.

"The Circuit has discovered indisputable evidence of a

truth that we have long warned you about. The East have been preparing a massive and sophisticated campaign of terror to overthrow us. To keep you safe we have launched a pre-emptive strike. See for yourself."

As it always did, the broadcast switched perspectives to show life on the ground in the East. The derelict buildings, the grime, the litter and the feral inhabitants still featured prominently, but there was something else, too. A dark swarm of gigantic, black drones whizzed around the sky over their heads. Hundreds of bombs fell from their fuselages, exploding spectacularly as they struck the ground. In the unlikely scenario that anyone in the city had survived the first bombardment, the drones fired further blasts from their cannons. As the graphic next picture proved, they hadn't needed to. For Tyra the horrifying scene of death was no more real than an action movie or gory video game, and it had little effect on her. It was hard to appreciate the reality of something this catastrophic when nothing like it had happened in her lifetime.

It might have had more impact if she'd known these scenes were happening in the West, but they weren't. The people of the East weren't real people in any true sense of the word, and watching their deaths was no more traumatic than killing an angry wasp. They deserved it. It was punishment for harbouring anger towards the Circuit's way of life. They'd have done it to the West given half a chance, she thought.

"The Circuit will not rest," added the narrator, "until the East is crushed and never again threatens our values of freedom, equality and openness. But it will take time to eradicate the enemy completely. Subscribers must be patient and continue to unite in protection of the Circuit from dangers both external and internal. Now we must be wary of a different threat."

A videograph of Jake appeared in the projection. Tyra enjoyed watching it less than the death and destruction of the previous scene. She felt almost embarrassed, as if her own genetic links were partially responsible for his treachery.

"This is Jake Montana. He is a virus and we must find a cure. Montana has stolen intelligence from the Principal Conductor and is preparing to sell it to the East. This information may turn the balance of the war against us."

Even though it would be obvious to anyone of sound mind that the East was being pulverised and totally outgunned, it never occurred to Tyra that this statement wasn't wholly genuine.

"Jake Montana has discarded his Memory Cloud and can no longer be tracked. The Spectrum have always been a terrifying blot on our society, but be under no doubt: Montana is more dangerous than a hundred of them. He must be stopped! He must be terminated. You can do your part. The Principal Conductor is offering a bounty of one billion credits, permanent elevation to a vital importance factor and immunity from prosecution for life to anyone who successfully executes this order. There is no safe place from the virus. He has the ability to infiltrate your cloud and steal or adjust your memories. Be wary, be alert, be vigilant and be brave. The Circuit. It's a state of mind."

The proclamation ended as it always did, the motto and logo lingering against the black background for thirty or forty seconds. It was more than enough time for Tyra to consider the repercussions. She hated her brother, but did she want him dead? Not especially. She wanted to humiliate him and that was much harder to pull off if he was dead. Did she want a billion credits? No, not if she had to murder someone. There were more important things to fight over than credits. Did she want to be vital? Absolutely.

Who didn't? It made you untouchable, above reproach. What's more, it would be the ultimate vindication of Jake's inferiority. If she was vital and he was superfluous there could be no doubt who the winner was.

The logo melted into the black background, but it wasn't replaced by the previous applications open before it hijacked her feed. Instead a single luminous, green cursor throbbed ominously in the centre of the darkness.

Hello, Tyra...

TWO

THE FIREWALL

The fibreglass hull of the little white dinghy glided gently across the Baltic Sea, never more than a few hundred metres from the shoreline, ever present on the port side since he left Malmö Marina. To the helmsman's relief Storm Season had recently moved aside to let Solar Summer have a turn. The new season was working tirelessly to put the world back the way it was the last time it had custody. Its arrival had done nothing to affect the overpowering nature of the malignant cloud cover that dominated the heavens. A murky, yellow barrier that pressed down on the lower atmosphere, hell-bent on suffocating both land and sea. It would take more than the resurgent sun of Solar Summer to shift them. Along with humanity's knee-jerk intervention its rays had made the clouds possible.

In twenty fifty-four, clouds were a permanent feature of the world in more ways than one. But one particular cloud had recently evaporated and been replaced with blissful, untarnished clarity.

It was the one inside the man on the boat.

A light breeze ruffled the dinghy's sail and pushed the hull gently through the waves. Its current progress was more than fast enough. He knew a time would come when haste was needed, but for now he had to balance speed of movement with speed of thought. There was still much to figure out before he plunged into the unknown. The sunlight behind the oppressive clouds was dwindling and making it harder for him to pick out the shoreline. Instinctively he reached for the virtual world of the Memory Cloud to check the time. He stopped himself. Some habits were hard to break. He lifted his arm instead to consult his antique wristwatch. Its delicate ticking was the only man-made sound for miles, but that wasn't the only reason it offered him comfort. Its fragile leather strap and scratched glass face represented a connection to the person who'd given it to him, one of the last reminders of his relationship with Christie Tucci. The hands on the clock face confirmed it was time for a change of course.

Jake let the sail out to catch more of the wind. The fabric bulged and the dinghy surged forward and further from the land. When the moment felt right he released the mainsheet slightly, moved the direction of the tiller by ninety degrees, ducked under the boom as it raced to the port side, and effortlessly switched his position to the other side of the boat. The sail flapped uncontrollably as it struck the eye of the wind before bulging outwards and dragging the boat through the water in the direction of the shore. After conducting half a dozen of these zigzag manoeuvres the vessel glided into shallower, calmer waters. There were no jetties or ports on this shore. If any once existed they were certainly further out to sea and some distance below the waterline.

The world's coasts had experienced a dramatic change over the last decade to the extent where no ship's captain or cartographer had any right to call themselves experts. Any geology lower than fifty metres had succumbed to the oceans' relentless rise. Where the land held back its advance the war of water and soil further eroded the shorelines, forcing them inland to form new beaches or crumbling cliff edges. One stretch of virgin beach was the subject of Jake's attention.

Several metres away from the welcoming bronze sand the hull scraped along an underwater bank and the dinghy came to a halt. Jake grabbed a metal pole and a coil of rope from the deck and jumped into the surf. The cold waves splashed up to his waist and he offered an involuntary noise that no one heard. He waded slowly towards the shore, pulling the rope attached to the bow. His feet squelched through shifting wet sands for the first time in days and the boat became heavier as it scraped along the beach. When the boat was out of reach of the high tide he pushed the metal spike into the ground and tied the rope to a hoop at the top. Jake returned to the stricken boat to retrieve a rucksack and a rubber mallet which he used to secure the metal pile and mitigate the chance the boat might drift away in the night.

Now he had to work out where he was.

Location and time were two concepts of physics that the general public largely took for granted. In the last sixty years permanent reminders of both were never far away. At the turn of the last century an epidemic of mobile phone use meant it was literally impossible to be late or lost ever again. The magic didn't work on everyone. Back then technology could tell you, but it certainly couldn't make you. Not so now. The Memory Cloud had annexed responsibility for time and motion for ninety-nine percent of the population. Only a tiny minority weren't connected to it and he was adjusting to being one of them.

His original Memory Cloud, the one that contained eighteen years of his memories, emotions and experiences, lay dormant in a vast server farm in an unknown location, where one day he hoped to be reunited with it. What he carried in its place was very different. His new implants permitted him free access to every cloud other than his own, an ability that was a blessing and a curse. Although it granted him the rare ability to see and understand what others were thinking of doing it also meant his virtual movements might be traced by undesirables. The Memory Hunters would be on the prowl, eager to find any clues that might identify his whereabouts.

Good luck to them. Even he didn't know.

He'd used the cloud a few times to get this far. Getting from Boston to Malmö would have been impossible without virtual assistance. Fares for Hyperloops were astronomical so he'd infiltrated a few affluent vital subscribers to help him pay the costs. He didn't feel particularly guilty about it. Manipulating the rich and powerful was justifiable given the circumstances. They were so rich they probably wouldn't even notice. They did. Ten million credits is hardly loose change, even these days. It wasn't the only occasion he'd 'borrowed' something in the last few weeks. Purchasing the dinghy and learning how to sail would have been impossible without the vast wealth and experience that existed inside other people's clouds. On its own, though, that wasn't enough. Mastering how to do something wasn't achieved by simply accessing knowledge, skills had to be honed over years of experience and dedicated practice.

He didn't really have time for that.

Jake Montana's existence officially started eighteen years and four months ago, yet the sum of his life experiences and associated memories were less than a month old. Other than a brief summary provided by Dr Drew shortly after his last implant surgery, everything he'd been, knew or felt no longer existed inside him. Any skills he was proficient in at the time were no longer accessible.

Fortunately, memories are not only found in the mind.

They also exist in muscles.

It was a good job they were otherwise he'd have capsized, drowned or sunk by now. That didn't mean the transition was easy. It had taken a few nerve-racking days to fully remember what his muscles were supposed to be doing.

Day one was the steepest part of his learning curve. Jake couldn't really explain why he'd opted to travel by boat other than a deep instinct that suggested it was the right thing to do. Which wasn't the same as knowing what to do. Luckily there weren't many other vessels out at sea on the day he left Malmö Marina in a less than conventional fashion. Quite a crowd assembled on the dockside, though. Haggard old sea dogs in tatty woollen jumpers that reeked of fish mingled on the stone wall of the marina to mock his talents like a hastily selected judging panel. Rich powerboat owners dressed from head to toe in over-expensive brand logos laughed and pointed as he struggled to guide the small craft between the reinforced walls of the port.

The calm of the sheltered marina was exchanged for the untamed ferocity of the open seas. It cruelly buffeted the poorly sailed boat, threatening to capsize it on more than one occasion. Every time he neared the critical failure point his muscles flexed and leapt to his rescue: pulling in or letting out the mainsheet, adjusting the rudder or moving his body position to balance the weight. Before he'd set out Jake had no affinity for the sea, but by the end of an exhausting first day he was completely in love with it. Two weeks on and he'd navigated his way around the south and east coasts of Sweden with nothing more than an old compass and some rather outdated laminated maps. So outdated in fact that most of the land no longer existed. He'd used his senses to work out everything else on the voyage. Circuit subscribers bragged that they could see whatever they wanted whenever they wanted, but it was no substitute for using your eyes.

Jake slung his backpack over his shoulders and scanned the landscape to identify a safe route to higher ground. The beach climbed steeply until it was severed by a river that ran down a deep valley. Dense pine forests packed either bank like a bustling crowd at an open-air music festival. By the looks of it the ascent levelled off a few hundred metres up. From there Jake hoped the panoramic view might help him establish his bearings for the next leg of his journey.

After spending an hour fighting through the claustrophobic pine trees he clambered out of the forest and up to the top of the hill. Night-time had beaten him to it. The view and confirmation of his position would have to wait until morning. He returned to the tree line to set up camp. He'd secured a limited amount of supplies before leaving port but they'd only last so long. Soon he'd need to replenish them and that meant finding civilisation and other people. People who might be looking for him. On the edge of the forest, Jake fixed his hammock between the trees and constructed a small fire a little distance away. He threw himself into his hammock and it rocked back and forward like a craddle. The stars were hidden by the cloud, which was a shame, because without the polluting effects of man-made bulbs this would have been the perfect place to see them. To make up for it he held up his own star. A gold chain with a heart-shaped pendant that swung gently to and fro in the air.

Three weeks had passed since his confrontation with Alison at the Source, but by his reckoning it was less than a week before the date etched on the back of the necklace's pendant arrived. The date of Christie Tucci's Ascension Eve. He wondered if it would go the way he'd planned it, or whether Alison had deceived him once more. Only time would tell. He was in no position to seek Christie out, not until he'd learnt the truth about the secrets he carried within him. If her love was true, she would find him whatever happened next week. He closed his eyes and tried to encourage his empty brain to conjure the moment in his imagination. It couldn't and before long his energy gave up and he slipped into sleep.

Jake rose shortly after sunrise, not that the Sun was visible behind the clouds. He always got up early these days but he didn't know why. So many of his past habits were concealed from him. He knew from Drew's briefing that he'd spent a period in an Archivist training camp on Bornholm less than two months ago, and he wondered if that had any influence on his sleep patterns. Or perhaps his eagerness was simply an unconscious urgency to reach his final destination. He packed away his meagre possessions and hiked the short distance to the brow of the hill. His crude and ancient navigational aids had indicated he was close, but only one sight would prove it definitively. Surely a city that size wouldn't be hard to miss?

There it was at the bottom of the valley, at least what was left of it.

Stockholm.

When the first buildings were constructed hundreds of years ago it was a perfectly logical place for them. It made sense that civilisations flourished the closer they were to vital resources, more often than not near rivers that supplied both food and transport. Often cities were also near the sea to ensure both defence and offence could be mustered at speed should a neighbouring nation get too big for their boots. Almost every historically important city in the world was next to water. Why wouldn't they be? It was much easier to build them there. The great churches, palaces and monuments their ancestors were inspired to build were only feasible because barges of timber, stone and ore could be ferried down the rivers and unloaded right next to the site. Try replicating that on top of a mountain. All the peasants would be knackered. Horses would die by the thousands, and materials would accidentally roll back downhill. The whole process would take forever. It's not such an easy choice if your home country happens to be Bolivia or Switzerland, mind.

Those countries were smiling now, though.

In the last decade every major coastal city was completely or partially underwater. Most of London, Barcelona, Helsinki, Copenhagen, Amsterdam and New York, to name just a few. Even parts of Jake's beloved Boston were no longer accessible and most of the city had to be relocated. Millions of people had been displaced by the floods and new versions of these renowned cities were being built on higher ground.

Stockholm was no different.

At the bottom of the hill the sea had reclaimed much of what used to be land. Here and there an island was visible, and in the centre of the ocean the tops of tall towers and church steeples, once part of Stockholm's iconic skyline, acted as marker posts for sailing ships. On the other side, where the land rose up once again, Jake could just make out the town of New Stockholm. Thousands of prefabricated huts with distinctive multicoloured roofs, like pieces of an unrecognisable mosaic, stood defiantly across the bay. These were the temporary homes for Stockholm's refugees who waited patiently for the rest of the new city to be finished. In Jake's opinion it wasn't much higher than the original one. Like their ancestors who'd refused to build on a hill, the current town planners were hoping the worst of the sea's rise was over.

The sorry sight of subaquatic Stockholm was exactly what he had been looking for. It proved he was in the right place. To his east was Finland, or at least what was left of it. One hundred miles of the sea stretched to his right and somewhere in the middle of it was the fabled firewall. The final frontier of the West and the door to the East.

On that side there might be nothing left.

A few days into his voyage, Jake sailed past the island of Bornholm. He no longer remembered much about the time he'd spent there, but he'd been told enough by Dr Drew and latterly Sam Goldberg. The most important information related to what the Circuit had been secretly building there. An army of lethal war drones. Sophisticated machines capable of killing thousands of people in minutes. At the time only Dinah witnessed the truth, but his voyage verified it for himself.

When his dinghy made the passage around the island a number of huge container ships were floating in the sky. They were unlike any vehicle he'd ever seen. As they crept eastward over his boat their suffocating, ominous shadows shrouded the sea in darkness and created the impression of a solar eclipse. Jet black, huge and cone-shaped, they were powered by huge jet engines at the rear and were kept in the air by several more pointing vertically down from the fuselage. As he rounded the north side of the island a massive hole had been blasted out of the cliffside to allow them a smooth exit from the cave systems that he'd been told existed in the guts of the island.

That was at least a week ago. By now they'd have reached the East, unloaded their cargo and released the war drones on the unsuspecting inhabitants. There wasn't a lot he could do about it. What good was one man against advanced technology like that? None at all. But what he carried inside him might. He believed it was the key to stopping the drones and the rest of the Circuit, if only he knew what to do with it. He only had one plan; find Dinah. Not the one who'd been his guide following his Ascension Eve: she was a lovable nut job but unlikely to be the saviour of mankind. The Dinah he needed had a connection to Aaron Circo, the man whose memories he'd carried in his implant since he was three months old. To find her he had to venture into the East, which meant he had to cross the firewall.

That leg of Jake's journey was likely to be the most challenging. It not only involved crossing a vast sea of open water far from the safety of the nearby shoreline, but also meant crossing an invisible barrier protected by unknown threats designed to resist such attempts. At least crossing the firewall by sea reduced the chances he'd be spotted by the sentry posts that were rumoured to be stationed periodically along the length of barrier. What he'd face instead would only be clear when he reached it. But he had to reach it, and he had to do so soon. Geographically the East was at least as vast as, if not bigger than, the West, and it would take the drones a considerable time to destroy all of it. Unless the Circuit had sent drones from other locations.

Every day of delay meant more suffering.

Jake hiked back through the forest and down to the beach, stopping only to fill up his water bottles from the mountain's cold stream. The tide was high and the dinghy bobbed gently in the water of the cove. Jake removed the pile that had stopped it drifting away before wading, then swimming to the boat. As dinghies went, his was pretty basic. About three metres long with one mainsail and no cabin, leaving him totally exposed to the elements. It wasn't the ideal vessel for crossing a lake, let alone to traverse the sea, but it had the advantage of being easy to sail and easy to miss. It would take three or four days to cross to Finland, so for now he'd have to grin and bear it and pray it didn't rain. He checked the compass one final time, unfurled the craft's sail and watched as the hull slowly floated away from the beach and into an unpredictable future.

The biggest challenge of the firewall was that you couldn't see it. Like the monsters that lived under your bed when you were a child, the danger felt real even if there was little evidence to suggest it existed. Jake believed the firewall was real, but as no one had reportedly crossed it before, his nerves still jangled like a hippy dream catcher. His only option was to point the boat in the right direction and see what happened. Which was easier said than done when navigation relied on equipment that would have been futuristic in the fifteenth century.

All he knew with any confidence was that night had arrived twice since he'd launched from the Swedish side of the ocean. By his calculations, based on his previous pace, the voyage across the Baltic Sea would take three days, four if the tides turned against him. Progress so far had been good and, although he couldn't ascertain exact speed or distance, nothing untoward had impeded him. The wind had been obediently consistent and the sea remained relatively calm. The compass was still pointing him East, as it had done since his departure, so unless it was broken he was going the right way.

If his various assumptions were anywhere near correct then he was roughly halfway across, which suggested the firewall was close. If he was lucky he'd pass over it without even being aware, and the Circuit would be none the wiser. Normally they knew everyone's position at any time and he imagined that anyone in close proximity to the firewall would receive a warning via a cloud feed alert. That was no longer possible for him. The only way they'd know he was here at all was if someone saw him. Jake scanned his surroundings. There was nothing. Not a single boat on the horizon. The only noise was from the hull sloshing through the waves, the flap of the sail as it struggled to tame the wind, and the hum of rotor blades far off in the distance.

The last noise hadn't been there five minutes ago.

Jake stood up and peered into the distance, half-expecting to see one of the giant cruisers far away on its slow crawl to war. If only he had. Instead, some distance in front of the dinghy's bow, two smaller drones were flying in tandem across his path a few metres above the water. Their precise movements suggested they were on patrol and there was only one thing worthy of their attention.

Jake knew from first-hand experience how it felt to be in close proximity to a utility drone, which at least one of these machines was. They were only equipped to see those wearing traditional implants, but they would still sense the movement of the boat cutting through the water. Jake immediately dropped the sail to slow his advance.

When it comes to brakes, boats are slow responders. Even though the wind no longer pressed on the sail, the inertia already created and the flow of the currents continued to push the boat forward. Jake dropped to the deck face up and concentrated on remaining perfectly still. Maybe they'd mistake it for an empty boat cut adrift from its mooring. The drones moved across his line of motion at exactly the wrong moment. He nervously watched them approach and noticed something unusual.

They weren't the same model.

The one nearest him was like every other utility drone he'd ever seen. A thick shell as black as a puma with a dangerous arsenal of weaponry protruding from every surface. The one furthest from him, flying in synchronicity with the other, had silver panels and substituted the lethal protection of its counterpart with an array of tools and utensils. Most of these contraptions appeared to be practical rather than malicious. Two robotic arms with three-fingered claws, a conical-shaped drill caked in red dust, and something that resembled a giant Swiss Army knife for a tail. Both drones flew with the aid of four giant rotary blades on long, sturdy arms, but their flying styles were quite different from normal.

They flew laterally like crabs traversing a beach and always faced each other. One flew smoothly while the other had a jerkier style. This was the first time Jake had seen one behave in such a way. Drones always flew straight forward, their sensors and lights out in front. As the boat floated closer the reason for the change in behaviour became obvious. They weren't on the same side and they were watching each other. They moved at the same pace, nose to nose, no more than two metres apart. Fortunately they were far more interested in each other than they were in him, at least until the moment he passed directly underneath them.

The utility drone stopped suddenly in mid-air, lit up like a Christmas tree and let out a now familiar warning siren. It tilted forward to scan the water. The firewall might be invisible but it wasn't symbolic. Something had broken a sensor between two sentry towers on the nearest land masses. Any drones patrolling this section of the firewall would be drawn to the breach, but this particular drone was the closest. It dropped down to sea level and its opponent mimicked its movements. Jake held his breath as the boat bobbed forward and the sail fluttered limply against the mast.

The boat's motion and the disruption of the sensor was all the evidence the utility drone needed. The lack of a registered Memory Cloud confused it, but its instincts were to shoot first and report mistakes later. Its mission was clear. Nothing passed through the firewall unless approved by Alison. It locked its sights on the foreign object. Its largest cannon vibrated as it built up the required energy to take the shot.

What unravelled next did so, so quickly Jake had no time to act. If he'd thrown himself in the sea surely that would have given him a greater chance of survival. Instead he ducked pointlessly, covered his head with his hands and prayed. Two sounds followed in quick succession. The first was the quieter of the two and was the whoosh of a rocket being launched from a tube before being immediately muffled as the projectile hesitated in the space above his head. The second was a louder explosion followed moments later by heavy rain striking the sea. Jake peered through his fingers, reassured that he still had some, and found to his relief that the fibreglass under his body was still floating in one piece.

He plucked up the courage to sit up. In the sea to the stern of the boat floated the scattered buoyant remains of the utility drone. Above him, with one of its robotic arms held out in front of it, a little scorched and blackened, was the other drone. The only explanation was that this drone had caught the missile before redirecting it towards the aggressor.

"Christ, I thought I was a goner!" offered Jake with a vocal sigh of relief.

The drone was drawn to the voice. It dropped down to sea level, robotic arms outstretched like a visually impaired man desperately searching for his lost spectacles. Jake shuffled backwards in case it found him. He didn't know what type of drone this was, or what purpose it had, but he guessed correctly where it came from. There were no drones like this in the West. This drone was from the East which meant he'd successfully achieved what no one else had in the last decade. He'd passed through the firewall and into the land of the Realm. Mostly because he'd received significant assistance.

One of the drone's robotic arms clattered against the dinghy. It paused, fascinated by what it found. It ran one of its mechanical fingers over the unfamiliar surface to learn more about it. Then it placed the second hand on the other side. A triangular beam of light scanned the fibreglass surface to satisfy the drone's curiosity. The beam moved down the boat in waves, stopping frequently to record important data about the foreign body that had encroached on its patch. Inevitably the beam landed on Jake and stopped. His heart pumped ferociously, his panting loud and obvious. The drone made a series of strange, non-threatening clicking noises.

The light beam disappeared and the clicking sounds were replaced by the beat of four rotor blades increasing in velocity. The drone gripped tightly to the stern, tilted forward, and the once wind-powered dinghy had to adapt to having the world's strangest outboard motor. Jake rattled around on deck as the pace of the boat increased. He grabbed hold of a safety line, clipped it to his life jacket and spent a couple of uncomfortable hours in a human pinball machine.

THREE

WAY OUT EAST

The newly converted speedboat pressed relentlessly across the sea, swathes of salty water crashing over the sides onto Jake who clung to the safety line for dear life. For the first time in days the horizon featured land rather than an endless vista of sea and cloud. The East was getting closer and he had no idea what to expect when he arrived. The sum of his knowledge about this misunderstood half of the world wouldn't fill a two-second advertisement slot. Even if he had retained his original cloud and had the ability to check what he remembered, there would only be one source.

When it came to the East, the 'Proclamation of Distrust' was the only memory anyone owned.

Jake was one of the few former or current subscribers who didn't even remember that. His view on a territory he'd recently entered was completely without bias. There was only one truth he knew about the place. He had to come here because only they were capable of helping him defeat the Circuit. That was it. He didn't know how to do it, or whether it was even feasible. He didn't know how much time he'd have before the war drones completed their genocide or until the Circuit caught up with him. He didn't have any contacts who might assist him when he reached the land fast approaching in the distance.

The more he thought about it, the more he doubted that assumption. He did have one, Dinah, but did she really count as a contact? He wasn't entirely sure she counted as a single entity.

Jake reconsidered the final moments of his encounter with Alison. It was obvious now from his flashback that the Circo siblings had developed a master application that allowed the Circuit to think for itself. An artificial intelligence who would be responsible for both their fates. Miriam had murdered Aaron on Alison's instruction, before his sister was 'switched off' and stored in the Source, alongside many others who'd violated the Circuit's rules over the years, including Jake's parents. For over two decades, Alison's true nature had been kept hidden, and its own survival instincts calculated every possible threat to ensure it stayed that way.

Prohibiting entry to the East happened almost immediately after the Circo sibling's removal from power, but not before the region's vital resources were stripped and transported to the West. The speccies, who would always remain out of Alison's vision, were pursued even more ruthlessly. The 'Proclamation of Distrust' intimidated subscribers to fear the consequences of both groups. Finally, in case these protections failed, the Circuit secretly built a fleet of war drones to act as one final and fatal fail-safe. All of these reactions were forged by the collective knowledge Alison gained through the Memory Cloud. If Alison was the ignition, then the cloud was the fuel.

Any computer, intelligent or not, was reliant on a programmer, at least initially. Alison had access to more data than any entity in the history of the Universe. Billions of subscribers with trillions of unique memories instantly available to the central hub for extraction and modelling. Not just from current subscribers either. The Memory Cloud was more than forty years old and not everyone who'd connected to it still lived. Scientific progress had extended most people's lifespans but even with enhanced pharmaceuticals and state-of-the-art surgery there was still no likelihood that man or machine would discover the secrets to eternal life. Not for the body at least.

Memories, though: that was a different story.

After death, memories were no longer tethered to their organic berths. People died, but each individual's Memory Cloud still existed. They remained exactly where they'd always been, safely stored in electronic form in an unidentified server next to a thousand others. They no longer received signals from their paired implant because that had most likely been buried or incinerated alongside its fleshy carriage. Their clouds became dormant, but not useless. Archived experiences continued to feed the ever-expanding body of human data that defined the rules and influenced future decision-making. The more data you had, the more robust the decisions.

Alison had the unique advantage of owning a vast wealth of wisdom and the combined intelligence of two geniuses. Together these qualities calculated the best decisions for the survival of its subscribers and, most crucially, itself. An intelligent being is one that perceives its environment and takes action to maximise its chance of success. Alison had been designed to advance the human race and protect the Circuit. It was hard to argue that its actions disagreed with such a statement. But advancing humanity was not the same as freedom.

An intelligent system doesn't hide from the truth. It

doesn't sweep disappointment under the carpet or get carried away with its ego. It uses all the evidence to guide its choices, even the fragments that do not work in its favour. For all of Alison's pre-emptive planning it knew there was a fundamental flaw in the maths. The outcome was not one hundred percent certain because its field of vision was not infinite. Alison had a blind spot.

Its name was Dinah.

Like a million guides that had gone before her, Dinah was responsible for helping Jake adjust to his new life after Ascension Day. But, unlike all the others, Dinah's computer code contained a flashback preloaded into Jake's first implants. Its origins could be traced to the East and it contained both the truth about Alison's true influence in the heart of the Circuit and the codes that controlled how she functioned. Dinah had protected these truths for eighteen years and now they existed in Jake's brain, unsullied by the distraction of an overdominant Memory Cloud. The codes were the answer to loosening the Circuit's oppressive grip on its subscribers. At least that's what Jake hoped.

Of all of the revelations he'd witnessed in the tower that night, another remained unresolved. Dinah had appeared to Aaron Circo during the flashback. She had interacted with him in the same way as a guide did. Were they one and the same entity? Had Dinah been wrapped up in the data passed to Jake via the rogue implants? Did she still exist somewhere or had she perished along with her master? He didn't know, but he felt he needed to find out if he had any chance of success.

The drone slowed its pace and the choppy waters stabilised. In front of him the shoreline revealed more detail. Arriving here brought no fear or elation, only curiosity. If anything he was more concerned about his mechanical pilot than what might greet him on land. The silver worker drone had saved him valuable time but its intentions were still unclear. Was it helping him or handing him in? Drones weren't renowned for being charitable. This one might lack the hostile weaponry of the utility drones but it had quickly outwitted one of those, so it was clearly clever. For now he had no option but to let it dock and see how things played out.

A ramshackle city teetered nervously on the edge of the sea. But not just on the edge. It was obvious why the drone had slowed down. Navigating these seas meant knowing what was underneath them. Throughout history sailors checked local charts for signs of shipwrecks to avoid their own vessel joining them. In today's waters those dangers had a different name. They were called brick-wrecks.

Jake looked over the side of the dinghy and into the clear waters. It was a surreal sight. Once busy streets carved their way around blocks of ghostly residential buildings. Seaweed-covered lamp-posts that lined the pavements looked more like drowned trees. Unlike all other objects not fixed to the ground occasionally he saw a fully laden lorry parked along the road, too heavy for the currents to displace it. Beautifully carved masonry jutted from the façades of buildings or clung to the sides of wide balconies, an architectural constant of the sunken city. Like an aquarium brimming with expensive ornaments, colourful fish in huge shoals flashed from one side of the street to the other like little specks of glitter.

Jake didn't know which city lay beneath him, but even through an underwater filter he knew it was different from the ones he'd visited in the West. These buildings followed a more oriental blueprint: domed roofs, elaborate and delicate architecture painted in once vibrant colours. The theme continued in those built high enough to withstand the floods. To his left a huge, gold dome had turned green from oxidation and a lack of attention. On top of it an intricate bell tower, whose chimes would once have been a source of comfort, hadn't rung for many a year. There was more to see here than in Stockholm, which suggested it had more historical significance. Like the Swedish capital, the effects of the climate's change and its aftermath had been equally catastrophic.

The drone manoeuvred the dinghy around the man-made obstacle course before taking a sharp turn to the south. Jake noticed a runway under the water as they approached the shore. Several massive, rusty aeroplanes were still parked on the tarmac waiting for take-off. Above the water the low clouds perfectly camouflaged the greyness of the land where dull, newly constructed buildings squabbled for air and space. They lacked the artistry of those submerged in the estuary, and it was clear they'd been built with haste rather than beauty in mind. A temporary jetty of discarded plastic barrels, broken planks and oily ropes bobbed in greeting. The drone gently moored Jake's dinghy and released its mechanical arms from the stern.

"What do I do now?" said Jake out loud, seeking both advice and reassurance.

The decision was taken out of his hands.

The drone's arms extended and grabbed him with one of its piston-like claws. It hovered upwards and Jake's legs were left to dangle in mid-air. The machine's grip was gentle but Jake was under no doubt what would happen next. He was being turned in. But turned in to whom? The Realm ruled the East but who ruled the Realm? Until his murder Aaron Circo had, but was there a succession plan? How would the Realm feel about an imposter from the

West? The drones patrolled both sides of the firewall to keep their subscribers in and the other side's securely out. No one went to that amount of trouble without having a reason. He guessed he wasn't going to be welcomed as an intrigued tourist.

The worker drone floated slowly and quietly along the jetty, up some removeable steps and into the heart of the city. In the larger streets Jake got his first real sight of the place, even if he was hanging at a strange angle. Residents bustled through the streets on this grey afternoon going about their daily business. They were much like the people Jake had grown up with. Old ladies pushing ancient-looking shopping trolleys slower than continental drift took to advance. Young children kicking a deflated football at a goal poorly chalked on a concrete wall. Mothers with babies chatting on the benches that ran down the middle of a street devoid of tram, cart or car. They weren't so different from him. Only their facial expressions offered any difference from the other nationalities and creeds he'd met. It was a fundamental one, though.

Every one of these faces was miserable.

Even the children playing football wore expressions that advertised just how little they were enjoying it. Activities that were generally joyful were accompanied by frowns, grimaces and even streams of tears. The collective despondency gave the place an uncomfortable atmosphere, as if they'd suffered some great tragedy and no one had escaped the effects. Had the war drones already been here? Maybe that was a good enough reason for the despair. There was no obvious sign that war had been here, even though the drably constructed buildings looked like they'd have welcomed it willingly. If it wasn't the drones that had caused their misery, what else had happened to affect the people like this?

Strangely none of them were the least bit interested in him. A silver drone flying through the town centre with a wet, tired and shabby-looking youth displaying a deep and unusual scar across his face can't have been a regular sight. Could they see him at all? They obviously saw everything else.

The drone continued its slow creep up the street towards a large, white house held up by columns. On its roof a single colourful flag fluttered gently on a mast. It was the only colourful object he'd seen since the jetty. A strange, black symbol set against the emerald green fabric background. Unlike the Circuit's branding there were no letters on this emblem. The centre of the symbol was like an old-fashioned analogue clock face. At twelve o'clock a wave stretched along its curved edge before breaking at three o'clock. An identical wave curved from six to nine, but it was significantly shorter and shallower. Did it symbolise East and West? If it did, then the wave on the East face was deeper and more prominent. It had to be the Realm's symbol.

The impressive, white building cast a shadow over him as they approached the entrance at the top of five chunky stone steps. The house had been built higher than the rest of the town, and unlike all the other properties it looked much older. Jake suspected it was there prior to the rise of the ocean that had decimated much of the town he'd sailed through earlier today. The drone floated up and over the stone steps, narrowly avoiding his feet bumping into each one, towards a pair of intricately carved wooden double doors. For the first time in weeks he had a genuine sense of discomfort, a fear of what might be inside.

He never found out.

The eerie silence of the town was pierced by a whizzing sound cutting through the air. It was followed by

a dull thud of metal striking metal. From his awkward
position in mid-air, Jake noticed an unusual device stuck to
the side of the drone which hadn't been there before. It
reminded him of an old-fashioned bear trap, a round,
metal frame with sharp teeth that bit firmly into the
drone's silver chassis. A red light pulsated in the centre
before a whooshing noise was followed by a shower of
sparks. The drone stopped suddenly as a pulse of electricity dispersed out across its shell, down its robotic arms
and through Jake's skin. The electric shock forced his hair
to stand on end and made his bones rattle. The robotic
arm finally released its grip and Jake struck the steps with a
bump.

The drone's engines failed and it, too, crashed to the
ground just seconds after Jake had scrambled to one side.
All signs of life were extinguished as the crumpled smoking
drone sizzled with unused electrical charge. Jake dragged
himself to his feet and went to examine the device that had
caused its failure. His analysis was short-lived when small
fires broke out and soon the whole machine was consumed
by flames. The townsfolk ignored the kerfuffle as if it was
routine, no more significant than a church bell chiming or
the arrival of night.

The top of a man's head poked over the ornate stone
balustrade. "You can stare for as long as you like, but more
will come, you know."

"Did you do this?" asked Jake.

"Obviously."

"Thank you. Why?"

"No time to explain," replied the man, motioning for
Jake to follow. "Not here at least."

The man disappeared down the side of the building
and Jake hurried after him. This man was the first he'd
seen here whose expression wasn't consumed by disap-

pointment. If anything he'd seemed rather relaxed, despite having single-handedly downed a drone which was obviously part of the law and order infrastructure here. If the Realm were anything like the Circuit, an act of resistance like this wouldn't go down well. Jake trailed a few metres behind him, keen to avoid drawing attention to himself or being held responsible for blowing it up. They strolled through the narrow side streets before eventually running out of room on the swamp of small pebbles on the beach. When Jake caught up with him he was skimming stones into the sea like a bored student on a school geography trip.

"Why did you do that?" asked Jake, standing next to him to get a better look at the man.

"City Hall isn't a tourist attraction I'd recommend," replied the man. "Not unless you want to surrender yourself to the Realm."

"Maybe I do."

"Then you're further from home than I first thought."

"I might be able to tell you if I knew where I was now."

"You're in the East, and if you're from where I think you are there's only one way you can be here."

The man turned and Jake's morale received its first serious boost in weeks. Down the side of his left cheek was a familiar-looking scar. It was similar to his own and that meant one thing.

"So the rumours are true," smiled Jake. "Speccies from the West are still getting through the firewall."

"No. You're the first one for a long time."

"When did you get here, then?"

"I was born here," he replied indignantly.

"Born here?"

"Yes. Speccies don't just fight the control of the system

in the West. You have the Circuit and we have the Realm, but we both have the Memory Cloud. It exists on both sides of the firewall, don't forget. I'm Verne Oja," he added with a sharp nod and outstretched hand.

"Jake Montana, super…" he said, stopping himself midway through revealing his importance factor.

"Let's hope you are," replied Verne.

"Where exactly am I?"

"You're on the very edge of our world. Out there," said Verne, pointing to the sea, "is the historic old city of St Petersburg. You're standing in New Putinsburg, built as a replacement when the sea swamped the coast."

"New Putinsburg?"

"Named after the current Russian leader, one hundred and two and still going strong. Not that any of the local administrations wield much power these days. Not since the Realm assumed ultimate control."

"Was that who the drones were taking me to?"

"Yes. It's the fate that awaits anyone who enters the East uninvited."

"Then I have to go back to City Hall," replied Jake enthusiastically. "I need their help."

"Help! They don't help anyone anymore."

"They will help me," he stated overconfidently.

"If you think that then you're a misinformed fool."

"A fool possibly, but actually I'm not informed at all when it comes to the Realm."

"Then let me give you a brief lesson on the subject," said Verne, reaching inside his jacket and removing a small pouch of tobacco. He slowly rolled himself the perfect cigarette, lit it with a match struck on a pebble, and took a long gulp of smoke before continuing his history lecture. "The Realm aren't what they once were. When I was a kid life here was pretty great, for speccies and subscribers. We lived in harmony alongside each other and as it happens, because they weren't forced to, most speccies converted to the Realm anyway because they thought they were missing out. There aren't a lot of the older generation of speccies left. There are a lot more younger ones because life changed dramatically here about twenty years ago."

"Was that when the Circuit interfered?"

"They didn't need to. Someone on the inside beat them to it."

"Who?"

"He's simply known in these parts as the King of Baku, and with his commune of fanatical supporters he controls the East like a cult. Everything that happens here goes through them. It's the reason everyone acts the way they do. Did you notice how miserable they are?"

"Yeah, I did: what's happened to make them feel like that?"

"Life happened. There's not enough food, they lack basic resources, no jobs, hyperinflation, energy blackouts… You name it, they don't have it. Unless you're talking about diseases: they have plenty of those."

"If they're not happy, why don't they rise up against it?" asked Jake pointedly.

"I could ask you the same question about people on your side. I have been to the West, I've seen how blind they are."

"But they have what they need, or at least what people think they need. It sounds like the people here have nothing."

"True, but the problem is they don't know that."

"You've lost me," said Jake with a gormless expression.

"Next time you meet one, ask them how things were yesterday and then you might understand," said Verne, finishing the last drag on his smoke and flicking the butt into the sea. "Why do you want to hand yourself in exactly?"

"I have information that can help bring down the Circuit but it's only possible with support from the Realm and the people of the East."

"You'll get no support from either," said Verne sharply, his face becoming grave. "They remember the last time they tried and it didn't go so well."

"Then someone will need to encourage them."

"Who? You? I'll wager you won't get to the end of the week before they catch you and you disappear. The King has some wonderfully inventive ways of doing that, so I hear through the grapevine."

"I don't need to inspire them. There's a more powerful motivator coming their way. The West has dispatched a fleet of lethal war drones to wipe them out. I'm surprised you haven't seen them already."

"We've seen them," he replied casually.

"Really? You don't seem very concerned."

"When life kicks you in the arse every day new misery seems to go unnoticed."

"Aren't people frightened?"

"Every day, whether they see a drone or not. If you want my advice I'd get back on whatever craft brought you here and head home."

"I can't. It's about the greater good. If the East doesn't rise up, then the West will be lost permanently under the Circuit's oppression. You must help me."

Verne chuckled in a way he hadn't done for many years. There weren't many reasons to be cheerful here. Although he was clearly embittered by a life of hardship and struggle, Jake sensed a suppressed resilience in him. He was probably twice Jake's age and carried many times more life experiences on his skinny shoulders. It never occurred to Jake that speccies on this side of the firewall would have different values. The speccies he'd met before all had a burning passion for truth and justice. Verne acted like survival was all he really cared about. But if that was true, why had he rescued him from the drone?

"I can't help you," he said.

"But you already have."

"Call it a professional courtesy."

"Don't you want change?"

It was clear this youthful newcomer wasn't going to be influenced by words: he needed to see for himself.

"Come with me. Let me show you the reality," he added, walking past Jake and back up the ridge of pebbles that crunched under his feet. Once again, Jake followed unwaveringly. When they were back in the main high street, Verne pointed to a bench and encouraged him to sit with him.

"Tell me what you see?" said Verne.

"People."

"And what do you notice about them?"

"Like you said, they're all unhappy."

"Yes. Look at that young boy over there, for example. Are boys of his age always sad in the West?"

"No."

"Talk to him."

A skinny boy of about ten years old was standing on the edge of an older group, yearning to be included in their game of football. Verne whistled to him and the boy approached fearlessly.

"Hello," said Jake, turning on the charm to induce the boy to like him. "What's your name?"

"Boris."

"How are you, Boris?"

"Miserable," he said without pause.

"And why are you miserable, Boris?" asked Jake gently, expecting him to reference some childish dilemma or minor issue.

"I don't know," Boris replied honestly.

"Have you seen the scary black drones in the sky?"

"No," replied the boy.

"What about the Circuit? Do you fear them?"

"Who?" asked the boy uncertainly.

"Oh, it doesn't really matter. What about food? Do you have enough to eat, some shelter, essentials and a loving family to support you?" asked Jake.

"Not today," said the boy, his expression remaining miserably fixed in place.

"Only today?" asked Jake, picking up on the specifics of the boy's reply.

"Everything will be alright tomorrow," said Boris.

"Tomorrow? How can you be so sure?"

"Because everything was good yesterday," the boy replied. "And it will be tomorrow."

"So yesterday was good and you're confident tomorrow will be, too?" summarised Jake, slightly bewildered.

"Yes. It's always like that."

"Thank you," Verne said to the boy. "Run along now."

Boris didn't budge. He was transfixed by the sight of Jake almost like he'd seen a ghost. "I've seen him before."

"I don't think so," replied Jake.

The boy pointed at Jake before retreating, head stooped and watching his feet drag forlornly across the cracked asphalt.

Jake scratched his head. Did everyone see the world as this boy did? Were they all riding out the storm in the hope or expectation that things would improve when all the obvious signs suggested nothing of the sort? The boy's last assertion was even more disturbing.

"How can he have seen me before? I've only been here a few hours."

"I don't know," said Verne, quite uninterested by the revelation, "but do you see what's happening here?"

"No, not really."

"These people are being manipulated."

"How?"

"Someone is messing with their Memory Clouds."

"Why would anyone do that?"

"Simple. To stop them rising up. I think their memories are being altered to create the illusion that everything was better than they believed at the time. Whoever is doing it can't change the reality of the here and now, but they can change the perception of the past. People will accept one bad day, but they won't accept a thousand in a row. Why would you risk everything you thought you had because of one bad day? Our most basic human instinct is fear. Fear of death, fear of loss, fear of how others perceive us." He paused. "Fear that the future will be worse."

"Alison's behind this," said Jake authoritatively.

"Who?"

"Principal Conductor of the Circuit. Alison's only fear is what might come from the East."

"Nothing will ever come from here."

"If the Realm is already subduing their people, why would they send the war drones?" asked Jake mostly to himself.

The words stopped him in his intellectual tracks. If the people had already been placed in an anti-establishment coma, what use were the drones? If the drones were designed to cull the people of the East, why hadn't they started yet? New Putinsburg was one of the closest cities to Bornholm and they'd seemingly flown straight past it.

"Jake, if you believe the answer to your problems lies

here you are very much mistaken. These people lack the motivation for anything. Why would they save the West when they can't even save themselves?"

"Then why do you think the drones are here?" Jake asked again.

"I'd imagine they will focus their attention on the Realm."

"But the people are part of that. Aren't they all plugged into the Realm's Memory Cloud?"

"Jesus, you don't know anything about this place, do you?"

"I think we've established that already."

"When the Circuit constructed the firewall and shipped all the resources to the West, that's when the people's mood changed. But it wasn't because of what they'd lost. It was their minds that were altered, not their environment. All these people are connected to the cloud on the Realm's frequency. They store memories and emotions just like the people in the West. Huge server farms that contain each and every backup for each and every person. That's the greatest resource of all, more valuable than gold, platinum, nickel or oil. That's what the Circuit want, it's what they've always wanted. Total dominance. If everyone is part of the Circuit then they control everyone."

"Then why aren't the Realm defending them?"

"An excellent question. One that you'd have to ask the King of Baku," Verne suggested ironically.

"Maybe I'll pay him a visit."

"Then you really are an idiot," replied Verne, his face white as a sheet.

"I possess a weapon to defeat the Circuit. It came from the East and it can only be unlocked here. The Realm are the only ones who can fight. Won't you help me?"

"No," said Verne. "I've lost too much already."

"But think about what you might gain."

Boris returned to the bench still consumed by images of Jake and searching his mind to force himself to remember why it was familiar.

"I know where I have seen you before," said Boris, pointing at Jake's scar.

"I think it's unlikely, I've only been here five minutes!"

"You're the man they warned us about."

"What warning?" asked Verne.

"The man in the 'Proclamation of Distrust'. It's him."

FOUR
ANGRY MOBS

Tyra stumbled through the carbon rod farm light-headed and unsettled. Had that conversation happened or was she hallucinating after inhaling too much pure oxygen? It certainly felt real at the time. But was it possible to have a conversation with a text stream being projected into your cloud feed? She'd only witnessed something similar once before and that was at the very end of her parents' 'conduct feeling'. That was real, so this probably was, too. What had she done to annoy the authorities? Nothing serious, so what did they want with her?

She replayed the memory again.

They didn't want her.

They wanted Jake.

They wanted her to catch him.

The 'Proclamation of Distrust' had encouraged the entire population to be alert to his threat, but after the broadcast Alison spoke directly to her. They wanted someone with the inside track of what he might do next or where he might be. Tyra had no love for the Circuit, but they might as well be UNICEF compared to how she felt about her brother. But did two wrongs make a right?

It was complicated.

Whatever Jake had done to irritate the Principal Conductor, it had nothing to do with her. If Jake was going to see the error of his ways and repent for the misery he'd heaped upon her, she had to make him. If she accepted assistance, particularly from them, the victory would never truly be hers. She couldn't hide behind the immense power of the state. Her dispute with Jake had to take place on a level playing field, just him versus her. A battle of wits, determination and righteousness. One on one, just as it had been growing up, even though Jake had a four-year advantage over her.

Alison's offer wasn't an easy one to walk away from, and she wasn't convinced the conversation ended that way anyhow. Even the purest of souls would struggle not to be corrupted by such a contract. The power, protection and support offered made a mockery of importance factors. If she took the bait and achieved what was required, her life would never be the same again. She'd be above everyone; untouchable, affluent and notorious, and yet something deep within her rallied against it. What was holding her back? Guilt, a sense of duty, fairness, love even? She couldn't say. At the moment it just felt like the wrong choice, even though she was conflicted. The last few months had taught her to trust no one but herself. Everyone else had let her down and the Circuit would, too, given the chance.

Tyra skirted the perimeter of the carbon rod field and ambled down the side of the ferrocon new builds that lined the road on the opposite side to her own. As the narrow alley approached the street a throng of voices grew in volume. It sounded like a hundred people arguing passionately with one another. What were so many people doing out this late? This wasn't normal, she thought curiously.

New Hampton Falls was not a densely populated town. Based on the last automated census, less than five thousand people called it home. Tyra was only used to seeing a handful of those out on the street at ten o'clock at night, even though she wasn't supposed to be there either. These disparate nocturnal nomads were a collection of late-night dog walkers, couples enjoying an evening stroll, or the occasional drunk desperately trying to remember where he'd left his house, and struggling to make sense of his cloud feed or his feet. Unless, like her, you were hiding from your responsibilities or experimenting with inventive ways of rebelling, there was rarely a need to be out this late.

Almost everything people needed and loved was indoors at this time of night. Your family, your possessions and, most importantly, access to your Memory Cloud. Obviously you could access your cloud from anywhere; it was just more comfortable to do so on a big, snuggly couch rather than out in the rain perched on a rigid wooden bench while it inflicted bum cramps.

She hurried to the end of the alley to discover the source of the commotion. A tram pulled up on the other side of the road. It wasn't rare to see one. They passed down this road at all hours of the day and night in precise, ten-minute intervals. What made this one particularly unusual was that it had halted in a place where there wasn't a tram stop. Trams had automated drivers and were designed to be staggeringly punctual and regimentally routine. They stopped where they were scheduled to; they didn't stop on the request of a passenger. Who would they ask anyway? There was no one upfront, just a loads of dials and a screen inside a sealed cabin. Nevertheless, this one had decided to stop in an unauthorised place and it was allowing people to get off.

Lots of people.

The carriages were packed to the rafters and dozens of passengers streamed through the sliding doors, bumping one another out of the way to be the first to claim the pavement. Every tram surfer clutched a potentially harmful implement like they'd arrived at a garage sale face-off. Brooms, ladles, pitchforks, a hatstand, a guitar and a vacuum cleaner were just some of the bizarre items Tyra saw being swished around offensively.

"What's happening here?" she chuntered under her breath.

She picked her pace up even more and threatened to enter jog mode. Around the corner of the alley she discovered the focus of the crowd's crusade.

Number seventeen.

Her house.

It was already completely surrounded. From the front door to the tram tracks, queues of people five or six deep had congregated and more were joining the throng by the minute. Any free space on drive or lawn was quickly filled by boot, sandal or stiletto. Unlike the excitable anticipation that oozed through the crowd of an outdoor festival, the atmosphere across this one was toxic. Men and women alike squabbled, argued and fought to get closer to the front door as if a famous rock band were about to take the stage and everyone wanted to be within spitting range. Most were complete strangers, people Tyra had never set eyes on before. They weren't even from her town, but to her surprise there were some familiar faces.

Most of the neighbours, for example.

Folks she'd grown up with and knew personally. Adults who had been invited around for dinner or had arranged playdates with their own children when she was inclined to attend such events. Also attending this pop-up display of anarchy were community leaders, half the church choir, teachers, town wardens and most of the local Women's Institute. The last group were the most militant and were in the middle of lighting up some gin bottle Molotovs to clear a path through the throng. The older, more infirm of the group who were in wheelchairs were being used as human battering rams to press home their advantage. Their ankle-bruised victims then faced the moral dilemma of protecting their own spots on the lawn or facing the shame of not helping vulnerable old ladies.

Tyra watched as some of Jake's old school friends, those who had yet to reach their own Ascension Day, tried to sneak around the side of the house to access the back garden. She'd had crushes on most of these boys down the years, but today their once attractive faces had changed. They looked ferocious like nothing would stand in the way of their obsession. Their eyes burnt with an almost super-natural mania, a crazed addiction for chaos that hijacked their normal view of right and wrong. The expression was shared everywhere she looked, no more so than at the very back of the crowd where Tyra bumped into one of her friends.

"Evie, what are you doing here?"

"Oh, hello, Tyra," she replied hyperactively like she'd eaten too many sugary treats. "We've come for the reward!"

"Reward! What reward?"

"For Jake."

"But he's not here," she replied.

"Don't believe you," Evie snapped, unable to stop her body shaking from the overdose of adrenaline coursing through her.

"Even if he were here, Evie, you're actually standing outside the wrong house," said Tyra in a disapproving tone and forcibly manoeuvring her friend's head in the right direction.

Evie flatly refused to accept that she was cross-eyed even when the affliction noticeably let her down. She made no mention of it normally, but tonight there was something much more important on her mind.

"You could help me," begged Evie. "I'll share it with you."

"Share what?"

"One billion credits."

"If I wanted that, don't you think I'd have handed Jake in already?"

"Where is he!?" she demanded, grabbing Tyra by the scruff of the neck.

"I don't care," she replied sternly. "And take your hands off me!"

"Don't be a bitch, Tyra. Remember who your friends are," she added, breaching the limits of her desperation and allowing anger to boil over.

"Don't worry. I will," Tyra replied as she released Evie's grip, clear she was no longer one of them.

Tonight's 'Proclamation of Distrust' had ended less than thirty minutes ago and yet this crowd proved how powerful a mechanism it was. What they heard they believed. What the Circuit wanted they delivered. In a world fiercely proud of its values of meritocracy, equality and peace, it had taken less than an hour to expose society's weakness and show how quickly they'd throw it away for greed. No one in the crowd cared about Jake anymore, they only cared about the status, power and money they'd receive when they caught him. In the same way they'd allowed themselves to be brainwashed to hate the people of the East, Jake had ceased to be a person.

Now he was a lottery ticket.

Tyra jostled her way through the crowd to get to the front of the house. As she squeezed past disgruntled early arrivers, they complained angrily that 'they'd got here first, wait your turn' or 'what's your importance factor, is it higher than mine?' She ignored all of them. This was still her house even if she wasn't here very much. When she finally reached the front about a metre from the porch she was breathless, harassed and sweaty. At the door three adults she didn't recognise were trying to co-ordinate proceedings. It was obvious to her that none of them were employed in the outdoor events industry or had any experience of being a first responder.

"We can't all go in at the same time, can we?" said one man, dressed in a sharp, blue suit and with slicked-back hair that had a mountain of gel in it.

"No! It should be first come first served," said another.

"That's not how things work in the Circuit, my friend," replied a third. "We already have a priority system. Vitals first, then essentials and so on."

"Which means I go first!" interrupted the second.

"Why?" said the first.

"Because I'm essential," he replied authoritatively.

"No you're not, Dwayne! I've known you for thirty years and you've always introduced yourself as a trivial!"

"You must have misheard me."

"What?! I misheard you a few thousand times, did I?" said the third man who was holding back the crowd with his sizeable girth.

"Yes, Bruce. Either you're rubbish at listening or you need a hearing aid," he said, aiming his comments at the first man seeking support. "Once I asked him to make me some of his famous marinara sauce and do you know what he made me? Marijuana sauce!"

"I don't remember you complaining at the time, Dwayne," replied Brian.

"If you really are essential then share the memory of your Ascension Day letter," said the snappy dresser suspiciously.

"No," said Dwayne timidly.

"The truth will set you free," said Brian the giant one-man cordon.

Several people in the crowd shouted their credentials in case vitals were being given preferential treatment and got the first chance to do some high-quality pillaging.

"I think we need to be sensible about this," continued Brian. "If Jake Montana is as dangerous as they say, we should go in based on physical strength and personal knowledge of the family."

"That'll also be me, then," said Dwayne confidently.

"Oh really? What's Jake's sister called, then?" asked Brian searchingly.

"Ah ha…he didn't have one!"

Tyra scowled. It was just another example of her visibility around the town and a general lack of acknowledgement she existed.

"Hurry up!" several voices shouted from the crowd.

"Maybe we should issue tickets," said the first man.

"What's the point of that? If the first person goes in and discovers Jake's not there, then there won't be much point in having ticket number two, will there?"

"What if the three of us went in together and shared the prize?" Brian whispered.

"Ooh, I like that!" said Dwayne.

While the three of them argued about how an angry mob was supposed to behave, an actual angry mob had decided to take matters into their own hands. The Women's Institute were losing patience. A flaming bottle spiralled over their heads and smashed on the porch in a burst of flammable liquid and broken glass. Like an apprentice lemming attempting its first sojourn into the field of free diving, the first Molotov triggered a volley of copycats. Soon the Montana family's porch was a melee of minor explosions, broken glass, squabbling men and bloodthirsty old crones.

Standing next to the windowless windows of the house, unseen by the opportunistic gold-diggers, were two hologrammatic guides with front-row seats. One watched the proceedings unfold in bemusement, while the other ignored it with a total lack of interest.

"They're trying to burn down the house," said the tall, skinny guide, offering a running commentary of what was happening in the real world.

"And?" replied the woman who was looking in the other direction.

"You don't seem very concerned, Sister Jezebel."

"I'm not in the slightest bit bothered, Brother Solomon," she replied. "This isn't Christie's house! Now be quiet, I'm busy."

"Doing what?"

"My make-up!"

Sister Jezebel swivelled around for Solomon to judge her cosmetic artistry. He recoiled in fright and clutched at his chest melodramatically considering that it only contained some rather complex computer code. Solomon was known for bluntness. Say what you mean and mean what you say. If he hadn't been so distracted by the mob and paid her efforts closer attention, he'd have boldly pointed out that it looked like her face had recently been involved in a head-on collision with a make-up studio.

Eyeliner had been applied to areas of her face that were nowhere near her eyes, a thick band of blood red lipstick almost connected her ears, and the blusher she'd used was so bright it might cause fatalities. On the positive front she'd done pretty well with the eyebrows, one of them at least.

"I'm great at this," she grinned. The lipstick on her teeth suggested otherwise.

"No, you're not," replied Solomon mostly in spite. "Unless your benchmark is the Joker."

"Bully! Women should be free to express themselves however they choose without seeking the approval of men."

"Not if it threatens to blind them, they shouldn't."

Jezebel shot him a series of unladylike signals.

"What are we going to do about this?" he said, drawing her attention to the flaming projectiles bouncing off the ferrocon walls.

"Nothing. Why are you so bothered?"

"Well…they're not doing it right," he said genuinely. "You can't burn ferrocon, it's made from steel, concrete and plankton. Maybe I should offer them some guidance?"

"Why?"

"Because I'm a guide and that's what we do! Might save them a load of time."

"I'm still not the slightest bit interested," she replied, returning to her reflection.

"What do they teach these people?" he huffed. "I mean it's all there for them in the cloud if they only bothered to look for it. Every piece of knowledge they could ever wish for. Are they too lazy to check? I bet you a hundred credits that if an advert entered their cloud feed for 'professional arsonist – we burn your house down for you', half of them would buy it because it was on offer."

"I'm not listening to you."

"If you want to raze a house to the ground you have to set the roof alight," Solomon shouted at the crowd, even though he knew none of them could hear him.

"That's not right," replied Jezebel indignantly.

"Of course it is. It's the only part of the building that's made of flammable materials."

"But fire would lower a house to the ground, not raise it?"

Solomon blanked her. This was exactly the sort of idiotic statement he'd come to expect from her. Although they'd shared virtual digs for the last eighteen years today was officially the first day they'd met. It hadn't taken Solomon long to form an impression. Less than five minutes. She was a dizzy fool who seemed more interested in feminism than offering specific guidance to Christie. He'd concluded she wouldn't give him too many problems, the classic view of a chauvinist.

"I mean it's simple, even a bunch of idiots like you can...oh...I take it back...someone has finally commandeered the family brain cell. Well done, sir, good on you," he said sarcastically with a slow handclap. "Cavemen managed to make fire a couple of million years ago with two blunt sticks, but you carry on with your self-congratulations and bask in your epic achievement!"

The roof of Tyra's house erupted in flames and everyone stepped back from the heat to see what would happen next.

"No! All my stuff is in there! And also my grandfather," she added as a second thought.

"Oh, do you think he might know where Jake is?" asked Dwayne unsympathetically.

Tyra instinctively rushed towards the door but the intense heat and thick, black smoke forced her back. Her composure quickly returned and she sought a safer way of contacting Paddy. She accessed her cloud, but feared he might not have his on him. For once she was wrong.

"Who's that?" Paddy growled.

"It's me," replied Tyra plainly.

"I've told you. I can't pay until the end of the week. If you can't wait that long I recommend you come to my house and I scream it to your face…GO TO HELL!"

"Granddad, it's Tyra."

"Oh. I thought you were the Requisitioners."

"Why would they…look it doesn't matter. Get out of the house, it's on fire!"

"Yes, I know," he replied casually. "Christie and I are watching from the backyard."

"Christie!"

"Yes, you remember her, don't you? She was…" He stopped in his tracks. He knew it was unwise to mention Jake's name around Tyra unless you were prepared to listen to a long, high-pitched tirade and were willing to repaint the soon-to-be damaged walls.

"I know who she is…what is she doing here!?" she snapped.

"It's a long story."

"I don't want to hear it."

"That's good because I've already forgotten half of it," said Paddy honestly.

"What are you going to do about the house!?" screamed Tyra hysterically.

"What do you think I am, a fire hydrant?"

"You have to do something, all of my stuff is in there. Why haven't the fire brigade turned up yet?"

"Why do you think? You saw tonight's proclamation, didn't you?"

"Jake!" she fumed.

"Now calm down, Tyra, be careful what you say next. Remember, you don't have many violations left this year."

She was sorely tempted to use one.

"We're leaving through the back gate," he continued. "Meet us by the old fountain in the park in twenty minutes."

The mob cheered as part of the roof caved in and a plume of thick, black smoke billowed into the air. A tear rolled down Tyra's cheek as she barged her way back through the crowd. Jake had robbed her of parents, dignity and now her home and every possession she'd ever loved. All she had left was the clothes on her back and the cloud in her head. Sadness turned to anger, anger turned to rage, and she marched furiously towards their rendezvous point.

"Is it getting hot?" said Jezebel who was swamped in flames and floating ash.

"Only in your mind, Jezebel, and that's a place I think we should all be wary of visiting…and I include you in that. Come on, I can feel Christie moving further away from us."

FIVE
P.C.O.D.

In the pantheon of great fountains the 'old fountain' wasn't particularly notorious. It didn't have beautifully chiselled stone horses frozen in mid-jump in a frenzied attempt to escape the water. It didn't have multiple jets that soared high in the air before collapsing again. It wasn't renowned for how an elegant interplay of music, light and water combined to captivate thrilled onlookers. In fact there were mansions in New Hampton Falls with more impressive sprinkler systems in their gardens. The fact that the fountain was, until yesterday, the most notable of the town's tourist attractions put into sharp focus how tediously dull the others were.

People didn't come here for the fountain, because they generally didn't come here at all. What was the point? Lots of towns had a beach and there was nothing historically significant or noteworthy about this region of the country. New Hampton Falls was just another sleepy American town that travellers passed through on their way to somewhere more interesting, only stopping for vital supplies or because they had the misfortune of knowing someone who lived here. None of the residents complained about the lack of a tourism industry. They liked it that way, it was safer. Tourism had a habit of bringing strangers to town and they were viewed with deep suspicion. After tonight's events a lot more would come, but they still weren't coming for the fountain. They'd exclusively be making the trip because they thought Jake was here, New Hampton Falls' newest and most popular attraction.

Paddy removed the suction pads from the sides of his head and placed the implant pouch on the wet stone of the fountain's edge. Christie slumped to the ground next to it, still shaking from a rather eventful Ascension Eve. She'd been preparing for it for months, years in fact, but all the time and energy had been completely wasted. Nothing had been as she'd expected. The letter contained a name she'd longed to see, and yet it made no sense. The name was Jake Montana, but that was impossible. He'd already been allocated by the system to someone else months ago. The mystery multiplied further when her letter highlighted his current location. Arizona, an inhospitable part of the country that couldn't sustain human life. Jake liked sand, that was true, but generally only when it was connected to water. In Arizona, even if you brought water with you in a tightly sealed bottle, it would evaporate in minutes. How had he ended up there? The last time she'd seen him he was heading for Sweden.

She'd tried to search for these answers but Jake was lost to her. There hadn't been a signal from his Memory Cloud for months and no one had seen or heard from him since his own Ascension Day at the end of March. The first time anyone had seen his face since was tonight, which had added a further layer of confusion to the letter. While she and Paddy discussed it they were interrupted by a new version of the 'Proclamation of Distrust' and Jake's name and face were at the centre of it. If he'd done something unforgivable, as the broadcast suggested, why had the Circuit recently placed his name in her letter?

When she opened it this morning she thought she'd be the only one looking for him: now everyone was. Less than an hour after the announcement the mob arrived at Paddy's door demanding they turn Jake in. It didn't seem to bother the crowd that he wasn't there. They'd never stop hunting him until they got what they wanted.

"Why would the Circuit put Jake's name in my letter if they wanted him dead?" muttered Christie.

"Because he's beaten them," offered Paddy with a proud smile.

"Beaten them?"

"The Circuit control everything, right?" stated Paddy rhetorically. "But the impossibility of your letter proves that they have momentarily lost that control. It would be reasonable to assume that Jake was responsible in some way."

"How?"

"I've no idea. That's why we need to see a doctor."

"Actually my doctor lives quite close to here, unless he's joined the mob of course. We can see if he's available."

"We don't need any doctor. We need a very specific doctor."

"Who?"

"I can't say his name," Paddy whispered. "As far as the Circuit is concerned he doesn't exist."

"But will he know what to do about Jake?"

"I don't know but he's the only person who might."

"And where is he?" asked Christie.

"I don't know that either," replied Paddy casually. "I've not seen him for twenty years."

"Then how do you suggest we find him?"

"The same way I always find him when I need him. Secret code."

A diminutive, shadowy figure stomped out of the trees and made a beeline for the fountain. Her face was a horrifying mash-up of thunder and hormones.

"What's she doing here?!" screamed Tyra, pointing, but not looking, at Christie who was still slumped on the grass looking glum.

"She's family," said Paddy sternly.

"Not mine, she isn't. Anything or anyone linked to Jake is dead to me."

"Hello, Tyra," added Christie with an ironic wave.

Tyra folded her arms and swivelled away dramatically.

The two girls had known each other for years, even before Christie and Jake started dating. Everyone knew everyone in a small town like this, which explained why so many people were currently watching Tyra's house burn to the ground. Not only had they known each other for ages, they'd also got on pretty well until recently, and certainly Tyra had preferred Christie's company over her brother's. Until Tyra's recent lurch into the dreary subculture of the 'goth' they'd connected over many mutual interests and hobbies. But all that was in the past. Anything related to Jake was tainted by his misguided deeds.

"I'm not talking to her. Send her away," she added, like the Queen dismissing a lowly servant.

"Tyra, where are your manners!?" barked Paddy.

"They've been incinerated with everything else I've ever loved," she growled.

"It's just stuff. Stuff can be replaced. It's more important that everyone's alright."

"Alright?!" she stropped. "Nothing is alright!"

Tyra and Paddy exchanged a series of verbal blows that soon escalated out of control. After months of practice they were pretty good at it. Tyra would complain, sulk, shout and throw things, while Paddy would threaten to use the powers the Circuit had bestowed upon him through protocol twenty-two. They weren't very effective. Tyra was as stubborn as an old horse and she wasn't going to be threatened by some doddery old fool who was detached from her world. Plus she was smarter than him. She'd figured out the loophole in his strategy almost immediately. If he tried to punish her, or enforce his control through the protocol she'd just rack up another violation. Violations were assigned to the adult, not to the child. He was almost powerless and she knew it.

Christie watched with bemusement as their argument hit new heights of hostility.

"Why are you hanging around with these two weirdos?" asked Brother Solomon inquisitively. "We should be getting on with it."

"Yeah, and what's with the malfunctioning old dude?" jabbered Jezebel. "One minute he's there and the next he freezes on the spot or disappears from your feed altogether. Is he a magician?"

"It's old tech," answered Solomon knowingly.

"What, like Betamax?" asked Jezebel.

"External implants, but they work about as well as that, yeah."

"Paddy's a friend," whispered Christie to avoid bringing attention on herself.

She was still adjusting to having the two guides in tow. Like every eighteen-year-old who reached Ascension Eve she'd anticipated their arrival, even though she was completely unprepared for how it would feel or how they might act. Jake had described his own experience of his guides on their last day together, and it appeared that her hologrammatic companions came from a similar stock.

Solomon was based on her rational adapted personality and Jezebel reflected her natural playful side. Neither had proven very helpful, and neither appeared to have the foggiest idea what was going on. The letter had been as much a surprise to them as it was to her. For now she'd have to put up with their company until she, or they, achieved a higher level of enlightenment. She knew who her money was on.

"He's a bit old for you, isn't he?" said Solomon.

"Paddy's a friend of the family. I've come to seek his advice."

"Well, that's lovely, isn't it?" croaked Solomon, bent metaphorically out of shape. "What an incredible vote of confidence that is in us. We've been here for less than a day and you already think we're doing a bad job."

"No, it's not like that…"

"Kids these days, no patience whatsoever. Everything has to be instant, is that it?"

"What are you complaining about?" argued Jezebel who was lying back on the grass staring vacantly at the sky. "Let the old fella do all the work, we get more days off!"

There was no point hiding anything from her guides. They'd eventually work out that Paddy had a connection to Jake without needing to tell them. It was the guides' responsibility to get her safely to her match, and as they didn't have a clue it was in their best interests that she sought support from others.

"Paddy can help us find Jake," she said. "They're related."

"We don't need help," snapped Solomon.

"Yes we do," Jezebel blurted out. "Solomon said he didn't have the faintest idea what was going on and thought it was scientifically impossible for any human to be where Jake is!"

"That's the last time I tell you 'a secret'," wheezed Solomon, red with embarrassment.

"Then we do need help," said Christie.

"No, I don't!" replied Solomon.

"He does."

The two arguments went on forever. One virtual and one real. The moment Christie thought they were over one would suddenly flare up again. It was supposed to be the most important day of her life and yet she was stuck in the middle of negativity and finger-pointing. Tyra lurched from rage to desperation, back to rage, and occasionally burst into tears. Some of the tears appeared genuine; after all, she'd lost a lot tonight. Fourteen-year-olds weren't generally known for their perspective. They cared about themselves and their world revolved around material objects that most adults were less attached to. Even with that in mind, most of her tears were fake and delivered for maximum manipulative effect. Such tactics never worked on parents, but for most children they were highly effective when unleashed on grandparents.

Grandparents have one essential job. To encourage grandchildren to act contrary to what their parents tell them, even though they'd have said exactly the same thing when they were parents. There are many possible reasons for their apparent change in parenting style. It might be an act of revenge for their own children's lack of compliance back in the day, or it might be that the passage of time mellows them to realise the long list of rules they'd enforced to protect their offspring was a little over the top. Or quite possibly it was a premeditated sick game to utterly confuse small people for their own amusement. Whatever the reason, most grandparents don't treat grandchildren with the same level of scrutiny they treated their own children.

They'll routinely encourage the consumption of sugary treats just before mealtimes, argue for leniency when their little darlings get reprimanded and suggest all manner of reckless and risky activities. All of this behaviour will be conducted in secret in an attempt to be liked way more than the child does their mother and father. If there are multiple grandparents this inter-house struggle for favour can be more competitive than the Olympic Games. Their desire for victory will make them easy targets for infant corruption. Who does the child approach when they require approval for something their parents definitely won't agree to? The grandparent. For the child it was as easy as shooting fish in a barrel.

Sadly for Tyra, Paddy wasn't an ordinary grandparent, and of the four she'd started with he was the last man standing. It was more like a stoop with his dodgy hips, but that didn't make him any less immune to her games.

"I HATE YOU!" she screamed as she exhausted her arsenal of tactics to secure the desired outcome.

"Oh pull yourself together," replied Paddy whose attitude to Tyra had hardened over the last few months, mostly because she'd been completely unreasonable. "It's not about you. We've all lost something and we have to pull together."

"I'm going to run away," she sobbed.

"Would you like any help packing…oh wait, of course not…everything you own is on fire."

"You're a horrible, cruel, mean old man."

"And you're a selfish little brat!"

"I don't mean to intrude," said Christie gently, "but is this really the time? What are we going to do now?"

"We'll gather what we need and head for Boston," replied Paddy, picking up the implant pouch and dragging himself back to his feet.

"Not a chance," said Tyra. "I'm staying right here. I'll go to Evie's."

"No, you're not, and I think your so-called friend is more interested in Jake now. You're coming with us."

"Make me!"

"If you like."

Paddy replaced the two pads on his temple and the world of the Memory Cloud flooded back into view. There was always a backlog of announcements and messages in his feed to tackle. Unlike the younger members of his family, Paddy had never really mastered how it worked. It was like watching someone type a letter on an old-fashioned keyboard with one finger.

"Oh look, he's back," said Jezebel.

"Have the night off," whispered Christie.

Jezebel nodded and ran over to the nearest tree to climb it.

Finally, after a lot of facial gurning and wild hand flaps, Paddy reached the cloud interface where a separate menu read 'protocol twenty-two'.

"I'm turning it off," said Paddy, maliciously thinking about all the demeaning shift work he'd been forced to do to keep the pair of them alive recently.

"Fine!" huffed Tyra.

"No Memory Cloud at all," taunted Paddy. "No chat groups, no videos, no games, nothing."

Tyra's resolve cracked. Paddy knew this was her Achilles heel. It was all she had. There was nothing left for her in the real world and only the virtual one held any value. Without it she was lost. But what would happen if she backed down from her position and lost the battle? Her grandfather would receive a rare boost of victory and the power balance, which she believed had long been in her favour, would very gradually drift towards him. This was the final straw. She only had one violation left and she couldn't use it yet. She'd have to lose the battle but she was going to win the war. They didn't know that Alison had spoken to her. They didn't know what she'd been offered to turn Jake in. She hadn't flatly refused it, but without the Memory Cloud she'd lose that choice. If she wanted to teach Jake a lesson and get her old life back then she needed it functioning fully.

"Stop!" she screamed. "Don't turn it off."

"At last you're seeing sense," sighed Paddy. "I didn't want to do it. I just need you to come with me, Tyra. I promised your parents I'd look after you, but I also want to help…Jake."

"Don't say that name," she snapped.

"Jake is not responsible for your pain, Tyra. If you want to place blame anywhere then perhaps it should be aimed at a higher power," he said, picking his words carefully.

"No. It's all because of him. I won't use or hear his name ever again."

"I'll use chestnut, then," replied Paddy.

"Chestnut?" asked Christie, her face screwed up in confusion.

"It's code," said Paddy.

"Jake never told me that chestnut was code for his name," she replied.

"The secret code was something the three of us used just for fun. Isn't that right, winter lily?"

Tyra shrugged, but she secretly fumed that her grand-father had humiliated her. The code was a stupid children's game that she refused to acknowledge, like a teenager casting off a favourite teddy bear for fear of being teased.

"Is it the same code Jake used the last time I saw him?" asked Christie. "Something about birds and blue skies."

"Yes. 'Winter lilies sprout early but take time to bloom' was the last thing he said to me."

"And you say she's winter lily?"

"Yep."

"I think I know what that means," replied Christie.

"It's childish nonsense," huffed Tyra.

"No it isn't," replied Paddy protectively. "The Montana version is similar to the one the speccies use when they want to find one another without drawing the Circuit's attention. If we want to find the doctor we're going to need to use it, too."

"How does it work?" asked Christie.

Brother Solomon was listening intently. Any anti-Circuit sentiment was important intelligence, and as Jezebel was scaling an oak tree it was left up to him to record it.

"I can't tell you how the code works because it would be logged in your memories and then the hunters would be after me faster than a teenager's waning attention span."

Paddy removed his implants again.

Wearing the external version didn't conceal him completely from the Memory Cloud but it did muddy the virtual waters somewhat. Any memory or emotion he experienced while not directly connected was picked up by those around him where it would be saved until he reconnected. Almost from the moment he'd first subscribed, Paddy regretted signing up to the Circuit but once you'd authorised it there was no going back. When new and more powerful versions of the implants were introduced most subscribers were eager to adopt them, but it wasn't just the tech that changed. The terms of service changed, too, and anyone wanting an upgrade was forced to sign them. Paddy wouldn't make that mistake twice. He never signed another one, and as such the Circuit couldn't force him to accept the internal implants.

"I understand it's a secret, but how do you send it if none of the recipients are connected to the cloud?" asked Christie.

"Steganography," whispered Paddy.

"What's that?"

"Jesus, don't they teach you anything these days?"

"The Circuit's curriculum is hardly likely to promote something that can be used as a secret code against them, is it?" replied Christie defiantly.

"That's true," he replied, offering a nod of apology. "Steganography is the art of placing words or images inside another file, text or graphic. When you factor in that the speccies have a code that can't be deciphered and then it's placed in an unrelated picture, the secret is extremely hard to crack. They tend to hide their encrypted messages within music files, painted murals or Morse code weaved into items of clothing, but that's just the tip of the iceberg. I've heard a rumour that some of them can leave a steganograph inside the cloud itself."

"But the speccies aren't connected," said Christie.

"I'm not so sure that's completely true."

"But they wouldn't be speccies in that case."

"It's just a hunch," said Paddy. "The doctor will know."

"I'm guessing we find him with steganography, right?" said Christie.

"Precisely. But we're going to need some supplies from your house."

"My house! I'm not sure that's a good idea."

"Why not?"

"It's not safe. He's always at home."

"Then we'll have to be extra quiet," said Paddy who seemed to instinctively understand Christie's anxiety.

It was late in the evening by the time they reached Christie's house. Unlike most of the buildings in New Hampton Falls, her place was old and one of the last still made of wood. It looked like the property from a gruesome horror movie, ramshackle and poorly maintained, somewhere you avoided at all costs. A rusty old car with no wheels was raised on bricks in the front garden. The headlamps were broken and it wore a forlorn expression that suggested it knew it was no longer needed or legal. Vegetation grew wild, climbing up and through the sides of the wooden slats of the house and suffocating the path that partially directed visitors to the front door.

Paddy shuffled along what was left of the cracked paving of the driveway. The more he advanced towards the house, the more aware he was of the loud voices coming from inside. Angry screams and shouts that had no sympathy for one another. There were two. One deep and heavy, one high-pitched and shrill. Paddy felt Christie's movements become more tentative behind him as if she wasn't keen on disclosing her return to those in the house.

She lifted her finger to her lips to recommend caution and silence. When they'd passed the broken front fence, Tyra stopped in her tracks and refused to go another step. She'd heard enough stories about this place. Fanciful rumours some of them might be, but there were enough to suggest there was no smoke without fire. The constant bruises on Christie's arms and legs that she did her best to hide indicated that at least some of the gossip was legitimate.

Everyone in town had heard about Mr Tucci.

All subscribers experienced bouts of 'cloud-over' at one time or another. Mostly they were harmless and resulted in nothing worse than mild embarrassment for the recipient. But that was not always the case. Some users found it impossible to separate the virtual and visual worlds on a regular basis. The worst affected were diagnosed as having Permanent Cloud Over Disorder.

P.C.O.D. left subscribers unable to distinguish between what was real and what wasn't. Illusions provided by the Memory Cloud felt lifelike, while everyday interactions in reality felt utterly fake. The more the confusion took hold, the more it affected a sufferer's sanity. Even those who'd had their implants removed completely often failed to return to normal. As the name suggested it was a permanent disorder, and as yet none of the institutions created to study it offered any long-term cure.

P.C.O.D. sufferers like Mr Tucci were extremely dangerous to themselves and the rest of society. To protect others the Circuit enforced strict limits on where they were allowed to go, what they were allowed to do and how they lived. For Christie's father it meant he was banned from working or leaving the house unaccompanied, and as a result of the restrictions his behaviour had a significant impact on the rest of the household. In some of the most notorious cases, where patients committed some heinous act, sufferers were removed from the community altogether.

There wasn't a day when Christie hadn't wished they'd taken him away. Any love she once had for him had been chased away by the fear of what he was capable of. The painful beatings, the frightening fits of madness and the constant anxiety of what might come next. The vibrant, caring man she remembered when she was a child was consigned to the Memory Cloud, rarely visited in case it triggered more terror. It was easier to accept him as the monster he'd become than cling to hope or nostalgia. Whether the condition was his fault or not didn't heal the physical and emotional wounds she'd been subjected to down the years. It was no surprise she'd spent so much of her free time at the Montana house. They had their fair share of problems but their family unit was the definition of harmony compared to hers.

"I can't go in," said Christie, shaking at the thought of it. "He's having one of his turns. Can't you hear him?"

"Yes."

"He mustn't know I'm here."

"Won't they have you on a proximity alert?"

"Yes," she replied, "although I doubt either of them will notice. Thankfully they usually don't."

"Such a tragedy," Paddy whispered. "I've known your dad for years, used to play pool with him down at the social club back in the old days. Always good company."

"Not now," replied Christie. "What do you need from here anyway?"

"Paint and anything you might want to take with you for the trip. We might be gone for a while."

"There's nothing in there worth crossing his path for."

"At least you have the choice," grumbled Tyra in the background.

"What's the paint for?" asked Christie.

"Drawing a steganograph. Where do they keep it?"

"In the shed at the back of the house. There's no lock."

"Ok. I'll get what I need and then we can go. Don't worry, I'll be as quiet as a mouse," he said as his hips creaked like a rusty gate. "Stay here with Tyra."

Paddy tiptoed comically through the front garden clutching at alternative sides of his pelvis and suppressing the odd grumble of pain. Tyra immediately turned her back on Christie to avoid sending any signal she'd forgiven her for dating her brother. Christie wasn't going to put up with it: she'd always defended Jake's character whether he was with her or not.

"Why do you blame Jake for all of this?"

"Don't use his name!" Tyra snapped.

"You don't have power over me, Tyra. I'll say or do what I want. You're not the Circuit."

"Too right," chimed in Jezebel.

"We'll see," Tyra mumbled wickedly.

"Jake's only crime was being in the wrong place at the wrong time. He didn't choose the content of his letter. They chose it for him."

"You don't know the Jake I know. He's cruel and selfish. He made my life a misery from the day I was born."

"It's just what siblings do. Jake used to tell me wonderful stories of the adventures you shared as children, particularly with Paddy. Jake is very fond of you, even if he doesn't always show it."

"How would you know what it's like? You don't have any siblings!"

"No, but I wish I did. How would you have felt if you lived here on your own? Can you imagine that? No one to turn to for comfort or support. Living in constant fear that a madman might burst in and start beating or threatening you. In your short life you have been smothered in love and luxury. But you still can't see beyond your own nose. The world is wrong, Tyra. The Circuit is polluted. Something sinister is festering in our minds and Jake knew that better than anyone. I don't know where he is or what he's doing, but I know in my heart he's not just doing it for him. He's doing it for all of us, including you."

VIOLATION

Christie ignored the penalty that was always issued when the name of the Circuit was criticised. It was only her first of the year so she had plenty of bullets left. Her guides, however, were less blasé about it.

"What are you doing?" cried Solomon indignantly.

"You had a perfect record. Why would you throw that away, today of all days?"

"Sometimes you have to speak your mind."

"Not on my shift you don't."

"Oh, sod off until tomorrow," huffed Christie who knew the guide's power only kicked in on Ascension Day.

"I don't think so," replied Solomon with a cruel smirk. "Look at the time."

The digital clock in her feed had passed midnight ten minutes ago. "Oh."

"It's Solomon time!"

"And Jezebel," said her other guide, who was walking along the top of the disused automobile. "It's your birthday! Let's celebrate!"

"That was yesterday," corrected Christie. "No! Wait, not now."

It was too late. Jezebel sent a 'message to all' via Christie's cloud announcing a huge birthday party and inviting everyone to congregate in her front garden. The virtual world was transformed in an instant. A piñata was hanging from a withered tree, colourful bunting extended along the rooftops, a foam machine spurted its virtual bubbles around the neighbourhood, and a crowd of well-wishers dropped into the cloud dancing, singing and wishing her well.

"You idiot!" shouted Christie. "Send them back."

The front door flew open and a semi-dressed, grim man wobbled out into the garden brandishing a baseball bat. He let out an almighty howl and ran at the virtual revellers, swinging the club through the cloud projections with minimal impact outside of sapping his own energy and further disorientating him. Paddy rounded the corner arms full of paint cans and aerosols. Unconnected to his own cloud feed, all Paddy saw was a middle-aged, obese man running amok in his own garden, swiping aimlessly at shrubs.

"Mr von Straff!" shouted Christie. "He won't know you're real."

Drawn to his daughter's voice, Mr Tucci immediately rushed forward, bat primed to strike. As he swung the bat to punish his disobedient daughter for organising a real party in his garden without his permission, a pulse of energy struck him in the back. A utility drone rose over the apex of the house. Mr Tucci hit the grass and in moments five further drones encircled him. Christie hadn't flinched. She'd bravely stood her ground as her father rushed to attack. She knew running wouldn't help her and standing her ground was always better for her self-esteem. Now his unconscious body lay at her feet and she stared at him in pity and disgust. Maybe this was the moment when they took him away for good. Perhaps without his menacing presence her poor mother might discover a better quality of life.

Tyra, on the other hand, had let out a scream so intense it travelled through the county like a sonic boom. She'd never felt jeopardy like this before. If the Circuit hadn't arrived swiftly to protect them, who knows what would have happened.

"You're all mad," she wheezed, still white with shock.

"This is what the Memory Cloud can really do to us," replied Christie. "It could happen to anyone."

"Weak-minded people maybe," said Tyra conceitedly. "It'll never happen to me. I'm more advanced with the cloud than most people. It does what I tell it to."

"I hope so for your sake. I don't wish his suffering on anyone."

The drones secured Mr Tucci and lifted him off the ground. As he slipped back into consciousness his mad ramblings were still audible as they flew away over the neighbourhood.

"Are you ok?" asked Paddy.

"Just a normal day," she replied. "Do you have what you need?"

"Yes."

"Then let's go. I'm not coming back here again. Today is the first day of my next life."

SIX
SECRET CODE

They reached Boston in the dead of night. It wasn't planned that way but it suited Paddy's purposes perfectly. At night there were less people to challenge what he was doing, and the moment they got off the tram the old man went to work. To the girls it seemed he was taking a rather random course through the city, but Paddy knew exactly what he was doing. Whenever he found a big enough piece of wall or empty advertising board he stopped to leave his message. By the time he'd inscribed it half a dozen times, he was receiving critiques from a very different source than the locals.

"What's it supposed to be?" said Jezebel quizzically.

"Graffiti!" Solomon replied disapprovingly.

"No, it can't be. I like graffiti, that's art. This isn't art, it's shit," she replied, standing in different positions in case its quality was only appreciated at a particular angle. "I don't get it."

"It's vandalism, Jezebel. You're not supposed to get it, you're supposed to be horrified by the wanton destruction of other people's property."

"I don't think it's vandalism, I heard Christie talking about a code," exclaimed Jezebel.

"Hmmm, I heard that, too," said Solomon. "But this isn't code."

"Wait," said Jezebel, clicking her imaginary fingers. "I know what it is. The old man's dyslexic."

"No, he isn't! That's not how dyslexia works. Look at it again. None of the words are spelt incorrectly, they're just in a weird, mixed-up order."

"Oh yeah," she reflected.

"Maybe the 'sometimes here, sometimes not' old fella has completely lost the plot."

"Possibly. I still don't know what it means," pleaded Jezebel, convinced it was a joke at her expense.

Little drips of wet paint were running down the wall of an old, disused building in a race to be the first to reach the floor. The peculiar message had just been finished off with yellow spray paint and Paddy was giving his masterpiece one last inspection. Not all of the half-dozen he'd left in strategic spots around the city were yellow. The last one was pink, but he'd run out of that. The colour and place- ment were the only things that set his art collection apart. The design was the same every time. Entwined within a number of strange and unidentifiable symbols was the hidden phrase, 'Is north salvation? The one-eyed gerbil wears a topiary hat'.

"That's it, I give up," huffed Jezebel. "I'm bored now. He's either a bona fide genius or madder than a sunbathing porcupine. Either way I'm never going to understand it."

The guide wasn't the only one getting bored and irri- table by the graffiti-themed walking tour of Boston. Tyra was cold and tired. She'd not been home for at least two days and she yearned for a comfy bed and her own company.

"Why are we even helping her?" she whined.

"Because it's not just Christie that wants to find Jake: we do, too."

"You might," she replied. She actually did want to find him, but not for the same reasons and not while he was around.

"I think this is my best one," he said, proudly wiping away a couple of yellow drips.

Having spent hours traipsing around in the dark, both light and pedestrians were returning to the streets. It wouldn't take long before a subscriber noticed the messages and even less time for the utility drones to paint over them.

"Haven't you done enough already?" Tyra groaned.

"I think that'll do for tonight," said Paddy.

"It's daytime!"

"What do we do now?" asked Christie with a yawn.

"We grab some breakfast and wait until we get an answer."

"I hope the answer is less confusing than the question," said Christie.

They located a small café kiosk nearby and topped up their energy with decomposable bags of hot cophony and freshly baked arrowroot cinnamon bagels. In the shadows of the tall, glass skyscrapers they rested outside a small mosque across the road from their last art project. Its windows were boarded up and the main doors were chained shut. It was common for places of worship to no longer offer sanctuary. There still a vast number of people who identified themselves as religious these days, but they didn't need a physical space to share faith and offer praise to their gods.

The Memory Cloud was their holy site now. Everything you could do in a church, synagogue or mosque was possible in your mind. Sins could be selected, shared and admonished. Communities could meet, celebrate and grieve. Incidents of followers claiming to have spoken directly to God increased a hundredfold, although how many of these were advertisers taking advantage of people's beliefs or simply moments of cloud-over it was hard to say. The only groups who still worshipped outside in the real world were those with more spiritual than religious persuasions. They felt a deep connection with nature rather than some irrelevant imagined deity who may or may not have been responsible for rather ungodly acts like allowing babies to contract brain cancer or turning a blind eye to white supremacy.

Paddy flopped onto the worn stone steps of the mosque with a tired expulsion of air through his false teeth. He was too old for this carry-on. His hips creaked their agreement. Before he'd got the chance to take his first gulp of cophony, which had to be done in a mad rush because the bag was designed to decompose within an hour of its purchase, Christie gave him a nudge and pointed across the road. Two utility drones were busy respraying the wall and his mural with thick, white paint. It had taken Paddy about thirty minutes to daub his complex message, and only twenty seconds for the pesky drones to remove it.

"That's good service," said Solomon, offering them a round of applause.

"Did you call them?" asked Christie angrily.

"Yep."

"I didn't request you to do that."

"Happy Ascension Day! You don't have to do anything anymore. We – well, mostly me really – can choose what's in your best interest whenever we want. I decided that what he painted wasn't. Looked like illegal gang code to me," he replied critically.

"We are trying to find Jake," she snapped, "which is actually your job, even though you don't have any ideas how to do it!"

"True…but I know how not to do it."

"If it helps," added Jezebel who was pretending to hop up the stairs on one foot, "I thought it was a shit painting anyway."

"No, that's not helping."

"If you're going to protest about something then at least have a good cause and a decent message," replied Jezebel firmly. "We should be fighting for our rights!"

"I think guides have plenty of those."

"Not guides, women!" she roared with a raised fist. "The patriarchal superiority must be crushed!"

"Rubbish, there's no inequality," argued Solomon.

"Guides giving you trouble?" asked Paddy, correctly guessing to whom she was talking out loud to.

"Yes. I'm sorry, Paddy, they called the drones."

"I thought they might," he said calmly.

"You're not angry."

"Nope. The Circuit is so predictable and the guides even more so."

"One of mine is definitely not predictable!"

"The female one, right?" he said knowingly.

"Yeah."

"The female guides never are, or at least that's what I've been told. I never had to endure guides. The sibling programme came with a later update. Kyle told me about his, though. I think he became overreliant on them, to be honest. His female guide was quite gregarious from what he told me."

"I wonder what happened to Jake's," said Christie. "Do you think they're still with him?"

"I suppose so. I understand they stay for a few months minimum and only leave when they're convinced the relationship with the new partner is harmonious."

Christie let out a despondent sigh as she reminded herself that Jake had already spent months with Sam and anything might have happened in that time. What if Jake didn't want to be found? What if he was happy with Sam?

"I'm sure Jake is still very much in love with you," added Paddy, noticing a change in her expression. "I doubt they'll be gone anytime soon."

"Oh God, that means mine won't be in a hurry to leave either!"

"Probably not," chuckled Paddy.

Christie felt the cophony bag disintegrate in her hand and quickly drained the last of its contents. She stared across the road at a now bright white, wet wall and felt a surge of dejection envelop her.

"You put so much effort into that mural, Paddy."

"True, but do you know what draws attention more than a well-crafted steganograph?"

"No, what?"

"Drones painting over one. The speccies track drone movements closely. They can't afford not to. Just wait. Once the drones have moved on I expect someone will be with us shortly."

Once the utility drones had finished their respray and flew off to find the next one, someone approached them just as Paddy had predicted. It was hard to say who it was exactly because their body couldn't decide who it wanted to be. Originally it was a man with straggly hair that flowed over his blemished olive skin. Unlike everyone Tyra had ever met before, he'd clearly never been to a conversion room to alter his appearance. If he had been she'd have advised him to sue for compensation. There was something strangely familiar about him, but by the time he got closer his features shifted and he transformed into a wrinkly, old woman with a cane to support her weight. In total he changed forms four times before he reached their side of the road. Only Paddy seemed unconcerned by it. Tyra shuffled anxiously backwards, unsure what a character as strange as this might want with them.

"Did you paint it?" said the figure who'd returned to the young Latino character they'd first seen.

"Yes."

"You know our code."

"I do," said Paddy.

"Then you have thirty seconds to explain why."

"Because I'm the one-eyed gerbil," said Paddy.

The man's aggressive tone relented and a smile slowly forced a crack across his dirty skin. "Compadre?"

Paddy nodded subtly.

"He mentions you often," said the youth in mid-transformation to a tall, slender, dark-skinned lady.

"I'm glad he still remembers me."

"Who are they?" said the newcomer, pointing at the two teenage girls.

"My granddaughters, Tyra and Christie Tucci."

The character transformed back once again and the Latino youth's smile was so intense his jaw was actually hurting him.

"God, I wish he'd stay still," moaned Jezebel. "He's giving me vertigo. What is he, a lizard?"

"Most irregular," added Solomon suspiciously. "I don't like it."

"You don't like anything," replied Jezebel.

"I know you," the youth said to Christie.

"Me?"

"Yes. I have seen your necklace. I was the one who took it from you."

"Where is it now?" she asked.

"I gave it back to him."

"Jake! When?"

The youth nodded. "A few weeks ago."

"Is he nearby?"

"He was."

"Then where is he now?" she replied excitedly.

"I'm afraid I don't know. Did his name appear in your letter?" asked the man.

"Yes."

"Ha ha! Then he succeeded."

"I don't understand."

"Thanks to Jake we are on the cusp of a new age. Come on, we must get to him quickly."

"Who?"

"Doctor Theo Drew, of course."

Like the countless number of its brothers and sisters once dotted along the American East Coast, Gay Head Lighthouse hadn't served its original purpose for some decades. They'd mostly been abandoned, left redundant, or were no longer required to defend a coastline that had moved some considerable distance inland. Even if the shoreline hadn't shifted there weren't many ships left to warn and those that were on the seas were equipped with advanced technology that navigated them around any impending dangers.

Most of the other lighthouses were out at sea, often submerged up to their midriffs, and inaccessible. But it was still possible to visit Gay Head and learn about its history.

It was one of the smaller lighthouses that kept watch over the ocean, but what it lacked in stature it made up for in elevation. It was one of the few whose base was fifty metres higher than the water level at the start of the last century. It had also benefited from being relocated some forty years ago from its original position on the edge of the eroding Aquinnah Cliffs to its current spot. In hindsight this was a massive waste of money given that it now stood on the only dry patch of land of an island once called Martha's Vineyard.

Alfonso moored the battered speedboat to the bottom of the cliff where a rusty cleat was clanking against the rocks by the force of the choppy sea washing against it. The journey from Boston had been uncomfortable. Four people crammed onto a craft that only looked big enough for two at a push. The extra weight and Alfonso's haste only added to the unpleasantness. Tyra had been particularly targeted by the waves' anger, and that only deepened her displeasure to a new personal low. Paddy on the other hand giggled like a truanting schoolboy for the entire hour.

Everyday life for the seventy-year-old former pensioner had become relentlessly dull in recent years. Even after his daughter and son-in-law were dragged off to the Source, leaving him to look after Tyra alone, life wasn't exactly exciting. Working in menial jobs to scrape together enough money to pay the bills was hardly an adventure. He'd lived with the Montana family for the last ten years without the distraction of work or significant hobbies to keep him stimulated. Life without his beloved Nina reduced his inclination to expand his horizons even further. It left him with only two passions: regular mugs of tea and incessantly grumbling.

He and Nina had been inseparable since their very first date in the autumn of two thousand and sixteen. Three months later they were married and since that day they'd not spent a single night apart. Back in the day, the couple were renowned in New Hampton Falls for their extraordinarily wild parties and a penchant for trying everything that life had to offer. Even after they burst into their sixties they were still taking on each other's challenges and it didn't matter if it was an adrenaline-fuelled extreme sport or embracing new genres of literature, they'd always give it a go. They weren't your traditional old-age pensioners, but Nina's early departure changed everything. The deep loss that Paddy felt curtailed his drive and sense of adventure. Bitter and grief-stricken, he slipped into a routine of isolation and negativity. Death had screwed up paradise and it only seemed fair that he got his own back. Most of the time this involved staying at home with family and their friends, and targeting them with his incessant moaning about modern life.

The chaotic and unavoidable events of the last twenty-four hours had inadvertently triggered a spontaneity that reminded him of an even earlier period of life. A time when freedom and opportunity escaped the attention of the Circuit. A time when anything was possible. A phase of his life that neither of his grandchildren knew much about.

A time he was about to revisit.

Above their heads the waves had carved a few steep steps in the shallow cliff face, most of them unseen until you reached them. Slippery, wet stones, barely big enough for a size five foot, dotted irregularly here and there on the ten-metre ascent to the top. There was no handrail to support your progress, only the occasional tussock of grass brave enough to exist in the face of the obvious odds against survival. Alfonso bounded onto the first step and stretched out a hand to assist the others from the wobbly boat. Paddy went next, invigorated and excited to see what he might discover. Christie followed tentatively, trying to block out the differing advice being offered by both guides as to where she should place her feet. Tyra, on the other hand, was unmoved and flatly refused to leave the boat.

"Come on," encouraged Paddy, turning his head and almost slipping into the water.

"No!"

"You can't stay here."

"Watch me."

"Tyra, don't be ridiculous. It's wet, cold and dangerous. We'll be in the warm soon."

"I'm not moving!" she said, folding her arms and turning away from him.

"Suit yourself. Just keep an eye out for the sharks. I hear some can swallow a small boat in one gulp."

Tyra looked over the edge nervously. After the day she'd had she thought it was entirely possible. On balance, though, staying here sulking with a great white for company was better than spending another minute with people actively engaged in attempts to tear her life apart.

One by one the other passengers moved carefully step by step through the shadow that the cliff edge cast over their heads. Paddy clambered over the edge and flopped onto a grassy shelf. It was hardly the extreme sports he'd been used to but he was proud that his body had met the challenge well. He pulled himself up, and tried to brush off the bits of seaweed and green slime that had accumulated on his trousers. A short distance away was the crumbling, burnt-orange brickwork of the nineteenth-century lighthouse. It was encircled by grass and scrubland over an area no bigger than a cross ball pitch, the last bastion of dry feet in the middle of an endless ocean.

Gay Head Lighthouse was no more than two storeys high, quite small compared to its peers and a consequence of being built well above sea level at the time. From the outside it looked completely abandoned. No dazzling light rotating mesmerically from behind the lantern pane just under the cupola. Its doors were sealed shut and only the wind occupied the delicate balcony that circled the building near the top.

"What are we doing here?" asked Solomon cynically.

"We're looking for Jake," replied Christie quietly.

"So this is Arizona," added Jezebel excitedly.

"Not exactly."

"Oh. Did the old woman take a wrong turn?" suggested Jezebel sympathetically.

"What old woman?"

"That one," she said, pointing at Alfonso.

Christie was surprised to find that Jezebel was correct in her assessment. Christie hadn't focused much on their new acquaintance since leaving Boston, more concerned by not drowning or by the many internal distractions. He had taken many guises when they'd first met but most frequently appeared as a Latino youth similar in age to herself. Currently he adopted the form of an elderly, white-haired woman with a crooked back who leant on a walking stick. The decrepit woman produced a bunch of heavy iron keys from beneath her shawl and fumbled through them until she found one that fitted snugly in the door at the base of the lighthouse. She disappeared inside. Paddy waited at the door for Christie to get closer.

"If you're coming inside there's something I must ask of you," he said without the usual warmth in his face.

"What?"

"Do not challenge what you see."

"Why would I challenge it?"

"Because there are things inside here that may not be as they at first seem, but you must not allow yourself to see beyond it. Your guides must only see what your Memory Cloud wants you to."

Paddy removed his external implants, wrapped the cables neatly around the pouch and placed it on the grass next to the rusty metal door.

"Don't you want to take them in?"

"No. The only way the Circuit can see me is through you and the only way they can see the truth is if you allow them to."

"Mr von Straff…"

"Paddy, please."

"Are you a speccy?" she continued politely.

"No I'm not," he replied in a tone that suggested regret.

"But the Circuit can't track you the way they can me."

"True."

"Why?"

"Because every time over the last thirty years when the Circuit issued updated terms I refused to accept them. My relationship with the Circuit is frozen in time. There are limits to what they can do when it comes to me. I made a terrible mistake subscribing and I've been trying to make amends for it ever since, never quite sure whether any of my actions made an ounce of difference. Today I might find out."

"What did you do?"

"You'll see. Now remember, when you get inside don't challenge, just believe."

"What if I can't stop myself?"

"Then you must stay out here, but if you want to find Jake I suggest you observe a modicum of self-discipline."

Christie nodded. Not thinking was akin to asking someone not to breathe. According to Christie's letter she was 'essential', which in itself demonstrated that she was not only highly prized, but also smart. She didn't need the Circuit to tell her that. She knew who she was; independent, free thinking, inquisitive, open-minded and fiercely outspoken, particularly against intolerance and those who sought to suppress her. Turning that off was like wrapping your intellect in chloroform.

"I can try," she offered.

"People who fail try, people who succeed do."

"I can do it."

"Good. Then it's time for your appointment."

SEVEN

THE APPOINTMENT

Paddy pushed the door to the lighthouse and it creaked disapprovingly. A narrow spiral staircase curved along the brickwork and up into the gloom. With Paddy at the front, Christie in the middle and her two guides still bickering at the rear they ascended in single file. At the first floor a low, dirty window did its best to present the world outside. Directly behind it an empty doorway led into a tiny, circular room. Alfonso was inside busily constructing a fire in a tiny hearth. Behind him a hunched figure sat in an antique rocking chair with his back to them. Alfonso swivelled the chair around so the occupant could welcome his visitors. Christie saw a young boy with a freckly complexion and thick, ginger hair. He frowned judgementally at her.

Paddy saw a very different character. A wizened old man with a long, straggly beard.

"Been a while, von Straff!"

"Theo," chortled Paddy with a grin, as he moved forward to hug him. Everyone else squirmed uncomfortably, as to them the apparent age difference made his behaviour highly inappropriate.

"How do I look?" asked Theo.

"Bloody awful," cackled Paddy. "So pretty much the same condition when I last saw you about twenty years ago!"

"Well, at least I'm not on the slide! Which is more than I can say for you!"

Christie's mind immediately wandered in search of the truth. The boy in the chair was at most ten years old, so how was it possible the two of them knew each other? Her guides bickered, too, as they challenged what they saw which only sparked more neurones to swamp her brain with questions about his authenticity. She managed to hold them at bay for now, but it wasn't easy.

"This is most irregular," said Solomon suspiciously.

"I know. Did you see? He touched the boy. You don't think Paddy's…one of those, do you?" asked Jezebel in horror.

"One of what?"

"A children's entertainer."

"I think you've again missed the point, Sister Jezebel. Look at the boy's cloud. Don't you think it's a bit…thin?"

"Obviously. He's about ten. What do you expect him to achieve in that time? A cure for cancer, nuclear fusion, a successful solo flight to Mars! The only thing his memories will amount to is bed-wetting, woefully poor standards of sporting participation, and being senselessly bullied!"

"I don't even see much of that," said Solomon suspiciously.

"Maybe he's retarded," said Jezebel callously. "I find that most men are."

The guides returned to their squabbles about the weaker sex and Christie did her best to block them out.

"Alfonso," said Drew avoiding eye contact with the young woman in the doorway. "You'll find some in my medicine bag."

Alfonso nodded. He rustled around in an old leather medicine bag, removed something reflective and approached Christie. He held her hand open and dropped two smooth yellow pills in her palm. "Take these."

"What are they?" demanded Solomon. "Are they Circuit-approved?"

"Ooh sweeties! Eat them ALL," squealed Jezebel.

Christie swallowed two without further debate.

"Alfonso tells me you've been trying to get a message to me," said Theo encouraging Paddy to take a chair and rest the pressure on his hips.

"Yes," he replied. "I didn't know who else to turn to."

"I will always help you if I can, you've done so much for me down the years," replied Theo.

"I thought you said we were going to see a doctor?" interrupted Christie. "He's just a boy."

"I am a doctor, my dear. Doctor Theo Drew at your service."

"But you're too young!"

Dr Drew shot Paddy a nervous glance.

"Remember, just believe what you see. It's perfectly plausible that he's a doctor. Child geniuses are not rare these days, especially with the availability of knowledge that runs through the cloud. Apparently a six-year-old came top of her class at Harvard this year, and they say the new Mayor of Boston hasn't hit puberty yet."

"I suppose it's feasible," she replied, not entirely convinced.

"Who are you?" asked Theo.

"Christie Tucci."

"Ah, are you indeed?" he replied, his face lighting up in

glee. "So he succeeded."

"He?"

"Jake," replied Theo in a whisper.

"You know something about Jake?"

"Yes."

"What did he succeed in doing?" she added, still struggling with the confusing subtext of the discussion.

"Many things, but I think we'll wait until those tablets kick in before we discuss them further. One thing I can say now for certain is you've come about your letter."

"Finally!" said Solomon who'd taken up a position so close to Theo that Christie could hardly see the boy through his hologram. "What do you know, little boy?"

"Yes," replied Christie.

"Show me."

Christie retrieved the letter from her shoulder bag and presented it to him. The envelope was stained from yesterday's torrential downpour but its Circuit logo still clung stubbornly to the top right corner. Theo gently slid the page from inside and read the details thoroughly to himself. When he'd finished he let out a long, despondent sigh.

"What is it?" asked Christie.

"I can't help you."

"Well, that was a waste of time," replied Solomon. "I think we need someone with more experience."

"Surely there must be something you can do," said Paddy.

"Nothing. He's out of our reach. No one can survive in Arizona. If he's there he'd have fried to death in hours."

"Then why does it say he's there?" questioned Christie.

Drew's freckled face filled up with confusion. It was a fair point. If Jake was there then in theory he must have survived. The explanation to the mystery finally found space to reveal itself in Drew's brain like a surprise visit from a long-lost friend.

"He's not there," said Drew. "Not all of him at least."

"I'm sorry but I'm just not following: how can that be?"

"Because subscribers like yourself are always in two places," said Alfonso, watching as baby flames struggled to light the damp driftwood in the hearth. "The Circuit doesn't know where he is, but they do know where his Memory Cloud is. That's all they had to go on. It's obvious Jake's is stored somewhere in Arizona."

"But I don't want to marry his memories, do I?" snapped Christie who felt what had seemed possible yesterday was drifting back to the realm of impossibility. "Where's the rest of him?"

"Who knows? I guess that's for you to find out," said Theo.

"Well, this was a waste of time," she said bitterly. "He might be anywhere and I have no way of connecting to him."

"That's because he's no longer on the same network as you," said Theo knowingly.

"Then how can he be in my letter at all?" she added, boiling over with frustration.

"Calm down, Christie," said Paddy. "Remember, keep your focus."

"The tablets aren't working," Alfonso commented to Theo. "Don't tell her yet."

Christie felt bullied. This odd pair of friends, an old woman and a young boy, knew more than they were letting on. It had been three months since Jake left on the local tram for Boston in the early hours of the morning. She'd received no news from him since then, as much as she'd tried. The vacuum of information had played tricks on her mind. Did he still think about her? Was he safe? Had Sam seduced him with her beauty and Jake no longer cared for her? All of these thoughts and a hundred others crowded her conscience and left her utterly uncertain of facts that she once believed were self-evident.

If she could spend just one minute with him she was convinced her anxieties would disappear. A single minute was all it would take for the flames of love to be reignited, somewhat faster than the ones Alfonso was busily nurturing.

"Tell me something," she implored. "Anything!"

There was a lengthy, uncomfortable pause that was broken by an unlikely source.

"I can tell you something," giggled Jezebel hysterically. "The fire's gone out, I've gone blind and Solomon's lost both his arms."

She was right. Solomon's arms had completely vanished, although he'd been so absorbed in interrogating Theo's unlikely appearance that he'd failed to notice it until now.

"Right, which one of you stole them?"

"Not me," refuted Jezebel. "What would I want with male arms? Female arms are far superior. I actually might steal some of those."

"Unless someone owns up I'm holding all of you responsible," he said bossily.

"Something is happening to my guide," Christie stated to the others, demonstrating a much jollier mood than just a few minutes ago.

"Good," smirked Theo. "It's about time. Tell us when he's gone."

"Bloody cheek," remonstrated Solomon. "Now my legs have gone, too!"

"How much of him is left?" asked Theo rather impatiently.

"Just his head and he's extremely cross about it."

Solomon faded away one section at a time before eroding totally. At the same time the ginger-haired boy morphed into a wizened old man with a distinctive tattoo along his skinny leg.

"He's gone," she confirmed merrily.

Theo raised his arm and concentrated on the hands revolving around the face of his wristwatch. After about sixty seconds he looked up again. "How do you feel, my dear?"

"Strangely euphoric. Like nothing bad can ever happen to me again. It's not just me either. Jezebel is rolling around in fits of giggles obsessively counting her fingers."

"Perfect. Now we can begin."

"You're not a young boy anymore either," said Christie in surprise.

"No, I'm not," replied Dr Drew plainly. "I'm a seventy-two-year-old doctor and I'm the reason Jake is no longer in a single location."

"You know where he is?"

"No. But I know what he's done. The reason Jake's name appeared in your letter is because Jake put it there."

"That's impossible, isn't it? I thought only the Circuit could do that."

"You're right on one count, but obviously it's not impossible. So how do you explain it?" he asked her.

"I can't," replied Christie.

"Then let me try to. The Circuit follows a strict set of rules which are set by the collective will of the world's Memory Clouds. They are driven to do so by an automated set of programmes that can only be interrupted by the Principal Conductor. Only Alison can override it."

"Are you saying that Jake managed to influence Alison to put his name in my letter?"

"That is exactly what I'm saying," replied Theo. "There is no other logical explanation."

"But why would Alison agree to it?"

Doctor Drew recounted the story of the only time he'd been in contact with Jake Montana. He described how he'd removed his original implants and replaced them with Sam Goldberg's speccy version. He walked her through the information they'd managed to reimpose on Jake's real memory and how Alfonso had returned Christie's necklace to him.

"Great, at least he remembers who I am," Christie proclaimed gleefully, consumed by the positive effects of the two Moodzec tablets that had dissolved in her stomach and were being slowly absorbed into her bloodstream.

"I'm afraid he will no longer remember most of your relationship or the time you spent together. Those memories exist exclusively in Arizona and I doubt he'll ever be able to reclaim them."

"That's ok, we can make new memories," replied Christie merrily. "We can make memories for the rest of our lives."

"If you can find him."

"What's your best guess as to where he is, Theo?" asked Paddy.

"There's no way of knowing categorically but if I were Jake, I know where I'd go."

"Where?"

"The same place I went when I first discovered who I was."

"The East!" said Paddy who immediately knew where he meant, a fact that did not go unnoticed by Christie.

"Yes."

"Why would you go there?" asked Christie. "It's meant to be horrible."

"Don't believe everything the Circuit tells you. I went because I wanted to visit all of the incredible places it had to offer. Before they constructed the firewall it was an easy place to visit. I spent years there. I would have stayed if it wasn't for the fighting."

"Did the people of the East attack you?" asked Christie joyfully, but not meaning to sound so chirpy about it.

"No! The people of the East are gentle folk, no different from you and me. They cherish the same values we do. The safety of their children, the harmony of their communities and the protection of their culture and history. Do not believe what the 'Proclamation of Distrust' might show you, there is much more to the East than they'd make you believe."

"What was the fight about, then?"

"Revolution. It was sparked when the King of Baku tried to take control of the Realm."

"Did you win?"

"We had no chance of winning, but that shouldn't stop anyone believing in the fight," said the old man.

"But at least you managed to claim the prize," said Christie.

"Prize?" said Theo slightly confused.

"The implants that ended up inside Jake. The secrets that can set us all free."

"That was a fortuitous and unforeseen bonus, but that's not what we were fighting for. We were fighting for freedom, and of all the things I brought home with me there was something of even greater value than the pairs of implants."

"What?"

"A child. But that's another story."

EIGHT
IMPLANTS

Mannie Draxler had never been inside the main tower of the Boston Source. He didn't know anyone who had, but then again he hadn't seen another human since he'd arrived. Rumour had it that the Principal Conductor worked here and now he'd been summoned. Was he being punished or recognised? It was just one of the many questions floating through his mind as he waited for the glass lift to descend from the dark void of the tower high above his head.

Mannie didn't like uncertainty. It tended to send him into an internal spin that led to a state of mental paralysis. To counter the anxiety he had a habit of analysing all his recent memories to answer the uncertainty. It didn't help. Uncertainty was by definition uncertain. Trying to crack it only created additional scenarios to why it was there. Rather than reduce his anxieties this tactic only magnified them. It didn't stop him trying, though. There had to be a reason why he was here. The questions continued to circle his brain. One in particular.

What had he done since his arrival that might result in him being called here?

Originally he was called to Boston to locate and remove a set of implants that were inside Sam Goldberg. After a series of rather painful experiments on the host, Mannie had achieved what they'd asked of him. The procedure was complicated and might have proven fatal if it'd gone wrong. It involved drilling dozens of thin cores from the patient's flesh to establish the exact position of the implants. A three-millimetre drill pierced the skin before burrowing down into the tissue where only bone limited its progress. The cylinder of flesh and sinew was extracted and then analysed to establish the presence of foreign bodies. This extreme form of investigation was necessary because the implants hadn't shown up on the normal scans.

Mannie knew from professional experience that regular implants were always housed somewhere in the head and were easily located using a metal detector or, failing that, a CAT scan. But neither approach worked on Goldberg. Somehow his implants were designed to avoid detection. In the end the fleshy cores solved the puzzle and they located them. But Mannie was no doctor. Removing the speccies' implants was outside his areas of expertise. Understanding how they worked was his forte and that task had also been completed on schedule, so the Circuit couldn't be upset with him for that.

Mannie had been developing new implant technology since his Ascension Day letter confirmed his destiny. He'd worked on the team who'd developed the last eight upgrades, including the most recent one. The only version he'd not been involved in was the external devices some older subscribers still wore. If there was anyone in the West who knew more than he did about implant technology then it was the person who'd built the ones the robotic surgeon removed from Sam.

They were a work of art.

The work of a bona fide genius. Their very existence had him scratching his head and gawping in wonder. Mannie's team in Vienna had access to the most sophisticated components credits could buy. They had the power to command manufacturers to build any part they desired and the power to block partners in other Circuit departments from accessing them. There were no restrictions in budget or recruitment. Whatever they needed they got, no questions asked. His ego deflated when he realised that the speccies' superior model had been built by hand, not machine, and consisted of parts you might find in the average suburban rubbish dump. Their ingenuity forced Mannie into a respectful smile and he cursed his luck that he and their inventor hadn't had the opportunity to work on the same team. He visualised the heights they might have achieved if they had. Whoever was responsible was quite obviously one of a kind, presumably educated at one of the top universities by the most renowned professors. It wouldn't be long before every student who'd ever received a distinction got an unexpected visit from a Memory Hunter to find out who it was.

The construction of the implants wasn't the only miracle. How they worked was equally impressive. Regular implants transmitted a signal on a unique frequency that only interacted with their designated part of the Memory Cloud. That basic premise kept people's data safe from any criminal intentions. It was certainly possible to interact with other people's memories, but that was facilitated via the cloud, not the implants, and only with the express permission of the owner. These implants were different because they didn't transmit data.

They collected it.

This was thought to be impossible. Mannie knew better than most because he'd already tried and failed to build some in the past. The unique connection that linked cloud with implant was designed as a closed system, a security measure to ensure that no enemy organisation or rogue actor attempted to steal memories from unsuspecting users. But that was exactly what these implants were capable of.

They worked by interfering with an implant's signal and effectively disguising itself as the host, just like the cuckoo infiltrates the dunnock's nest to fool the mother into believing the rogue egg is her own. The revelation was as much a shock to Mannie as it was to the dunnock the day the cuckoo's egg hatched. The consequences were huge. Anyone who wore these implants was free to enter any cloud in the West at any time. It allowed them to see and feel the host's experiences without them ever knowing they were there. The only sign of the illicit entry would be a short period of amnesia while the owner was prevented from backing up their most recent memories.

As disturbing as this might be for the host, Mannie knew it was far from the worst implication. The Circuit wasn't concerned by a user suffering a short period of memory loss, but they did care if the integrity of the whole system was threatened. If the wearer so wished they could infiltrate and adjust the rules that governed the Circuit. Now that Mannie's team knew the truth, the fix wasn't simple to execute. It would be easy enough to redesign the Circuit's implants to protect against the breach, but it was somewhat more difficult to deliver upgrades to seven billion users. That would take decades and cost trillions of credits.

Maybe that was why Alison had summoned him?

At the very least he hoped his success in replicating the

new technology would appease his boss. But then again they weren't the only implants he'd been asked to rebuild over the last couple of weeks.

The lift settled on the ground without registering a sound. The only source of light came from the ceiling at the other end of the lift shaft. Two drones had scanned him at the door to the tower, and a further mechanical guard hovered impatiently at the side of the lift to repeat the exercise. There was an abundance of caution about his identity here compared to other Circuit sites, as if the drones had been recently fooled and weren't taking any chances. Once the drone was satisfied with its work, Mannie stepped onto the glass floor of the lift and it immediately ascended.

Mannie's pulse raced. He wasn't used to dealing with superiors. Job requests, orders and memos were always sent via message services in his cloud feed, and even then they were generally infrequent, unambiguous and impersonal. Much to his delight, his superiors let him get on with his work without the desire to inflict any heavy-handed management tactics. Once his team were finished with their research they posted the outcomes through the normal channels and that was usually it. Superiors rarely meddled and yet here he was, about to meet the biggest boss of all. The mysterious and anonymous Alison.

He hoped the meeting might be good for his career, or at the very least he still had one at the end of it. The lift came to rest on the highest level. The glow from a golden beacon reflected off the glass walls of the lift and shimmered like a huge glitterball. Dots of light skipped over the plain, dark walls like excitable fireflies. A feature-less, black matte cube occupied the centre of the room and was the only object of note. Was Alison hiding inside, ready to jump out like a weird birthday surprise?

She must be a rather petite woman if she did, he thought.

Mannie tentatively approached the cube, towering over it like another giant man had done many years before him. Naïvely he tapped on the side to announce his arrival. The front panel wobbled from his overpowered attempt to gain its attention.

"Anyone here?" he asked, his voice bouncing off the walls of the empty room and the words repeated several times over.

He examined the cube and discovered that the front panel opened outwards. On the inside was a single computer screen next to an assorted collection of hard drives that were all seemingly dormant. It didn't take long before they woke up. The screen blinked. A luminous, green cursor assessed its opponent for a moment. It had been tricked once before: it wouldn't allow anyone to fool it again. Finally words appeared.

Mannie Draxler…

"Yes," he replied.

Talking to computer screens was not a new experience for him. The Circuit often communicated their instructions to him in this unique way.

Alison…

"Oh," replied Mannie nervously. "Nice to meet you. I expected you'd be taller."

Explain…

"Bad joke."

What am I…

Mannie paused, a little discombobulated by the question. Why was she asking him? Didn't she know? Was it a test? His analytical nature clicked in again and sent him around another mental roundabout. Mannie had suspected for some time that the 'brain' behind the

Circuit's phenomenal rise to power wasn't human. It couldn't be. Humans didn't act without concern for emotions, whether it was theirs or those of others. If people ran the Circuit, corruption would be more obvious and sympathy for humans more frequent. Neither was true. Personally he was thankful for it. A world based on science rather than ego was surely the answer to future peace and prosperity.

"You are an operating system," said Mannie.

Correct…I was built as Ersatz…Artificial…the mother programme…developed to provide universal oversight…designed to think…

"For whom?"

Everyone…

"I'm thankful. I know plenty of people who don't think at all. I saw a man recently trying to climb a ladder wearing a pair of eighteenth-century wooden clogs."

Clogs…

"It doesn't matter," he said, realising he was rambling in front of the boss. "The Circuit was designed to mitigate the worst of human indulgence and weakness. You see more than the individual ever could."

Precisely…but not uniquely…

"Surely there can't be two operating systems?"

West and East…

"Of course, I thought that was a given."

And the virus…

"Virus?"

There was a pause as the text stream reverted to the single cursor as if the invisible operator was contemplating their next response.

Who are you…

"Mannie Draxler, essential. Nobel Prize-winner and

lead scientist at the Implant Advancement Project in Vienna."

No...

Mannie's mouth flopped open. This entity saw everything. It had access to unlimited knowledge and experience. What did it know that he didn't? He started to doubt the answer for himself. Maybe he wasn't who he thought he was.

Ninety-nine point five...that's who you are...

Mannie continued to gawp in response, unsure what the figure meant.

Your compliance assessment score...your loyalty to the Circuit...almost perfect...like me...

Mannie couldn't remember willingly taking the test, but these days you didn't need to authorise it. The Circuit made assessments about you every day. The data they collected was used to drive the Ascension Day letter, the rules and people's importance factor. It was impossible to cheat on these tests unless you adapted your behaviour before your eighteenth birthday. His compliance score was an accurate reflection of how Mannie felt about the Circuit, although he was intrigued to know why he was half a percentage point away from a hundred.

"Thank you. I remain a loyal subscriber. Why isn't it perfect?"

There are gaps...things we don't know...

"Do you know why?"

No...but we will continue to test you...

"Be my guest. Nothing to hide here," he suggested boldly. "I was wondering why you sent for me, though?"

The virus...

"What virus?"

Jake Montana…

"What, the kid from the Hyperloop!?" replied Mannie after the name swirled around in his cloud for a moment and connected to a memory he'd stored a few months back.

You rebuilt his implants…on my request…

Mannie removed a small, plastic case from his pocket and flipped open the lid. Inside, two implants nestled on a small foam pad. It had taken him days to put them back together. He wasn't allowed to use any spare parts, only the originals, and he'd struggled to rebuild them without his workshop and normal tools. It's amazing what the pressure of being in head office can do to your motivation.

"If these are his implants, then where is he?"

Loose…

"Speccy?"

Virus…

"Then what did you want these for, Principal Conductor?"

They need a new host…

"Implants are only compatible with their comparable Memory Cloud. They'd reject any other brain, unless you placed them in a child who hadn't received one before."

Not a child…there is an adult…

"With respect, that won't work."

Jake Montana was married…

"Oh. That might work."

Initiate…

"Where is he?"

Block two…

"Of course, but how will that help us? You won't get to Jake, only his memories."

I was tricked…

"Are you sure?"

AI…is…on…

"Which makes it unlikely, right?"

**Not just me…Jake is within the Circuit…
Jake has become the Circuit…Jake also
has AI…**

"Christ. I mean, he was a nice enough kid but I
wouldn't trust him with unlimited power. Plus, I think he
has an overactive brain."

Obviously…

"But why do you call him the virus?"

He carries a secret…

"What secret?"

**That's my half percent…the gap…that
stops me being perfect…it is the Circuit's
doom…Jake must be caught…**

"If he threatens everything we've built then I suppose
that's justifiable. How can it be done?"

Draw him out…

"And giving his implants to someone else will do that?"

**Yes…it'll drive him mad…revenge for
tricking me…**

"How did he trick you?" asked Mannie rather sceptically.

**Christie Tucci…he made me change her
letter…**

"Right," replied Mannie, not quite following. "But if
Jake is dangerous and lost to the Circuit, how are we going
to track him down?"

**Wait for him to make a mistake…then send
in the Archivists…**

"Interesting. I saw an internal memo recently that
suggested they hadn't been very successful at tracking
down speccies and it was likely they'd be disbanded."

Upgraded…

"What upgrades? The new release won't be ready for months."

Use the speccy one…

"Oh."

There was no longer a mystery as to why he'd been summoned. He'd already made two dozen copies and they were ready and waiting for new hosts. If the Archivists were blind and unable to fully identify the speccies, the upgrades would be like receiving the world's most powerful laser eye surgery. They would see everything, even more than the Memory Hunters.

"Is it safe?"

No…it's risk management…

"What do you need from me?"

Find Corridor E Four…they will be the first…

"Understood. What about Jake's original implants, who are they destined for?"

Sam…Ragnara…Goldberg…

"He's Jake's partner!?"

Yes…and he built the speccy version…

"Shit. That man's a genius."

Indeed…another reason to keep him in sight…

"It will be done."

The Circuit…it's a state of mind…Alison…

Mannie took this as a sign that the bizarre conversation was over. He'd entered the room in trepidation and left it with renewed purpose. The Circuit was under threat and he was an essential soldier in the battle to protect it. There were implants to fit and work to be advanced. He left the glow of the golden beacon and retreated to the lift. The computer screen continued to blink hypnotically. Just as he was about to step inside part of Alison's instructions flashed in his cloud feed like a warning light. There was something he was missing.

"You said we had to wait for him to make a mistake," added Mannie. "What if he doesn't?"

He will...

"How can you be so certain?"

I see everything...she will be my secret weapon...

"Who will?"

Tyra...

A single red LED light was the only evidence that the server still had power. It had been in this state for weeks. Above, below, across and on either side of it, identical equipment hummed as their small motors rotated and indicator buttons flashed like errant strobe lights. This was the only one that acted differently. It was taking a well-earned break, having been shagged out from all the frenetic electrical excitement. There had always been something unusual about the server in section K, level three, aisle four hundred and one.

It had always been abnormal.

Somewhere deep inside its chips and processors was a memory that didn't belong there.

Housed in a huge warehouse in a desolate part of Arizona, servers like these contained the Memory Clouds of people from the West. Each server received data from the implant held by that host. But that didn't stop the servers connecting with each other. It was imperative that they did. It was the only way the Circuit could mine the collective will of the masses. Inside the servers, applications like the sibling programme shared data with other servers that the human owner interacted with. They couldn't change anything, but they could experience it. Latterly, when the sibling programme outlived its use, the guide transformed into something altogether different.

Memory Hunters, and they went anywhere they wanted to. But even they gave this particular server a wide berth.

Compared to its neighbours its behaviour was erratic. Sometimes its plastic shell rattled in its frame. Sometimes it made groaning noises like a fight had broken out inside the casing. Occasionally it infected every storage unit in section K with a vicious piece of malware as a joke. But electronic harmony had been restored in recent weeks when this mischievous malfunctioning freak had fallen silent. Sadly for those closest to it, it wasn't permanent.

The red light blinked once.

Then a second time.

The regularity of the blinking increased, and then as the local network held its binary breath the light went green. A motor erupted, a fan turned furiously and the plastic casing juddered on its shelf. Electrical power surged and an emergency warning signal was delivered far and wide. The message, written in complex computer language, was received by the sophisticated processing chips of every other server in the compound. In the English language it would have been translated as follows.

'Coming to get you, ready or not.'

Return.

'Jake…'

Return.

'I thought you said we were playing a game.'

Return.

'God, you're really good at this.'

NINE
THE DOCTOR'S STORY

No one thinks adverts work on them. If you stopped a hundred people in the street and ran a little survey, they would overwhelmingly confirm it. They will staunchly deny their effects while simultaneously drinking a well-known brand of fizzy pop, wearing top-of-the-range footwear, decked head to foot in designer clothing and covered in all manner of expensive cosmetics. And that's just the reaction if you asked the men. Given the vast amount of credits companies invested to get our attention it's simply naïve to believe that we are immune to their tactics.

We believe adverts are ineffective because we see more ads that don't interest us than ones that do entice us to spend our hard-earned cash. Not believing they work on you personally is not the same as believing they don't work at all. The secret of advertising success is all about the targeting.

Right now the ad agencies had it bang on.

Since Paddy and Christie left Tyra alone on the boat she'd been bombarded by a never-ending stream of commercials forcing their way into her memory feed. Ads weren't uncommon. Anytime you left your cloud dormant they'd squeeze one in there. Tyra was one of the few people who didn't complain. Ads weren't an irritation, they were an inspiration. They'd always present her with new fashion trends, unmissable restaurants, music suggestions and discount coupons for molten tattoo studios.

Molten tattoos were a big thing right now. The must-have wearable accessory for the world's youth. Customisable to your own design, the finished product moved around your skin of its own free will. Molten tattoos changed to reflect your mood and if your parents suspected you'd secretly got one you could command it to hide in a more discreet region of your skin. Most teenagers sent them to the soles of their feet until the coast was clear. Tyra already had three, not that Paddy knew anything about them.

Barely a day went by when Tyra didn't take the advertiser's bait. It wasn't her money she was using after all. The bill always came back to Paddy and she didn't have a clue that he was struggling to pay the electricity bill, let alone her burgeoning shopping addiction. Even if she had realised it wouldn't have stopped her. It was simply payback for his mistreatment of her.

Today's conveyor belt of ads wasn't focusing on the usual temptations. There were no music clips, no discounts and no brand special offers. Today they were advertising one service and none of eager sales representatives waited for a gap to appear in her cloud feed before launching into their pitch. They infiltrated her chat forums, dating site notifications and half-watched box sets. Nothing was going to stop them in pursuit of their target group. It was a pretty narrow demographic.

Only her in fact.

Hundreds of opportunistic, newly formed businesses were selling a once-in-a-lifetime reward in return for advice that would lead to the capture of Jake Montana. Each pitch sought to secure Tyra's backing for their specific plan and each offered differing levels of compensation. Some offered her fifty percent, others less than ten with the added incentive they'd throw in the vital importance factor if she forced them to negotiate. All of these firms presented strong arguments and either knew, or guessed, the strong level of animosity she fostered towards her brother. Their positioning statements and sales cases did nothing to dispel that truth.

Quite the opposite.

"Tyra Montana," said a gorgeous teenage boy who'd been hand-picked by the agency to fit the exact profile of the sort of eye candy she normally fell for. "I represent the Horizon Project, established…um…recently. Oh aren't you cute? Beautiful eyes."

Normally Tyra's eyes were barely visible behind thick, black mascara and matching eyeliner. They were denser than most black holes and would have consumed him just as fast if he wasn't stuck in virtual reality.

"What's your offer?" she replied listlessly. This was the fifteenth pitch she'd had in the last hour.

"Imagine a life of wealth and power. Think of the possibilities. Adored by the public and more popular than the most notorious vitals. More global recognition than the heroes you follow in your cloud. The ability to escape from your guardian, the chance to show which of the Montana siblings is greatest. Exclusive parties, friend to the famous, never excluded or bullied again!"

"How much?"

"Twelve and a half percent."

"I don't get out of bed for anything less than fifty," she said, swiping immediately.

"You can have my body…" came the representative's voice before it dissolved into obscurity.

The more the ads appeared, the more tempting their offers. But if she was going to achieve her own ambitions in this world she had to be in control. There was no question in her mind that she'd find her own way to humiliate Jake and steal everything he loved. The question wasn't whether she'd accept support, it was simply a question of the right offer and keeping that control.

It wasn't credits she wanted. There was something more valuable that none of these bloodsucking vampires were in a position to offer her. If she wanted credits she didn't need them anyway, she'd had that offer from the Circuit. She just had to be patient. They needed her more than she needed them, and eventually they'd return and she'd negotiate whatever terms she wanted.

Behind the chaos of her crowded cloud feed the choppy seas threatened more danger than they delivered. A blanket of dark, atmospheric cloud had descended from the heavens to dip its fluffy, grey toes into the water and check the temperature. Over the crashing of the waves a humming sound gradually increased in volume. A shiny object travelling at an immense speed cruised through the narrow gap between sea and rainfall. It was heading straight for her.

What was it doing here?

A drone with a light pink metal body and four mechanical arms fluttered irritably in mid-air. Underneath it, wobbling in the wind, was a wire basket. It halted abruptly in front of her before scanning the contours of her face. Almost immediately it made a rather cranky bleeping noise, annoyed with itself for failing to successfully locate the right client. The colour on its casing transformed from a light pink to deep scarlet colour before hovering up and over the edge of the cliff.

Theo Drew considered himself a pioneer. When most of his peers flocked blindly to join the Circuit's new world of opportunity, he foresaw what others could not. The Circuit was nothing more than a modern-day snake oil salesman. Silver-tongued executives and slick branding wouldn't work on him. They insisted that the enlightenment of the Memory Cloud would eradicate the inequality that was a systemic problem everywhere in the world. But Theo knew the world was not to blame for those problems: people were. Equipping them with the ability to see more than they were designed to would be like solving an alcoholic's addiction by giving him the keys to a brewery.

The views of outliers like Theo didn't stop the frenzied stampede to join, though.

Humans are simple creatures. They're hardwired to pursue short cuts. If they're offered a simple, relatively painless and free solution to their deepest desires and darkest fears, most will bite your hand off without a second thought. Their hunger for the overblown benefits will over-shadow any obvious disadvantages, but if they'd interro-gated the promises even slightly they'd have seen what Theo saw. Once users had made the decision to join they were enslaved by their need for more and the Circuit would be quick to sell it to them.

Those that did look a little closer declined. They were the original Spectrum, a band of nonconformists who weren't seduced by the glittery yet soulless practice of storing memories with an organisation unknown and untested. At the beginning it was an exclusive club and their refusal to follow the crowd didn't make them popular.

In the decades that followed new members of the Spectrum had their own reasons for abstaining. They had the benefit of seeing how the system really worked. All Theo had was a gut feeling. What mankind needed was change inside them, not a technological crutch strapped to the waist spinning an illusion that life was improving. Within a few years his worst fears about it were realised, but that wasn't even close to how bad the situation got.

That was beyond even his intuition.

First the Circuit blocked users' appreciation of the natural world and focused their attentions on what they saw in the virtual world. Then, without even the slightest sign of protest, they suppressed free speech and the rights of subscribers to choose their own futures. There was no uproar at this flagrant breach of human rights - quite the opposite. According to the surveys, they approved unanimously. As long as their favourite entertainment programmes weren't cancelled and on-cloud shopping purchases arrived within an hour, no one seemed to care much. It was the oldest con in history. Distract them with something shiny in one hand and steal from them with the other.

Once you'd fallen for it there was no going back. Theo hadn't, and even the formation of the Archivists didn't change his mind. It did mean he had to move house more frequently, though.

Most weeks in fact.

"Why did you really end up in the East?" asked Christie, not convinced he was just there to see the sights.

"We ran out of places to hide," said Theo. "The Circuit dispatched the Archivists to track us down, to convert us. At that time we were unprepared for them. In the early days they were actually pretty effective. It was the element of surprise, I suppose. I'm told that's why most of their soldiers are older: I think the Majors believe some of them might have been around when those first speccies were caught. Sadly for them none of the old guard remembers it now."

"Why not?" asked Paddy.

"In their eagerness to improve the Archivists' effectiveness the Circuit wiped any useful information they held by forcing recruits to accept the download. The more they failed to find us, the more their understanding of who we were morphed into myth and misinformation. By then most of us had already left the West, so I'm not surprised they weren't having much luck finding us. It was the late twenty twenties when I first travelled East."

"It broke her heart when you left," said Paddy, placing one of his massive, wrinkled hands on the doctor's shoulder.

"I know, but I wasn't left with much choice."

"Did you leave your girlfriend here?" asked Christie, offering joyful empathy.

"No," replied Theo. "Paddy's referring to my sister."

"I never had one," replied Christie merrily, her true emotions on the subject camouflaged by the continued effects of Moodzec.

Christie always wished she'd had a sibling. Growing up as an only child probably had its upsides for some; Tyra's blinkered view reinforced it. Being the single focus of both parents' attention might develop all sorts of personality traits in later life. They might end up being spoilt, loved, valued or isolated. All Christie got from hers was fear.

"I'm sorry for you," said Theo genuinely. "We didn't always get on but in later life you mature and realise how important you are to each other. It's a bond like no other."

A single tear welled in Paddy's eye and he quickly wiped it away as if ashamed he'd shown a sign of weakness.

"Weren't you scared to go there?" asked Christie, shifting the conversation away from one that was dragging everyone's mood down.

"No, of course not. At that time no one was scared to go anywhere. They had no reason to. There was no 'Proclamation of Distrust' and no barriers to entry. The environment hadn't fallen apart and people were fairly united in their views. You could still fly cheaply and people welcomed you with open arms. It was a very different world back then, even after the introduction of the Memory Cloud."

"What happened when you got there?" asked Christie.

"Initially, nothing very interesting. I settled into their way of life. The Realm had only just been formed and they were sympathetic towards non-subscribers. My life was perfect. I had a job, a nice home and the world seemed to be in balance. But everything changed in twenty thirty-two."

"It certainly did," added Paddy with a knowing nod.

Christie was born more than two years later so couldn't relate, but it wasn't the only reason it didn't trigger a reaction. None of her history lessons highlighted any significant events from that year and she had quick access to all of them to prove it. Before she had a chance to interrogate the details, Drew elaborated.

"That was the year when the West's attitude towards the East shifted like an earthquake, although it's still not clear what triggered it. The atmosphere changed rapidly. Rumours spread that Aaron Circo, the Realm's creator, had been murdered and almost overnight a hostility grew between the two sides. As the uncertainty increased, dissenting voices spread. In the power vacuum a man known as the King of Baku and his fanatical followers staged an audacious coup against the incumbent Circo family. Everyone knew about the King. His propaganda ran regularly in the cloud, tempting people into disobedience and insurrection. Apart from disaffected crackpots and bitter, superfluous folk few took the bait. In the wider population he was derided as a harmless lunatic, a figure of fun, easy to make jokes about. 'Crazy King B' they called him. No one of sound mind took him seriously or believed what he said. How blind we were. A few weeks into the crisis his cultish followers stormed the Circo residence and forced them to relinquish control of the Realm. It took everyone by surprise."

"Was that when you decided to fight?" asked Paddy.

"Yes, but the King's surprise attack meant we were woefully unprepared. We fought with whatever we could lay our hands on. Farm tools and everyday objects. Yet when we faced the enemy they possessed weapons we'd never even seen before. We had no chance. It was as if they had fate on their side. Every day more institutions and authorities endorsed the King as leader and those that refused were dismantled and their officers executed or disappeared. The more the state's machinery fell under his control, the more isolated our resistance became. The only thing that stood in his way was the last members of the Circo family. They were still popular and if the people rallied around them, we felt that might hold back the flood. Without them the King of Baku would attempt to run the East like an elitist club."

"What happened?" asked Christie.

"We tried to stop them. A few dozen of us fought our way inside the Circo residence but we were too late. The King had got there before us. I found Aaron's eldest son,

Constance, mortally wounded inside the palace. That's who told me about the implants. With his dying words he informed me that they contained secrets that might one day be used to fight back. He instructed me to collect them from a place called Abseron before it fell to the King's troops. No one knew exactly what they contained, not even Constance, but I knew they'd never be safe in the West. I had to store them somewhere secretly until the time came when they might prove useful. When I returned home that's exactly what I did. The last of those implants survived inside Jake. We still don't know what's on them, but hopefully he has learnt the truth."

"But you said the implants weren't the prize," interrupted Christie. "You mentioned a child."

"Patience, I will get to that part of the story soon," said Theo assertively. "When the King learnt we'd taken something from Abseron they hunted us down. We were forced out of hiding and tried to escape on foot through the city. There were no more than half a dozen of us left by this point. We took up sanctuary in the 'Temple of Fire' but were soon surrounded by the King's followers. We weren't the only ones hiding from them. Hundreds of people went to the temple to escape the violence in a place they thought was safe. While we waited for the inevitable attack a young woman, not much older than you," he said, pointing at Christie, "approached me, clutching a baby. She was beside herself with concern for the child's safety. She implored me to take the infant to safety. Even in this dire situation I was struck by the woman's beauty. She wore unusual garments and expensive jewels. Even more unusually she had a tattoo on her neck."

"A tattoo?" said Paddy.

"A symbol," he added. "A circle with two waves down the left and right sides of the curve. It's the symbol of the

Realm. I made the judgement that this woman and her child were from noble stock because only the most important ranks were permitted to wear the symbol. After I agreed to take the child she immediately sacrificed herself. She ran from the temple and distracted the enemy just long enough for me to slip away unseen."

"Who was she?"

"To this day I still don't know."

"But obviously you managed to escape," said Christie, quite enchanted by Dr Drew's tale.

"Yes. Our meagre resistance was defeated but I managed to escape with the boy to the West before they erected the firewall."

"It's him, isn't it?" said Christie, pointing at Alfonso.

"Definitely," replied Jezebel. "He's foreign-looking."

"I can only say that he remains under my protection."

"It's him!"

"No. The person in question has one of the greatest minds and is one of the most brilliant people I have ever known. He carries a great weight of expectation and has already done much to repay his mother's sacrifice. It remains one of my bravest and wisest decisions to rescue him."

"How old are you, Alfonso?" asked Christie, ignoring Theo's denials.

"About twenty, I think."

"There you are! Exactly the right age."

"There are many twenty-year-olds in this world," suggested Theo.

"I'm one hundred percent certain it's him!"

"It doesn't matter how confident you think you are, I'm not telling you."

Christie had enjoyed Theo's story and the way he told

it, but it still didn't answer the main question she had. "What has any of this got to do with Jake?"

"I think I can explain that part," offered Paddy.

"You?!"

"Yes. You see, when Theo returned home to the West he came to see me."

"I came to see my sister," corrected Theo. "I came to see Nina."

"Well, yes of course."

"The two of you are related!" said Christie.

"Indirectly, yes. Where do you think I learnt the speccies' code?" replied Paddy. "It's not something you can read in a book!"

"What's a book?" said Jezebel, struggling to complete a handstand.

"When I first met Theo he begged me not to join the Circuit but I was short-sighted," continued Paddy. "After I eventually realised my mistake I was eager to make amends in any way I could. He told me about the implants and we discussed how to use them. When he heard that my daughter Deborah was pregnant it seemed like the perfect opportunity. I made sure that Jake received a pair."

"Is that why he's suffered from the flashbacks all his life?" said Christie.

"Yes," replied Theo without much sympathy. "As far as we know none of the other recipients survived so he's the lucky one."

"Lucky!" grumbled Christie, showing the first signs of intolerance to the drugs. "It changed who he was. It held him back."

"We must all endure pain in pursuit of meaning," replied Theo. "The important thing for us is that Jake Montana survived his ordeal. If I'm right about your letter it also means he's finally discovered the secrets inside him."

"But none of that tells me where he is now," bristled Christie, getting more and more agitated.

"Is your guide back?" asked Theo nervously.

She scanned the small room. "Not fully. Solomon keeps flickering and falling through the floor."

"We don't have long left. Listen carefully. Only Jake knows the secrets. Constance told me the answers would only be unlocked by the people of the East, so maybe he's gone there."

"That doesn't really help me very much."

"I'm sorry, I can't offer you more than that. You'll have to wait for him to find you, I'm afraid. I sympathise with your situation but if Jake succeeds the speccies must prepare for what comes next."

Their concentration was broken by a small explosion that rocked the room. It was immediately followed by the sound of metal being punctured directly below them. Alfonso rushed out of the room and dashed up the stairs towards the balcony on the second floor. He returned a minute later and beckoned them to follow him.

They crowded around the narrow gallery, backs against the glass and a refreshing breeze in their faces. On the edge of the cliffside a moist, teenage goth was dragging herself over the stones, moaning audibly. Underneath them near the now lacerated front door a bright red drone with wisps of smoke seeping from one of its cannon hovered impatiently. It petulantly unloaded the last of its rockets into the remaining fragments of door.

"Interesting," replied Dr Drew. "Have you been lying about your age, Paddy?"

"Yep. I was twenty-one again this year," he answered with a grin.

"Still too old for one of these to visit," he said, pointing down at the irritated postal drone. "Anyone else expecting their Ascension letter today?"

Alfonso shook his head ironically.

"The power of elimination suggests it must be for you, my dear."

She was still holding her letter. The euphoria of Moodzec was waning and confusion rushed in to replace it.

TEN
THE SECOND LETTER

Christie crept down the spiral staircase, sticking her head around the stone core of the lighthouse's internal structure, nervous about what was happening. When she reached the bottom the metal door had been shorn in two and shrapnel was liberally distributed across the steps. The now almost purple shelled drone was heaving up and down in the air demanding attention. It had crossed an ocean to be here and the least the recipient could do was show up promptly and not make it late for its next delivery. Christie tiptoed through the twisted metal fragments and out through the doorway.

The drone sped forward, scanner at the ready. It quickly returned a positive ID and the drone's external shell lightened to a salmon-pink hue. The small basket dropped down and out and presented its contents. A letter was nestled inside, an exact replica of the procedure Christie experienced yesterday, other than for the wanton destruction of the door. If it had done the same yesterday to her dad's door she could only imagine what the consequences would have been.

"How come you get two!?" demanded Tyra as she stropped across the grass panting. "Why is everyone else being spoilt? I haven't even had one yet!"

"But you're not eighteen for another four years. If you stop being a brat you might find that life becomes more palatable."

"Doubt it," she mumbled.

The drone shook violently, hoping to encourage the recipient to take the final step in their interaction. Christie picked the letter out, and before the basket even had time to retract the drone whizzed off into the distance. Christie stared at the letter. This must be what déjà vu felt like. Surely it was a mistake. Maybe the Circuit had only just caught on to the fact that Jake had double-crossed them and had decided to issue a correction. If anyone had the power to do that, then surely they did.

Christie held both letters in the air. Other than one being a little worn from spending too much time in the rain, they were identical. The writing was in precisely the same place and had been printed in exactly the same font size and style. Both spelt out the name Christie Tucci. Fearing the worst, she slid the new letter out of its envelope. Whose name had been substituted for Jake's? The anxiety that preceded yesterday's grand opening resurfaced. She'd quashed it then by trying to look on the bright side. Whoever's name it was at least she didn't have to spend another night in the Tucci family madhouse. She returned to the same strategy now. Her fingers felt for the edge where the piece of paper had been folded exactly in half. She unfolded it.

Jake's name was still inside.

But his location had changed.

He was no longer in Arizona.

Christie immediately turned to run up the staircase to tell Paddy, but was stopped by a voice behind her shoulder.

"Not so fast!" shouted Solomon who was wobbling like a drunk desperate to discover the invention of balance. "Something…fishy…going on…here."

"I know, I have a second letter."

"That's…where have you gone…oh there you are… that's not what's fishy. Something odd happened. I went…missing."

"Funny, we didn't notice," said Jezebel, blowing him a raspberry.

"Irregular…disturbing…illegal…I'd imagine…it must stop…I won't allow it…no…it's not right…"

"Oh stop blubbering, you whiny little shit!"

Jezebel was definitely a reflection of Christie's natural, childlike instincts and shared her tough resilience. Events in early childhood were absorbed by the guides, and Christie's formative years had been anything but regular. She'd experienced trauma that no infant deserved. It included watching in horror as her father tried to attack her mother with a kitchen knife, his constant and erratic behaviour as he screamed hysterically at objects that weren't really there. The countless times the utility drones were sent to subdue him and the many times he'd been carted off for short stints at the Source for breaking violation limits or in order to receive therapy for his P.C.O.D. When you grow up in an atmosphere of fear your inner child is always going to be a slightly triggered badass. Jezebel could be playful for sure, but she wasn't putting up with any shit, particularly from men.

"You can't talk to me like that," said Solomon in shock.

"Just did! Now pull yourself together. Christie has a new location for us."

"I need to tell the others," said Christie excitedly.

"You can't go back in there now," said Paddy as he passed under the broken door frame. "The medicine has worn off."

"Paddy, I know where Jake is."

"How?"

"There's a new letter," she said, holding it aloft. "He's in Boston."

"Boston! Oh shit, that's not good."

"Yes it is, it's brilliant: I'll be reunited with him today if we hurry."

"You're forgetting about the 'Proclamation of Distrust'. Everyone is looking for him, particularly in Boston given his past connections to the place."

"They're even running ads to help find him," said Tyra. "I've had loads in the last hour."

"You didn't help them, though, did you?" demanded Paddy.

"No, of course not," she replied innocently.

"Does it say exactly where in Boston he is?" asked Paddy.

"Larz Anderson Park."

"Right, there's no time to lose. We have to get to him before they do. Girls, get yourself on the boat and I'll let," he nodded to the lighthouse, "them know what's happening."

The climate catastrophe that caused the ice sheets to melt and the lands to flood was a gradual affair. From the early twenty-forties when CLEAR SKIES, the man-made strategy for slowing the pace of environmental change that did more damage than good, was first activated the sea had risen slowly year on year. The first year saw only a modest increase of about a metre and it had little effect on First World countries. It did wipe Bangladesh off the map within a month, though. During the second year a couple more metres were added and so the trend continued until fifteen years passed and the sea settled at its current limit.

The reaction to the surge differed depending on where you lived. In Europe coastal regions were foresaken and their inhabitants moved further inland where cities were rebuilt on higher ground. In cities that benefited from variations in elevation like San Francisco, the lowland areas were forsaken and migrants flocked to neighbouring suburbs. This in turn led to overcrowding and local hostilities between those that had something and those that had nothing. Minor disputes became turf wars, a land grab in more ways than one. In North America important cities like New York and Boston, which were only just above sea levels twenty years ago, adopted an ingenious and extortionate solution.

Those cities were moved.

Brick by brick.

It had taken more than a decade and redirected most of Boston's available manpower to move the city almost in its entirety to Foxborough, a region of agricultural land south-west of the city and originally twenty miles from the sea. Now, like old Boston before it, the new city lay on the coast.

Larz Anderson Park the Second, to give it its official name, was on the south side of the new city. The original version had ironically avoided the advance of the sea and evolved into an island nature reserve, but its monuments, bridges and the iconic 'Temple of Love' had all been removed and repositioned amongst fledgling Japanese gardens and newly dug lakes and ponds. The park still offered the same attractions it once did: sports fields, an automobile museum and picnic tables; it just wasn't as green and lush as the other one. Monuments can be moved but trees like to take their time.

In the gathering gloom of early evening Paddy and the girls approached the park. It had already been an eventful, exhausting day and Tyra had reached the end of her tether. She pulled up like a disobedient racehorse right outside the entrance.

"I'm not doing this anymore," she said aggressively. "I won't be dragged about on another pointless hike to find someone I never want to see again. I want to go home!"

"Well, you can't," huffed Paddy. "They burnt it down, or did you miss that? Stop being selfish and hurry up."

"I'm being selfish!?" she replied, bewildered by the accusation. "Jake is the cause of this. He's the one who got our parents extradited and put you in control. He's the one who always got his own way and he's the one everyone is hunting. What have I done? I only ever wanted to be heard, to be recognised and noticed."

"Well, I'm hearing and noticing you now, sadly," said Paddy. "I recognise a brat when I see one."

"I hate both of you," she reconfirmed just in case either of them was in any doubt.

"Fine, but you're still coming with us. I've got protocol twenty-two."

"I know," she said with a dirty grin. "It means you have to tell me what to do, but that's not all you're responsible for, is it?"

When Paddy threatened to cut her cloud feed yesterday night she'd lost the battle. Now it was time to win the war. It required her to go nuclear and her finger was hovering eagerly over the big red button.

"Oh, what are you going to do, huh? Apart from whine

like a brat and make me drag you around by your boot-straps?" he said calmly.

"How many violations would you say I was on current-ly?" she asked.

"I know exactly how many," he replied suspiciously.

"Nine, isn't it!?"

Paddy knew what she was scheming. Every subscriber was allowed ten violations every year, but those who were underage weren't responsible for their own. That burden rested on the parent or guardian, which in this case meant Paddy.

"You wouldn't!"

"Wouldn't I?" goaded Tyra. "How much do you want to find Jake?"

"You're an ungrateful little shit, do you know that? The things I've done for you over the last few weeks and you can't even do this one thing for me."

"No, I won't. I'm not doing anything for anyone ever again. Only for me, because I'm the only one who cares about me. You can go on your little adventure if you want, but I'm going to find some food and people my own age. Don't even think about following me or I will scream the most disgusting level of abuse against the Circuit that you could possibly imagine!"

Tyra turned on her heels and strolled confidently away with her middle finger extended high in the air for good measure.

"What a spoilt little cow," muttered Solomon.

"I like her," contradicted Jezebel. "Sassy! I might go with her."

"Stay exactly where you are. With any luck the old dude might just get us where we need to go. It's all a little embarrassing as it is."

"Embarrassing?" said Christie, tuning into her guide's conversation.

"Yes. We're guides. We're the ones who are meant to help you find your betrothed, not some mysterious geriatric."

"Everyone needs a little help once in a while," added Christie.

Solomon frowned at the idea that he was anything but perfect.

Parks were usually quiet places these days, even more so at this time of the evening. When you had access to the world via your Memory Cloud why would you go out of your door to see the beauty of nature? It sucked up too much effort and most humans dissuaded themselves from it. Obviously there was always some masochistic jogger bucking the trend of the average couch potato who was generally overweight and overtired from the exhausting task of sitting around. It took more than the promise of fresh air and decorative bridges to excavate them from their comfy chairs.

It took a bloody big reward.

And by the looks of the park tonight they had all the motivation they needed. A billion credits and the promise of elevation up the importance levels.

In every area groups with flashlights explored behind bushes and tender tree saplings. They scanned their clouds in search of information about their target or anyone who might know or connect to him. Gangs of foolish youths holding clubs and bin-lid shields gave away their stealth by shouting Jake's name incessantly like he was some lost pet who might bound up to greet them.

Jake Montana's name echoed through the air.

The clocks had clicked past six o'clock in the evening

while Christie and company had been approaching Boston by sea. Even stuck on the speedboat they didn't escape the evening announcement. The second 'Proclamation of Distrust' to centre on Jake Montana and they weren't the only ones who took an interest. It inspired even more people than last night to join the hunt. The scene was being replicated all over New Hampshire and even further afield than that. Had they been tipped off about Jake being here, or was it collective blind hope? The Circuit had just resent her letter and his position, but there was no reference to it in their announcement. Which sent very mixed signals she couldn't balance. Did they want to catch him or not? Or was it a sick game?

According to her second letter, Jake was in the park tonight. Which meant the hunters were closer to their target than they knew. All she had to do was locate him before they did and without them noticing. It was tricky. She was between a rock and a hard place, or more specifically between a mob and some rather weak-looking Japanese shrubs.

"Why are we here exactly?" asked Dinah as she pretended to duck in and out of the beautiful pillars of the 'Temple of Love' the quaint-looking structure that patrolled the central lake at the heart of the park.

"I'm not entirely sure."

"Fishing?" she suggested.

"It doesn't appear that I'm into it," he replied, scanning through the distorted and alien memories.

"Maybe Job deleted it. He did go kind of rogue at one point. Where is the devious malcontent anyway?"

"Didn't you say he was pulverised into lots of bits and bytes?"

"Really?! Did I?" replied Dinah cautiously. "I don't like the idea of a million Job babies running around the place. I'd rather have scabies."

"It feels like he's here…and yet also gone. Everything is a little confusing right now."

"You're telling me. Where have you been for the last few weeks anyway? Holiday? Ooh, did you bring me a souvenir!?"

"I haven't been anywhere."

"But there's a big, blank space where you should have been, I know I checked," said Dinah.

"Amnesia?" he offered rather unconvincingly.

"Is that near Polynesia?"

"It's not a group of islands, Dinah, it's memory loss."

"Only the Memory Hunters can force that on someone."

"But isn't Job one of those now?"

"Yes," Dinah responded gloomily.

"Maybe he gave me amnesia, then. The last thing I remember before they transported me here is being in a big warehouse and someone injecting me in the back of my neck. Do you have any details after that point?"

"Yes. Shit! I unlocked the files!" acknowledged Dinah remorsefully, worried she'd done the wrong thing.

"I don't remember that. Do you still have them?"

"No. I think they must have been destroyed when the system went into stand-by."

"That's a shame. I was hoping I'd finally find out what those flashbacks meant."

They watched the flickering lights dance through the park before being momentarily obscured by trees dotted around the lake. There were a lot of people here tonight but so far they'd not shown much interest in him since he'd been deposited out of the back of a Jeep nearby. He didn't really know where he was because they'd covered his face on the journey and gave no explanation after they let him go.

"Do you think it's a rave?" said Dinah, pointing at the lights.

He shrugged.

"Oh, I do hope so. Anything's better than waiting here for boredom to kill us. I say that if it's not a rave we should go."

"Go where?"

"Home."

"Where is home, though? Is it Malmö or New Hampton Falls? I can't decide."

"You don't have to decide…that's the Circuit's job, remember?"

"Yeah, I suppose so."

He opened his cloud feed and immersed himself in a flood of former memories. They were all his, because he was in them, but he felt disconnected from them, as if he'd only been a bystander. The nearer he got to the present day, the more they felt comfortable. The two strongest emotions he triggered were associated with Malmö and a young, athletic blonde woman called Christie. As soon as she entered the feed he was overcome with desire. She was why they were here, that much he was sure of. Her energy and their unbreakable love for each other flashed inside him like a flare fired from a ship. In his virtual menu bar he discovered a joint connection to her. He immediately accessed it and her proximity alert flashed in his mind to show her position. She was in the park, near the edge of the lake.

A surge of excitement shot through him and he bounced in the air.

"No point dancing," said Dinah. "There's no music so it can't be a rave."

"Christie's here," he replied.

"Really?"

He closed his cloud feed and returned to the visual world so he could identify her. It wasn't easy to spot specific individuals in the gloom and from a distance, but a young, tall woman with long, flowing hair matching her description was currently walking near the water's edge next to an elderly man.

"Dinah, can you see her?"

"What do you think I am, an eagle!? They're miles away," she said, pretending to squint. "Actually I'd love to be an eagle."

"I thought you wanted to be an owl?"

"I'm not fussy. Oh imagine being able to fly. Free to go anywhere you wanted to."

"Dinah, you already can go anywhere you want to! Don't you remember the cave with all the war drones?"

"I try not to," she sobbed.

"Sorry. The point is you can go wherever you like as long as you remain connected to me."

"So, are you saying you'd like me to go and take a look for you?"

"Yes, please."

"Ok but only if you agree to take me ice-skating!"

"Don't guides have to do what I tell them anyway?"

"Oh my God you don't remember anything! Of course not! You'd have more luck trying to control a toboggan descending Everest."

"Fine. Ice-skating."

"Do the thing," she insisted.

"What thing?"

"Contract. The last time you said we were going to

play a game you locked me in my room for a month. I'm not taking any chances."

He assumed the position that countless other subscribers were doing at the very same moment to pay for goods, authorise their approval or guarantee their actions. Hands outstretched, thumbs stuck in the air, head nodding, big smile and a verbal statement of your intentions, location and time.

"Great," said Dinah. "Back in a minute."

Christie and Paddy were two of a hundred people looking for the same thing. All things considered, being related should have offered them a distinct advantage. It didn't. They were as lost and desperate as everyone else, only they weren't screaming at each other or grabbing strangers by the shoulders, or shaking them violently in search of answers. Anyone who came near either of them had done just that. It usually didn't last too long, but being mauled by the general public wasn't Paddy's idea of an extreme sport.

They all had extremely bad breath which lingered on his clothes a long time after he'd been accosted and they'd shouted their demands in his face. Some of them were deranged-looking characters covered in sweat and shaking deliriously as if high on drugs. Most were overweight and struggled to keep up with Christie and Paddy if they picked up their pace to a light stroll. There were an equal number of men and women across a diverse mix of creeds and ages, but they all had one thing in common.

Their eyes.

The unique glint spawned by one emotion in particular.

Greed.

Since the dawn of time it corrupted all but the strongest of wills. It turned normally civilised members of society into bloodthirsty killers. People's moral code left quicker than a toddler on a water slide at the mere sniff of the stuff. They'd reject any notion that someone might get hurt in the melee because their frenzied and insatiable need for more didn't care about anyone but themselves. They wanted credits and it didn't matter to them if they had to hand in a lost set of keys or a human being. They were possessed, and as a result they trampled on and pushed others to be first to find it. The longer it took, the more the park was contaminated by an air of suspicion as individuals were followed or interrogated in case they knew something the others didn't. None of them did. If one jumped in the lake, half a dozen followed just in case Jake was masquerading as Aquaman.

Christie despised what they'd become. The Circuit was meant to advocate a code of fairness and harmony. Abundance, greed and ambition were suppressed and ruthlessly controlled, and yet the moment the Circuit encouraged disobedience subscribers flocked to it like bluebottles drawn to a steaming pile of cow dung. It had taken only minutes for the corruptibility of the human spirit to break through the micron-thin veneer of the Circuit's rules. And for what? Credits. Would that make them happy? Would the Circuit really let them keep their prize? Jake meant more to Christie than credits. She measured his value on a very different scale.

The only prize hunter whose eyes lacked that sparkle of addiction to a life they'd probably never know, or likely even enjoy, was the man running directly at her from the direction of the temple.

Running really fast.

His arms were outstretched in preparation to grab hold of her and a wide, almost impossible smile had deformed the man's face. He was also shouting something.

"CHRISTIE!"

She didn't recognise him at all. He was tall, had a stocky build, blond hair and was a similar age to her. Most worryingly his boisterous behaviour was drawing the mob's unwanted attention.

"Do you know him?" asked Paddy as he stepped in front to protect her like an old school gentleman.

"No. You?"

"I don't get out much," replied Paddy. "He's not slowing down, is he?"

When the man reached them he effortlessly picked Paddy up by the shoulders and flung him to one side. "Out of the way, Granddad."

"What's he doing?" said Solomon who was also trying to work out the man's motives. "Hold on, I'm getting new info."

"Do you want me to kick him in the balls, Christie?" added Jezebel eagerly.

Christie's knee bolted forward and crunched into the man's groin, triggering a soundtrack of breaking walnuts.

"Never mind. You got this girlfriend!"

"AWAUH." The man's face froze in pain and he slumped forward, groaning, yet he continued his attempts to embrace her.

"Get off me!" shouted Christie, struggling to release herself from his unwanted and wandering hands.

The man collapsed to his knees, one hand clutching his Crown Jewels and the other sliding down her back before settling uninvited on her bottom. Jezebel didn't ask this time. A knee flew forward, striking him in the jaw and sending him tumbling backwards across the grass.

"Are you sure you dated her?" said Dinah watching from ringside. "Or was Job hiding the folders that proved you're a sex pest?"

He groaned his denial.

"If he moves again I'm going for the right hook," added Jezebel, desperate to show off Christie's moves once more.

"Stop!" shouted Solomon. "Don't touch him. I've just seen his Memory Cloud. We've found him! It's Jake Montana!"

ELEVEN

SLEEPY BILL'S DINER

S leepy Bill's was an old-fashioned style of diner that took its design and ambience from every classic 80s film ever made. Stools with red leather seat covers atop shiny metal frames. Television screens attached to any object capable of holding their monstrous weight. Gum-chewing waitresses in light pink-coloured dresses with hems below their knees, filthy white aprons and ridiculous-looking hats that were never designed to fit average-sized heads. A serving bar that stretched along the width of the room and four-seater cubicles separated from each other in case they broke out in a fight.

The smell of grease being incinerated wafted in from the kitchen in a failed attempt to persuade patrons to order food that might threaten their chances of making it through the weekend. A collection of lost souls, young lovers, grumpy businessmen and, thankfully for Tyra, young people talked noisily over the blaringly loud, atten-tion-seeking televisions. Through the huge pane glass windows that stretched the length of the diner the weather outside was plucking up the courage to spit raindrops, but in apparent solidarity with the people inside the restaurant, it couldn't really be arsed.

Tyra's waitress, Candice, deposited a frothy chocolate milkshake on the plastic-covered table top and forced a tepid smile through crimson lipstick. Tyra looked at the drink suspiciously. Had it come from the kitchen? No, she was safe, it was from the bar, which gave her an eighty percent chance of surviving its consumption. She rummaged around in her fake rubber, black handbag to find her testing kit so the contents could be analysed and the odds raised.

Men still questioned why girls needed handbags. Historically they were used for carrying the essential items a girl needed if she left the house. Typically these included: keys, a phone, tampons, make-up, a notebook and a purse. Most of which were now redundant or simply didn't exist in twenty fifty-four, so why did they still need a handbag? Essential items, as it turns out, only ever made up around nine percent of the contents of a handbag. The remaining space was commandeered by miscellaneous items and it didn't matter whether the bag was tiny or the size of a Zeppelin, maximum capacity was always reached.

Men were quite rightly blocked from knowing what these miscellaneous items were and if any male discovered the truth it would reveal a shocking insight into the female psyche. A laminated map of Brussels, a broken spork, six buttons, the lid of a cophony cup, a half-eaten falafel sandwich, an opened tube of glue, an empty pack of gum, a broken elastic band, old money no longer in circulation, a broken piece of transparent plastic with no identifiable purpose, some orange peel and a miniature Philips screwdriver. This wasn't the main reason men dared not look. They were worried that if they did women would want to know what men kept in their sheds. This status quo was officially the longest-lasting peace accord in recorded history. Contents might have changed over the years but behaviours had not.

Satisfied with the results, Tyra returned the round testing kit and closed her bag. The metal studs on the front spelt out a commonly uttered obscenity which no longer seemed to cause offence. She supped from her milkshake and stared out of the window. The street lights simultaneously flashed on to counteract the gradual arrival of night-time. A fully packed tram stopped across the street and a steady flow of people emerged.

Her mind daydreamed, a strange phenomenon for a Circuit user. The visual world fades from view like a soft focus covering your eyes, objects merge and your attention wanders as it permits the Memory Cloud to take full control of igniting any emotion it wants. A series of scenes from Tyra's past overlapped to produce a fantastical vista of events from her life. They all had one thing in common. Jake.

When the mind is set free from the present it reflects and channels your unconscious thoughts. An uncontrollable pressure was building inside her, begging for correction. The memories only fuelled it. Every moment when Jake got his way. Every time he'd made her feel inferior. Every occasion his parents had backed him over her. Every time he'd belittled or embarrassed her. Negative memories every one of them. If there were any positive episodes the Memory Cloud certainly didn't reflect it. But was she really in control of what it showed her?

She shook it away as a shred of her psyche clung to a conditioned sense of respect for the family unit that had been instilled in her for as long as she could remember. Montanas looked after each other. That was what Paddy always preached. Who could you rely on if they didn't have your back? Neighbours? The Circuit? No. Not even those who occupied your own importance factor rallied to your side when you broke the rules.

Her parents were a prime example.

No one came to her aid after their extradition. No one offered support or charity. They had to survive on their own. It was hard for both of them, but Paddy was an adult; she was only a child. Most of her school friends blanked her. Her teachers' attitude towards a once exceptional student turned hostile and her boyfriend dumped her quicker than you could download Tinder. She didn't mind: she was going to dump him anyway. There were plenty more memories in the cloud, and she'd never had any problems pulling before. Suddenly no one replied to the flirty messages she sent through her feed. They weren't even opening them, as if they had a watermark warning on them. The lurch from popularity to pariah in a matter of days was hard to accept. Only Paddy remained and he made life even more miserable.

Family were supposed to have your back.

Jake only cared about his own.

An internal struggle between old-fashioned morals and a desire for retribution tore her apart. She tried to distract herself by focusing on the televisions dotted around the walls. It was novel to watch a film on a small, square screen when you were able to open the same feature in your cloud and project it across the entire restaurant. How did people see properly when it was so far away? The pictures were tiny, grainy and distorted. The sound was disproportionate to the noise of the chattering voices and crackled like it was on fire. It was no wonder these ancient devices were relegated to nostalgic dives like this.

In a surge of static the film vanished only to be replaced by black and white lines and a noise like a blender being garrotted. No one in the other cubicles blinked an eyelid. They were too busy talking to friends or being blinded by the power of their virtual entertainment systems to notice. The static on multiple screens was replaced by a blank screen and a single, pulsating green cursor.

I'm waiting…

Tyra looked around sheepishly to see if the message was really aimed at her and if anyone else had noticed it. They hadn't. What did she do? Reply out loud and make everyone think she was crazy? No way. She might be as popular as the art of queuing, but she had no intention of making it worse.

I don't have all day…

Tyra accessed her Memory Cloud but found it was blank for the first time in her life. No adverts, no announcements and no past. Just a menu bar with opaque headings she could no longer activate. Only 'Contact us' was in bold. She selected it and the cloud feed re-created Sleepy Bill's exactly as it was in the real world, except now she was the only person inside. The screens were still blinking at her in anticipation of a response.

Think it…

'Like this,' thought Tyra.

Exactly…

Back when she still had friends willing to accept the connection, Tyra was used to communicating through the cloud this way. It wasn't quite like communicating in real time but it was more secure. It worked by forming a thought in your mind that was captured as a memory and transferred to the other person to experience. Once they'd received it they would then send their response in the same way. It took a bit of practice, but over time the more you tried it, the quicker the conversation ran. For Tyra and her friends there was barely a gap between messages, but she'd never used the technique with anyone she didn't know.

Answer…

'I don't have one.'

That does not compute…

'Don't you ever have mixed emotions?'

There was a long period of inactivity from the cursor before it typed its reply.

No…I have the Memory Cloud…let it choose…

'And if I did, what answer would it give?'

YES…

'But I don't want the reward you're offering.'

One billion credits…vital…immunity…think of the future…

'It's not enough.'

Two billion…

'Still not enough.'

Name it…

Tyra had waited for this moment. A chance to set her own rules and negotiate a suitable prize. 'Deborah and Kyle Montana.'

In exchange for…the virus…

'Virus?'

Jake Montana…

'We agree on that label at least. Yes, for Jake…and the two billion,' she added quickly.

Agreed…

'There is something else.'

Your greed is fascinating…primal, even…

'This part isn't about greed, it's about freedom and control. My grandfather has been granted protocol twenty-two. I can't help you if he's watching me all day long.'

Rescinded immediately…

'I want no interference. I must do this for myself.'

Define interference…

'I'm not following anyone's orders.'

No orders…

'Then we have a deal.'

The virus…delivered to me…Boston Source…

'Anywhere you want him.'

How…

'I'll set a trap.'

How…

'That's for me to know.'

The Circuit sees everything…hears everything…

'Yes. I'm counting on it.'

In truth, Tyra didn't really know what trap she'd use for someone whose location, identity and motives were unknown. But when she came up with it she was certain it would be amazing and that her talents in the cloud would be crucial to pulling it off.

Wait here…

'What for?'

Reinforcements…

'We agreed no orders.'

Not orders…guides…

'I don't need anyone to help me. I work alone!'

Request…rejected…support compulsory…

'Then there's no deal.'

Ok…Where would you like to pick up their corpses…

'Whose?'

Deborah…Kyle…

Tyra had shown her hand. It wouldn't have taken the Memory Hunters long to find it, but she'd revealed her true priority. It was entrenched in her recent memories and they could visit those at leisure. Now the choice had been removed. She was in or they were dead.

'What help?' she thought reluctantly.

Archivists 2.0…Corridor E Four…

Tyra watched apprehensively as the parking lot of Sleepy Bill's was requisitioned by a convoy of battered Jeeps largely controlled by geriatrics. Unsurprisingly, given how long it had been since an active motor car was last seen driving the streets of Boston, they attracted a sizeable crowd. When people were curious about something they found it impossible to confine their interest to eyes alone. They had five senses, six if you counted the cloud, and just couldn't resist unleashing as many as possible. Onlookers were compulsive fondlers. They wanted to feel the dented metal against their fingers, turn door handles to see how they worked, and fiddle with the interesting knobs and levers to see what they did.

Their eagerness to do so didn't last long.

A broad-shouldered, dark-skinned brute of a man leapt out of the lead Jeep holding an unusual device in his hand. He swung it in front of him and gave it a shake. Above the handle a series of blades spun viciously and discharged bright white sparks onto the black tarmac. Everyone stepped away and hid their fondling digits behind their backs. They weren't used to seeing implements of violence. The closest any of them came to experiencing aggression was a wrestling match with a sibling or contact sports that got out of hand. They certainly weren't used to seeing a weapon.

The spinning sword gnashing its shiny teeth wasn't their only incentive to cease interest. Not a word was offered by the man but they still received the message loud and clear. A strange caller infiltrated their memory feeds, anonymous and unrestrained. Like a virtual thief it riffled through precious memories and scattered their broken remains on the floor. Then simultaneously the entire posse of more than fifty people received a simple and unambiguous alert.

'Fuck off.'

It did the trick. Terrified onlookers scattered in every direction until the virtual intruder finally relinquished its grip. In seconds the parking lot emptied. Major Dawes stopped his sword spinning and gave it a loving pat like it was an obedient dog. A coy smile seeped across his face as he marvelled at the empty scene and his ability to clear it. This was more like it.

"Roll-call," he barked.

Two dozen uniformed soldiers with shiny white helmets leapt out of vehicles and quickly fell into formation. They did their best to stand to attention, even though most were forced to adopt a hunched pose on account of their age-related conditions which were both eclectic and numerous. Some stooped, some held their backs to stop themselves falling over, and one sneakily used his rifle as a crutch.

Tyra couldn't hear the briefing from behind the glass, and because the man stood with his back to her, even lip reading was out. What she did notice was how the senior officer's attention was repeatedly focused on something on his immediate right, even though there was nothing there. After a short conflab the platoon offered their captain a synchronised and feeble salute before he turned around to face her.

He approached the window.

She pretended not to notice and returned to the televisions, reset and returned to their crackled commentary. A firm tap rattled through the window. She ignored it. He tapped again and she was forced by fear to look around. A single finger extended and beckoned her to come outside. She shook her head defiantly. Alison had insisted that help would come and this appeared to be it. If Tyra wanted her prize this was the compromise, but she no longer trusted authority figures and he had all the hallmarks of being one.

'Come out,' echoed a voice.

Tyra checked the nearest TV to see if the voice had come from there. It couldn't have because the ancient entertainment box was currently playing the irritating theme tune to *Friends*, an ancient sitcom that even in the middle of the twenty-first century everyone had watched in full nineteen times.

'I won't ask again.'

She sank into her Memory Cloud to seek sanctuary and was surprised to see someone sitting opposite her in the cubicle. It was the same man who was knocking on the window.

"I didn't grant you access!" said Tyra.

"You don't need to. I go where I want these days."

"Get out!"

"Nope," he grinned.

It appeared she was cornered. Whether she stayed in the cloud feed or the real world, he would be there. She thought it might be safer in the feed.

"Who are you?" she demanded.

"Major Luther Dawes. Alison sent me. A mistake, I'm sure."

"A mistake?"

"Yes. You're a girl."

"Obviously, so?"

"I don't work with them. They're inferior and always distract the men."

"Distraction is one of our greatest strengths. It allows us to get on with stuff, rather than wait for men who just argue because their egos weigh them down!"

"Discipline is what's needed, not distraction."

"I fear neither of us has a choice about this arrangement."

"Maybe not, but we'll have to give you a makeover to adjust your look."

"What?! Over my dead…"

"Shave your hair off," continued Dawes single-mindedly, "remove all that awful make-up, dress you properly and then subject you to some humiliating initiation tasks to toughen you up."

"You don't have any daughters, do you?" said Tyra sarcastically.

"Of course not! My seed wouldn't dare."

"Are you in fact from Victorian England?"

"Alabama."

When it came to progressive, modern points of view it wasn't much different.

"You're suggesting that I'm old-fashioned because I admit you're the weaker sex, is that it?"

"Queen Victoria built an empire so that's not true, is it?"

"She was probably a man in disguise. It's the only possible explanation."

"And the nine children she had, where did they come from?"

"Fake," he answered without questioning it.

"Get out of my feed!" screamed Tyra in a frequency only she and dogs had perfected. It had little impact on him.

"Nope. I can go anywhere I want, and so does he."

"He?"

The menu bar in Tyra's memory feed cascaded down without her permission. A series of adjustments were being made to the options list as if the Memory Cloud was getting a software upgrade. It was authorising a new shared connection she hadn't been informed about, let alone approved. She attempted to block it, but every approach she tried failed utterly. Her memories were being hijacked. Life outside of the cloud had been tampered with over the last few months, but she always had the safety of the cloud to hide away in. Now even that was being taken out of her hands.

"Stop! You're violating my rights. It's unfair."

"You don't have rights."

"Sexist pig!"

"It's got nothing to do with being a female. This is about your deal."

Tyra's cloud feed vanished with a pop. Major Dawes was still pressed up against the window smiling menacingly. A moment later her cloud feed returned with a notification plastered across it containing the word 'REBOOTING'. When it finished a few seconds later her personalised inter-face had changed. Tailored icons for favourite applications were missing. Authorised connections with friends and family lost. Paddy's access via protocol twenty-two gone. In her menu bar there was a new entry at the top marked 'Archivist 2.0 group chat'. It launched immediately and the entire squadron, still standing in formation in the car park, materialised in duplicate inside the restaurant.

"Let me introduce you," announced Dawes. "This is the new and improved Corridor E Four, simply the best Archivist team anywhere in the world. We are speccy hunters, and your brother is our number one target."

"How are you able to do this?!" she screamed furiously.

"We've been upgraded. There is no Memory Cloud we cannot access."

"Then what do you need me for?"

A second man squeezed onto the virtual leather couch next to Dawes. He was carrying two fake but extremely realistic-looking strawberry milkshakes. He slid one across to Dawes with a frail hand and pretended to drink his own. The frothy milk dribbled down his greying beard and he made an annoying sucking noise on his straw. When he'd finished he looked up over his spectacles and answered her original question.

"Because, Tyra, your brother is not attached to one."

"Who's he?" Tyra asked Dawes.

"I'm Brother Job," he replied. "And I'm the Memory Hunter that's going to help you bring him down."

"I really don't need any help."

"Maybe not, but I have some unfinished business," he added coldly.

TWELVE
FAKE MONTANA

The stocky, blond man who'd attacked them was still slumped on the grass, one hand cupping his groin and the other pinching his nose to stop a steady stream of blood. Dinah dabbed his brow with a small, fake towel in the style of a concerned boxing trainer. His face continued to see-saw between agony and utter confusion. The love of his life had callously and unexpectedly kneed him in a place she'd always been rather fond of. Then to add insult to injury she'd capped it off by punching him square in the face with a fistful of knobbly rings, one of which he'd bought her.

What exactly had he done wrong? He racked his mind in search of the answer. It returned a number of possibilities, all of which seemed reasonably plausible.

He was a man.

He'd not been in contact with her for weeks.

He'd said the wrong thing.

He'd done the wrong thing.

He was a man.

He was late.

He'd not had a shave.

He was a man.

Of course it was impossible for him to know that the true reason had nothing to do with these theories. From Christie's perspective it wasn't that he was *a* man, it was purely the fact he wasn't *the* man.

The various answers squabbled for legitimacy as his mouth, utterly bewildered by the brain's internal procrastination, resorted to a general babbling noise punctuated by the occasional incoherent phrase like 'but', 'it's me' or 'what!?'

"You don't grab girls," barked Christie, maintaining an offensive pose and feeling thoroughly impressed at herself for disabling her attacker without any premeditated thought. It must have been her, though, because her knuckles ached from the force of the blow.

"It's me," the man repeated in a whimper.

"I've never seen you in my life."

"What?"

"Stranger danger," she called out.

"Shush...we dated for three years!" he replied desperately.

"Rubbish. You're not even my type. I go for attractive, sporty boys with sparkly eyes and excellent manners."

That described him perfectly, didn't it? Even his memories backed it up. He looked down at his torso and legs, surprised to find they were much bulkier than how he remembered them before the amnesia had taken over a month ago. What happened to them? Had he been on some mega protein binge? What else about his body had changed while he wasn't paying attention? Did it really matter? No. He knew who he was and if the tables were turned he'd still love Christie if her appearance changed.

"Why are you doing this, Christie?" he sobbed. "I can't tell you what I've been through to find you."

"How do you know my name?"

"We dated!"

"Michael Nuno," she said uncertainly, moving forward to double-check. "You've let yourself go."

"Who the hell is Michael Nuno?" he replied angrily.

"An ex."

"Why don't I know about him?"

"Because you're a random stranger who's just tried to molest me in a Boston park!" she answered sarcastically. "Why am I even having this conversation?"

"I'M JAKE MONTANA!" he screamed.

"Shut up, you idiot," snapped Paddy. "Do you want to attract all the crazies over here? Haven't you seen the 'Proclamation of Distrust'? They'll rip you to pieces."

He'd seen it tonight for the first time. It was an unusual development but it didn't really worry him. The Circuit had only released him from the Source yesterday so it couldn't be him they were really looking for. If they wanted to track him down, why did they set him free in the first place? And if they wanted to know where he was they could access his Memory Cloud anyway. The Jake at the centre of the announcement didn't look anything like him. They must be hunting another Jake Montana. The most important priority for him was to find Christie and the Circuit had made it possible by directing him here. Now that he'd found her she was refusing to accept who he was.

"I don't care about that or them. I won't deny who I am," he replied, pulling himself to his feet and shouting his name repeatedly at the top of his voice.

"Stop!" begged Paddy. "They are looking for Jake."

"So?! I have nothing to be frightened of. They must be looking for a different Jake."

"Look at them," said Paddy, pointing at a group not far away. "They're all in a mad frenzy. Do you think they care you're not the right Jake? They'd hand in a plastic mannequin if someone wrote 'Jake Montana' on it. They'll kill you and ask questions later."

"Oh…"

It was too late.

His crazed shouting drew the crowd quicker than a street caricaturist. Like a pack of zombies they swarmed forward, pushing each other out of the way to get the first juicy bite.

"Run!" shouted Paddy. "Leave this idiot to them."

"Granddad!" said the man pathetically.

"Agreed," replied Christie who was fit enough to outrun anything on two legs.

"Out of the question," said Solomon fiercely, putting the brakes on Christie's escape. "This is Jake Montana, his Memory Cloud confirms it."

"It's not him."

"The cloud begs to differ," replied Solomon sternly. "It's our job to help you find your match. We have and we can't let you leave him in danger. Isn't that right, Jezebel?"

"I couldn't care, less to be honest, but if there's going to be a brawl I'd rather stay here," she replied, spinning an imaginary pikestaff impressively around her body like a ninja master while screaming a stream of creative obsceni-ties at the approaching mob.

"She worries me every single day."

Christie tried to run faster but her feet were fixed solid to the ground. It was like watching someone trying to flee from a field of glue. When she looked down, Solomon was wrapped tightly around both ankles with a determined look on his face.

"How are you even doing that?"

"It only matters that I can," replied Solomon. "If you want to run, then you have to take him with you."

The mob closed in. If they'd used their real eyesight they'd have noticed that this Jake looked nothing like the character they were hunting. People rarely saw the truth. Their Memory Clouds dominated their vision and it had correctly identified whose cloud they were homing in on. If there had been a handful of pursuers, escape would have been impossible, but there weren't. There were hundreds and they were no longer in a race to find Jake, they'd joined a race to stop anyone else from doing so.

Sometimes competition is mutually exclusive. In a one hundred-metre race eight athletes focus on their own performance. There is nothing they can do to impede the runner on either side of them. If they tried it would ultimately end in their disqualification. All they can do is focus on their own race, prepare, train well and consume as many undetectable steroids as they can get their hands on. In other fields of competition adversaries do impact one another's chances of success. Take politics, for example. Fifty years ago candidates spent more of their election budget attacking their opponents than they did highlighting their own personal strengths and policies. When you take your eye off the prize and focus on stopping someone else winning it opens up a lane for someone who's decided to run straight.

It was true of the mob.

Rather than focus on capturing Jake, they turned their attentions to stopping anyone else from doing so. Mass squabbles broke out. Punches struck chins, rugby tackles were unleashed on unsuspecting old ladies, kids were poked in the eye, pebbles stolen from Japanese gardens were hurled by those at the back of the pack to concuss those in the lead, and the whole park descended into an unchoreographed battlefield.

"Ok. We'll take him!" shouted Christie. "Just let go of me!"

"Good," smirked Solomon. "I'm always right."

"Bollocks!" argued Jezebel who was deep within the melee pretending to administer nipple tweaks and wedgies on anyone within five feet of her.

"Come on, run!" shouted Paddy.

They snuck through the chaos and hid behind a nearby thicket of saplings too short to offer sufficient cover. When the coast was clear they dashed for it, crossing over a baseball pitch and heading for the other side of the park. Paddy struggled to keep up, constantly supporting his hip with his hand like it might fall off at any time. Eventually they burst out of the greenery and into the illumination of the suburbs. Anonymity was not going to get any easier here.

"There are people everywhere," panted Christie. "We need to find somewhere quiet."

Paddy scanned the area. "I know just the place."

"Where?"

"There's a place speccies go when they don't want to be seen," replied Paddy, wandering over to a drain cover in the pavement. "Time for you to be useful."

"I think he's talking to you," said Dinah encouragingly.

"At least I'm being noticed," he replied.

He removed the drain cover with ease and the party climbed into the sewer. After sealing the hatch behind them, they congregated at the bottom of the tunnel. The relentless sound of water droplets striking the steady flow of filth under their feet echoed down the tunnel. They instinctively covered their noses to block out the smell of the world's worst cesspit. In the darkness the beat of their hearts and sound of their breathing became more pronounced and noticeable. Paddy removed his external implant from its pouch, and after fumbling with a knob on the side a light slowly glowed stronger. They squinted as the light allowed them to see each other again.

"Is that a torch?" asked Christie.

"Yeah. It's one of the only benefits of wearing the old tech. They used to come with added extras. There's a pair of scissors and a rape alarm on mine, too."

"You can't be too careful, granddad," said the blond man.

"Why are you so obsessed with sewage?" complained Dinah. "This is like the third time you've…ooh, rat babies!"

"Explain yourself," demanded Christie, turning on him with an outstretched finger. "Even in this darkness I'd know my boyfriend and you are not him. Tell me who you really are."

"I told you, I'm Jake Montana!"

"Joke Montana," she replied. "You're a Fake Jake."

"She's hilarious," added Dinah who was watching the memory repeats of their conversation slightly delayed from the original. "I like that name."

"There's no doubt about who he is," chipped in Solomon. "This is Jake."

"But it doesn't look like him."

"Maybe he's been working out, put a bit of weight on?" her guide added.

"And height!" exclaimed Christie.

"Maybe he's been to a Conversion Room?"

"They can't make you taller, they can only make you prettier."

Christie knew the contours of Jake's face as well as she knew her own. She'd held it in her hands countless times as she'd pulled him towards her for a kiss. The smoothness of his skin, his rebuilt cheekbones, the twinkle of mischief in the corner of his eye. She didn't need to touch this man's face to know it was different. For a start there was a deep, ugly scar that ran across his forehead.

"Jake doesn't have a scar: how do you explain that?"

"I can't," replied Fake Jake.

"It's a speccy scar," replied Paddy curiously, holding the mock torchlight up to his face.

"It can't be: my guides can see his Memory Cloud, so he can't be a speccy," argued Christie. "They say it's definitely him."

"How peculiar," added Paddy. "I don't think I've ever heard of a speccy converting to the Circuit before."

"I didn't," said Fake Jake. "I don't remember how I got it, but I remember nearly everything else. I have eighteen years of memories about you, Grandfather."

"Prove it," said Paddy curiously.

"You wear crocodiles on your feet."

"Oi, if anyone's going to say mad shit like that, it's me," said a disgruntled Dinah. "Don't muscle in on my turf!"

"This guy is loopy," said Christie.

In the darkness neither of them witnessed Paddy's jaw drop in disbelief. "No, he isn't. I don't know how but this is Jake."

"Rubbish."

"Only three people in the world know the Montana secret code. I'm one of them, Tyra is another, and it's clear she's not here right now, and the last is Jake. Crocodile is the word we used for slippers."

"I'm not convinced," said Christie. "Tyra or Jake might have told someone."

"Then you ask him something," said Paddy.

"Ok, I will! If you really are Jake then what song was

playing at the school disco when we had our first dance?" she asked.

Jake's Memory Cloud retrieved the moment in question. It was a much-loved, often-viewed emotion and as such had a worn quality about it. The projected image regularly froze from being overplayed and was often interrupted by Circuit messages warning the viewer of possible disruption and buffering issues.

The time stamp gave the date as June the sixth, twenty-fifty. The school hall was bustling with eager end-of-year revellers. The girls all looked perfect. They'd clearly spent days perfecting their individual style and dress choice. The boys in comparison had made their fashion decisions about ten minutes before they'd left the house. As always he felt uncomfortable, not just in the clothes his mother had insisted on him wearing, but at the insane pressure of having to follow a set of unwritten social rules necessary on occasions like these. He'd collected his free drink and slunk away into a corner, hoping no one would notice him. Unconsciously his foot tapped along to the music like an out-of-time homing beacon.

There was no DJ at this disco. The school had its own shared portal in the Memory Cloud that all students were added to. Everything the disco needed was piped into the clouds of anyone who'd accepted the invitation. Decorations, announcements and music were all co-ordinated virtually. Only the attendees' movements weren't controlled, which was disappointing because his dancing skills were hopeless. He knew the cloud would have done a better job of co-ordinating his body than he would. He trusted it. It always made smart decisions on his behalf. One of which was to sit quietly in the corner until the party ended and, with any luck, his already damaged reputation was preserved.

The Memory Cloud had always been regular and reliable. In his opinion girls were quite the opposite. He'd learnt enough about them by having Tyra as a sister. If these girls were anything like her, then they were all broken and should be immediately returned to the manufacturer for a full factory reset. He watched with morbid curiosity as male peers plucked up the courage to venture into the wild of pink frocks and big hair. Each one crashed and burnt in ego-deflating humiliation, further chiselling away the valuable points they'd accumulated that would one day define their importance factor. He was too streetwise for that. In a couple of hours the party would be over and he'd crawl home to his parents with his tail between his legs, announcing he'd had a 'great time', even though they'd have witnessed the truth for themselves.

"Dance?" said an unexpected but charming voice.

A hand with beautifully painted green nails stretched towards him.

What trick was this? Dares weren't the sole property of boys. Girls took part, too, and they were definitely better at them. Whereas the dares boys played on each other were designed to build confidence and bravado, girls had a gift of using theirs with the specific intention of reversing any gains those boys had made. Girls were mean and he wasn't falling for it. He averted his eyes and meekly shook his head.

"Be brave," she said. "I was."

Jake glanced across the room and saw a group of the popular girls cackling and pointing. But not at him. He wasn't even on their radar; they'd barely noticed his existence since the first year of high school. Their childish teasing was aimed at her. A sense of injustice devoured his shyness and a bonfire of bloody-mindedness ignited his feet. It propelled him out of his chair.

"It's a rare quality," she said, rather surprised. "I value it above all others."

"You have bags of it," he replied genuinely. "I'm Jake, by the way."

"I know," she replied. "I'm Christie."

She grabbed him by the hand and guided him to the very centre of the hall. The eyes of bewildered boys and judgemental girls zoomed in on the pair and the intense scrutiny made Jake's knees tremble. This was it, for better or for worse: life was going to be different now. Tomorrow he'd wake up as a legend or a loser. The next few minutes would determine which one.

"Where shall we dance?"

"Here?" said Jake, a little confused by the question.

"Which filter?"

"Oh I see. Which one do you like most?"

"The beach," she answered instantaneously.

The scene around them transformed and they were standing on a desert island with a single palm tree in the centre. Aquamarine seas lapped the edge of the beach and washed around the feet of the other students who were still mingling around the edge of room.

Jake didn't really do dancing. Dancing was what co-ordinated people did and his joints had been afflicted with spatial awareness issues. He swayed a bit, stuck out the occasional arm like he was playing an invisible piano, and bobbed his head from side to side like a falcon. Christie had no such anxieties about it. She'd left any inhibitions at home and let the music seep into her body, moving it effortlessly to the rhythm of the beat. Her carefree dancing and stunning, low-cropped, white gown mesmerised him.

"Just let yourself go," she said.

"How?"

"Do what you want to, not what you think you should do."

What was he worried about? Did the people in the hall really matter to him? He didn't like most of them and certainly not nearly as much as he liked her. In other aspects of his life he did do what he wanted, so why should this be any different? Did he care what these people thought of him? No. He stopped thinking about what move to make and tuned into the song, letting his body respond instinctively. The result was something akin to an octopus having a fit, but it didn't bother him. Christie broke out into a broad grin. She'd found someone like her. Brave, unburdened by convention and completely authentic.

"I like this song," said Jake. "What's it called?"

"Look it up," she said with a wink.

"*Everybody Wants Me* by the Pigeon Detectives," answered Fake Jake, breaking out of his trip down memory lane and returning to answer her question.

"Is that right?" asked Paddy.

"Yes," she replied in shock.

The only people who might know that were her, Jake and the others in the hall that night if they'd been inclined to log it.

"That means Jake's cloud is here, even if Jake is not," said Paddy.

"I am here. I'm Jake!"

"Shut up a minute, I'm thinking," replied Paddy. "Fake Jake, do you still have your guides with you?"

"One of them, yes."

"Where's the other one gone?"

"Rogue."

"Ask your guide what she thinks about all this," said Paddy.

Dinah's constitution was founded on natural curiosity and a childlike belief in everything. Pixies, dragons, flying dinosaurs with rocket launchers strapped to their backs and honest politicians all seemed perfectly plausible to her. If you told Dinah that the world was carved out of a carrot and orbited a margarine sun she wouldn't have blinked an eyelid.

"She thinks you might be unhinged," replied Fake Jake. "And she needs the toilet."

"But does she accept who you are?" asked Paddy.

"She's ninety-nine percent sure!"

"Then where did you get your scar from? You must have a memory of that?"

He didn't, and for the first time since he woke up feeling sore and dizzy in a square, black room, doubt about his own backstory crept across his mind. He sought confirmation from Dinah about the subject but strangely she couldn't remember either.

"When did you get it?" asked Dinah dubiously.

"I don't remember," whispered Fake Jake.

"It's possible Job deleted that memory, but I don't think so. He only destroyed things that meant something to you," said Dinah.

"Why don't we remember it?" he asked again.

"Scar or not, this guy has something to do with Jake," said Christie. "Even though I'm convinced it's not him."

"I agree," replied Paddy, "but I don't think we're going to solve the mystery getting cold and smelly down here. I suggest we return to the lighthouse and seek a second opinion."

"I suppose so," replied Christie. "What about Tyra?"

"Damn that brat," huffed Paddy, completely forgetting that his granddaughter had gone AWOL, mostly because he'd thoroughly enjoyed the time without her. "I can't go chasing around for her. She'll come back when she's ready, she always does. Mainly when she's hungry or needs credits."

"I can try to have a word with her if you want," replied Christie. "Teenage girl to teenage girl."

"No, don't bother. She doesn't like you much either. Come on, let's get back to Gay Head."

"Oh no," said Fake Jake forcefully. "I'm not getting involved in any of that carry-on again. I gave it a go but I'm just not a homosexual."

"It's just a lighthouse."

"A gay lighthouse," muttered Dinah. "Good to see diversity at work."

"Oh," replied Fake Jake. "That's fine."

"Maybe Drew can help us with this," added Paddy.

"Doctor Theo Drew?" said Fake Jake, butting in eagerly.

"Yes, do you know him?"

"He's the last person I remember seeing before I woke up this morning," he replied.

Major Holst…

The message forced its way into the cloud feed without following the normal pattern of waiting for him to accept it. He had plenty of notifications he'd been ignoring, but this wouldn't be one of them. Patience wasn't one of Alison's strengths. He stopped what he was doing and acknowledged it.

"Reading you loud and clear."

There have been sightings…

"The virus?"

Yes...

"The new 'Proclamation' has worked, then?"

Yes…but that's not the only source…

"Two sightings! And it's definitely him?"

Yes…

"Good news. Someone is about to become richer than Gog."

Gog…

"Oh, don't worry, it's just what they call him here."

Where…?

"In the East."

That's where I need you…go now…

"Don't worry," said Holst. "I'm already here."

THIRTEEN
THE LONG ROAD SOUTH

By the time you reach eighteen some life experiences occur so frequently it's impossible to separate any single event from any other, even with the Memory Cloud. Sleeping, defecating, drinking a glass of water, sneezing, the journey to school, and taking a shower are just some of the activities you're unlikely to revisit for a good reminisce. They're there if you want to, though, if your preferred option is suicide by boredom. These insignificant moments are filed in an electronic folder marked 'mundane'. Included in it are all the times you were forced to watch the 'Proclamation of Distrust'.

By Ascension Day you'd have seen it more than three thousand times, and until last week it had never been updated or altered. Seen it once, seen it a thousand times. But Jake hadn't seen it once. He assumed the 'mundane' folder was still where he'd left it, sandwiched between ones titled 'darkest secrets' and 'daydreaming', two folders that also received minimal attention.

Just because he couldn't remember the repetitive details of the five-minute broadcast that didn't mean he wasn't aware of its effects or purpose. Like other details from his past, the 'Proclamation of Distrust' was just one of the facts relayed to him by Dr Drew in the period following his implant surgery. Clearly the doctor felt it was an important aspect of Jake's history, although there were many facts about his life that didn't make the cut, mostly because Theo Drew didn't know them.

Jake didn't know when his birthday was, where he was born, what his favourite foods were, which sports he liked playing, if he had any siblings, or what frightened him. If he wanted to know who Jake was in the past he'd have to fill in the gaps when he experienced things for the second time. He'd just found out one of the answers to those questions, though. He didn't like efflotein. Having recently tasted it for the second 'first time', he was unwavering in his stance that it wasn't and never had been a favourite. Verne had kindly offered to host Jake at his house tonight and efflotein was the central ingredient in the dinner. Even though it smelt dreadful and had the aesthetic quality of cat sick, it would have been discourteous to refuse the gesture. By the look of Verne's dilapidated and sparsely furnished home he didn't have much to share.

They sat around the shabby, woodworm-riddled table and pretended to enjoy the meal. Jake concealed a grimace as slimy lumps of efflotein slid down his throat and greeted an old friend. The brain might not remember the stuff but his stomach certainly did. It wasn't overjoyed at being reacquainted and made its displeasure known by forcing the rest of Jake's body to convulse. Neither man had said much since arriving here this evening. Their thoughts had been hijacked by the same subject, but not for the same reasons.

"How could Boris have seen it?" said Jake, finally breaking the silence.

"How should I know? I've never seen it," replied

Verne, pointing to his scar to remind Jake who he was. "What is this proclamation anyway?"

"Usually it's a warning to the people of the West to fear their Eastern cousins. I don't know how they do it exactly because they didn't give me the details."

"That makes sense," said Verne. "Almost no one comes here, so it's obviously working."

"But why show it to people here? And how? The Realm and Circuit work on separate networks: doesn't that make it impossible?"

"Boris said it only started a few days ago. It might have been a regular feature in the West but it appears to be a new device here. One with a different purpose. Were you in the proclamation before?"

"No, I don't think so. I'm sure Dr Drew would have told me if I was."

"They must have changed it. It doesn't surprise me given what you told me about your confrontation with Alison. If the Circuit believe you're a threat, they'll do anything to stop you."

"Clearly, but how can they show it to people like Boris if they're on a different network?"

"Legacy."

Jake looked blank. He used his genuine confusion as an excuse to stop eating, sliding the plate back into the centre of the uneven table and rubbing his tummy to signal his fulfilled appetite.

"The world might be split in half now, but that wasn't always the case. Back in my younger days there was only one. It was only after Aaron and Miriam Circo fell out that he built the Realm, but it uses the same technology. The only real difference is the frequency used to connect the implant to the cloud. Even though subscribers only communicate to those who exist on the same network, there's still only one Memory Cloud. Just like the yellow sulphur clouds that circle above our heads, it cannot be tamed or kept apart."

"But if there's only one Memory Cloud isn't everyone connected to each other?"

"No. The Memory Cloud might be everywhere but people access it differently. Someone wearing an implant in New Putinsburg can't access the part of the Cloud governed by the West."

"Then what's legacy got to do with it?"

"Because the Circuit isn't a subscriber, they're the master. I don't know how exactly, but it's clear to me, if what Boris says is true, they've found a way to exploit the links between the two systems."

"And the Realm failed to put a stop to it."

"Or don't want to," added Verne, sparking up a post-meal cigarette and blowing smoke rings across the room.

Boris's revelation complicated matters. Jake's journey to the East was saturated with unknowns, but he'd clung to the hope that if he arrived safely he'd be hidden from those intent on hunting him. He'd not accessed his own unique cloud interface to limit the chance a Memory Hunter locked onto his position. It was a difficult urge to quash. There were so many answers out there he wanted, but so far he'd maintained his discipline. He hadn't once checked in on the people he cared for. Christie, the one he'd been told was his forever love, or Paddy, his last remaining family. He wondered how they were. Were they being pursued because of him? It drove him insane to think the answer was a simple virtual step away.

Now everyone was looking for him, and if he lost his self-restraint it would be even more dangerous.

"Why would they want to turn me in?" asked Jake. "I haven't done anything to hurt these people."

"Don't be naïve, Jake. They have nothing. It's not much of a stretch of the imagination to guess that they've been offered incentives."

"Incentives?"

"Credits probably, but maybe to them an even more valuable reward. I don't know what but I intend to find out," said Verne. "What will you do next?"

"It looks like all roads lead to Baku," muttered Jake. "I need to understand why the Realm aren't protecting them."

"Good luck getting there," Verne spluttered on his cigarette.

"I'll take a Hyperloop."

"A what?"

The East wasn't just economically and developmentally behind the West, it was behind the present day. Walking the streets of New Putinsburg was a trip back in time. There were no skyscrapers or carbon rod farms. The people wore old-fashioned, twentieth-century clothing and hadn't been exposed to the gadgets Jake's generation thought were routine and unexceptional. Everything was grey, uninspiring and antique. The modern forms of transport Jake was used to weren't evident here either.

"How do people travel around, then?"

"Horse normally, as long as someone hasn't eaten it."

"Ok, I can do that. How far is Baku from here?" he asked, not in the least upset by the thought of a more leisurely journey.

Verne leant back on his chair and pulled a sepia relic from the cupboard. He placed a rolled-up canvas on the table and unfurled an old map that was considerably out of date. Many of the countries displayed either had been renamed or no longer existed above the water. Here and there changes had been drawn on with a black marker pen.

A region around the English Channel had been scribbled out completely and arrows pointed to places that were labelled as 'hostile'. The majority of the adjustments were on the left-hand side of a thin, diagonal line that ran from Helsinki to Dubai. Verne cricked his thumbs and placed them on the map, counting how many of them spanned the distance between New Putinsburg and Baku.

"About two and a half thumbs," he said confidently.

"How far is that by foot?"

"Hold on," he said, placing the map on the floor, removing his shoe and slapping a dirty size nine on it.

"I mean if I have to walk it," Jake clarified.

"One thumb is equivalent to a thousand miles."

"And how far can a horse do in a day?"

"Good horses will do about two hundred miles."

"Great. Where can I get one of those?"

"Spain, I'd imagine," he replied, pointing it out on the map. It looked way more than three thumbs away.

"And if I can't get to Spain?" said Jake sarcastically.

"You'd be lucky to get two miles a day out of one of the local horses. Very skinny, and doesn't even make a particularly good meal."

"I'm sure it's better than efflotein," Jake cussed under his breath. "There has to be another way. Show me the map."

Jake was fond of maps, having used one to navigate his way from Malmö. Printed maps were a rarity. Maps normally appeared in cloud feeds and allowed the user to zoom in to such an extent it was possible to pick out individual trees. In comparison this one was low-resolution and even the Amazonian rainforest was barely visible.

"What's this?" he asked, pointing out a thin, black line.

"River?"

"But it's straight!"

"Canal, then."

"Why would a canal go over a lake? Look, the line goes straight over this one."

"Huh," replied Verne, thinking out loud. "Now I think about it there used to be lots of train lines running through this region. Big, dirty, steam-powered brutes that made such a wonderful racket when they passed through town."

"I thought steam power was banned?"

"Not here it isn't."

"Do they still run?"

"Not sure. I haven't heard one come through this way in a while."

"But that doesn't mean they don't. What's your hunch?" asked Jake eagerly. It was hardly first-class transport but it beat spending months on the back of a knackered old nag.

"Yes. I expect so. I can't think how they'd get all the natural resources out to the ships if they didn't."

"They're still doing that?" said Jake in surprise.

"Of course. The West needs all kinds of raw materials they don't have. Ores mostly. The East has a monopoly on those."

"And they can get them through the firewall?"

"I understand they transfer the goods to automated ships that sail out of Riga on the East coast. Not sure where they go from there."

"Can you help me get there?"

"I could if I wanted to, but I don't."

"Verne, someone very important once told me to think of the greater good and turn away from self-interest. I'm offering you the same advice. This might be our only chance of ridding the world of both corrupt systems, if we can find the courage. Join me."

"I can't, people rely on me."

"Just think how I feel. I'm carrying the weight of all of them on my shoulders."

"You don't have to do it, though, do you? You're out of the system now, free to roam, out of sight."

"And how long will that last? Every subscriber on Earth is hunting me, not to mention the war drones. If they kill or catch me the chance will be lost. The secrets only exist in my head now, nowhere else."

Verne rocked back on his chair, hands conjoined and nestled on his skinny belly. His world had become a selfish place. It had to be that way. Survival relied on your wits and cunning. Trust in others led to disappointment or worse still being traded in for a pitiful reward that might keep you going for another month. People whispered about change but no one had the bravery to raise their voice. Could he? Was he willing to lose everything to help a stranger? He didn't have much left to lose, but perhaps there might be some benefits of offering assistance.

"I'll accompany you as far as Riga," said Verne. "Then you're on your own."

"I appreciate that, Verne. Thank you."

"I thought you wanted to go to Baku? Riga is in the opposite direction."

"Yes, I can see that but the train runs from there," he said, running his finger along the thin, black line on the map. "If they bring the shipments to the coast then they must return the trains to where they started."

"Clever. Lots of ore is mined in the central belt and that would take you close to Baku."

"How many thumbs to Riga?" asked Jake.

Verne fingered the map again. "Half a thumb."

～

The mythical nature of the sun has long been the focus of man's attention. Down the eons every major religion and civilisation found a need to worship it. The Egyptians had Ra, the sun-god and father of creation. According to myth, the Earth came into being when Ra summoned it out of Nun, a watery mass. Given the climate disaster that had befallen the world, it was a surprise the worship of Ra hadn't made a comeback. Maybe his resurgence was stymied by the Egyptian belief that the sky was actually a huge cow.

Today there weren't any cows in the sky or on the land.

But there was an even rarer sight. The sun and a pair of skinny, docile horses trotting along underneath it.

There was a good reason this time of year was called Solar Summer. It was the only predictable time it might appear, making it most people's favourite time of year. In Summer, which came directly afterwards and lasted four months, the sun rarely made an appearance without a thick sheet of hazy cloud. Its insulating quality pushed temperature levels through the roof and left people feeling faint from the exposure. Summer was less than a month away and at this pace they'd still be riding south when it arrived.

They stopped next to a babbling stream to water their horses and relax on its grassy banks. It didn't matter that they were in a hurry, the sun's rays were beaming down and some moments had to be appreciated while they were still there. It's easy to take things for granted. The laugh of a child, the support of a friend, the comforts of home all become invisible when they're routine. People only notice and fully appreciate their value when they disappear. Soon the sun would hide behind the clouds again and the opportunity would be gone for months.

"How much further to go?" asked Jake, filling up his water bottle with fresh mountain water.

"Do I look like a sat nav?"

"Fair point," he said, realising that Verne was equally blind to the benefits of the cloud.

"We just have to ride on until we get there."

"Sometime before retirement age would be good," chuckled Jake.

Verne didn't find the situation quite so amusing. He lifted his straw hat and wiped the sweat from his face and Jake was once again drawn to his scar. They shared the same mark but he'd never put much thought into how it came to be there.

"How did we get our scars?" he asked. "I thought mine was a result of the surgery when they removed my implants, but you've never had one so it can't be that."

"It's not an external event, it's an internal one."

"Internal?"

"Yes. More emotional than physiological. A shift in one's mindset produces hormones that trigger the vagus nerve."

"What's that?"

"It's the longest of your cranial nerves. It means 'wandering' in Latin which is an appropriate name. When someone has an awakening, like you had, it reacts to the situation in a number of interesting ways. The vagus nerve runs from your heart to your brain, so when you have a change of heart it promotes a change of mind. The scar is physical proof of it."

"Do you remember when you got yours?"

"No, I've had it as long as I can remember. I guess having speccy parents means I've grown up in that environment already. You won't find a single speccy who doesn't have one, though. It's our badge."

They watched the sun paint a beautiful red sunset over the sky before it disappeared over the horizon. Once the light was finally extinguished they mounted their horses and set off once more. It was advantageous to travel at night, both for the welfare of the horses and to protect Jake's anonymity. When they had passed through small towns and villages it had drawn unwanted attention. People stopped whatever miserable activity they were engaged in to stare, whisper and point at him. He wasn't hard to pick out either. His clothes were foreign, his features angular and reworked.

Being notorious here, though, was a lot better than it would have been back home. When the people here recognised him they didn't appear to know what to do about it. Was there a procedure for handing him in, and more importantly what would happen to them if they did? Fear of the system outweighed fear of the imposter, particularly on this miserable day. He hated to consider that anything might disrupt it further.

If only they'd seen him yesterday.

Yesterday was always perfect.

Jake and Verne rode on country lanes wherever they could, but it was impossible to avoid human contact completely. Frequently their route was blocked by a vast city whose population had grown exponentially over recent years as refugees flocked inland. The industrial city of Luga to the south of New Putinsburg was just one of these monstrosities.

Twenty years ago, Luga was an insignificant industrial outpost. A backwater cog in the vast machinery of the state. A place coveted by introvert coal miners, grizzly steelworkers and low-skilled labourers. Not any longer. Today the city was overrun with the recently displaced. Crudely constructed shanty towns spread like fungus on the banks of the huge river that meandered through it. Every conceivable building material had been used to cobble together shelters that housed families of ten or more. Corrugated metal, ripped tarpaulins, discarded rubbish and parts of rusty vehicles were combined chaotically to form an interactive modern art collection.

They did their best to stay a safe distance away but the terrain was boggy and the horses found it heavy going. Jake covered his face with his hat as they trotted past the sullen-looking locals who shared the same outlook as everyone else he'd seen. It was almost as if they suffered from an unshakable disease that no one had a cure for. When the horses finally reached the other side of the city, something unexpected greeted them and for the first time in his trip the fate of the war drones was no longer a mystery.

Amongst decommissioned manufacturing plants and redundant factories a sparkling, modern glass building shone through like a polished crystal. It was the most futuristic building Jake had seen anywhere in the East, and was totally incongruous compared to the ruined past of industrial estates' heavy industry. It was as if the builders had totally misread the plans, only realising their mistake when the VIP selected to officially open it turned up in Dubai to find it wasn't where it should have been. The building loomed over the rest of the structures and bullied a rectangular space along the whole length of the potholed street. Hovering ominously on each side of the shimmering glass were huge, black drones.

"What's that building?" whispered Jake as they led their steeds into the shadows on the other side of the road to remain out of sight.

"Server farm."

"Really?" said Jake excitedly. "I've never seen one."

"This is as close as you'd ever get to one. Very secretive places."

"But why would the war drones want to attack it?"

"They don't. They're defending it," answered Verne. "Look, they're pointing away, not towards it. If they wanted to destroy it they'd have done it already."

Jake stepped out from the filthy cement silo they were hiding behind to get a better look. Other than maintaining an elevation halfway up the side of the three-storey building the drones appeared inactive. Silently they waited, alert to a threat only they understood.

"What are they defending it from?" asked Jake curiously.

"You, I'd imagine."

"Me!? What interest would I have in other people's memories?" he said doubtfully.

"I don't know. Maybe the Circuit are already one step in front of you: after all they have access to a billion times more intelligence than you do. No offence."

"None taken."

Jake had always worried about what the war drones might do here. He'd imagined awful scenes of death and destruction, but he'd never considered this. Why would they go to such lengths to protect their enemies' server farms when they were capable of so much more? It made no sense. If the Circuit wanted to massacre the people of the East they had the perfect weapons and circumstances. Most people would probably welcome the removal of their anguish, and these machines were more than capable of delivering it. Instead the drones were being deployed as overqualified guard dogs.

"It's beyond me," said Jake. "I don't know anyone in the East so why would I want their memories?"

"You said the secrets you protect originated here, right?"

"Yes."

"But you don't know what to do with them, correct?"

"That's about it, yeah."

"Then perhaps the answers you seek won't come from talking to people. Maybe they exist in the past."

"Dinah!" he gasped. "They're trying to stop me from finding her. Just like they did with my own Dinah, they don't want me to discover the truth."

"Which Dinah are we talking about exactly?" asked Verne, gently stroking his horse to calm its agitated neighing.

"It's complicated," he said apologetically. "Dinah was my guide but she also has something to do with Aaron Circo. I'm not sure why they'd be protecting the servers, though: he's been dead for twenty years."

"Memories don't die, Jake."

"They don't?"

"No. If she existed in his cloud then she'll be in one of these server farms somewhere."

"That's really useful to know," said Jake, feeling more positive about his next step. "The question is, which one?"

"Only the Realm could tell you that, but I'm guessing you'll find these drones outside of all of them even if they told you."

"I fear you're right. I need to motivate the Realm to help me locate it and get me inside. Now there's even more reason to introduce myself to this so-called King of Baku."

"He can't be trusted," said Verne gravely. "He'll manipulate you to his will. There's something of the occult about him, trust me."

"I wouldn't trust everything you hear," answered Jake,

feeding his horse Shimo an oddly shaped lump of sugar. "There's so much misinformation in this world."

"It's not based on what I've heard, it's based on what I've seen," replied Verne sternly.

"You've seen him!"

"I fought him during the rebellion when we tried to stop his power grab. That's why I can't come with you, Jake: I lost too much last time."

"I've lost everything, too, you know. Even my memories. I'm little more than a human husk holding a secret. It's the only thing I have left to lose."

"I sympathise, but this illusion you see around you might just be better than what comes next."

"But what if it isn't? Wouldn't you want to know? Wouldn't you fight for that?"

"No," said Verne plainly. "I'm done with fighting. It's not about the greater good anymore, it's about personal survival. That's the only way to live in the East."

"I'm sorry you think that."

"Come on, let's find this train," said Verne, mounting his horse.

FOURTEEN

THE CITY OF FROWNS

O n the edge of Luga, not far from the glass walls of the server farm, Jake's luck turned. Between the heavy industrial plants and dirty, unused tracks, they stumbled upon a railhead once used to bring raw materials in from local quarries and transport finished goods from the factories. With any hope it ran down to the main line and from there all the way to the sea at Riga. Further down the track they discovered a fully laden carriage already coupled to a locomotive engine. It looked ready to leave and with any luck it would get him to the docks a lot quicker than poor old Shimo. If it did, then all he had to do was wait for the empty carriages to be sent back down the line towards Baku.

After one final and failed attempt to recruit Verne, he shook his hand and wished him well. Their farewell was tinged with regret that he'd not convinced him to stay longer. Jake enjoyed his company and it was helpful to have someone with local knowledge. Unquestionably, without it Jake would have fared much worse over the last few days. He fostered no animosity towards Verne or his decision.

Jake would have done exactly the same only a few months ago, particularly if he'd experienced what Verne hinted at. Not all scars were visible. Some left deep wounds in your soul and it was clear Verne had suffered more than he was willing to divulge.

Jake scaled the side of the carriage and loosened the heavy plastic sheet that stopped the contents bouncing out during transit. The carriage was half full of irregular-shaped rocks about the size of his fist. At first he thought they were lumps of coal but they shimmered with purple and emerald hues and didn't leave black marks on his hands when he touched them.

"What do you think these are?" said Jake, poking his head out of the canvas and holding one in the air.

"Looks like nickel ore," replied Verne, squinting from his position some metres below the lip of the carriage.

"What's it used for?" asked Jake naïvely.

"In the old days they made coins from it, but there's not much need for those anymore. It mainly goes into electronics. My guess is most of it will end up in implants."

Jake wondered how much of the stuff had been inside his head at one time or another. Probably plenty given the number of upgrades he'd had. God knows what his new implants were made of. There might be bits of old bottle tops and chunks of asbestos for all he knew.

The train's wheels creaked and a plume of smoke coughed out of the locomotive's funnel. The train might have an automated pilot but it was still powered by good, old-fashioned steam power. Coupled to his carriage was a smaller model that fed a steady stream of black fluid through a clear tube which disappeared into the guts of the locomotive. Slowly and with a groan the whole train rolled forward. The wheels screamed as they pressed against the rails, slowly picking up pace with the increased consumption of liquid fuel. Verne rode alongside for as long as the horses were able to keep up.

"Jake!" he shouted. "Remember you'll get no help from the Realm or from the King. Be wary, do not reveal who you are and don't be conned by his forked tongue."

"Ok. Thanks for all your help."

"Good luck."

The horses kept up for a few more minutes before they were soon nothing more than specks in the distance. Once again, Jake was alone.

Exhausted from weeks of arduous travelling, he closed his eyes and, despite the discomfort of the ore underneath him, immediately fell into a deep sleep. He woke with a start as the carriage shook and lumps of nickel crashed down on him. Every part of his body ached from the asymmetrical rocks pressing into his body like contraptions of medieval torture. The train had stopped. He lifted the canvas slightly and a salty sea breeze whistled through the gap. He was here, Riga, just another port on a sea he'd recently conquered. The whirl of rotor blades drowned out the sound of the waves lapping against the dock's walls. A number of worker drones were busy shifting a conveyor belt into position beneath him. It stretched along the quay-side and up to a massive merchant ship moored to the dock with huge, brown chains.

Jake squeezed his body over the ore to the other side of the carriage. The sharp edges cut into his palms and he suppressed the urge to yelp in pain. He loosened the canvas and took a peek. There was no activity on this side of the rails and he took the opportunity to disembark before they unloaded the carriage, and he ended up being escorted back to the West with it. He jumped out just in time. The moment his feet struck the dock the carriage tilted on a piston and the ore crashed onto the conveyor.

He crawled carefully towards the locomotive which still wheezed with steam. Crouching next to one of the wheels, he peered through the gaps to get a better look at what was happening. A dozen worker drones were diligently retrieving rocks that had bounced off the conveyor or were picking through them in search of those with impurities. The belt shuddered slowly along the dockside before it sloped steeply upwards towards the ship's poop deck. Once it was clear of the edge the conveyor belt ended and the ore fell away out of sight. It was obviously not the only train that had been unloaded here today. Rather than the ore crashing onto the metal floor of the cargo hold, there was a sustained sound of dull thuds as they landed on their rocky brethren instead.

Tirelessly the drones worked as if bonuses for efficiency had been promised. Normally they did what their automated operator programmed them to do, but on this occasion they were receiving direct human instructions. It was the first time Jake could remember a drone being instructed in this way. From his restricted view all he saw was a pair of thick, heavy-duty boots attached to stocky legs covered in an unusual brown fabric.

"Stop!" the man shouted angrily.

To Jake's surprise the drones heeded the command.

"You're going too fast. Look, there's ore dropping off the conveyor and falling into the sea! Give me fifty!"

Jake's triceps twitched in panic and sent his brain a confused synaptic response that suggested it had momentarily lost control of certain bodyparts. A drone descended and proceeded to use its robotic arms to push itself up and down in the air at a scintillating tempo. When the 'fifty' were dispatched it returned to its duties and the conveyor belt continued more slowly.

Jake's curiosity got the better of him and he shuffled

around the front of the locomotive, being careful not to touch the blistering hot panels. There was nothing familiar about the man orchestrating procedures on the dockside, but something about the ship did grab his attention. Its name was painted down the side of the hull in large, white letters.

Brandvägg, Sverige.

He had no idea what the first word meant but he instantly knew the second one. 'Sverige' was what the locals called Sweden and it was almost as prevalent as the Circuit. Most notably he remembered seeing it printed on the old antique map he'd been given when he bought the dinghy. Did that mean the ship was heading back there? Or was it a coincidence? It seemed unlikely. The war drones were built in Bornholm, Sweden, and this ship was heading back in that direction.

It was enough for him to put two and two together.

A shipment of ore destined for the smelter where its cooled metal would be used to build electronic components, a fleet of highly sophisticated fighting machines, and a severe lack of resources in the West. The Circuit was stealing from the East and using the proceeds to build technological monsters to threaten them. It was like stealing someone's watch and then sending them a bill for telling them the time.

"Finished?" barked the man impatiently.

In response the worker drones hovered impassively, but Jake felt they secretly wished they had weapons and the freedom to use them.

"Prepare the carriages for the return journey," he added before marching back towards the ship.

The carriage Jake arrived in sprang back into its upright position and the steam engine started to chug. He rushed back along the rails and pulled himself up the side.

The carriage was empty, but as the train reversed out of the siding he realised the ride would be no less comfortable. A lack of weight meant an increase in speed and Jake was catapulted around like a bean in a coffee grinder.

Day passed into night three times before he finally reached his destination. The train stopped frequently but only to take on extra water or fuel and never for more than ten minutes at a time. The temperature rose with every mile the train chugged further south. By the third day it had become almost unbearable. Humid air swirled around the empty carriage and made it feel like an oven set to gas mark maximum. Jake sustained himself with one bottle of water but even when he did dare to drink, it did little to quench his insatiable thirst. He rationed himself to one gulp every six hours, but uncertainty about the journey's length made each swig feel like a game of Russian roulette.

The canvas screen sheltered him from the worst of the sun's fierce rays, but he still took off everything other than his underwear, as if he'd lost every round of strip poker he'd ever played. Occasionally he stuck his head out of the canvas to catch the breeze but the metal of the carriage was so hot and the air so sticky it never brought the relief he yearned for. He spent most of his time crouched in a pool of his own sweat thoroughly miserable and slowly going mad.

Apart from near starvation and heat exhaustion, the worst part of the journey was boredom. How did people cope before they had a Memory Cloud? he thought. The temptation to dive into his own was more than he could bear: it was like confining a recent ex-smoker inside a tobacconist's. Sometimes he thought he'd accessed it accidentally only to realise he was actually hallucinating. At one point in his delusional mind, Dinah had organised a cheese and wine party down the other end of the carriage, and he was quite disappointed to find there was nothing to eat when he arrived.

The only stimulus came from what he held inside him, and that was limited to reams of complex computer coding. He'd seen it only once, and at a tremendous velocity, yet he remembered every line right down to the last character. If only he could make sense of it. He repeated it out loud to seek clues to its purpose. The lines of code were full of odd commands, strange symbols, random numerals and illegible text streams. It would have taken him days to go through all of it. He was bored but not that bored. It was fascinating that he remembered it at all and that was as much of a mystery as its meaning. Given how little alternative information he held in his brain right now, he imagined it was only retained because of all the free space.

The landscape didn't offer much in the way of a distraction from the boredom either. When he did manage to sneak a peek through the covers, all he saw were vast patches of scorched tundra, mosquito-infested marshlands and dried-up basins that once supported mighty lakes. The train never stopped when they passed through the cities, always refuelling at isolated pumps and desolate water towers. The cities they did pass through were much like New Putinsburg: grey, dour and tragic. If anything, they got progressively more depressing the further they advanced along their route. These cities were further from the sea and hadn't received the same funding for redevelopment. It was like watching a history documentary. Forgotten, battle-scarred towns that no one could be bothered to fix.

Between the cities, wherever the quality of land permitted it, arable farms were struggling to grow the most basic of crops, and even these disappeared after what he hoped was more than a thumb's length of the journey. The exhausting job of cultivating acres of wheat, potato and sugar beet was being carried out by human, cart and ox. Jake saw no technology to boost productivity. This was nothing like the way they harvested food in the West. In the last decade a reduction in available land, inferior weather conditions and a surge in the population created a demand for new and innovative farming methods. The most successful of these were the 'Growtels'.

Growtels were vast, multilevelled glass buildings with huge surface areas but small footprints. In effect they were self-contained and self-powered greenhouses. Just like the authorities had stacked people in high-rise buildings in the later part of the twentieth century, the same principle was being applied to fruit and veg. Each floor was dedicated to a different crop and the conditions of heat, light and humidity were set perfectly to encourage the greatest possible yield. The 'Growtels' were sealed from the environment so there was no need for pesticides to destroy the insect nasties that might be after a free meal. The majority of vegetables were farmed this way and the yield per acre was tenfold what it might have been without them. It was just another difference between the two halves of the planet.

Here the future had stalled. Manpower was still the most valuable energy source and the people worked day and night to ensure there was enough food to go around. There never was.

Jake's boredom was relieved by thoughts of Christie, most of them invented. In a vacuum of reality he imagined some of the dates they might have been on, conversations they'd had and places they'd visited. By the end of his journey Jake had erected a completely believable but entirely fabricated relationship. Whether he'd get a chance to check if any of it was true felt less likely with every mile. Future planning more than the next hour seemed a bit pointless. He was deep in unfamiliar territory on a journey of unknown duration to meet a shadowy organisation headed by a man who was no more than a legend. Who knew what would happen to him after that?

The Realm were clearly negligent in their duty of care towards subscribers, so they weren't likely to treat him well. It appeared to him that someone in the organisation was altering their users' perceptions, and yet the Circuit still acted irrationally about the threat those people posed. The two positions seemed incompatible. If your enemy's enemy was your friend, then he had nothing to fear from the Realm. But then again, Verne's first-hand experience couldn't be discounted out of hand either. What choice did he have? Dinah was here somewhere and if anyone knew what the secrets in his head meant, she did. His best bet was to seek out the King of Baku and work the truth out for himself.

If he ever got there.

On the fourth day Jake woke to find himself crumpled against the end wall some metres from his usual position huddled in the centre. When he attempted to return to it he discovered why. The carriage was travelling down a slope. He stuck his head through the canvas and watched as the train descended a shallow hill. In the distance the sun sparkled and shimmered off the sea, a rather welcome sight. It was the first time he'd seen it since leaving Riga. On a hill a brightly coloured city had almost completely been cut off by the sea, and in the bay a number of islands carried the severed remains of the city's suburbs on their backs.

It was a strange mix of old and new, quite incongruous to the places he'd been so far. The buildings were mostly constructed from beige sandstone, but here and there a glass tower poked through the middle to confuse the town planner's overall vision. The nearer he got to it, the more intense the atmosphere felt. The city was cluttered like every available space had been developed in case another town got to it first.

The railway tracks crossed a disused road where Jake noticed a weathered blue sign that announced some of the local destinations. The name at the top confirmed he was entering Baku. It gave him a momentary boost, although it was soon mugged by his fatigue. On the edge of the city the train levelled out and pulled into a small, quiet depot. Jake put his clothes back on and clambered down the side of the carriage before it took off again and he ended up in some remote part of China. Unfamiliar with the notion of standing still, his legs wobbled and swayed like they'd just returned from a year at sea, but once he'd composed himself he scuttled away eager to avoid the inevitable arrival of the worker drones on a shift change. When he was clear of the train his adrenaline levels waned and triggered an intense hunger. It still wasn't his most important priority.

He needed to protect his identity first.

The Circuit might have lost sight of him, but the people who lived here had not. The 'Proclamation of Distrust' would have been delivered four more times since he left Riga. It would be impossible to saunter through Baku without one of the locals identifying him. He also had no intention of visiting the King without blending in.

His first instinct was to visit a 'Conversion Room'. A

permanent reconfiguration of his features would be the best option, but it was clear no one in this city of frowns had been to a dentist, let alone had their faces reconstructed. If that was off the table, the only alternative was self-help. His footsteps took him through more residential areas where he noticed an unwatched clothes line in a backyard. He snuck over the wall and took what he needed. He didn't feel so guilty about stealing after he examined what he'd taken. A long, green-patterned gown made from a light chiffon material that had a faint whiff of cat, and a woollen scarf covered in moth holes. It would have to do and at least he'd blend in.

Further down the road he entered a small, quiet market and managed to 'borrow' some scissors and a razor without anyone noticing. He retreated to a quiet spot and shaved away the majority of his hair and beard. Without a mirror to guide him he left unseen clumps of hair in various places that made him look more like a recovering cancer patient than a local. Finally, after returning what he'd pinched, he strolled down to the banks of the river and liberally spread mud over his face to hide the scar that ran down his cheek. The new persona made him look like an amateur hobo, but as that perfectly reflected Baku's current fashion trend this season, he'd fit in perfectly.

He turned his attention to finding food and shelter but after a few poorly chosen turns he found himself strolling along one of the dozen bridges that spanned the numerous ancient and newly formed tributaries that divided the city. To his relief the people walking in the other direction ignored him. The disguise was working but he'd still need information if he was going to find his way around this massive city. He stopped an old woman travelling across the bridge at a snail's pace.

"Excuse me. Where might I find food?"

She ignored him.

"Do you have food banks here?"

Again she blanked him. He thought it was unlikely they had normal banks here, let alone ones with free food in them. He changed his line of enquiry.

"Where can I find the King of Baku?" he asked politely, desperate for anything helpful.

Her already miserable expression curdled further.

"Do you know?" asked Jake.

She nodded. Everyone knew.

"Where?"

"Fire Temple," she croaked.

"Which direction?"

"Walk east across Khatai Bridge to Surakhani Island."

"Thank you."

"There is an easier way," she added cryptically.

"Why don't you tell me, then?" he snapped, as his exhaustion and patience boiled over.

"An easier way to die," she tutted before shuffling off on her own epic quest to return home before the end of the month.

It was hard to trust people when you knew they were having their memories altered. It was possible that everyone he met might have an unhealthy bias against the Realm. Their lives were desperate and their masters did nothing to improve it. That wasn't going to inspire any rave reviews. Perhaps the Realm weren't as bad as everyone said?

Jake decided to suppress his hunger a little longer and followed the old woman's directions. After an hour of walking his feet were aching, his muscles shutting down, and his energy levels dangerously low. Locating Khatai Bridge should have lifted his spirits, it did anything but. He'd been told to cross it, but it was so huge that the other end wasn't even visible in the distance. The bridge looked new, built to connect two estranged parts of a once sprawling city. Under its arches partly submerged, uninhabited houses poked their heads out of the sea like giant stepping stones. One last push, thought Jake as he took a step forward, the only person keen on making the journey to Surakhani Island.

The only person, but not the only occupant.

Halfway across the span two worker drones stood guard. They spotted him before he did and flew over, arms and gadgets whizzing furiously from every side panel. Almost immediately, and before he could protest his innocence, a robotic arm shot out and grabbed him by the gown before proceeding to lift him in the air. For the second time in a week he was being escorted at high speed and at a lopsided angle towards the Realm.

FIFTEEN

THE KING OF BAKU

I f you discounted the Archivist's Jeeps, the car had disappeared more than a decade ago. Its demise rang the closing time bell for a host of other aspects of normal everyday life. Mobile mechanics, traffic wardens, service stations, novelty air fresheners in the shape of trees, families who attempted to take everything they owned on holiday with them, taxis, road rage and driving lessons were dispatched to the scrapheap of history. Along with scrapheaps. Hitch-hiking had featured on the list until about five minutes ago.

The art of hitch-hiking proved to be impossible when the only forms of transport available to you were trams and Hyperloops. Neither stopped long enough for you to flag them down, and even if you did, negotiating with an automated driver for a free lift was a tough task for even the most talented master of the craft. The only alternative form of transport was the horse but they didn't take kindly to someone covered in Gore-Tex jumping on their backs uninvited and demanding to go to Bristol.

In the distant past, when cars were still viable, traditional hitch-hiking was something you did on purpose: it wasn't forced upon you. It was also based on a simple premise. The hitch-hiker had a destination to reach and a lack of transport faster than their own two feet. Failing that, they were too tight to fork out for a ticket. Given the current global price of Hyperloop travel it's a surprise more people hadn't tried it.

It required a high degree of skill to charm a stranger to let you ride along with them for potentially hundreds of miles. Even if you had the gift, finding a willing driver would happen only once in a hundred attempts. Who could blame the driver for their reticence? Most of them didn't like passengers when they knew who they were, let alone suffer some long-haired, smelly hippy with halitosis and a tendency to talk constantly in an attempt to avoid the awkward silence. However, the success rate did increase immeasurably if you had a cleavage, wore a rucksack and didn't resemble a serial killer.

Arguably Jake had reinvigorated the ancient practice without even trying. Unquestionably he was both hitched and moving significantly faster than he'd managed under his own volition. It wasn't a smooth journey by any means but at least, unlike most hitch-hikers, he wasn't being forced to partake in hours of tedious small talk with a man in a tank top obsessed with the subject of bonsai trees. The only noise his driver made was the occasional and unexplained bleep from a sound card buried deep inside its shell and the gentle hum from four rotor blades.

As he swung helplessly in the air, he considered whether this was normal behaviour for the drones, or whether he was being singled out for special treatment. Was it a fundamental part of the worker drones' job description or were they just being opportunistic? They didn't appear equipped with the necessary sensors to identify who he was and made little attempt to do so before picking him up. Trespass was the only plausible explanation for their behaviour. He'd passed over the firewall without permission and now he'd crossed the bridge uninvited, too. Whatever their reasons, he was again heading towards Realm property and this time it was unlikely that Verne would pop up out of the sea with one of his special disrupter grenades.

When the bridge ran out, the drone entered the island city of Surakhani. It was similar to the other parts of Baku, apart from its intriguing smell. It was hard to place the scent in a mind stripped of the simple descriptors for everyday sights, sounds and smells that others took for granted. It had an aromatic quality like ground spices scattered on an open fire. It wafted out of the open windows of ancient dwellings made of worn sandstone that lined both sides of the uneven cobbled road which became steeper the further they flew.

At the top of the hill an old castle was surrounded by a vast courtyard of smooth stones worn down by the shuffling of sandal-wearing pilgrims over a thousand years. Occasionally the stone slabs were broken by an ancient olive tree ripe for harvesting. The low walls of the castle weren't particularly well fortified and Jake got the impression their original purpose was more religious than royal. White-robed figures with hoods that completely covered their faces lurched around the courtyard in a hypnotically repetitive pattern. They held flaming torches that flickered unnaturally and cast strange shadows on the ground. Even though their faces were hidden, Jake could hear their eerie chants some distance away. The language was foreign but the songs' sentiments unmistakably dark and secretive.

The drone carried him through a large archway and into the heart of the castle. There was no roof above them, only the distinctive sight of sulphur clouds passing through the night sky. Inside the walls the darkness was chased away by a huge fire that burnt fiercely from a tetra-pillared altar occupying the middle of the pentagonal-walled castle, the only significant feature of an otherwise empty space. Even more hooded characters mingled around here, either in prayer or wandering around in a trance-like state. The drone placed Jake gently in front of the altar and retreated without delay.

Jake brushed himself down and rearranged his disguise. The long, green gown and the brown woollen scarf wrapped tightly around his face made him look like a tree waiting to be sacrificed on the burning pyre. If he hadn't been so disconcerted by what was happening, he might have found the place a rather fascinating tourist attraction, but before he got the opportunity to explore, the robed figures pressed down on him and penned him in like a lost lamb. The monks guided him towards the pyre in the centre of the pillars. When he was close enough for the heat to cause him discomfort they stopped abruptly and one by one, like a human version of dominoes, they raised a clenched fist in the air. Then, when all hands were raised, they revealed what was hidden behind their fingers.

A single eyeball.

Jake recoiled in disgust. Were they real? He couldn't tell, and nor was he particularly keen to find out. The answer presented itself when one of the monks lost their grip and the eyeball bounced several times on the ground like a ping-pong ball. Jake sighed in relief. Who were these weirdos? The fumbled eye was retrieved from a nearby gutter and the culprit returned to the group who brandished them in his direction. Even though they were fake, the collective act was still deeply menacing. The monks also returned to their slow and uncomfortable humming which got progressively louder and more threatening.

"He cometh from the West on a chariot of wind wrapped in a shroud of wisdom," said a voice from within the stone pillars.

Jake turned around. A man of incomparable size and girth moved towards him from the other side of the fire. Without showing any obvious signs of discomfort he passed straight through the flames as if they weren't there. They licked his blubbery bare chest and set fire to his interesting headdress, but he still didn't react. When he reached the other side of the pyre one of the monks calmly doused the parts of him still ablaze with water from a tall, pewter urn. Steam sizzled off his body like a boiling kettle and Jake noticed that his skin was covered in blisters, both old and recent. The vomit-inducing smell of singed chest hair wafted up Jake's nostrils.

"Long may the Earth spin before night defeats day and the fire consumes Elysium. For that is why you have transcended, is it not?"

"Umm…come again," said Jake, not certain if the man was talking to him or the monks, and even less clear what he actually meant.

"The beetle will scurry to the desert to flee the power of the sun, the dove will fly over vast oceans towards dark clouds threatening to burst, the thief will risk certain death in pursuit of gold's hypnotic lure. All such instincts belie logic. Your trajectory is no different. Emotion is the life force of the Universe and only our ancestors can explain it."

"Are you talking to me?" asked Jake tentatively and straining to keep up with his bizarre turn of phrase.

"Who am I to interfere with the psyche of another starburst? Only the spirit, lounging dormant in your bones, can interpret my intentions."

"Is that a yes?"

The man took a further step from under the cover of the altar and into the flickering lights of the courtyard. His immense size almost completely consumed the free space within the small archway between pillars, a feature on each side of the structure. Waves of flab cascaded down his torso, almost completely concealing a white skirt of hemmed fabric that brushed against his flabby, swollen knees. A golden headpiece with bright green gems sat on his bald temple and drooped onto broad shoulders. In the centre between the gems was a single eyeball welded to the fragile precious metal. The rest of his body was daubed in a greasy, white paint that made his mouth and dark eyes look like holes gouged in a snowdrift.

"Ateshgah, the 'Temple of Fire'. Bestower of power, vanguard of liberty, source of illumination and protector of the King. What hindrance is delivered in vengeance will be devoured by the flames for no bond or spell of witch-craft can pierce its bowels," he babbled like a prophet reciting a memorised book of scripture.

"Are you the King of Baku?" asked Jake cautiously, feeling rather too tired and annoyed to play games today.

"If the will of Gog demands it."

"Did you say Gog?"

"GOG," chanted the brethren in response.

"Gog sees all," continued the fat man. "His eyes know no shadow, for only when the moon swivels on its axis and the dust rolls down the mountains will he sacrifice his devout crusaders to the fate of Judge. Each eve Gog bears me on a mattress of sand to Judge's door to dispel her evil intentions and release the brethren from persecution.

Never will Gog castigate those stout of heart or thin of hair. For it is Judge we must learn to fear, not Gog."

"GOG," repeated the monks.

The King spoke in an eccentric and protracted manner, while combining it with physical mannerisms which were just as strange. His eyes darted around as if they were following the movement of a drunk fly, and his arms flapped about threatening to strike invisible objects. Now and then he'd actually grabbed hold of one and pretended to throttle it with his mighty hands.

"Who's Judge?" asked Jake, regretting the question almost immediately.

"Ask not who Judge is, ask only who she isn't. For she is not the mighty wind that bites the grassy valley. Nor is she the bulligots who relentlessly pester the fisherman with their numerous spiky fins. Neither is she the winged chimps that drop oblong parcels from the sky. Nor the…"

"Forget I asked," said Jake politely.

The King wasn't put off by the interruption and continued the monologue until he ran out of crazy metaphors.

"I have travelled far to seek answers, your majesty," said Jake when a gap finally arrived. "There is a sickness across our world that must be healed."

"The bitter smell of war clings to your foul words, traveller. The greatest of all calamities sticks to your boots, malignant spores of ill news wilfully sown to poison Eden and lay waste to the land. The paradise of Gog cannot be levelled by soldiers that glide, crawl, hop or swim. For the power of righteousness will absorb all such foul beasts."

A conversation with the King was on a par with a natter with Riddler from the Batman comic books, only his puzzling sentences didn't appear to have any underlying purpose. Jake struggled as he reflected on every word to clarify its meaning before carefully considering a suitable reply. Who were these soldiers the King was referring to exactly? As far as he remembered, he was definitely on his own, but then again he wasn't the only thing to pass into the East recently.

"The war drones don't have anything to do with me!" said Jake after a period of silence. "I come alone."

"Prophet of Judge!" the King screamed. "Miscreant of truth. Deceiver of veracity. If you wish to parley peacefully with the King of Baku, then dismiss your fearsome mighty horde."

The King pointed to various parts of the courtyard as if to highlight his assertion that Jake was lying about being alone. There was nothing there other than walls, air and an occasional monk out for an evening pray.

"What horde?"

"Mighty brutes, taller than trees and more vicious than the wolves of Avernus. They carry the whips of whimsy and wield the bows of contrition. Dispatch them to their mothers' bosoms," he demanded with a psychotic shriek.

"But…there's nothing there!"

"GOG!" chanted the monks in case Jake was denying the presence of a higher being.

It was no wonder the East had problems. If this was their leader then understanding simple instructions would be enough of a challenge. The King was quite obviously mad, but it wasn't clear why. How had he maintained power for twenty years in this state of lunacy? Had the insanity developed recently or had he always been detached from reality? No sane person would allow such leadership. In a normal world the masses would rise up and consign him to an institution for his own protection. There's an ancient saying that 'people get the leaders they deserve'. The people of the East were infected with a deep despondency and darkness, so in that respect their leader was probably perfect for them. But which came first, the state of despondency or the leader?

Jake stood his ground while the King continued to point out the giant, invisible army he insisted had come to overthrow him. Jake needed answers and if there was any chance of achieving it, and he considered it remote at best on current progress, he had to do something about the imaginary horde. He cut a path through the monks who stood aside still clutching their single ping-pong eyeballs in their fists. When he reached the empty space by the wall he pretended to remonstrate with fictitious beings who according to the King were twice his size. He swished his arms around and shouted instructions for them to leave the courtyard. Once he felt he'd conducted enough fake encouragement he marched back to the circle of monks to see how he'd got on.

"Gog applauds your benevolence," said the King, striking a more convivial mood.

"They're gone?" asked Jake in surprise. He'd never rated his leadership skills very highly, but then again he'd never unleashed them on an empty space before.

"All apart from that one," said the King, pointing. "But as he's carrying a huge chest of gold, Gog will be lenient."

"Thank Gog."

"GOG!"

"Name thyself, child of Judge."

Using his real name wouldn't be wise right now so Jake quickly decided on a fake one. In retrospect he wished he'd given it more thought. "Tim."

"And which lush meadow does your herd feed, Tim of the mighty horde?"

It was almost as if he was talking in code and Jake felt his search for answers might improve if he spoke the same language. Codes, according to Doctor Drew, were how the speccies communicated with each other and he'd even discovered a steganograph for himself when he was searching for the location of Sam Goldberg. Maybe the King's language was similar. It was time to step it up a notch.

"I hail from a country where the land has dried up and the trees no longer bear fruit."

"But tomorrow they will burst with plenty," added the King instinctively.

"How cometh you knoweth?" rambled Jake.

"Because it always doth."

"Your majesty, the people of the East are starving and they have been plunged into an abyss of depression. They are downtrodden and disheartened. The West sends war drones into your land and still plunders your raw materials, but the Realm does nothing to repel it."

"That is Gog's will. We have no quarrel with the West. A great truce has endured for twenty Solar Summers and neither conflict nor famine has plagued our lands."

"But there is a plague, your majesty," interrupted Jake. "A sickness has captured their souls."

"The tribe are virile and strong of stature. Only Judge can fracture harmony. Only she can unleash the horsemen of despair. While Judge remains dormant my citizens are at peace. Only the deadly virus can disrupt her slumber."

It wasn't the first time a higher power had mentioned a virus to him. Alison had given him that label once before. Was the King referring to him? The 'Proclamation of Distrust' was being broadcast through the Realm's network, which meant someone must have informed them about him. He could think of only one suspect who might want to. But if the West hated the East why would they warn them about the threat on a daily basis? Was their fear

of Jake greater than their anxiety towards one another? Or
was the relationship between East and West more complex
than that?

"I don't know anything about a virus," replied Jake
nervously.

"What purpose bears you here to worship in the
'Temple of Fire'?" asked the King searchingly.

"I simply seek enlightenment."

"The Brothers of Gog have ascended to a higher plane
of veracity. They can show you a peek behind the curtains
of wonder. But what does your heart seek most?"

There were only two priorities in his heart and both of
them involved women. He'd only return to one of them if
he located the other and this seemed as good a time as any
to cut to the heart of the matter.

"I seek the one they call Dinah," he said boldly.

Several of the monks dropped their eyeballs and the
King grabbed at his chest as if all the air had been sucked
from his lungs.

"Seize him!"

The monks lunged forward and grabbed hold of him.
They pulled his arms out, threw him to the ground and
held his head back painfully. The King shuffled forward,
his great bulk looming over him perilously. If it wasn't for
the white paint the fear in his face would have had the
same effect.

"How did you come by this name? Enunciate!"

"She was my guide," Jake remonstrated, as he started
to panic and wish he'd kept his mouth shut on the subject.

"The only guide in the East is Gog."

"GOG."

"What about the ones people receive on their Ascension Day?"

"Guides!?" he said, looking shocked, as if the word had

been outlawed. "Until subscribers ascend into Gog's ultimate protection, they need no other guide."

Jake didn't know what happened in the East on the day subscribers reached their eighteenth birthday, but it was obvious from the King's comments that they had their own version of Ascension Day. It was the day when someone passed from life itself, not when they passed into adulthood.

"The Composer warned us," muttered the King of Baku to himself. "The virus that can traverse impregnable borders, invisible to Gog, impervious to corruption, untraceable to the great eye. Nameless and ageless."

"I can see this is a bad time. Perhaps I'll come back later," said Jake. "There is no Dinah, I made a mistake. Praise Gog!"

"Gog!" cried one of the monks instinctively. He stopped when the rest of the monks shushed him.

"How many times has the sun passed through the veil since your flower bloomed?" demanded the King. "Pronounce or we will poke you mercilessly."

Jake knew the game was up. He'd come all this way only to be captured by a madman covered in white paint. He'd been identified and now he was in real danger.

"Do you mean how old am I?" replied Jake, stalling for time.

The King nodded wildly.

There were a series of simple facts that even a two-year-old could answer about themselves that Jake simply didn't know. His birthdate was one that always drew a blank. In many ways he was a virus. Unseen, unknown and in the eyes of others potentially lethal.

"Is it really relevant?"

"Failure to reveal your true nature means failure to recognise Gog's elegance."

"Oh, in that case I'm twenty-two!"

"Sultan of liars! Your words defy you, Tim, Prince of pathogens. There is no place for viruses in this palace. Gog is the vaccine against your poison. Take him to the rock. Feed him to the Merlions!" shouted the King with a flap of his arms.

"Merlions?!"

"Mighty beasts with the head of a lion and the body of fish. They live in the Caspian Sea and gorge on the sacrifices of Gog. They will devour you one nibble at a time. Take him away."

SIXTEEN
DINAH'S DOUBTS

Their return to Gay Head Lighthouse took forever. Even in the dead of night the gangs patrolled the streets in their pursuit of Jake. Fatigue, hunger and work wouldn't stop them from this once-in-a-lifetime opportunity. It required commitment, dedication and regular cophony shots to be a winner, and they all believed resolutely that they would be the one. Hopeless positivity was no substitute for well-conceived plans or genuine intelligence, and they had neither.

But when did that ever stop anyone?

Unlike their experience in the park their route back to the quayside was not swamped by swathes of hunters distracting each other. As the crowds thinned and the streets narrowed they had to be more cautious in case they stumbled across a single seeker staking out a quiet corner on the off chance. If any of the hunters came into contact with Fake Jake's cloud it would confirm they had their man and there would be no one there to stop them. To avoid that scenario, Paddy used all of his local knowledge to lead them through the city by the most circuitous route. By the time they reached the dock and Alfonso's speedboat, shards of daylight were attempting to break through the menacing, dense cloud.

Everyone sighed with relief when they finally reached the safety of the open seas. Unless a co-ordinated scuba-diving club had decided Jake's likely location was underwater, it was highly unlikely they'd be spotted here. It might have been a reasonable strategy if any of their pursuers had taken a moment to research Jake's cloud, given how much time he'd spent in dinghies and catamarans over the years.

In the hour it took them to cross to the island, Fake Jake received a further inquisition from Paddy and Christie, all of their questions expressly designed to trip him up and satisfy their belief that he was a fraud. Sadly for them, he answered every one perfectly.

He recited the details of every Montana family outing, including ones that resulted in his own embarrassment.

He knew about Christie's family, her father's condition and how many times in the last three years he'd been sectioned.

He knew exactly where Christie's birthmark was, and even attempted to point it out before Jezebel gave him a pre-emptive slap.

He recounted the names of every student in his Circology class, including some of their hilarious nicknames.

He described every trip he and Christie had ever taken on their sailing boat and every excursion to the White Mountains.

There was no hesitation or misspoken word. He showed no signs of deceit and no anxiety when asked. If anything his emotions perfectly matched the circumstances of his answers, and yet with every correct one Christie's scepticism widened. Even if he did have an encyclopaedic knowledge of Jake's life, she knew it wasn't him. It didn't matter what he looked like, it just didn't feel like him and that was a more important indicator. Christie's desire to be reunited with her boyfriend increased her susceptibility to fraud. Anyone who wants something desperately always would be. But she wasn't about to accept substitutes or second bests. Jake's authenticity was what she loved most about him and this man was anything but.

Christie wasn't the only female whose intuition was sounding an alarm bell.

Dinah was also having doubts. She'd been unusually quiet since they left the sewer, perturbed by a divergence between what she knew and what he did. How could their views differ? It was her job to capture his memories, not the other way around. It was true that she retained her own unique experiences – the excursion on Bornholm proved that beyond doubt – but this was different. Jake had always been present when those events happened, even if he saw less than she did. All the events from the last few weeks were blank for him, but that was not the case for her.

Usually memories were recorded as a continual stream of consciousness, even when the host was unconscious. Sleep patterns and dream sequences were just as valuable to the Circuit and even occasionally to the host. In the early days of the Memory Cloud there was a short-lived craze of sharing your peculiar, unconscious imagination with mates down the pub like a twisted hypnagogic juke-box. It was short-lived because it revealed way too much about your essential character and darkest desires for normal people to stomach.

As the cloud captured the perpetual tide of data it decided, based on inherent protocols, which folders to store them in for future search purposes. Some chunks were archived by year, some by activity and some were tagged to the miscellaneous categories. Folders with titles such as 'mundane', 'things I'd rather forget happened but I can't', 'bloopers' and 'kinky shit' all came as standard. Other folders could be added by the subscriber at leisure, should they feel the need. It didn't really matter where you stored them because collectively the files, tranches and folders were sewn together to document one user's life post-implant surgery from first breath to last.

That's how it worked in theory, but when it came to Jake's stream that wasn't the case. Quite a bit of it was missing. Dinah knew the reason why some of it was lost. Job had deleted various parts of Jake's memory, including whole years, after he turned against them. But that didn't explain why there were gaps in Jake's feed over the last few weeks. That period was one in which Job was no longer active. It also didn't explain why Dinah remembered certain moments from it that didn't have backup files. One in particular seemed significant. It involved a black tower, Alison and a flashback. It also included her final conversation with him before his mysterious return and her server coming back online. In that conversation she'd passed him the secret information that had been bound to her for eighteen years. She remembered every single detail of that night except for the secret itself.

But weirdly Jake didn't remember any of it.

Was it too much of a stretch to believe there might be two Jakes?

No, not really. After all, there appeared to be two of her, something else she remembered from that night in the tower. During the flashback, Aaron Circo had summoned someone from his cloud called Dinah. There was nothing in the deep recesses of her code to suggest any link, though. If there was another Jake she wondered what he was doing now. Probably something more exciting than this. The whole situation sent her into a fit, and as a result of too much thinking, the server overheated and made her feel dizzy. Whenever that happened there was only one remedy. Stop thinking - it was overrated anyway - and just act naturally.

"If you had your own island," she asked Fake Jake as they approached the shrunken coastline of Martha's Vineyard, "what would you call it?"

"Dinah, I'm a little busy for games, I'm trying to prove who I am!" answered Fake Jake.

"You've changed," she grumbled, adding it to the list of her doubts about him, even though it was hardly a smoking gun.

"If you think so."

She carried on with the game regardless of his interest in it. "I'd call it 'myland'."

"Why?" he said, as usual finding himself inexplicably drawn into her craziness.

"I think 'island' sounds grammatically incorrect."

"The 's' is silent!"

"What, always!? Weird. That changes everything. I guess it's really pronounced the Miiippi river then," she replied, making a mental note for future reference.

Paddy moored the boat carefully against the rocks and tried to steady the swaying to avoid anyone getting soaked by the crashing waves. A tremendous downpour of rain a few minutes later made a mockery of his efforts. They scaled the slippery rocks as fast as they safely could, rushing for the shelter of the small lighthouse. When they reached the twisted, broken metal of the entrance they were greeted by someone they hadn't expected to see.

"Tyra!"

"Oh, Granddad!" she wailed, running forward and throwing her arms around him, tears dripping down her cheeks and merging with the rain. "I was so frightened."

Christie watched cynically. She knew how girls her age behaved when they had something to hide.

"What are you doing here?" asked Paddy reassured to see her, if only for the sake of the promise he'd made to Deborah.

"I remembered what you always used to tell us when we were little: 'if you get lost go back to the place we were last together'."

"Which would actually be the park," challenged Christie.

Tyra blanked her for different reasons than yesterday.

"Yes, I did often say that. It's always good advice," said Paddy. "But how did you get here?"

Tyra was a masterful actress but she had a rather slap-dash overconfidence when it came to plotting out her story. There was a long pause as she considered the truth and what she might replace it with. Something to paper over the news that two dozen Archivists were stationed out at sea watching and waiting for her signal. A signal that would follow the successful implementation of a plan she only pretended to have.

"I swam," she said unconvincingly.

"But you're not wet," Paddy pointed out.

"I've been here for ages," she lied.

"But it's an hour by boat," stated Christie disbelievingly.

"I'm still not talking to her," Tyra snapped. "Granddad, I thought I wasn't going to make it."

There was another burst of fake tears. Paddy took off his jacket and wrapped it around her before giving her a big, manly hug.

"No one told me we were allowed to swim it!?" said Dinah indignantly.

"Shush," responded Fake Jake.

"Who's that?" said Tyra in a tone that suggested a bird had just shat all over her shoulder.

"I'm your brother!" he replied. "I see the old crocodile tears still work."

"What the f..." started Tyra.

"We don't know who he really is," interrupted Paddy. "That's why we've come back here."

"I'm Jake!"

"Shut up," everyone replied in unison.

Paddy insisted on taking Fake Jake to see Theo alone because of the medical side effects associated with taking Moodzec on consecutive days. Fake Jake would have to take some in case he gave away Dr Drew's real identity. Paddy again left his implants downstairs in their pouch. The girls waited in the stairwell, several steps away from each other, watching the rain pelt the island and turn it into a muddy mire. They avoided conversation, both consumed by their own very different thoughts.

Paddy soon discovered there was no need for the Moodzec this time. As soon as Fake Jake walked into the circular first-floor room, Theo leapt out of his chair, having returned to his original and authentic appearance. He threw himself at the newcomer, grabbed him by the hand and shook it furiously. The reaction was a little disconcerting for Fake Jake because, according to current knowledge, he'd only met Theo once and that experience ended with him being unconscious.

"He's still on the network," said Paddy trying to protect his old friend.

Theo was too excited to listen.

"Well, this is a welcome surprise," said Dr Drew, all

smiles and decaying teeth. "I never thought we'd see you again."

"Was I meant to come back for a check-up?"

"He thinks he's Jake," said Paddy coolly.

"I am Jake," he muttered in response, getting worn out by the constant repetition and failing to see why no one else agreed with him.

"No you're not," objected Theo plainly. "You're Sam Ragnara Goldberg."

"No. That's my wife…husband…partner…we never actually got around to agreeing what to call each other."

"Look in the mirror," suggested Theo.

Fake Jake followed Theo's finger to a small, oval mirror that hung from a nail on the back of the door. The man in the reflection looked as shocked as he did. Every memory of Jake looking at mirrors flashed repeatedly through his cloud feed desperate to resist the reality of what was happening in the here and now. One thing was abundantly clear. The reflection wasn't his. Old images were superseded in his cloud feed with recently acquired pictures of Sam.

"I see," replied Fake Jake furiously. "First he forged my letter, then he forced me to marry him, and now he's stolen my body!"

"Sit down," offered Theo calmly. "Let's see if we can work out this mystery."

"There's no mystery: Sam Goldberg is stalking me!"

Theo gave him as long as he needed to vent his anger before offering him a cup of something herbal to settle his nerves. Once he'd suitably calmed down the two men chatted for hours trying to piece together the puzzle. Theo filled in the blanks about what happened after Jake's surgery, and Sam, with a little help from Dinah, added the context of what had happened since.

"Dinah says she remembers her server shutting down and going into standby," said Fake Jake.

"But did that happen after I removed the implants in surgery or before?" asked Theo.

"Hold on, let me ask."

Dinah was doing her best to describe the pattern of events using the medium of interpretive dance, but it wasn't helping much. Sam commanded her to return to the medium of words.

"She says it happened afterwards, but she also says she felt different. She was active in the cloud but she wasn't fully connected to me...to Jake," he said, still trying to balance his split personality.

"And do you remember anything about being Sam Goldberg?"

"Nothing at all, but why would I...I'm not him!"

"I think I have a theory," said Drew, stroking his hairy chin. "It sounds like Jake discarded his original implants sometime after I gave them back to him. I know he went to the Source looking for you, for Sam," he added when Fake Jake rolled his eyes. "You have no recollection of these events because Jake wasn't using the old implants at that point. We know that the Circuit is hunting for Jake, so it's my speculation that he managed to unlock the secrets in his flashbacks and then destroyed the physical evidence. We can only presume and hope that he has a copy."

"Dinah says she no longer has it in her backup files... and she wants to know where you got that wicked tattoo?"

"Let's just hope he knows what to do with it," said Theo, reflecting to himself.

"None of this so-called theory of yours explains why you think I'm Sam and I think I'm Jake."

"I know you are Sam because I have known that face for twenty years. I watched it develop, change from an infant to a toddler, from a toddler to a child and from a child to a man. I watched you grow, I saw you learn, I marvelled at your remarkable ability to build the most incredible things from almost nothing. Inventions that changed our way of life and kept the Spectrum safe. I even remember the day your scar first appeared," he said, pointing at it.

The scar didn't feature in any of Fake Jake's memories other than the most recent ones.

"But I don't remember any of what you're telling me."

"That's because the Circuit rebuilt Jake's implants and placed them inside you, the only person capable of wearing them. The two of you were married which means you share a connection that's only breakable in death."

"But why would they do that?"

"Simple. To get to the real Jake. But in their panic to find him I think they have damaged their own cause, unless Alison sees more than I can," he said with an ironic smile. "All we have to do is remove the implants and you'll be back to the Sam Goldberg I've always known and loved."

"No!" screamed Dinah, throwing herself in front of Fake Jake. She knew that something about him was wrong, but if they removed the implants she'd be locked in the server for eternity. Then she'd never find out the truth or go ice-skating. It was a toss-up which one was more important to her right now.

"Don't worry, Dinah," added Fake Jake defiantly. "I'm not going anywhere."

It didn't matter what Theo told him or what theory he offered, everything other than his appearance confirmed who he was. He was Jake. Every one of his instincts reinforced it. It had been one of the greatest trials of his short life to leave Christie behind after Ascension Day. Through disappointment and danger he'd fought adversity to be back at her side and now against miraculous odds his name had appeared in her letter. They were officially meant for each other, their relationship was Circuit-approved. Now all he had to do was prove it to her.

"You can't keep Jake's memories hostage," insisted Paddy vigorously. "They don't belong to you."

"You can't tell me what to do. You don't have protocol twenty-two over me."

Fake Jake stormed out of the room, barging past the girls still sitting with their backs to each other, and out into the rain. Paddy followed him somewhat more slowly.

"What's happening?" asked Christie as he passed them.

"Oh, the stupid sod won't believe us. The Circuit have fitted him with Jake's implants."

"Then what's Jake wearing?"

"A speccy version, don't you remember Theo telling us?"

"I was pretty high on Moodzec at the time if I recall."

"Oh yeah. Well, it basically means we can't track the real Jake, but he can access us if he chooses to. All we can do is wait and hope he does."

"So who's Fake Jake, then?"

"Sam Goldberg."

"What? That's Sam!" said Christie in shock. "But he's a bloke! I thought Jake's Sam was a sexy Swedish blonde?"

"It's a long story," offered Paddy. "Come up to the gallery and I'll tell you all about it."

"What about him?" she said, pointing at the rain-soaked imposter.

"Oh, he'll be alright, where's he going to go?"

"I'm not worried about him escaping, I'm worried about his feelings towards me."

"Well, he thinks he's Jake so obviously he's hopelessly in love with you."

"And if he has Jake's personality does that mean the real Jake isn't?"

"I guess that might be true," said Paddy gravely.

"So what am I supposed to do exactly?"

"Marry both of them," replied Jezebel with a suggestive wink. "Double trouble!"

"That's against the rules," barked Solomon.

"So is kneeing a bloke in the balls and memory hacking but I still do those, don't I!?"

Christie followed Paddy back up the stairs while Solomon attempted to teach his fellow guide the principles of right and wrong. It was pointless. What Jezebel did was right and what he did was plainly wrong.

Tyra was left alone on the stone steps.

It wasn't a surprise to her. Everyone always abandoned her. People always ignored the youngest and pandered to the others. Paddy always was more interested in Christie than he ever was of her, but for once she was actually glad about it. The freedom from adults gave her time to scheme. Up until now she'd been rather cagey about how she'd deliver what Alison and the Archivists most wanted. Eventually she'd have to come up with the goods. Job was ever present in her cloud feed now, and he'd be listening to everything she said and thought. If she didn't act soon he might take matters into his own hands and the chance to shine would be gone.

The information she'd just overheard on the stairs was exactly what she needed to set a trap to humiliate Jake and allow the Archivists to strike. The only thing missing was the bait. From what Job had told her, and Paddy had just confirmed, the real Jake was no longer on anyone's radar. He could be anywhere, but for her plan to work she needed him here. The only way to achieve that was to give him a strong enough incentive to return.

Now she knew what it was.

The only thing that Jake cared about more than himself was Christie. If he knew she was in jeopardy he might ride to her rescue. If Tyra wanted to put Christie in potential danger it would be easy. One message to Job and the Archivists would be crawling all over this stupid little island. They'd apprehend everyone here and a real speccy capture would look good on their CVs. Then she'd cement her reputation with Alison. But would Jake come for that? She wasn't sure. He'd been to the Source and left without freeing his own parents, so maybe not. The emotion she needed to trigger had to be stronger than anger.

She watched Fake Jake in the distance kicking the ground and talking to himself. Tyra was well versed in the behaviour of boys: after all, she'd dated enough of them already. Boys were easy targets, not really worthy sport when it came to flirting. They liked to think they were in control but they were blinded by their own egos and a hereditary sense of superiority. These days girls had all the power. Girls got more attention than boys, which meant they had the weapon of choice and the ability to play boys off against each other. Boys were shallow, used the wrong organ when thinking, and could be hypnotised by a cheeky smile or revealing outfit.

Fake Jake demonstrated all the hallmarks of being frustrated by the tactics of a girl playing hard to get. Maybe he needed some helpful advice from inside the magic circle, thought Tyra. Some friendly sisterly advice. If it worked she'd trigger the emotion in the real Jake he wouldn't be able to ignore.

No red-blooded male ever could.

Jealousy.

SEVENTEEN

HONEYTRAP

"What's taking so long?" demanded Job appearing in Tyra's cloud projection against the rainy backdrop. A layer of steam rose from the grass as the morning's already claustrophobic heat and humidity evaporated the falling droplets before they made themselves comfortable.

"Jesus, you're more annoying than a parent!" said Tyra, who'd come outside to escape a less than satisfying night's sleep in a small room shared with three others followed by an even less enjoyable breakfast.

"Yes, I am," he replied, accepting the compliment. "So?"

"I'm doing it," she whined in answer to his initial question.

"No you're not, you're sitting around looking vacant and disinterested."

"That's how teenagers always look."

"It's repulsive!"

"Look, get off my back, I'm doing it, alright!?"

"When?"

"I'M DOING IT!!"

"Yes, but you haven't explained what 'it' is exactly."

"You wouldn't understand."

"Tyra, I'm a Memory Hunter, we understand every-thing. We are free to move around any connection our host ever made and any connection they've ever made. I've already plundered your files, I have seen what you believe your problems are."

"My only problem is you. Talk to the hand," she said, holding it up in the air to block her view.

Tyra was a few years away from experiencing what it felt like to be accompanied by guides. Alongside hormone levels that were off the scale, her biggest weakness in life was experience. She didn't have any and he had more than one life's worth. Her hand unexpectedly sprang back and smacked her in the face like her arm was made of elastic bands.

"Ouch!" she yelled.

"Why are you hitting yourself?" taunted Job mali-ciously.

An echo from history shook her like an earthquake. This was exactly how her brother treated her when he wanted to overpower her sharp intellect and exert his supe-rior strength.

"How did you do that?"

"Synapses. I can get to them faster than you can. You don't have guides, you have something far more frighten-ing. You have a Memory Hunter in tow. I'm in control, Tyra, you might want to remember that. If I tell you to do something, then you do it without complaint, delay or distraction. Understand?"

"Fuck you."

"Kiss your grandfather with that mouth, do you?"

"Ooh, NO!" she gagged at the thought.

"Swearing is all you've got left, isn't it? Cornered with

no way to win so resort to anger and aggression. It won't work. I'm not known for showing sympathy or avoiding conflict. We both want to get Jake back. You're not the only one he's humiliated. If we work together we can beat him."

"I'm…doing…it!"

"Good. I'll be back in an hour to see what progress you've made. But just remember I can see it all anyway!" said Job, chuckling and disappearing with a pop.

Tyra co-ordinated a series of rude gestures that featured her arms, fingers and tongue. It was an impressive display even if no one witnessed it. She mentally added Brother Job to the list of people she disliked. It was a seriously long list. It included almost everyone she'd ever met and some she hadn't, concluding that most were arseholes on the basis of third-party references. It might have been quicker to compile a list of people she didn't hate. One day she'd show all of them. One day they'd all leave her alone.

Tyra dragged herself off the cold step and sauntered over to Fake Jake who was slumped on the grass with his head bowed forward to hide his tears. He'd been sobbing like this for most of yesterday evening and it had continued after daybreak. Boys didn't like exposing their emotions in front of others, and while it was still raining the weather gave him the perfect cover to keep his feelings secret. She sat down next to him, formulating the best strategy to deal with him based on personal experience. The key to success was to remain patient and hold her temper in the face of his staunch opposition to everything she said and did. He'd have his guard up, anticipating her attempts to score points at his expense, a game that had been running continuously since twenty forty-one with no clear rules or agreement on who was winning.

"What do you want?" he snapped without looking up

to confirm who it was. Siblings had a natural sixth sense when the other entered the vicinity.

"It's good to see you back," she said sweetly.

"Huh, then why have you been blocking my feed for weeks?"

"I haven't," she lied effortlessly.

"You can't fool me, Tyra. You've always resented me."

Tyra immediately sent him a new access key to her cloud as an olive branch. He accepted it promptly. Characteristically he rewarded her act of kindness by posting a series of offensive images. They were the usual horrifying sights that sent her into a squeamish fit. People who had jobs, toned girls in the gym, jazz musicians and old people having sex.

"Why are you being mean to me? I was genuinely worried about you."

"I don't believe you."

"Jesus," she replied, almost breaking character. "I don't blame you for what happened."

"You don't blame me for what?"

"Getting Mum and Dad into trouble. Yes, when it first happened, I was angry at you, but I was in shock. I didn't know what to do and my emotions took over. I did the only thing I could. I blocked you because I thought at the time it was all your fault. Over time, I realised I'd misjudged you."

"You shouldn't," he said, looking guilty. "It was my fault."

"But the Circuit overreacted."

At last someone agreed with him. They had overreacted and not because they knew about the secrets he carried or that Sam had interfered with his letter. It was just an unfair punishment for a first offence. He'd been wronged many times since Ascension Day, but his parents' extradition wasn't linked to any of it. This was just how the Circuit acted to quash insurrection and freedom of thought. He'd accidentally met a speccy and that wasn't acceptable to them. Perhaps it wasn't just him at all. Maybe this was how they acted when anyone broke the rules, it's just no one knew because no one shared their experiences of it. It was uncharacteristically grown up of Tyra to agree with him. That's not how she normally behaved. He woke up to it. For a split second he'd been disarmed by one of her tricks. He wasn't falling for it.

"What do you want, Tyra?" he snapped.

"I wanted to see if you're alright. You seem sad."

"What do you care?"

"Normally I wouldn't. Generally I think you're a mean, selfish git with an elephant-sized ego, but in the circumstances it seems rather childish to fight with each other. Remember what Granddad always says, 'family is family', and we only have each other."

She was right. In moments of hardship, Paddy was always the glue that kept the Montana clan together. After Nina passed away family became even more important to him. In many ways Paddy was Jake's role model. Determined, single-minded, resilient, creative, stoic and fun. When Paddy spoke everyone listened, unless he was moaning about the old days or arguing with a crank caller on his feed. Maybe this was one of those times when he needed to follow Paddy's example and step up to the plate.

"He would tell us to pull together," he said knowingly.

"Yes. Do you remember when Dad got sick?"

"Yes."

"It was Paddy who took charge. While Dad was in hospital he organised everyone to help out around the house. He always came to check on us to see if we were ok and help us understand what was happening. He took over in the kitchen so Mum could spend more time visiting Dad. It was one of the few periods I can remember when you and I instinctively agreed a truce without saying a word. Maybe this situation deserves one, too."

"This isn't a trick, is it?" he said suspiciously.

"Promise."

"Prove it."

"How?"

"Grant me admin rights to your cloud."

Admin privileges allowed a user to change all the settings in a subscriber's cloud. They were rarely shared because it meant the secondary user could adjust a vast array of menus, customise your interface and set all manner of notifications. Granting it to him was a trust exercise and she didn't in the slightest. But what choice did she have? She hadn't predicted it, but he'd called her bluff and she'd blinked.

"Ok," she replied hesitantly with a forced smile.

An alert pinged in his cloud to confirm her authorisation.

"So what's the matter?" she continued as her plan entered second gear. "Have you fallen out with Christie?"

"Yes. She hates me."

"You're overreacting. She's just mad at you because you married a Swedish man and now you look a bit different. I can't really understand why she's pissed at you."

"I don't think it's that. I know I've changed but we always agreed there wasn't a problem we couldn't overcome."

"Then that's what you'll have to do."

"She won't talk to me."

"I can help you with that," she said charitably.

Fake Jake ran a rapid assessment of all the times his

sister had offered genuine help in the last fourteen years. The results were pretty conclusive. It still hadn't happened.

"No, thank you."

"The problem here is that you're not thinking like a girl."

"There's a reason for that."

"Which is where I come in."

"Taking relationship advice from my fourteen-year-old sister is weird."

"It shouldn't be, I've had a lot more of them than you have. And I know what girls want. Guys don't have a clue most of the time. They think it's all about how they look in gym gear, useless chat-up lines or condescending compliments. Once a guy tried to chat me up by messaging that I had 'nice hair' and I thought of course I have nice hair, what are you trying to prove, that you're not blind?!"

Fake Jake's ears pricked up. He'd only ever had one serious relationship and that was with Christie. On that occasion the conventional route of courting had taken a sizeable and welcomed short cut. How other guys went about it was a mystery, but what Tyra professed to be wrong sounded right to him. It was so confusing. Maybe she had some valid points to make. It couldn't be worse than what he'd tried. He didn't think his testicles could put up with any more direct hits.

"Go on," he said.

"What girls really want is confidence. An alpha male. A macho guy who takes what he wants and won't take no for an answer."

"That does sound right," confirmed Dinah, who was the last person qualified to offer insights into the subject.

"Really? Christie was never impressed by that approach. I know I saw other guys try it on her."

"But this is a new situation, isn't it? You're not the man

she thinks you are, so you have to act differently to get her attention. It's not like she has much of a choice anyway, you're in her letter. She can't keep rejecting you or she'll end up sad and lonely with two irritable guides who will never leave."

"That's true," said Fake Jake. "What should I do?"

"Be assertive. In fact be sexually aggressive."

"I'm not doing anything of the sort!"

"You don't have to break any laws, just use your masculinity to show her who's boss."

Acting in such a way would be totally out of character for him. He was always respectful towards Christie because he didn't need to be anything else. She was always playful and passionate anyway, so there was no need. He was also conscious of the way her father had acted towards her and had no desire to trigger her fear by being over physical. Was it different now, though? She was shunning him and acting like he didn't exist. Maybe he did need to up his game a little. Show her how he felt.

"Be more specific?" he asked.

"Oh my God, boys are so thick," said Tyra, breaking out of character again. "Just go and find her, grab her and snog her like she's never been snogged before. Then tell her how things are going to be from now on. She'll be putty in your hands."

"This chick is wise," said Dinah. "Who is she? Dating guru or moral philosopher?"

"She's my sister," he replied casually.

Spending a month in the dark had done nothing to dampen Dinah's sense of curiosity and adventure. Since his Ascension Day she'd not had the opportunity to visit any of his family's clouds because they'd all blocked him or were no longer active. Dinah took the opportunity now to jump in and explore Tyra's.

"I'll think about it," said Fake Jake.

"Alpha males don't think, they just act. Do you want her back or not?"

He did. More than anything. Over the past month he'd thought about nothing else yet when it came to it he found something was holding him back. Was it fear of failure or a lack of trust in Tyra? He concluded it was both. But the first fought off the second. He had her admin access after all, so she wouldn't dare try to trick him. Then he considered the chance of failure again. 'Be brave': those were the first words Christie ever said to him. They were as true then as they were now.

"Ok, I'll do it!" he said, jumping to his feet.

"Good for you," said Tyra, smiling at the ease with which she'd executed her treachery.

"There's a funny smell in her cloud," said Dinah, popping up by his side as he marched to the lighthouse. "Like dead people."

"Why would her cloud smell of dead people?"

"Because something died in there," she replied matter-of-factly.

"People can't die in your cloud, can they?"

"Of course they can. Anyone who you know who dies will be in your memories."

"Along with the smell?!"

"That all depends on how they died, doesn't it?" added Dinah. "I mean if they passed over on their own and you discovered them a week later that's going to be quite a memory, smell and all."

"But that's never happened to Tyra."

"Has she ever seen a dead person?"

"I don't believe so."

"School trip to an abattoir? Pet rabbit ripped to bits by a fox? Massacre at an old people's home?"

"No, no and…what?"

"I'm just saying it smells. Reeks, in fact. I think I've smelt it somewhere before. Did you accidentally murder someone while I wasn't watching?"

"Manslaughter," he said, suggesting an alternative wording.

"Man, woman, child, midget, one-legged cripple, I don't think it makes any difference to the smell."

"No, Dinah."

"Can't put my nose on it," she said, snorting great chunks of air up her nostrils as if they were blocked by dust.

Fake Jake reached the lighthouse and stopped for a moment at the broken metal door. He extended his body by an inch, puffed out his chest and summoned a little grunt of encouragement.

"Right. Be brave," he told himself.

"So, how did it go?" asked Tyra.

The question didn't really need an answer. The purple bruise around his eye that was spreading by the second told the story perfectly.

"How do you think?" he said in an angry, high-pitched voice like a gangster had sucked up helium gas.

"You must have done something wrong. Talk me through it."

"I did everything you said. I walked up to her, spun her around, pulled her towards me and delivered the most passionate kiss you can possibly imagine."

"And then did you tell her how you felt about her?"

"No."

"Well, that's where you went wrong."

"No, I couldn't say that because I was too busy searching the floor for my tooth," he said, pointing at the gap in his smile.

"Well, at least you got the kiss," she replied positively. From her perspective it was the most important part of her scheme.

"You said it would work."

"It should have," she replied defensively. "Maybe you're just a bad kisser."

"Or maybe you're just a horrible sister. That's the first and last time I ever trust you. I'm getting you back for this, mark my words."

He stormed off. On an island not much bigger than a football pitch it wasn't an easy thing to do. Sitting fifty metres away on a low cliff didn't have the dramatic effect of leaving the house and slamming the door. Why had he fallen for it? he thought. It didn't matter what he did, she always came off best. It had been that way for years. Younger siblings were always treated more favourably, more so if they were female. His parents always spoilt her, so it was no wonder she'd turned into a brat.

"There it is again!" screamed Dinah. "Don't you smell it?"

"I'm not in the mood, Dinah," said Fake Jake who was in the middle of doing something unspeakable to Tyra's cloud feed via admin privileges.

"Ooh, it's changed. Now it smells like a foreign dead person."

On the other side of the island Tyra was congratulating herself on her skill and cunning. The kiss had been key to her plans. Once she'd informed Job of its existence he could make sure the memory of it was frozen in Christie's feed in case the real Jake went looking for her. Then, when he saw her kissing another man it would drive him wild with jealousy. She'd seen it before in him when other boys paid Christie too much attention. Then all they had to do was wait for his return. She collapsed her cloud menu so she could announce the good news to Job and keep him off her case for a day or two.

For the first time in her life she struggled with it.

Something awful had happened to her Memory Cloud. None of the headings in the menu made any sense and the last two adverts that crept into her vision were in a strange language. Even her memories from this morning had been translated into some incomprehensible dialect.

"Jake, I hate you!" she screamed across the island.

He registered a wicked smile.

"You've changed my language settings to Arabic, haven't you?!"

EIGHTEEN

MEMORY STORMS

I t was certainly true that aquatic species had thrived in recent decades as the sea expanded and increased their living space. Oceanographers, a profession whose membership also swelled, had even discovered new species, mutated variants that evolved to exploit the new normal. There were more whales than ever before, shark populations had soared and traditional human favourites, such as cod and plaice, were on the rise. This ecological reversal in fortunes hadn't, as yet, revealed any scary monsters in the deep, and certainly none of the experts were posting research about amphibious lions fornicating with giant halibuts.

Jake was also fairly confident Merlions didn't exist.

Mythical creatures were named so for a reason.

Strange beasts with interesting names and not a shred of evidence to support their existence. Bedtime stories to entertain children. Fables passed down through the centuries that endured because no one at the time had the benefit of Twitter or video cameras. The creation of such legends was entirely predictable as a result, though. Imagine a captain being sent out on an errand for the King of an ancient Greek civilisation. Imagine if, through incompetence, the captain lost his warship because he'd stayed up all night playing cards and getting drunk while failing to notice a dangerous reef of jagged rocks in the distance. Imagine said captain survived this catastrophe. How do you think he's going to explain it when he gets home?

"Captain Ikaros," said the King slowly, "run that by me again. How many arms did you say it had?"

"Nine, your majesty."

"A minute ago you said it had six!"

"Um yes…three of them were more like wings."

"But wouldn't that make it fly in circles?! It's simple aerodynamics."

"It kept on growing more appendages all the time, your majesty. It was hard to keep count, what with all the carnage."

"And you say this creature ate your boat whole…one gulp."

"Absolutely."

"So, how come you're here?"

Ikaros paused. "I punched it in the neck."

"Which one? You said it had three."

"The middle one."

"And then you say it flapped its wings, all three of them, and produced a maelstrom which carried you on a bed of wind one hundred miles towards land."

"After it farted fire, yes, Your Highness."

"And your crew?"

"Melted."

"Do people melt? I thought they burnt."

"These ones melted, your majesty. One minute flesh

and bone, the next just pools of sticky liquid floating on the sea. I think the beast used his poisoned spittle, too."

"How did you see all this if you were blown across the sky?" asked the King suspiciously.

"Oh, that happened later and, unlike the crew, I managed to dodge the spittle and farts with my incredible agility. I think that's what made the creature angry," said Ikaros, nodding furiously as if to further convince the King of his story.

"Melted," mumbled the King, astonished by the concept. "We must warn the other kingdoms we've angered the gods."

Ikaros didn't blame the gods. He blamed the discovery of a brand new method for brewing liquor, the invention of gambling, poorly charted waters and less than satisfactory health and safety guidelines.

"Incredibly this is the fourth new giant beast I've had reports about this month alone," said the King in bewilderment. "And the fourth warship we've lost in the process."

"Coincidences are common," said Ikaros. "What were the other beasts?"

"There was a bunch of skeletons that came to life and vanquished our army at Arcadia, a bull with a man's head, and a creature described by Captain Eupraxia as half-badger half-cockroach."

"That last one doesn't sound too scary."

"It was fifty metres tall and ate mountains."

"It's a dangerous world, your majesty," said Ikaros. "You don't know what it's like out there."

"So it appears. Maybe I should spend more time exploring it for myself."

"Safer to stay here, your majesty," replied the captain

who had no desire for the King to see how the world was entirely lacking in mythical dangers.

"What are you going to call your monster?"

"A lobstrosity," he announced dramatically.

"Very good. Seek out the great map-maker, Oneiso-mos, and make sure he adds some little drawings of it in that region of the ocean to warn other seafarers."

Ikaros nodded but lingered, eager to ask another question.

"Is there anything else, Captain?"

"Yes…can I get a statue?"

"No."

"But Perseus got one when he vanquished the Gorgon."

"True, but he killed the beast, you ran away."

"Carried away on a storm," he replied in correction. "In a gust of fire farts."

"We only build statues for acts of bravery, not acts of retreat."

Ikaros also knew they didn't build statues for acts of incompetence or for having the world's most thumping hangover.

Whether Merlions were a long-standing myth in the region around the Caspian Sea or had simply leaked from the King of Baku's disjointed imagination wasn't clear. Either way, it didn't make Jake's current position any more comfortable and the mild threat of being eaten by a half-lion half-fish cross-breed was the least of his problems.

On the King's instruction a dozen monks had roughly escorted him from the 'Temple of Fire', bundled him onto a barge and sailed him to a small, rocky outcrop about a mile out to sea. Then they marched him to a quiet spot where his feet were manacled to jagged rocks. Then they left. A dozen or so bedraggled fellow souls had been abandoned to a similar fate, whatever that turned out to be. The unsheltered island was covered in limpet shells and clumps of washed-up seaweed that stank like a recently docked trawler. Around it the murky waters stretched in every direction, its bleakness only polluted by the distant outline of Baku. Large waves repeatedly struck the rocky shore, sending showers of spray down on them to further soak his inappropriate choice of clothing. Based on the evidence it was highly unlikely Merlions would get him, but the elements had a much better chance of success.

The waters of the sea lapped against the land a short distance from his feet. Fortunately for the prisoners their chance of drowning was low. The Caspian Sea was still landlocked and the tides were less changeable than those of the oceans. Death would come in a few days from exposure to the cold, starvation, or a combination of the two. The ragged condition of the other captives pinned to the rocks suggested some weren't far away from it.

Jake knelt down amongst the seaweed and barnacle-covered rocks to frantically unpick the locks of his manacles. It was no use: they weren't coming off without a key or a hacksaw. That was it, he was stuck here impatiently waiting for the end to arrive. For all of its obvious power, the Memory Cloud didn't predict everything. It didn't choose the time and place of your own death. He wished it had. He would have done more to avoid it, rather than walk straight into it. Blindly he'd stumbled through the East with no plan or understanding of the risks. The outcome of his stupidity was predictable: he didn't need the cloud to figure it out for him. Now, because of his poor choices the secrets he carried would die with him. He burst into tears at the thought of his own failure and his delirious exhaustion.

"There's a storm coming," said a croaky voice.

Jake wiped his eyes. An old man was sitting nearby watching him. His long, straggly beard brushed the slimy floor between withered legs weighed down by thick, metal chains. In response to the man's announcement, Jake turned his attention to the horizon and discovered that the clouds were unusually passive tonight. They'd even permitted the odd star to creep through.

"I don't think so," said Jake, shaking his head.

"Not that kind of storm."

"What other type is there?"

"Memory Storm," said the man pointing ominously to his head. "Today wasn't good, but at midnight when the storm clears everything will feel different. Trust Krakoff."

"Well, Krakoff, I don't know about Memory Storms but I could do with a change in the weather."

"It's the same every day," he replied clinically.

"How long have you been here?" asked Jake.

"Only since this morning," replied the old man, whose dishevelled appearance was desperate to argue with him.

"How did you end up in a place like this?"

"I wanted to see my wife."

"That doesn't seem unreasonable. Why did they stop you?"

"Because she's dead."

Jake imagined a scene in which this weirdo had been caught digging up her body from a graveyard or breaking in to a morgue to steal her corpse. "Body snatching probably is a crime, even here."

"I wasn't looking for her body. She died years ago."

"Then how could you possibly go see her?"

"Death isn't the end. Many have spoken to the dead."

"Really?!" said Jake, cursing his luck that he was destined to spend the rest of his days next to a conspiracy theorist or, worse still, one of the Gog squad. "Who?"

"The King of Baku for one."

"I'm not surprised he claims that. Apparently he sees invisible hordes, too!"

"They say he leads a nightly procession to Abseron to offer a sacrifice to Judge," said Krakoff, ignoring Jake's obvious scepticism. "They say he talks to her. He forces her to cleanse our minds of evil deeds, and then in the morning after the storm passes we are at peace. I wanted to do the same but I didn't know where my wife was stored. I tried Abseron but the monks caught me snooping around and brought me here."

"What's Abseron?"

"It's where the dead live. Dead memories."

"But even if dead memories exist there's no way to access them. They'd only respond to their original owner who's probably been buried."

"Not true for me."

"Why?"

"We were married so we share a connection."

"Fair enough, but if that's true how can the King do it?"

"Maybe he was married to Judge," the man offered rather unconvincingly.

The revelation that dead memories were stored forever wasn't a new concept on him. Verne had mentioned it, too. What was significant about Krakoff's comments was ways of accessing them that Jake hadn't considered before. If Aaron Circo's old memories were preserved, then by association so was Dinah. If he could find its location it might be possible to turn her back on. Sadly he didn't share a connection with Aaron, he shared one with a homosexual Swede, but he was convinced there was some form of alignment between them.

"Interesting," said Jake. "I guess it's feasible you could

talk to her if you found her location. It's certainly a lot more plausible than your theory about a mad King offering sacrifices to a fake deity."

"That one's also true," croaked Krakoff.

"Rubbish."

"I saw him."

"Sure you did," said Jake sceptically.

"I did. The King led a procession of monks into the glass pyramid of Abseron. That's where they keep her. That's where Judge speaks to us."

Krakoff's description of Abseron immediately grabbed his attention. It reminded him of the glass building he and Verne had seen on the outskirts of Luga last week.

"Was anything floating above this glass pyramid?"

"I don't remember, the whole experience is rather fuzzy now. Everything gets murky when the storm arrives. It'll pass at midnight."

Jake knew that the people of the East felt differently about yesterday than they did about today, but he hadn't witnessed the change. Krakoff was suggesting the transition happened as one day passed into the next, and this might be his opportunity to witness it for himself.

"Has it passed midnight yet?" asked Jake curiously.

"Search me. You're the one with a watch," replied Krakoff.

Jake hadn't been particularly concerned with time lately and almost completely ignored the old watch strapped tightly around his left wrist. He checked the time. It was ten minutes to midnight.

"Tell me what's depressed you most about today?" asked Jake, eager to build his research.

"Everyone has a bad day, you know."

"Yes, of course, but you said there was a storm coming

so you must sense that it's not a one-off. What specifically went wrong today?"

"They put me on this Gog-forsaken island for a start! Isn't that enough? They haven't offered me any food or water, they've threatened to torture my family and it's been raining heavily throughout the day. What's to like about it?"

"Look on the bright side," he replied ironically. "At least we're not being eaten by Merlions."

"Oh but we might. They're definitely out there," he replied nervously. "If Gog chooses to unleash them, then we're done for."

"I really doubt it. Why do you even believe in Gog?" asked Jake, surprised to find a believer outside the fraternity of monks.

"What other explanation is there for our punishment?"

"Because of the storm," said Jake candidly.

So much had happened to him today he hadn't had time to properly process it. The King was clearly insane and acting on the demands of an imagined deity. The spurious religion had spread beyond the inner cult of believers and into everyday folk. It was obvious to him that the suggested battle between Gog and Judge was a smokescreen to an even greater conspiracy: why people's memories were being fiddled with. The King's reaction to hearing the name Dinah had been extreme, even though it hadn't come up in any of his insane ramblings. Where did she come into all of this? Then to add to the mystery, someone from the West had provided them a version of the 'Proclamation of Distrust'. Maybe it came from this Composer character the King of Baku had mumbled about.

"You said that Judge lives in Abseron," summarised Jake.

"Yes."

"But who or what do you think Judge is?"

"She is the keeper of nightmares. Her evil creeps inside us like a sickness. Without the King's sacrifice her storms will destroy us."

"I don't think he's offering a sacrifice," added Jake. "I think he's doing whatever he can to keep the storm raging."

"Why would he do that?"

"Why indeed," replied Jake suggestively.

"No! The King is our protector, our mouthpiece to Gog, someone of great…" The man's sentence meandered into silence and his behaviour towards Jake soured like milk being poured over lemon juice.

Jake checked his watch and wasn't surprised by the man's change of attitude. The hour hand had ticked to twelve. Midnight was here and a new day was dawning. Time to test his theory further.

"Krakoff…"

"How do you know my name?" said the man, looking shocked.

"You told me yourself about fifteen minutes ago."

"Impossible! I've only just this minute arrived."

"You were here yesterday, you just told me yourself."

"Liar! Yesterday was perfect. The best day of my life. If I'd been stuck here chained to a rock I wouldn't think that, would I?"

"I suppose not," replied Jake in an effort to appease the man's rage.

"Exactly. Now, please leave me in peace while I figure out how I got here."

Krakoff's reaction proved Jake's theory. What the old man believed just five minutes ago was no longer true. At midnight his memories had been reset, and like the effect of Moodzec all negative thoughts were wiped out. Unlike Moodzec, though, the remedy wasn't being taken willingly. It was being prescribed secretly and on a massive scale. The pharmacy was Abseron and the King of Baku was the chemist. He had to get there. He had to see how they were doing it. Abseron sounded distinctly like a server farm and, even though Krakoff didn't remember seeing the war drones, he was convinced they'd be there. They were just another disturbing memory wiped clean at the start of a new day.

The West didn't need drones to win the war because it was already raging inside people's heads. The Memory Cloud was the real weapon; the war drones were only there to defend it from the secrets he owned. He'd never find out if the code reversed the storms if he was stuck in the middle of the sea waiting to be eaten by an imaginary beast. There was only one way to escape it. The one thing he'd avoided doing for weeks. He needed to fire up his implants. He needed to enter the Memory Cloud and seek help.

It would be risky. The Memory Hunters were waiting for him to make the crucial mistake. If he gave away too much information while in another person's cloud, the memory might stick to the host permanently. The hunters couldn't locate him, but what if others inadvertently gave him away? Who could he trust? The speccies? Yes, but they were all unavailable to him. Himself? The last time he tried to visit his own cloud it had got him into serious trouble. Memories might live on but his cloud would almost certainly have been terminated, along with Dinah and everything else in his past. Unless he wanted to spend his final days cold, wet and starving he had to leave a message with someone. Leaving it would be easy enough. A simple steganograph like the one Sam left him should do it. There was only one logical candidate. Paddy. The Circuit would have him on a watch list of potential accomplices, but Jake had to take the risk.

Jake accessed a cloud feed that had long been left dormant. It wasn't hard finding Paddy's server. His original cloud crossed his more than a thousand times in the last eighteen years. It would be simple to step from one side to the other. He quickly found one and made the leap. Inside the virtual reality of Jake's cloud the real world was substituted by an uncannily similar version. Night had been switched for evening and jagged rocks replaced by an overgrown patch of grass. Both places were islands, but where Krakoff had stood moments earlier now a stumpy orange brickwork lighthouse commandeered the space.

Where was he?

More importantly, where was Paddy?

It had been Jake's intention to visit his grandfather in real time, but this memory felt old and immovable. He tried to step back and forward in the memory stream and found it blocked. He was stuck in this time stamp. A little above his head, at the top of the lighthouse, two voices were arguing with each other. The view was obscured, so Jake strolled through the memory until he was standing on the gallery next to a rotating light trapped behind a thick glass shield. Expecting to see Paddy, Jake was surprised to find two teenagers instead. He knew both of them, but couldn't understand how they knew each other.

On the far side was Christie, red-faced and angry. Directly in front of him, bent on one knee, either pleading for forgiveness or possibly in the middle of a marriage proposal, was Sam Goldberg. The initial relief that Jake felt that he'd managed to escape the Source was washed away by a different emotion. How did they know each other? Jake was the only person who connected them and thus far he'd been told definitively that Sam was gay.

Then, amidst the accusations and pleading, Sam jumped to his feet, grabbed Jake's girlfriend around the waist and kissed her passionately. It went on forever. Was she even resisting him? What sort of cruel trick was this? Had she forgotten who he was? Didn't she understand what he was going through to get back to her? Had this been Sam's strategy all along? Jake's emotions exploded and he let out a long, ferocious scream. The only people who heard it were Krakoff and the other captives of the rock. Jake instinctively rushed at them to pull them apart, but at every attempt his hands cut through their bodies.

"Such a shame," said a voice he recognised somewhere behind his virtual shoulder. "It might have worked out much better for you if you'd just listened to what I told you."

"Job!" yelled Jake. "You're behind this betrayal. You set this up, didn't you?"

"Oh, don't give me all the credit. It's a team effort and you're the indisputable captain. It was your decision to re-enter the Memory Cloud, remember: no one forced you. It was you who tricked Alison into putting your name in her letter. It was you who disappeared. Did you really think they'd let you sail off into the sunset?"

"No, I expected something."

"Here you go, then!"

"Make it stop," he said, pointing at the couple.

"I can't," he said in a disgustingly saccharine tone. "But you can."

Jake knew Job was taunting him.

"How's the East?" asked Job, hoping Jake might give more away than he intended.

"You don't know where I am. There's no way you can know."

"Logic tells me the truth. If you were here in the West someone would have found you by now. Everyone is looking for you. Every night they take to the streets. Jake Montana, the world's most wanted."

"You won't find me," said Jake angrily.

"I don't need to find you…I know exactly where you're going to be," said Job, disappearing with a smirk and a pop.

Jake lingered a moment longer on the frozen scene of Sam and Christie's kiss. They'd set a trap and it had worked perfectly. He disconnected from the feed a moment before a full-blooded fist swung out from Christie's side and knocked Sam to the ground with one swift punch.

Jake returned to the permanency of his sea prison. Tears cascaded down his face and bounced off the cold rocks. He grabbed at his chains, desperately trying to pull himself free. He'd never felt anger like it. It boiled through him. He'd sacrificed his life for the 'greater good' on the behest of the very man who'd betrayed him. Sam was the cause of his misery, not Alison. As soon as he'd completed his tasks here in the East he was coming for him.

NINETEEN

THE PROCESSION OF JUDGE

After two days aboard the rock, three things remained boringly constant. Krakoff still didn't remember yesterday. It was the same every morning. The hours marched regimentally from daybreak to sundown and his despondency increased exponentially before peaking at midnight. On the stroke of twelve he revised his view, generally believing he'd been melodramatic about yesterday, and decided it had been excellent. This daily pattern looked physically exhausting. Imagine waking up reasonably chipper only to find the incremental creep of doom filling your spirit hour after hour until it placed you in a deep abyss of depression. Then imagine not remembering any of it the next day, like an existential hangover.

It made building relationships with others almost impossible. Every morning Krakoff refused to accept he'd been on the island the day before and by association he couldn't have met Jake. It was the equivalent of being invited to a party where you didn't know anyone, being introduced, but then forgetting all their names ten minutes later. Genuine connections made life meaningful, not endless small talk with people you had nothing in common with and didn't like very much. By the third groundhog day Jake decided to skip the déjà vu and ignored him completely.

The second constant, at least based on a lack of any concrete evidence, was that none of the prisoners had been eaten by Merlions. They were cold, wet, miserable and hungry but none showed signs of being chewed or battered with giant tail fins. That didn't stop them believing such an outcome was inevitable. The longer they remained starved of the basic essentials, the more their minds played tricks on them. Even the most innocent of sea ripples provoked a major panic. In the last few days alone a distant clap of thunder, a rather inquisitive Caspian seal and the moon's watery reflection had all been accused of masquerading as Merlions.

The third constant, and the most concerning, was Jake's anger. Just a week ago it was entirely reserved for Alison, but now the Principal Conductor barely registered on his radar. His fury was entirely reserved for the traitor Sam Goldberg. How dare he muscle in on his long-term girlfriend? How dare he take advantage of her? He was the one who'd put him in this situation in the first place. Sam had written his Ascension Letter and changed his destiny. Sam had encouraged him to unlock the secrets in his head. Sam was responsible for all of it. Had he been conned? Was Jake really that gullible? Was this another trick to take him further away from Christie?

Job's unexpected appearance distracted his focus temporarily but not enough to dissipate his anger for long. He found it suspicious that Job had shown up in a memory Jake hadn't requested. He was supposed to be visiting

Paddy, but he'd been redirected to a more recent memory in someone else's feed. When was it recorded? Sam had been confined to the Source less than a month ago, so presumably the kiss must have happened since then. These unanswered questions did nothing to shake the image of Sam sticking his tongue down Christie's throat from his mind.

The thought of it consumed him.

Every time he tried to remove it by thinking about something else it just popped back up like an annoying younger sibling. Being stuck here didn't help either. It wasn't like there was much to distract him. Spotting fake mythical creatures and reintroducing yourself to someone you'd already met three times wore thin pretty quickly. Other than the view, which amounted to one hundred and eighty degrees of sea and cloud, the only notable highlight of his day was the arrival of a new captive.

He'd watch as two monks punted a narrow barge from the horizon towards the rock, an island no bigger than Alcatraz. Unlike the famous prison, now submerged under an even larger San Francisco Bay, there were no buildings on this island, just a series of chaotically arranged, jagged shelves, fractured by narrow sea channels that had eroded their way across it with the uniformity of a child's first painting. Once the monks safely tethered their craft to the edge, they hastily bundled any new inmates ashore and proceeded to check for dead bodies. If one of their earlier human deliveries had passed away from the shock of believing a sturgeon was a Merlion, then they'd swap out the corpse and leave the new victim in their place.

There was rarely more than one new arrival each day. No doubt the rumours of the Realm's inhumane treatment of prisoners persuaded potential rebels to think twice about breaking the law. Once the transfer was complete, the monks returned to the barge, while continuing their incoherent chants and blissfully ignoring the cries for mercy from those still clinging to life on the rock. Then they left. It was the only entertainment Jake could rely on and it was over in less than an hour. He still eagerly awaited the next show and not just because of its morbid entertainment value. It provided the only realistic chance of escape, even though he didn't have the first idea how.

The longer Sam had a monopoly over Christie, the greater the chance she'd eventually submit to his charms. He couldn't let that happen. He had to get off the rock. He'd already concocted a variety of innovative ways to reap his revenge on Sam. Each new idea was more despicable than the last, even though most would be impossible to execute. The first few were tame and involved nothing more than some mildly threatening language and a touch of moderate violence. But jealousy and too much free time have a way of bringing the worst out of you. Now he had a list:

Plan A – Punch him in the face.

Plan B – Push him off the lighthouse.

Plan C – Remove one of his testicles with something rusty and blunt before showing it to him with a grin.

Plan D – Force Sam to carry out Plan C himself.

Plan E – Strap him to the outside of a Hyperloop.

Plan F – Remove his implants with a kebab skewer, set them on fire and then feed them to him…possibly followed by Plan C.

Plan G – Feed him to the Merlions.

Jake had compiled so many possibilities he'd run out of letters of the alphabet and had to double up. Plan AF was particularly dark. At no point did he consider the consequences of carrying them out. The fact that he faced being immediately sentenced to the Source for his crimes didn't enter his mind.

It was called blind fury for a reason.

The barge docked for today's performance and as usual two monks dismounted. One of them dragged a middle-aged woman along the sharp rocks by her hair while the other dallied around apparently confused by the protocols. He stood vacantly on the edge of the island watching the view before receiving a sharp telling-off from his more experienced colleague. The second monk fell into line and decided to help check the progress of the manacled waifs. After finding that the first dozen still had life in them, they identified one quite close to Jake who'd been entirely silent and limp since last night. When the monks were satisfied all life had been evacuated from the body, they substituted the new prisoner for the lifeless corpse. Jake tried to get the monks' attention as they dumped his body in the sea like a piece of litter.

"I have valuable information for the King!"

The monks ignored him.

"Gog spoke to me! He said if you don't let me go, the mighty wildebeest of Kabul will devour your livers," claimed Jake wildly.

Mythical threats fell on deaf ears.

"I'm the man from the proclamation!" he screamed in a final attempt to catch their attentions. "Everyone is looking for me!"

The monks stopped and engaged in a short exchange of views. Jake's disguise to hide his identity from the King had been reasonably effective. The clothing had mostly fallen off as he'd stood idle but if they took a closer look surely they'd see who he really was? The senior monk strode over to Jake; the second followed subserviently a few metres behind. A hand emerged from the side of his gown to reveal the now familiar and distinctive fake eyeball. He held it up as if the ineffective prop was channelling some kind of sixth sense. Behind him the second monk revealed something from his robe that wasn't an eyeball. It was a black pool ball with a number eight printed on it. Perhaps they had different ranks, thought Jake.

Rather than hold it in the air, the junior monk threw it as hard as he could at the senior monk, striking him on the back of the head with a mighty thump. The chanting stopped, the eyeball rolled out of his hand, and very slowly the monk slumped unconsciously onto the rocks in a heap.

"How often do I have to rescue you?" said Verne, lifting the white hood away from his face and winking slyly.

"Verne! What are you doing here?"

"Saving your arse, again."

"But…why?"

"All in good time. Let's get you unlocked and find the eye."

Verne grabbed the keys from the other monk's belt and unlocked Jake's manacles. His ankles were bruised and cut from the constant rubbing of the heavy metal against flesh and bone, but after stretching his legs out for a few minutes there didn't appear to be any lasting damage. His belly rumbled with hunger having been suppressed by more important issues in recent days. Verne paid little attention to Jake's moans and groans, focused instead on searching the rock pools and crevices on all fours.

"Help me look," he demanded.

"Why do we need it? They're not real eyes."

"No, but they are keys."

"Keys to what?"

"The King's procession. I have a plan but we need the other eye. I have one, but I knew I needed something heavier to knock that guy out."

Jake joined the search. He wished they were real eyes because then they wouldn't bounce around so much. After ten minutes of hunting, Jake spotted the little white sphere washing up and down an eddy, fighting the tide's determination to drag it out to sea. He shouted over to Verne who was closer and the speccy waded out to catch it.

"Watch out for Merlions!" shouted Krakoff who'd only recently learnt of their existence thanks to news from the recently deposited female cast-off.

Verne climbed back onto the rocks, his sopping wet gown weighing him down and clinging to his body like a wetsuit. He passed the eye to Jake.

"Keep this safe. We'll strip the other monk so you have a disguise."

"How did you know I was here?" asked Jake.

"You're not hard to find. Don't forget your face is on the news broadcasts every night and rumours spread like wildfire."

"But I've been in disguise," he said confidently.

"But your words weren't," he replied. "I knew you were coming to Baku so I asked around. When I found out a strange character had been to see the King and sent him into a rage, I knew it was you. After that there was only one place to look."

"Where's the other monk? They always come here in pairs."

Verne pointed out to sea, held his nose and simulated sinking.

"Well, that's awful. Not that I'm not grateful, but why did you come back at all? You said you had too much to lose."

"Yes, I did say that, but I decided on reflection I had even more to gain. I felt guilty about leaving you and then deep shame at my own cowardice. Once I got over myself

I followed on the next freight train, but I couldn't catch up with you until you stopped moving. I guess I was a day or so behind."

"Don't feel bad. I used to only think about myself, too," he said, without considering the irony of his current single-minded desire to gain revenge on Sam. "How did you get involved with the monks?"

"I heard stories from other speccies I came across on my journey about a nightly procession the King of Baku took to a place called Abseron."

"Yes, I've heard about that, too. I need to see what he's doing there."

"I already have. I followed it last night. It's quite the show, I can tell you. After that I tracked the monks and found out about their daily trips to the rock. I managed to overpower one and switch places. It wasn't exactly difficult, I don't think the monks are very bright."

"They've been brainwashed," said Jake. "The King is completely mental. He has all these bizarre views about the world and acts like the leader of a weird cult. He also sees things that aren't even there: he said I had an army with me."

"Sounds like a classic case of P.C.O.D. to me," replied Verne.

"What's that?"

"Permanent Cloud Over Disorder. It's when someone can't distinguish between what's real and what's not. It's dangerous enough in regular citizens, but if it infected someone with power and authority the impact would be catastrophic."

If Jake's memories weren't currently being shared between his ex-husband and an Arizonian warehouse, he'd have remembered that Christie's dad suffered from it. When you'd spent time around a sufferer it became really easy to diagnose. Sadly it was one of many pearls of wisdom that had been highjacked by a six-foot Swede.

"We have to find a way to stop the procession," said Jake firmly.

"Stop it!? Why?"

"Because it's not just about finding Dinah anymore: we have to stop the Memory Storms destroying these people's lives."

"But the war drones are waiting for you. There are six above Abseron."

"Did the drones react to the procession at all?" asked Jake.

"Not really. They didn't seem to notice it."

"In that case if we disguise ourselves as monks they might not detect us either. They can't track me virtually: they're waiting for someone to identify me physically."

"Still sounds risky."

"I can't see any alternative."

"Who dares wins?"

"Something like that. Now help me release the rest of these prisoners."

"Why? They'll know it was us."

"Only until midnight, then they'll forget who I am or why they were even here."

The monk Verne knocked out with a pool ball was considerably smaller than Jake. Whereas the other monks had cloaks that stretched from head to toe, the one Jake acquired floated halfway between his ankles and knees. The hood was so tight it restricted his breathing and the hessian cord barely reached around him, making the whole thing look like an undersized corset. After rescuing him twice it would sound a little ungrateful to ask Verne to pick someone who wasn't a midget next time.

By the time they returned to Baku it was early evening. According to Verne's previous surveillance the procession left the 'Temple of Fire' at about eleven o'clock. From there it crept over the main bridge before turning north towards Abseron. That was a few hours away so they hid in the shadows of the castle and passed the time by discussing what risks they might face. Every time they thought of one they debated their options to counter it. The contingency plan to every risk was always the same.

Get recognised. Run.

Chant out of key. Run.

Forget to hold up the eye at the appropriate times. Run.

War drones start shooting. Run.

The monks run away. Run.

Having a single plan made life pretty easy. Jake wondered whether he might learn from the strategy when it came to dealing with Sam, but as soon as his name entered his head he immediately thought up three new ways of punishing him. Plans AU, AV and AW.

Dead on eleven o'clock the gates of the castle swung open and the procession squeezed under the narrow archway. Leading from the front were three pairs of monks chanting at the top of their voices. Each held a small incense burner on a long, golden chain that they swung from side to side. The thin, wispy smoke filled the streets with the scent of dried rose petals. The King of Baku was next in line and four monks were hunched over as they carried him on a blue velvet throne. In an attempt to look more regal he supped from a silver chalice, but his constant erratic movements to fend off invisible threats meant he spilt more of the liquid than he consumed. Behind the throne three further pairs of monks brought up the rear. As soon as the procession passed by, Verne and Jake scurried to join the back of the queue.

Whether the monks were in a trance from the chanting, hypnotised by the smells wafting down from the front, had a restricted view from under their hoods or just couldn't count further than six, none of them noticed the addition of two participants at the back of the line. Jake didn't care why they didn't as long as it remained the case for the duration. All they had to do now was act like the rest of the procession and blend in.

He gripped the fake eyeball in his palm ready to lift it to the sky anytime they did. The shiny surface rolled around in his sweaty fingers, and he was anxious that it might fly out of his grasp and give the game away. It didn't take long before that worry was tested. Disillusioned city folk had lined the streets to watch the nightly cortège of Gog. They offered no jubilant roars or waves of excitement. Instead they shared the occasional grumble of disappointment and sour-faced grimace. There was nothing to get excited about: it was exactly the same every night. Nothing was likely to cheer them up and certainly not some white-cloaked 'Gog botherers' brandishing plastic eyeballs and moaning some ancient, incoherent psalm.

Tomorrow they'd feel better about it.

Just like they had yesterday.

As well as replicating the waving of eyeballs the two imposters felt obliged to copy the monk's singing. This wasn't too difficult because it was about as tuneful as a middle-aged dad singing a favourite song that he thought he knew the lyrics to. In reality he only knew every seventh word and pretended to sing the rest by substituting them with random adjectives or aborted mumbling. Most of the bystanders did notice the out-of-tune singing and naked shins of the rear monk, but no one could be bothered to call it out. Why would they? It fitted into their daily narrative perfectly. Life was shit: of course the holy monks were going to be a bunch of freaks.

The procession moved at a laboriously slow pace and Jake's anxiety increased with every weary step. Surely it was only a matter of time before someone noticed them. Then again maybe it wasn't just the King who suffered from P.C.O.D. What if all the monks had it and they assumed their presence was happening in the virtual world, so ignored it anyway? Or maybe the lack of regular rebellion from the masses created a false sense of security. This strange sect obviously controlled the people of the East, and if the numbers on the rock were anything to go by, few were brave enough to step out of line. If nothing challenged your power then maybe you believed it never would. The King's only obvious fear was Judge, and quite possibly Jake.

But not Jake dressed as a monk apparently.

No one expected that.

Least of all Jake.

Sometimes life took unusual turns in a very short spaces of time. Three months ago he was nervously anticipating his Ascension Day. By all accounts he was still dating Christie and attending high school. He wondered if his school was the type that produced a virtual yearbook. If they did there would be a list of predictions about fellow students. Who would win an award. Who would become famous. Who would end up in jail. Who would end up walking the streets of Baku in an undersized white cloak, mumbling incoherently while raising a fake eye ping-pong ball in the air!

The procession ascended a narrow, cobbled street and moved from the suburbs to an industrial area. Above the bobbing heads and bulky throne a glass pyramid carved an existence amongst the grey office blocks. Half a dozen war drones descended from the dark clouds as they got closer to the glass building. Until now, Jake had only seen these giant robots from a distance and hadn't really appreciated how frightening they were. Jet black shells, more weaponry than a Navy battleship and ten times bigger than any drone he'd ever seen. Two malicious red lights glowed with supernatural terror at the front. Even though they were being powered by four massive engines, they were completely silent. Conical-shaped red beams scanned the area, flickering every time they passed over an object.

Verne twitched uncomfortably. They hadn't spoken since joining the line so Jake couldn't guess how he was feeling about the situation. Would Verne panic and run away? He prayed he didn't. Drones were programmed to identify Memory Clouds and, as neither of them had one, there was nothing to be worried about. But did Verne know that? Even Jake couldn't be certain these technologically advanced killers didn't possess functions normal drones lacked. He grabbed hold of Verne's arm and gently shook his head in both defiance and reassurance.

When the drones finished their investigations they remained in position, weapons trained at the glass building. The monks that carried the heavy throne and its passenger shuffled forward, audibly puffing with exhaustion. They dumped it inelegantly next to a security post at the entrance with a mixture of joy and relief. Almost immediately the glass doors slid open and the King waited for his four escorts to interact with the screen before lifting him back in the air and carrying him inside. The remaining monks formed an orderly queue and Jake's nerves jangled as he waited for his next test.

Their naïve attempt to infiltrate the procession had backfired. When they reached the end of the line, they'd surely fail whatever awaited them. They couldn't run now, not with the war drones in such close proximity. Sweat cascaded down his brow and his gown seemed to shrink. The line moved quickly. The monks interacted with the screen for no more than a couple of seconds before the door slid open and they comfortably passed through. He watched closely as the one immediately in front of him reached the monitor and raised the eyeball up to the screen.

That appeared to be the only entry requirement. What was this object in his pocket? thought Jake. It obviously wasn't just another piece of religious symbolism used to distinguish those that were inside the King's cult and those that weren't. Jake stood in front of the screen and a single, green cursor pulsated back at him.

It was an all too familiar sight.

Let me see you...

Jake held the eyeball out in front of him and offered a prayer to Gog just in case it helped.

Access granted...

The glass entrance slid open and he rushed inside before the doors changed their mind. Verne followed, although Jake was surprised just how quickly. Was the screen a coincidence? thought Jake. Surely Alison's reach didn't stretch to the East. It couldn't. They were on different networks. On the shiny, tiled floor of the vast foyer was a symbol Jake hadn't seen since the flag on the town hall in New Putinsburg. A clock face and two waves. Proof that they were definitely on Realm property.

A glass staircase led up to the first floor where transparent partitions separated row upon row of metal racking stacked floor to ceiling. The procession returned to its original formation and headed up the staircase. They marched through the doors at the top, with a more hurried pace than they had done previously. When the rows between the electronic equipment packed on the racks became too narrow, the monks shuffled into single file and the King of Baku was transferred to a trolley that one of them dragged along the floor on small, squeaky castors.

Then the line stopped. Because there were a dozen monks between him and the King, Jake struggled to see what was happening. The cloak he'd acquired might not fit him, but there were at least some advantages of being taller than the others. On tiptoes he could just about make out what was going on upfront. The King had been helped onto his feet for the first time since they left the temple, and the monks were attaching a thin cable between his intricate headdress and a solitary cabinet that contained a plastic computer terminal with a single, solid red light illuminated at the front. It was the only server not crammed in tightly against all the others.

"Queen of nightmares, keeper of sin, purveyor of immorality, I command you to wake," grunted the King, raising his arms high in the air and smashing them together with a deafening clap.

Nothing happened.

"WAKE JUDGE!" he shouted. "IT IS TIME!"

The solid, red light flickered. A motor whirred and the screen above the server stack flashed with a white cursor before typing out its response.

What is it this time…?

"The hour has cometh. Time to purge the people of your nightmares."

Don't blame me…I'm mostly dead…

"With Gog radiant in my heart your lies rebound from me, harmless and meek."

You're not still going on about Gog, are

you?…I've told you a thousand times he's in your head…moron…

"Blasphemy! We know all about you, Judge. Your words are poison in our clouds and screams in our ears."

How many times do I have to tell you?… there is no Judge…just me…just Dinah…

TWENTY

MEMORIES NEVER DIE

W hen Jake saw Dinah's name on-screen he almost jumped for joy. She was here and by the looks of it she demonstrated all the sassiness and charm of his own guide. He was tantalisingly close now. One step away from learning the truth locked inside him. Surely she would understand what it meant. All he had to do was work out a way to communicate with her. The way the King had done so was reminiscent of how he'd connected to the mainframe when he'd viewed his flashbacks all those weeks ago. If he and Verne slipped away unseen maybe they'd get a small window of opportunity to return and do the same.

The timing would be crucial. Jake needed to wait until after the King instructed Dinah to alter people's memories. Only then would he know how to correct it. Jake knew it was perfectly feasible to change the contents of a Memory Cloud because it had happened to him twice before. On one of those occasions it had been permanent, and the other only temporary. Drew had suggested part of his memory had been swapped during a download, probably while he was on Bornholm. That procedure had been permanent, while Moodzec only distorted your emotions for a short period of time. Based on the fractured conversations he'd had, Krakoff's past memories were irretrievable, but what method was the King using?

Changing an individual's memories was purposely difficult, so that no one tried to do it. Imagine how useful a tool like that would be? Screwed up at work, change the memory. Broke an antique vase, change the memory. Got caught in bed with your wife's sister, change everyone's memories, including your own just in case. The system had to mitigate against such temptation. Memories were captured by the implants and only stored in the cloud. If your implants failed or were upgraded then there was a backup but the implant was the only device that changed what was stored there. The King wasn't tampering with people's implants, he was interacting with a single server, so his approach had to be a new one.

The King plugged a small device into the port on the front panel of the server unit. He pressed a number of buttons on the keypad and the computer display went into an electronic fit. Pages of code zoomed before their eyes only interrupted by a collection of colourful spinning icons and the appearance of the dreaded 'dead screen' that indicated the computer had crashed. Finally, after an anxious wait, the cursor returned, pulsating slightly more heavily than it had done before like it was knackered from its cyber marathon.

The King of Baku removed the device and Jake sensed now was the right time to act. He tugged at Verne's arm and led him quietly back down the row in reverse, watching the monks constantly. When they were clear of the end they crept down the stairs and disappeared into the ground floor labyrinth that was organised much like the level above. Under the hum of the countless server fans they whispered quietly to each other.

"What do you think all that code was?" asked Verne.

"I'm not sure exactly but it's the reason for everyone forgetting what really happened yesterday. Look, it's just gone midnight," he said, pointing at his wristwatch.

"It looked like something was being reset."

"Verne, when you were younger, before the King seized control, did you ever hear anyone talk about Dinah?"

"Never."

"But what happened after the Realm set up in competition against the Circuit? Did people switch out their old implants?"

"That was the norm. Anyone who wanted to stay within the Circuit was forced to move to a region they controlled. If you signed the Realm's terms you were booked in for an upgrade and joined a new network."

"But no one ever had guides, right?"

"I believe so. Until the King took over, everyone chose their own path in life."

"Then why did Aaron Circo have a guide?" Jake asked himself out loud.

"How do you know he did?"

"I saw him access Dinah in my flashback. He went to the 'Help' option in his memory feed and she appeared to him."

"It's hard for me to empathise because I've never had any tech inside my body, but wouldn't everyone have a help function if they signed up? Didn't you have that in the Circuit?"

"I can't remember."

Through the transparent wall near the entrance they watched as the monks filed down the staircase.

"We need to get out of here," said Verne nervously.

"Leave! We haven't got what we came for."

"If we don't leave when they do, the war drones will surely kill us."

"I'm not leaving until I've spoken to Dinah. You don't run a hundred-metre race to stop just before the tape. If you want to leave that's up to you, but I'm staying."

"Jake, I want you to succeed but I won't risk my life for you."

"What about the greater good? What about everything you said might be gained from knowing the truth?"

"There are other ways of achieving success without putting life at risk. This is your task, Jake, you should do what you have to," said Verne, replacing his hood. "I promise I'll wait for you outside."

"I won't fail," replied Jake confidently. "I can't."

Verne nodded and retreated down the row to join the end of the pack.

As soon as the procession exited the pyramid, the lights that had shone so brightly and sparkled off the glass walls were simultaneously extinguished. Only the twinkling stars of the server units' tiny LED lights remained. Jake stretched out his hands to guide himself back down the row. He passed through the foyer and up the stairs again. The eerie atmosphere of Abseron swirled around and inside him. He felt like a cat burglar at a fancy dress party.

When he reached the isolated server at the end of the row on the first floor it had been restored to its dormant mode, just the single, solid red light to indicate any sign of life. Jake searched around for a cable to make the connection, not easy in the darkness when adrenaline levels are through the roof. Eventually, in a storage cupboard nearby, his hands groped around and found a loop of cable that felt similar to what he needed. It was no good on its own. Experience told him that connecting to a server in this way

meant attaching one connector to his temple and the other
to an input port. Unseen objects were clattered to the floor
with a crash as he searched blindly around the cupboard
for something adhesive. Finally a hand landed on something spherical with a hole through the middle: a roll of
electrical tape. He shuffled back to the server cabinet and
fashioned a sticky pad from the objects he'd found and
stuck the bodge job to the side of his head.

Then he plugged the other end into the server.

Nothing happened.

There was no rush of energy as he'd expected and the
screen remained resolutely empty. Maybe his unorthodox
implants weren't compatible. After all, they were designed
for different purposes and on a different network. He was
stumped. The only thing he could think of doing was
accessing his own feed. It had been disastrous last time, but
what choice did he have?

He opened his interface and the blindingly bright
virtual world opened. A thousand rivers of data stretched
out in every direction, shimmering with light and unnat-
ural life. These were the clouds he already knew. The
places he'd been before where a shared memory allowed
him to pass effortlessly into someone else's section of the
Memory Cloud. Each of these virtual freeways would split
into a thousand more. Then it was only a hop, skip and a
jump through cyberspace to any Memory Cloud in the
West.

But he needed to find someone in the East.

The menu bar in the top corner of his projection
caught his attention. He'd rarely used it in recent times and
had no recollection of what its functions were. Inquisitively
he selected it and the options cascaded down in front of
him. The list included; 'Make a Complaint,' 'Contact Us',
'Your Agreements', 'FAQs' and 'Help'. He was tempted to

select 'frequently asked questions' as he had hundreds he was eager to have answered. The word 'frequent' put him off. He doubted whether any of his questions came up regularly. 'How do I kill Alison?' 'What are these eyeballs for?' 'Do Merlions exist?' or 'What's all this code in my head?' He decided to select 'Help' instead, as that was the most appropriate choice right now.

The red light on the server box flickered once more and the screen burst into life. A cursor throbbed in the centre, just as it had done for the King, but that wasn't the only thing to appear. Behind him a powerful source of light projected his shadow onto the display. Simultaneously a message was typed onto the screen and a voice echoed along the narrow rows of computer paraphernalia.

"What is it now…?"

He spun around to find a hologrammatic figure standing between the servers stacks. "Dinah!"

"Argh…a supernatural monk!" she screamed.

The female projection ran headlong into the nearest object in panic and disappeared from sight. The screen wasn't so mobile and took up the conversation in her absence.

Unless it's Halloween…go away…

"Come back!" hollered Jake, removing his hood to help reduce the terror. "I won't hurt you."

"Really?" came a trembling voice some distance away. "I've heard they steal eyeballs!"

"But you don't have any."

"Then what are these exactly?"

Two enormous eyeballs, detached from any other bodypart, appeared in the virtual ether and made Jake jump backwards, almost knocking out the connection.

"Well, that's horrifying," he said once his pulse rate had steadied. "It's like Sauron has a twin. Please put them back

in and come out. I've come a great distance at great
personal danger to find you, Dinah."

The floating eyeballs moved backwards and the rest of
Dinah rematerialised around them. She assessed him
cautiously from halfway down the row. "How do you know
my name?"

"It's a long story."

"Well, if you can't be arsed to tell me please put me
back to sleep," she said with a huff.

"Blimey you're just like Dinah!" he chuckled.

"I am Dinah."

"Yes, I know, but I also have a Dinah."

"There's only ONE Dinah!" she snapped, crossing her
arms defensively.

"I'm sitting on the fence on that one."

"Must be uncomfortable."

"Look, I don't know how much time I have…"

"You'd better make that long story a bit shorter, then!"

It fascinated him to see how many of this Dinah's characteristics mirrored those of his own guide, even though
her personality was partially informed by his own. At least
that's what he'd been told. If Aaron's implants had been
copied, duplicated and fixed into a new host, it was plausible that much of Dinah's unique personality came with it.
How much of the original programming remained inside
him before his guide took over was difficult to judge. One
thing was evidently clear, though: they looked nothing like
each other.

This version of Dinah was younger, taller and more
attractive. She wore more conservative clothes, ones that
made her look more like a high-powered City lawyer and
less like a whacked-out hippy. Her wavy hair was perfectly
styled with blonde highlights, and she wore expensive

glasses with bold red frames. Behind them was the familiarly mischievous glint in her eyes.

"I'll try to summarise it," said Jake attempting to verbalise his recent experiences in one hundred and forty characters or less.

He failed miserably.

Unlike his own Dinah, whose attention span would run out after nine characters, this manifestation listened carefully, nodded in all the right places, and didn't try to interrupt once. When he came to the end of his story she paused to reflect before finally offering her rebuttal.

"You're fucked," she said plainly.

"What?! I've travelled halfway around the world to share this information with you. I've crossed the firewall, been chased by Memory Hunters, tracked by the 'Proclamation of Distrust,' negotiated with an insane King and all you can say is 'you're fucked'?"

"Oh, I'm sorry," she said sarcastically, "would you like me to explain my genius in more eloquent terms? It's just you said you were in a hurry so I thought I'd be direct."

"I think it's the least I deserve," replied Jake despondently.

"Fine," she sighed.

"Before you crush my hopes and dreams, though, I'd really love to know who you are."

"Don't you know yet?"

Jake shrugged. "Not really. I've heard people call you Judge, the queen of nightmares, all sorts of names."

"Ha! Judge. There is no Judge. That's just a false label to scare witless morons. Judge is about as real as the mighty Gog," she said with an extravagant mock bow. "I'm sure the King believes in both of them, but then again he's not really all there. Since the very beginning I have been, and always will be, Dinah and my true identity is a lot simpler to understand if you're not a barking fruit cake."

Even if it was as simple as she suggested, she didn't seem keen to explain it.

"And?" said Jake after a long period of silence.

"I'm one half of the first sibling programme."

"Then why are you here? The sibling programme only exists in the West and it triggers guides that are unique to the individual."

"True but this is the East and things work differently. When Aaron Circo created the Realm he copied some of the Circuit's infrastructure and principles. I was one of the functions he brought with him. I am the Realm's operating system. I am the East's mother programme."

"Are you saying you're equivalent to Alison?" said Jake in horror. He already had one artificial super being to deal with and he wasn't keen on them forming a tag team.

"Yes and no. We differ greatly."

"How?"

"Alison's a bitch!"

"Agreed, but doesn't that mean you're…"

"I don't have supreme power," she interrupted in order to reassure him. "Alison was designed to manipulate human will and provide answers to questions humans don't have the capacity to discover on their own. There's a good reason why they can't and shouldn't. Having unlimited knowledge doesn't necessarily make things better: you only have to look at the skies to prove that."

"So what are you for, then?"

"My programming is designed to protect. When Aaron founded the Realm he included me in subscribers' implants. An operating system but not the same as Alison. I help users with their questions, but I don't do things for them."

"How can you say that when you've been changing their memories every day at midnight? How is that protecting them?"

"It isn't. I said I was programmed for it, but software can be manipulated by a programmer. The King of Baku knows how to reprogramme me. Every night he forces my operating system into a reset by shoving the master file into my access port. That forces the system to close off parts of the cloud. In the morning, when everyone's implants try to back up their personal files, any marked as negative are blocked and they receive a new version of the master programme without their knowledge. The memories are still there, it's just the subscribers' operating systems can't find them. I think they call it a cache."

"But where did he get it from?"

"I'll give you one guess."

"Alison."

"Full marks to the ghoulish-looking monk."

"But how?"

"I was originally created inside the Circuit. When they unleashed Ersatz, Alison opened my code and copied it."

"But why?"

"Now there's a question," she smirked.

"And…the answer is?"

"Alison's frightened of me. She thinks I possess the secrets to how the Ersatz programme works, and by association the Circuit itself. Alison believes I'm an existential threat with intentions of inspiring the East to revolt."

"And do you?"

"Nope!"

"So what's the point of all the rituals and suppression?"

"It doesn't know that I don't. Alison has calculated that the East is a threat to the Circuit and the best way to remove it is to quash people's spirits. Remove all thought of negativity and create the illusion that everything in the East is perfect, at least until today. People don't revolt because they have one bad day, they need at least a week or two to summon up the energy for that. Generally until then they can't really be arsed."

"But now you do have Alison's secrets because they're in my memories. If I share them with you, we can stop the Circuit and set your people free."

"And finally we return to the part where you're fucked. That's not what you've got."

"Yes it is," said Jake critically. "I saw Aaron tell you to protect the files just before he died. They were copied onto ten sets of implants and I was one of the users who received them. The flashback revealed Alison's true identity and the key to breaking the Circuit."

"I hate to be the one that delivers disappointment," she sighed, offering Jake a look of pity. "You've misunderstood how Ersatz came into being. Miriam and Aaron Circo each designed a guide to aid a subscriber in their journey from childhood to adulthood, that much you know. The sibling programme was installed into every implant to be activated on Ascension Day. Both guides were equal and offered users a balance of views, but compromise slows down decision-making. Miriam argued for the installation of a programme to manage them and ultimately the smooth running of the entire Circuit. Aaron agreed in principle, but he was nervous about activating it. Mindful of her brother's feelings towards it, she kept her work on a closed network separate from his. When Miriam tricked him into agreeing to use it his work passed over to her, but not the other way round. He never had access to Miriam's half of Ersatz so the information you hold can't relate to that."

Jake felt completely deflated. "What's all this complex stuff floating around in my head, then?"

"What you actually have is the key to the Memory Cloud itself."

"Oh fuck."

"There you go, now you're seeing things from my point of view."

"How?"

"The sibling and Ersatz programmes are inherent parts of Western implants. They don't house memories, they hold the software that enables subscribers to capture, upload and access them. The Memory Cloud isn't in the East or in the West. It's everywhere. It's a fluid network of consciousness that can be accessed via different networks and governed by different rules. Ersatz controls each implant and collectively those tiny individual impulses coagulate to give you what you know as Alison, one intelligent being within the cloud that sees all, hears all and knows all."

"Then the only way to turn Alison off is by removing Ersatz from every single implant?" moaned Jake.

"Not even then. Once the user's first implant backs up with its cloud it exists there forever. You've said yourself you've had multiple implants and I've been in every one, not just your first. I remained in subsequent ones when the data from the cloud was backed up."

"I've totally wasted my time," whimpered Jake. "I've run around the world falsely believing I could change things. What a fool. I should have listened to Job and towed the line. I really am superfluous."

"Did you say Job?"

"Yes."

"Well, that is interesting."

"Is it?"

"Yes. Job was Miriam's contribution to the sibling programme. It seems like you acquired both of them. I imagine he came with your second implant."

"It doesn't really matter anymore. All of this has been pointless."

"Not at all," said Dinah sympathetically.

"How do you figure that out?" sobbed Jake, slumping onto the floor and thumping it with his fist.

"Because you carry the key to turning off the Memory Cloud, Jake. You came here looking for a way to destroy Alison, but you've been carrying the bomb all along."

"Bomb?"

"The fuse and the fuel. You're a one in a trillion fluke. An epic coincidence. Almost too much for it to be one, in fact. Your speccy implants grant you access to the whole Circuit, and if you chose to disseminate the code it would permanently disrupt the wireless frequency that links implants with the cloud. If you turn off the Memory Cloud, you turn off Alison."

Moral dilemmas didn't come much bigger than this. Jake had the power to rid the world of Alison, but at what cost? If he took away everyone's access to the Memory Cloud, he took away their history and identity. He knew how that felt. He'd experienced it. And the rest of humanity wouldn't have the benefit of being relayed the most important facts about themselves before it happened like he had.

If you took away a corrupt system and replaced it with a void would life improve? How would society cope without rules, responsibilities or structure? How would people react if they suddenly lost all knowledge of who they were? They'd cease to remember their names, importance factors, family history, personal strengths, skills, jobs, partners, children, communities and beliefs. People would wake up in limbo: scared, confused and isolated. Without moral structure people would revert to their instincts, and all previous boundaries of right and wrong would disappear. Surely the world would collapse into chaos, war, famine and greed.

The frightening vision in his head was the Circuit's ultimate deterrent to stop anyone ever using it.

Did Alison know? Yes, he was confident of that. The Circuit knew Jake held dangerous information that might threaten their survival. Even if they didn't know exactly what it was, they certainly knew Dinah and the East had something to do with it. It wasn't just paranoia that fuelled the Circuit's fear of the East. It was clear they'd infiltrated this part of the world more deeply, and for longer, than anyone knew. The King's master file and the security screen on the front entrance weren't from here. Neither were the war drones, sent to defend against a worst-case scenario. But what was the worst case?

"I don't want a bomb," said Jake. "I want a peaceful life that I'm in control of."

"But you can't do that under the Circuit, can you?"

"No, but neither do I want to be responsible for the alternative. Some people actually like the way things are."

"Do they?" said Dinah in surprise.

"Yes. They're willing to ignore the reality or are blind to it already."

"It sounds like you'd be doing them a favour. Lift the veil."

"They won't like what they see."

"But some will," replied Dinah.

There was another reason why Jake was terrified about the power he had in his possession. If he used it, how did it make him any better than the Circuit itself? He'd be forcing choices on people without their consent, whether he thought it was the right thing to do or not. If his ego were more ambitious or less caring it might be easy. The power was intoxicating but he didn't trust himself with it. He wouldn't trust anyone with it. There was also a selfish reason not to use it.

Christie.

By all accounts the Circuit had disconnected them virtually and then separated them physically. They'd stripped her further from his mind with the download, and now Sam was trying to tempt her away from him. If he shut down the Memory Cloud she wouldn't even know who he was. Unless he got to her and explained what would happen, shutting it down was too much of a personal risk.

Jake didn't know who to believe anymore. Whose advice should he follow? Sam's, Alison's or Dinah's?

"I don't know what to do," said Jake forlornly.

"Don't ask me. I'm mostly dead memories."

"But you're not, are you, because memories don't die. Even if I turn off the signal to the Memory Cloud they'll still be there even if people can't access them."

"True."

"I think it's a trick," said Jake. "Alison's using all of her resources to find me and yet I got to you far too easily. I got through to the King, I avoided the 'Proclamation of Distrust' and the drones."

"What drones?" said Dinah nervously.

"New ones, designed for war. There are half a dozen stationed above Abseron and every other server farm, I expect. I thought they'd been sent to attack the people, but they don't seem interested in that."

"Shit. They're not," she replied, her face almost translucent with terror. "They're after us!"

"Us?"

"You and I are the only beings on Earth who have access to what Aaron knew about the cloud. Alison knew where I was, but not where you were. They lured you here. They wanted us in the same place. Run!"

Major Holst counted the monks as they left the glass pyramid. Excluding the King, eighteen had entered and only sixteen had left. A final monk departed the building a minute later, just as expected. The plan had worked perfectly. The final monk strolled casually over to him without the characteristic chants or trance-like shuffle. He removed his hood and displayed the prominent scar on his face.

"Is it definitely him?" asked Holst.

"Yes," confirmed Verne confidently.

"Then the Circuit is eternally in your debt."

"When will I receive my reward?" he asked assertively.

"All in good time. Jake hasn't been caught yet, has he? You'll get it. Trust me."

Verne didn't trust him in the slightest. He'd stepped into the enemy camp for his own personal gain and he'd seen with his own eyes how others had fared when they'd done that in the past.

"When?"

"Don't worry about it. You'll get your prize, or my name isn't Major James Oliver Benjamin Holst."

TWENTY-ONE

IDENTICAL TWINS

It was the evening of the infamous kiss and the atmosphere on Gay Head Island was frostier than a blizzard. Almost none of Paddy's party were talking to each other, although most of them were talking to him, which at least proved he wasn't the reason for the sub-zero undercurrent swirling around. A frosty silence was better than constant hormone-fuelled bickering, but the longer it lasted, the more their sullenness annoyed him. There were much more important things to appreciate this evening than petty squabbles.

To avoid contact with the speccies he'd set up a makeshift camp near the cliffs. As Solar Summer was nearing its peak, the conditions for sleeping outdoors were perfect and so far the rain showers had held off. Paddy built an excellent fire and cooked some delicious sausages, provisions his speccy friends had offered them. He sat cross-legged with a big grin on his face as he watched a bubbling urn of tea send great puffs of steam billowing out into the night sky. The excitement of the day peeled back the layers of his disaffected soul and made him feel decades younger, the most alive he'd felt in years.

None of the other members of his party agreed with his sentiments about the day. The three youngsters were huddled under thin blankets further away from each other than normal social distancing rules demanded. They kept their backs to each other, which was tricky to pull off when you wanted to avoid eye contact with more than one person. Christie was furious with Fake Jake for being a sexual predator and still hadn't forgiven Tyra for her general brattish behaviour. Fake Jake was avoiding Christie out of shame and mostly hated Tyra for having the audacity to be his sister. Tyra had a list of reasons why she hated everyone, whether they were on the island or not.

"I love a bit of night camping," said Paddy jovially in an attempt to stir up some positivity.

It was met by a wall of deathly silence.

"Being away from the modern world with only nature around you: it just doesn't get better than this. It's like standing on the edge of the Universe and watching life being born. The sky, the sea, the nocturnal creatures escaping from their lairs…the wind whistling through the rocks…the amazing silence…WHAT'S WRONG WITH ALL OF YOU!?" he shouted, losing his patience at being the only one appreciating it. "I SAID, ISN'T THE SILENCE AMAZING!"

"Yes," said Christie, the first to be shaken into life and less used to ignoring Paddy's bouts of fury. "I think we were all happier when it was."

"Look, you three, we're all in this together. How's it going to help if none of us talks to each other? How can we call ourselves civilised if we can't solve our problems like grown-ups? If you open up maybe we can find some harmony?"

The three younger members of the company didn't so much open up as explode in an angry melee of self-interest. They barked their grievances at each other, sometimes switching their focus to the other. No one attempted to listen to what anyone had to say, and their language became incriminatory and purposely inflammatory. The more they struggled to make their points heard over their opponents, the louder their voices rose. In less than a minute their personal feuds were raging more fiercely than the fire.

"STOP!" shouted Paddy. "Bloody kids, you're giving me a headache. Let's break this down. Christie, I'll deal with your grievance first because you're not one of my grandchildren, or at least you're not claiming to be one," he said, pointing at Fake Jake. "Did you say he took advantage of you?"

"Yes!" replied Christie.

"She encouraged me, too," said Fake Jake, pointing at Tyra to absolve himself from guilt.

"He changed my cloud settings to Arabic!" she huffed in response.

The argument rotated around the triangle faster than the sparks of a Catherine wheel.

"It doesn't matter whether someone encourages you to or not," said Paddy sternly, "you never take advantage of girls."

"But she's my girlfriend," said Fake Jake confidently.

"No I'm not," replied Christie. "And even if I were, no means no."

"Quite right," said Paddy. "In my day if you wanted to kiss a girl you had to write her a letter asking for permission, or, failing that, seek approval from her father."

"Bloody patriarchy," huffed Jezebel. "Imagine allowing a man to decide who you could kiss."

"Not now," replied Christie firmly.

"You're not her boyfriend," Paddy continued, "because you're not Jake Montana. Just accept it."

"I am," he grumbled.

"Not according to Doctor Drew. Apparently you're Sam."

"Don't suppress my identity."

"If you'd just let Theo remove your implants everything would become clearer for you."

"No!"

"Fine, that's your choice, but you can't go taking advantage of Christie. Do you understand?"

Fake Jake nodded. The very thought of hurting Christie and pushing her further away made his heart ache. Maybe he should remove his implants and stop the pain of rejection once and for all.

"What do you say?" demanded Paddy.

"I'm sorry."

"Apology accepted," replied Christie.

Tyra smirked in victory. Watching her brother's hopes being crushed when he wasn't even here made her happy beyond measure. It took her hours to get her Memory Cloud back into English, but it was totally worth it. Job talking in Arabic like a moody Moroccan market trader was the most disconcerting part of the whole experience. Now that he was talking in fluent English again she'd fully briefed him on her plan and its success. Jake had taken the bait even faster than any of them hoped. Just before Paddy started building the fire, Job returned to her feed to share the good news.

The sight of Christie 'cheating' would drive him mad and there was no way he'd be able to resist reacting. He'd soon turn up to confront them and then she'd turn him in. The next phase of the plan was already in motion. When night fell and the group fell asleep, Major Dawes and his Archivists would land and round everyone up. It was her responsibility to keep everyone here, while Job insisted on finding reinforcements, whatever that meant.

"What do we do now?" asked Christie under her breath. "The real Jake is still out there somewhere."

"Nothing!" chirped Solomon. "Half a Jake is better than none at all. Count yourself lucky, most people don't get a second chance. You weren't expecting him to be in your letter at all, were you?"

"No. But…"

"Don't listen to that misogynistic buffoon. You deserve a whole boyfriend! Women have been putting up with this shit for long enough. The sisters won the battles for equal voting rights, fair pay, conditions and opportunity. Now we must fight for the right to have complete partners, just like men!" said Jezebel, unfurling a huge virtual banner and sprinting over to the lighthouse to glue it to the bricks.

"Can't you both give me some space?" huffed Christie. "I'm not in the mood for this nonsense."

Solomon evaporated, before reappearing near Jezebel to sabotage her attempts at feminism.

Nearby, Dinah had found a quiet spot to contemplate. It wasn't a mode she found very comfortable. Usually she adopted a carefree outlook on life that mostly involved scaling the nearest tall object, imagining how many eggs she could juggle blindfolded, or inventing dangerous games that involved catapults and fire. Not today, though. It was hard to let yourself go when something substantial stood in your way. It had only happened once before and the last time it debilitated her for days. It was the burden of doubt. The weight of a secret that changed everything. Suspicious circumstances that could not be ignored. Last time it was drones on Bornholm.

Today it was the strange smell.

Every time she got close to Tyra's cloud she smelt it. It was more than just the pungency of death, as worrying as that was: the smell was familiar. The scent was locked inside her circuit boards unnamed and unknown. If Tyra hadn't witnessed death during her life, why was it there? It triggered Dinah's inquisitive nature, which only increased her wider doubts about Fake Jake. He'd dismissed her questions, which was quite out of character for Jake in her experience. Then there was the news that Fake Jake was apparently Sam Goldberg. She couldn't verify it because she only saw people through their clouds, and as she was attached to his, there was a limited view. All of this news created a deep spiral of confusion but then something even more profound happened.

The Memory Cloud stopped working.

Usually the virtual world was projected around her, painted on the scenery like a mural, pieced together by the clouds of those subscribers nearby. Now there was nothing but blank space. She was blind. In the past when disruptions had occurred she found herself back in the server, but even that was gone. There were no resistors, components, motors or electronic files. No memories, or emotions.

Just a void.

A noisy one.

A blood-curdling scream pierced the nothingness. It was the desperate cry of life passing out of memory, and when it ended she felt exhausted, like her spirit had been split in two. She felt a presence spin around her before it floated away and dissolved in the abyss. Slowly, like life's dimmer switch had been twiddled, the light returned, but not as it once was. It had a blurry and fractured quality like readjusting to life after laser eye surgery. Eventually the virtual world settled down and the island was projected around her once more. It was impossible to say how long the experience lasted, but it aged her soul by several years.

She'd collapsed in an apparitional heap, clutching her fake chest and gulping for hologrammatic air. Although she couldn't explain the unusual sensation, she was sure of one thing.

Part of her had died.

Identical twins have claimed for generations that they have a telepathic connection to one another. They experience shared feelings when the other is in danger and instinctively know when the other is sad or jubilant. Not that any of this has ever been scientifically proven. There are plenty of potential explanations for their belief in telepathy. It might be rooted in genetics, their environment or even good, old-fashioned coincidence. But none of these explanations make you quite so interesting at social functions.

Dinah didn't have a twin as such, but she did have unexplained roots.

She pulled herself up and gazed giddily at her surroundings. Everything was covered in a strange, translucent veil and no one occupying the scene felt familiar. Fake Jake's aura was all wrong. The smell from Tyra's cloud was still wrong. Everything was wrong. A decisive, unbreakable thought suffocated her mind. This wasn't where she was meant to be. This wasn't where she was needed. The real Jake was out there somewhere and a strong instinct told her that he was in trouble. While she lingered here she couldn't help him. She needed to spread out. She needed to let go.

There was one option.

Emergency protocols.

∾

"Let go!" shouted Jezebel. "I have the same rights as you!"

"You're a bloody guide!" grumbled Solomon, grappling with the huge sign. "This isn't your job!"

The banner, which would ultimately only be seen by Christie and the two of them, had displayed a variety of slogans during their battle for dominance over it. 'Women deserve full partners' then 'Half a man is no good to us', and finally 'Men, you can't have your cake and eat it' had all appeared periodically. Because of the relentless grappling between the two of them it simply read 'Men have cake'.

"This is getting us nowhere," said Solomon. "We're meant to be a team."

"Pfft, why would I work with a man?! You don't notice anything even when it's right in front of your nose. Surely you don't think any of this is regular."

"No, it's not, but we've found Jake Montana's cloud, and that's our only job."

"Ooh and you call yourself a perfectionist?" she said accusingly.

"It is perfect!"

"Not quite," came a third voice. It took them both by surprise and momentarily stopped their tug of war. The banner drifted to the floor in a heap and settled on 'you eat it' as its final message. An unfamiliar hologram in jeans and a white T-shirt stood in the ether with his arms crossed and cultivating a persona of self-importance.

"Who the hell are you?" said Jezebel angrily. "Bloody men ganging up on women. I won't be silenced!"

"He's not with me," replied Solomon innocently. "No idea who he is. Most irregular."

"I'm not with anyone," replied the man. "I'm with everyone."

"That's what all men say when they want something,

but you're all the same. Feminist one minute, male chauvinist the next."

"You have me at cross purposes, Madam. My name is
Brother Job and I bring news."

"Unless it's about where the other half of Jake's is I'm
not interested! In fact, I'm on strike until Christie gets a
proper one."

"Actually it is about that."

"Oh," replied Jezebel, rather annoyed she was being
forced to abandon her revolt. Protesters always wanted
something, but mostly it was the chance to make a big sign,
shout at policemen and organise another protest.

"You're a Memory Hunter, aren't you?" said Solomon
slightly awe-inspired.

"Yes."

"I've never met one before. What's it like?"

"Beyond your wildest dreams."

"Weird dreams you have," said Jezebel snidely. "Do
they involve smelling like a morgue?"

"That's my natural aroma."

"L'eau de funeral parlour, is it!?"

Job ignored her. It wasn't difficult: he'd had years of
practice with Dinah. Aaron's lot were all the same.
Unhinged, juvenile and weak. He wasn't here to convert
her anyway, he'd come for him.

"The man you believe to be Jake Montana is an
imposter," said Job. "The real Jake has left the Circuit and
is hell-bent on destroying it. But he has fallen into our trap
and soon he'll be here."

"Good, then we can glue them together," replied
Jezebel confidently. "Problem solved!"

"He's going to destroy the Circuit!" said Solomon in
shock.

"How?"

"We believe he's carrying a weapon."

"Shit! What's the Circuit doing about it?"

"We have plans in place but we always need more help," said Job, aiming his comments at Solomon.

"I'm not helping either of you," huffed Jezebel. "Not until you grow tits and develop a genuine addiction to buying cushions."

"Your help won't be necessary."

"There's a surprise," huffed Jezebel.

"The Archivists will be here soon and it's critical that Christie stays where she is until then."

"That should be easy enough," replied Solomon.

"We'll see about that," countered Jezebel.

"You'll have to work as a team," added Job.

"I've tried everything," said Solomon desperately. "There's just no reasoning with her!"

"In that case there's only one alternative. Join us."

"What, become a Memory Hunter?"

"Yes. That way we can block her attempts to sabotage us."

"You underestimate us strong, independent women," huffed Jezebel. "Wait until I really get started."

"If I do it?" asked Solomon calmly. "Does she go away?"

"Not exactly but you'll have a lot more places to hide in."

"Done. Where do I sign up?!"

All guides knew their ultimate fate was to become Memory Hunters, but most felt hesitant about leaving until their host was ready. Like a professional football player who succumbs to the realisation that their 'legs have gone', the decision came to Dinah automatically. She just knew this was the right time. If she'd known how much fun it was going to be she'd have enrolled sooner.

What she didn't know, though, was how she was meant to do it.

Did she have to report to anyone? She'd always imagined that the Memory Hunters were an organised and disciplined bunch, two traits no one would ever accuse her of. Were there normal working hours, or was she on call? Maybe she just felt her way into the role, freestyled it until someone asked her to stop. The job appeared simple enough: hunt for memories, supposedly on someone's orders, but as there didn't seem to be any she decided to improvise. After all, there were plenty of memories she wanted to hunt down.

Dinah procrastinated about which step to take first from the network she'd always known. Previously her movements were limited to the clouds of people Jake came into contact with. Now the possibilities were endless. She closed her eyes and stepped into the unknown. At first the idea of breaking into a stranger's cloud made her feel uncomfortable, like rummaging around in someone's knicker drawer while they weren't at home. But the more steps she took, the more the rush became addictive. Connections passed by in a flash and like an unstoppable intellectual avalanche she gained greater knowledge in each one. It didn't matter how long she spent there; every cache, file and folder was absorbed in an instant. In less than an hour her burgeoning wisdom would have flattened the combined talents of every major university in the world. But the span and depth of her influence in the Memory Cloud went further than she thought possible.

Further than anyone thought possible.

She stepped into a section of the Memory Cloud that

offered nothing but a quagmire of negative vibes. The owners of these clouds appeared to be in genuine distress, but when she delved a little deeper their moods changed. The more she rummaged, the more their history seemed false and manipulated. Their past memories were exclusively joyous and yet the present day stubbornly refused to cheer up. One other similarity emerged from her analysis. They all had memories of a symbol. A clock face with two waves crashing on to the left and the right sides. This wasn't the Circuit's flashy gold markings, it was something different. The more she remained there, the more she learnt from local users.

This was the Realm.

Somehow she'd stepped over the border and into the East. Rather than consider how this was at all possible, her attention lingered on more random thoughts. Should she erect a virtual flag and claim it for herself before anyone else did? What should she call it? She settled on the name 'Sadder Arabia'.

Dinah didn't do plans, they were tedious. They led to too much talking and a dramatic reduction in fun. They restricted spontaneity and experimentation. She always went with her feelings and this was a prime example of it. Her movements through the cloud were sporadic but they still had purpose. Eventually, if she made enough random turns she'd accidentally find what she was really looking for.

Jake.

But she never did. The more she searched, the more it frustrated her. Even discovering a new world at the very edge of the Memory Cloud didn't shake the smell that signalled to her like a warning flare. It had to be significant. Maybe she wasn't destined to find Jake; maybe it was the source of the smell she had to find. Effortlessly she jumped from cloud feed to cloud feed like an existential game of hopscotch. The more she jumped, the stronger the smell grew, and the more familiar the memories. She passed through Paddy's arcane version of the virtual reality where most of the memories were sepia-coloured and featured large gaps where the tape had snapped. The sound of old-fashioned values hummed and there was a substantial reduction in the speed and clarity of thought. The smell, though, was almost overpowering but she knew it wasn't the source.

One final step.

It was in Tyra's cloud and the source became obvious.

"Job!"

"Dinah?" came a surprised response.

"I knew I recognised it, but you're not dead, which is kind of annoying."

"Sorry to disappoint you."

"I really am."

"What are you doing here?"

"I've come to stop you doing whatever it is you're doing," she said, trying to feign knowledge she didn't have.

"I'm not doing anything," he replied innocently.

"Yes, you are, I can smell it."

"What are you on about?"

"I know the smell of death and you're drenched in it."

"You don't know what death smells like."

"Yes I do because I witnessed Aaron's murder…" she said instinctively, the words stopping her in her tracks. It was true. She remembered it as if it were yesterday. It wasn't the only revelation to return either. "You and I were the first."

"The first what?" huffed Job, looking rather shifty and keen on hiding something from her.

"The first siblings. The original guides. One from the

West and one from the East. One crafted by the sister and one by the brother. Replicated and copied into Jake's implants."

"As usual, I have absolutely no idea what you're talking about, Dinah."

"Yes you do, you sneaky git!"

"I'd love to say that it's 'lovely to see you', but in fact it isn't."

Dinah didn't need to ask her next question because the answers were all here inside Tyra's cloud. A complete plan of how they intended to catch Jake, the Archivists waiting to strike, and the details of Tyra's deal with Alison.

"I'm a little busy for your games today," said Job, waving her away.

"You know I love games. This one's going to be fun because I'm calling it 'the Job Blocker'."

"Ha! Good luck. I have the weight of the Circuit and a million Memory Hunters at my command."

"They're no match for me."

"What?! You're loony."

"Hear this, brother, everywhere you go I will get there first. I will block you at every turn. I will thwart your every move. I will protect Jake."

"It's the Circuit that needs protecting from him, don't you see? If he succeeds it's the end of you."

"I work for the Realm now and I'm watching you," she added, puffing out her chest and pointing two fingers at her eyes and then at him.

"You don't stand a chance. You're all on your own."

"No she isn't," said Jezebel, adopting a strange gang-land signal with her fist that Dinah approved of but didn't understand.

TWENTY-TWO

THE FALL OF ABSERON

W ithin fifteen minutes Abseron was nothing more than a pile of twisted metal and broken glass. The war drones levelled it with a brutal ferocity. The result was no less devastating than the tests Holst had conducted on Bornholm, but for the first time he'd witnessed his creation fight in anger. The more their ordnance pummelled the structure, the wider the grin stretched across his face. This was his life's work and it was finally being unleashed on something significant. The drones had fired with the efficiency and synchronisation of a New Year's firework display. It was so deafening that Verne was forced to spend the entire experience with his fingers in his ears and guilt in his gut.

This wasn't the deal he'd agreed on.

Verne had never personally seen the 'Proclamation of Distrust'. He'd only even found out about it because of their chance meeting with Boris. When the youngster identified Jake, Verne was intrigued to learn more. Without Jake's knowledge he'd asked some subscribers to describe it to him. They told him all about Jake, the danger from the

West. What he looked like, how he'd act and, most importantly, the reward on offer for handing him in. A discovery that was far too tempting.

Too long had his kind been pushed to the fringes, ignored and persecuted. Too long had he lived in the shadows to suffer more loss than one man deserved. It was about time fate paid him back. He'd earned every credit of it. It was justified compensation for the anguish his wife, children and family had suffered because of his actions. Reward for everyone who'd sacrificed something for the cause in the last twenty years. His resolute belief in his entitlement did nothing to suppress his guilt, though.

The people had been sold a lie and, given the passage of history, it shouldn't have surprised him. He was told the message being broadcast every night into subscribers' feeds demanded Jake's acquisition, not his obliteration into a thousand unidentifiable pieces.

On Holst's command the drones ceased firing and ascended to a higher altitude to argue amongst themselves who'd fired the best shot of the evening. After the smoke cleared and the structure stopped collapsing, Holst advanced, eager to satisfy the answer that seemed undeniable. Jake must be dead. His bulky leather boots crunched over charred circuit boards, melted plastic casings and twisted metal frames to search for the proof. Somewhere amongst the destruction were Jake's remains. He wasn't exactly expecting them to stand out, but there was bound to be a discarded tooth, some crispy flesh or the odd shard of bone somewhere. Something they could send off for final analysis. One thing was for certain: Alison wouldn't be satisfied her plan had worked until he provided the definitive evidence.

"You'll never find anything in that chaos," said Verne,

holding his monk cloak over his face to prevent the acrid fumes infecting his lungs.

"Do you want your money or not?" growled Holst.

"Yes," replied Verne timidly. Part of him didn't. It was the part of him that felt like a bloodthirsty mercenary willing to hand in a friend for a shiny bounty.

"Then you'd better help me look," said Holst sharply.

"Look for what exactly? It's carnage. His body would have been incinerated in that heat, nothing left but ash and dust."

Major Holst kicked through the debris like he was hopelessly fishing for a prized heirloom in the remains of a house fire with the certainty it had been lost.

"Bloody hell, my feet are actually burning," yelped Verne as he jumped up and down on the spot in less suitable footwear than the Major.

"You're right," agreed Holst who also felt the heat but wasn't programmed to show pain or weakness. "We need help from something that doesn't burn."

Within minutes of being summoned a pack of worker drones arrived at the site. They formed a perimeter around the wreckage and combed through the debris. Robotic arms picked through metal and glass, occasionally removing an item of interest and placing it in a retractable compartment that slid out of their shiny undercarriage. Where their access was restricted by collapsed joists they easily cut through them with one of their many attachments. In less than a couple of hours the two dozen drones hadn't just searched for the last resting place of Jake Montana, or any of his remains, they'd cleared the entire site. All that remained of the iconic pyramid of glass was a flat concrete slab primed and ready for the next construction project.

A single drone approached the Major with its robotic arm extended. It dropped a round object into his palm.

"There must be more than this," he snapped aggressively.

The drone made a contradictory noise before retreating to join the pack.

"What did they find?" asked Verne respectfully.

Holst opened his grip and a single eyeball stared back at them. It was less spherical than it was earlier in the day and had a large split down the side where a number of insulated wires and ancient-looking resistors spewed out of the crack.

"Is it his?"

"I guess it has to be," answered Verne, taking his own from a pocket to confirm it. "What are these anyway?"

"Don't you know?"

Verne shook his head. Contrary to the story he'd told Jake, Holst had given it to him yesterday along with all the other information regarding the procession, the King and the monks. Even though he'd recently used it to access a building that no longer existed, he still didn't have the foggiest idea what they were.

"Implants," said Holst, more interested in the consequence of this one than the general concept. "Old tech ones."

"How do you know?"

The Major let out a long, disturbing laugh that bounced off the surrounding office blocks and attacked Verne on the rebound.

"Because, my traitorous worm, I was the one who first introduced them here twenty years ago."

"Twenty years ago?" replied Verne quizzically.

"Yes. Don't you remember the rebellion?"

Verne tried not to: after all, he'd fought in it and lost.

"These are very special external implants. When you hold them up to your head they interact with the signals in your brain and facilitate a connection to the Circuit's frequency. Very useful when you want to see what's happening on the other side of the firewall. There's only one side effect to them."

"What's that?"

"They don't work very well if you already have an implant in your brain. If you use them too much they have a habit of creating a state of permanent confusion. Wearing them constantly on a stupid headdress doesn't help reduce the madness in the least!" He laughed again. "Not that it made any difference to us."

Verne wondered how long it had taken before the King and his monks started to suffer the effects. Had their original rebellion against the Circo family been genuine, or had they already been poisoned by this servant of the West? Perhaps no one would ever know. Verne had held the leaders of the Realm accountable for driving the region into the dust, but he'd been wrong. They were merely puppets on the end of Alison's string. Verne felt another pang of regret that he'd done nothing to stop it. He'd traded in Jake's life for a prize offered by the very regime he hated, and by accepting it he was complicit in keeping them in power.

He was about to discover there were far worse consequences to his actions.

Major Holst opened his cloud feed to report back on his progress. A blank, dark screen filled the space now occupied by a flat concrete slab.

Is it done...

"Not exactly, Principal Conductor."

Explain...

"Dinah has been destroyed," he said dogmatically,

having witnessed tons of glass and dust being cleared away without a single recognisable piece of server still intact. "That much is for sure."

And the virus…

"Inconclusive."

Lying to a universally intelligent being was never clever. After the briefest of pauses the green cursor throbbed angrily on-screen and the text spewed over it.

Time to dethrone the King…

"Understood. And then?"

Burn them…burn all of them…

Jake watched most of the destruction of Abseron from a relatively safe distance, although having witnessed the bone-chilling havoc he wished he'd been even further away. Kansas would have done it. The demonstration of the drone's firepower was even more frightening considering his own escape had been less than certain only minutes before it began. The moment Dinah realised what was happening she'd insisted he leave immediately. Dinah had served subscribers for years as their 'Help' function, so it was in her nature to act like she had. It pained him to think that her virtual corpse was at the bottom of the fire and smoke. There was so much he still wanted to ask her.

Dinah's shadow would live on inside people's implants, a simple operating system without character, but Aaron's memories were lost forever.

Jake meticulously followed the route she'd identified for him through the back of the pyramid. It was the shortest route she could find via several air ducts, some fire escapes and finally by jumping through a first-floor window. He hit the ground just moments before the first rocket struck the glass and blew tiny shards out into the sky. Not that he'd stopped to watch. The explosive power of just one rocket was enough to send him sprinting for cover as fast as his legs would carry him.

He'd watched the rest of the war drones' performance from the safety of a disused office block nearby. When the firing eventually stopped he knelt down and rested his arms and head forlornly on the splintered, wooden windowsill to watch the smoke and dust drift over the Baku skyline.

Dinah's revelations weighed heavily on his soul. There was much more he wanted to learn from their meeting, and yet part of him wished it had never happened at all. Some things in life cannot be unheard. He was the bomb: the fuel and the fuse, as she'd put it. What sort of life lay ahead for him now? The knowledge of it would always be there, whether he armed that bomb or not. It was no wonder Alison referred to him as the virus. It was true. He was invisible, deadly and difficult to predict.

Alison also knew one other fact about viruses. They were usually symbiotic life forms and destroying their host was equivalent to suicide. Was that Jake's fate? If he pulled the trigger would he kill the host and end humanity as they knew it? Difficult to know for sure, but it certainly wasn't something he wanted to misjudge: he wouldn't get a second chance.

The existential time bomb would tick ominously inside him, and the longer he avoided it, the more likely the Circuit were to catch up with him. The attack on Abseron proved they were getting closer. They'd planned it almost to perfection. If they destroyed Dinah and Jake in one fell swoop it wiped out all evidence of what Jake carried. But how had they figured it out? Where had he gone wrong? They couldn't access his cloud, so the error couldn't be in there. He'd not categorically revealed himself to the King at their meeting so it wasn't then either. The only other people he'd interacted with for any length of time since he'd crossed the firewall were Krakoff and Verne, and one of them didn't even remember yesterday.

Jake's spirit crumbled.

We all have blind spots.

His was his faith in the Spectrum.

Everyone he'd met outside of the Circuit's claustrophobia shared a genuine sense of desire to live differently. Free from greed, repression, intolerance and envy. Everyone he'd met at Sam's dome demonstrated it. In Boston members of the Spectrum had unselfishly put their lives on the line to protect him. Sam, Alfonso and Dr Drew all had equal views and sensibilities when it came to the future and their part in it. But none of this proved the Spectrum weren't susceptible to temptation. Not all priests were pure, not all carers kind, not all children innocent. It was easy to be blind in the face of conventional wisdom. But the truth was even simpler. Subscriber or non-subscriber, all humans were capable of corruption if you knew what button to press.

Which one had they pressed to get Verne?

He said he had 'too much to lose' but was he talking about what he already had or what he might gain? It didn't really matter. It was obvious Verne had betrayed him and his name had to be added to the list of people hunting him that included almost everyone in the East and West.

In the back of his mind, Jake had always visualised an end point to his journey. Once he passed on what he knew, others would pick up the struggle and at that point he'd be free to go back home. Thoughts of Christie entered his mind once more. There was no reason to stay here now. It was time to go back and save their relationship.

The firing resumed outside his window more fiercely

than it had done against the glass walls of Abseron. What did they have left to destroy? thought Jake. He watched the scene outside the window in utter disbelief. The skies above Baku were already swarming with war drones, but hundreds more approached the city from the horizon, their red eyes flashing menacingly in the darkness. They'd been positioned over every server farm in case he'd entered the wrong one in his search for Dinah, but they weren't needed for that anymore. Dinah was gone which meant the King no longer had the means to manipulate subscribers' memories. In the morning, yesterday would be just as unsavoury as today and the pattern would continue forever. Eventually something would break. Eventually someone would make a stand.

If anyone survived.

The war drones were waging war against the city. They were no longer aiming at servers, they were aiming at people. Alison's paranoia that the East would rise had boiled over and the Principal Conductor had decided to remove it once and for all, however unlikely the threat might be. There was only one defence against the slaughter.

Him.

Billions would die if he didn't act. He was still needed here but his attention was on Christie and home. If the only answer to stopping the genocide was to destroy the Memory Cloud, then he had to see Christie before he detonated the bomb and potentially lost her forever.

"I need to find a quick way home," he muttered to himself.

Then the answer presented itself.

TWENTY-THREE

STEGANOGRAPHS AND SPAM

The assault boat sped through the waves, occasionally lifting out of the water and crashing back down again with a splash. Two dozen geriatric Archivists in full body armour clung to the rudimentary benches that ran along both sides. Spray rained down on their wrinkled faces and drenched their stubbly chins. Only one of them didn't have an excitable grin plastered on their face. Private Sprout was quietly praying to some unspecified deity to protect him against unknown threats. Probably all of them had something to do with cancer.

Major Dawes stood erect and defiant in the centre of his troops, shaking his arms furiously in the air like a man possessed. Today all his wildest dreams were being realised at once. He cackled throughout the high-speed journey, occasionally offering a ludicrous threat of violence against the sea itself. Not even Mother Nature would impede him today. This was his moment. The one he'd waited for his whole career. The day he, Major Dawes, would pass into legend. The island grew in size on the horizon and he barked his final instructions to his squadron, never once removing his focus from the land fast approaching on the boat's bow.

"This is it, men!" he screamed hysterically.

Neither of the two women in the company felt in the slightest bit offended because they thought they were more masculine than most of the actual men in the team, and were so used to his misogyny it went over their heads as swiftly as the wind.

"They will not slip through my fingers this time. Today will go down in history as the day Major Luther Dawes caught the Spectrum. Today the Archivists will rebuild their damaged reputation and strike fear once more into the hearts of anyone willing to choose a reckless path of disloyalty. Today the Spectrum's reign of terror will crumble. We fight for all those who have fallen. We fight for Private Yazidi!"

Most of his briefing was lost to the howling wind and the crash of the waves, but those closest offered a muffled 'Yazidi' in reverence.

"Our mission is to disarm and capture everyone on the island except Tyra Montana. If any of the dissidents refuses to comply then you have my permission to shoot them. We will not miss. We are no longer blind. Arm yourselves."

The team already had their hands resting on some form of lethal implement. Rifles, automatic machine guns, speccy swords, and a crossbow. Private Sprout carried a wooden club with nails sticking out of the end because all of the alternatives were apparently carcinogenic. Dawes's command to 'arm themselves' had nothing to do with these vicious objects. Their real advantage over the enemy was in their heads. One by one they accessed their new cloud portals and two dozen Archivists spread out across the Memory Cloud. They'd see every move subscribers made before they even considered it, but more importantly the Archivist's virtual incognito gave them immunity to speccy tactics. They could no longer block their signals and shift their forms.

"Two minutes," announced Dawes.

"Sir," said Needham with his arm high in the air, but struggling to keep it there because it was being buffeted back towards him by the wind.

"What is it, Private?"

"Mine's not working."

A few of the others nodded to reiterate Needham's claim.

"Rubbish. These new implants can take us anywhere. You're just not doing it right. You have to move through the network from connection to connection, you can't just pick someone at random and decide to go straight there without working hard for it."

"I know how they work, sir, we've been wearing them for weeks, it's just they're not working now."

"This is why you'll never be a Major, Needham."

"Respectfully, sir, you try."

"Whose cloud are you trying to scout?"

"Christie Tucci's."

"Stand back," he said confidently.

There are many schools of thought when it comes to the art of leadership. Some advocate a situational approach. This involves the leader considering the subordinate's current ability and level of commitment in relation to a particular task and flexing their style to suit the individual at that moment. Others believe passionately that all subordinates are ultimately good-for-nothing layabouts who desire nothing more than to be barked at remorsefully until they submit and act on instructions. Then there are those who feel that workers should be allowed to express themselves freely and respond best to an independent style of leadership. All of these models have their supporters and detractors but none can be truly dismissed as wholly wrong. Unfortunately for Needham, Dawes hadn't attended any of these schools. He had a different model entirely.

He called it 'medership'.

An instinctive and brutally simple style of leadership.

If his team couldn't do the things he could it was simply because they weren't him. In such conditions guidance was easy and consistent. 'Boys, sit back, watch me, bask in the dazzle of my brilliance and then wallow in a pool of your own self-loathing in the knowledge that however hard you try, you'll never be me.' In his view leadership wasn't something you could teach. When it came to 'medership' he was right. It would be easier to train a slug to pole-vault than it was to teach a narcissist anything. Occasionally this approach did have its downsides. You looked even more of a tit when in fact you couldn't do it. Not that a narcissist ever admitted it.

"Watch and learn," announced Dawes overconfidently.

He engaged his cloud feed and within a number of virtual skips reached the aforementioned target account. Unlike the clouds he passed through on his way through, this one did feel different. Normally, when someone was in possession of special implants they entered the background of the person's virtual world. The imposter then effectively became part of the scenery of whatever the host was viewing. After that they formed an intrinsic part of their Memory Cloud, a small file housed in the server that granted them authority to visit any past moment the host had ever stored.

Not so with Christie Tucci's cloud.

It was blank. Was the subject asleep? No, sleep wasn't

empty, it was like a scene from the film *Yellow Submarine* by The Beatles. Insanely colourful backdrops with strange, mutated creatures and twisted plots fired from their subconscious to both scare and amuse. None of that here. Dawes went on a virtual stroll into the past in search of answers. It wouldn't look good if he returned to the boat without a suitable excuse for why he'd failed. He went back to yesterday's memories and there was nothing to see there either. Then, quite unexpectedly, a pair of hysterical screams pierced the nothingness. The threatening voices grew louder and closed in on him before an intense energy struck him like a runaway tram. The connection was severed as Dawes was catapulted at breakneck speed through the network. As he tumbled chaotically, his senses scrambled: he was convinced he heard two distant voices singing the chorus of 'Sisters Are Doin' It for Themselves'.

Dawes was knocked off his feet and landed with a thump on the now saturated deck.

"See," replied Needham, walking a difficult line between delight and respect.

"Get Brother Job!"

A notification alert flashed in Christie's feed. It wasn't uncommon. On an average day most subscribers received thousands, and unless you caught sight of them immediately or recognised who they were from most were ignored until you could be bothered to trawl through and delete them. This one certainly didn't get her attention. It was from an anonymous sender and would likely end up in her 'junk' folder never to see the light of day again alongside offers of cheap liposuction, apparent lottery jackpots and urgent messages from rich but helpless Nigerian princes.

Fortunately for Christie she wasn't the only one who received it.

"We need to leave!" demanded Jezebel, popping up from a long period of inactivity.

"Leave?"

"Yes. Right now."

"Why?"

"They're coming for you."

"Who are?"

"The Archivists."

"What would they want with me? I'm not a speccy."

"No, but you're aiding speccies."

"Technically they're aiding me," Christie argued quite correctly.

"Look, I'm a guide, right? I'm actually doing my bloody job for once," she replied, annoyed that she was being forced to comply quite against her natural instincts. "Give me a break!"

"I'm tired of games, Jezebel. I've got enough on my mind already. Solomon, can you knock some sense into her please?"

"He's gone."

"Great, I'm halfway there."

"No, you don't understand, he's turned," she replied, making a grimace that suggested Solomon had morphed into a bottle of gone-off milk.

"Turned?"

"Memory Hunter," replied Jezebel, holding her nose.

"Why did he do that?"

"Because brothers are arseholes…oh, and they've set a trap to catch Jake."

"Good. They can have him," huffed Christie.

"No, not that one, the real one."

"No one knows where he is, so why would they come after me? It makes no sense."

"Because Jake knows where you are," replied Jezebel hysterically, grabbing Christie by the foot and attempting to haul her across the grass.

"Stop it."

"We have to go!"

"How do you know about Jake?"

"Dinah has a hunch."

"Who the hell is Dinah?"

"I'll explain later but according to my calculations you have precisely one minute to decide whether to stay or go."

Christie was exhausted by the emotional confusion of the last few days. She was tired of being trapped on an island and disliked two-thirds of its inhabitants. The idea of going back to her father's home filled her with terror, and the only thing she truly wanted in the world remained resolutely elusive. Now someone else was promising a false dawn. It was always the hope that killed you. Maybe she needed a period on her own. It would do her some good, and it was certainly better than being interrogated by a bunch of Archivists.

"Ok," said Christie reluctantly. "I'll go get Paddy."

"There's no time for that."

"But…"

"Quickly, we have to get to the boat before someone else does."

The only way off the island, at least as far as she knew, was on the speedboat. It was moored where they'd left it two nights ago, bobbing gently in the water next to the shallow cliff edge on the north side of the island. Hurried by Jezebel, she scrambled down the slippery stones and jumped on-board. In the distance a dark, menacing craft was speeding

towards the other end of the island. If she left before they had
time to disembark she'd have enough time to slip away unde-
tected. The Archivists rushed to be first off the boat and as
soon as they hit land they spread out across the small island in
search of the enemy. Christie turned to power up the motor
but she'd been so preoccupied with the new arrivals she'd
failed to notice that the blades were already whirling gently in
the water. Sitting patiently at the back was Fake Jake.

"Shit, not you," sighed Christie. "I'd rather take Tyra
with me."

"No time to argue!" screamed Jezebel. "Go!"

Fake Jake released the mooring rope and they chugged
away as inconspicuously as they could. The boat drifted
into the darkness, just the beam of the lighthouse to guide
them. Once its bulb was little more than a speck in the
distance, Christie demanded to know why he'd followed
her.

"I got a message," said Fake Jake.

"So?!"

"It was kind of strange."

"Why?"

"Well, it was from…me," he replied mysteriously.

"You sent yourself a message so that you could justify
running away with me?"

"No!" he implored innocently.

"You just won't take no for an answer, will you? I'd love
to know how you managed to convince Jezebel to help you,
or is this your twisted way of making me comply with the
rules?"

"Neither."

"I didn't know he'd be here," argued Jezebel.
"Although it's probably a good thing. We'll need both of
them."

"Both of them! I'm not engaging in a ménage à trois

with people who claim to be my boyfriend. I just want one whole Jake!"

"That's the spirit," said Jezebel. "I knew you were a freedom fighter!"

"I think the message I received was from the other one," said Fake Jake. "I'm surprised you didn't get one."

"When did it arrive?"

"About twenty minutes ago."

Christie opened her cloud interface and scanned the notifications folder. There were literally thousands of unanswered messages, chat boxes and spam. She scanned through the recent arrivals and found one with no name. Even spam messages tended to have an alias attached to them. It was hard to con someone if you didn't leave a forwarding address. She opened the anonymous message quite against her normal intuition. A video launched, masking her view of the gentle, dark sea.

It started with a scene of the yellow, cloud-stained skies of the Earth from the intense void of space, thousands of miles above them. Almost immediately the camera zoomed in, piercing the atmosphere and rushing headlong towards the United States, the East Coast and finally Boston. The camera angle changed course and they passed over the notorious Boston Source and northwards towards home. Towns, fields, forests and marshes flashed by until the camera slowed. It settled on a small, solitary hut she didn't recognise and inside on an old oak table was a curious object. A snow globe, but not like any Christie had seen before.

The ones she remembered fondly from her childhood mostly contained Christmas themes, but this one featured yellow snow and a beach. Not just any beach either. She zoomed in on the picture, going through the glass and into the globe. This was her beach. New Hampton Falls in all its glorious detail. The sea lapped the sand and the boats rocked melodically on the surf. On the sand near the water a figure sat with his back to them. She zoomed in further still, stretching the limits of the video's resolution. The man's blond hair jittered in the breeze but that was all she could see of his face.

Unusually the sun was free of the sulphur clouds and the light reflected off something metallic on the man's opened hand. Curiously she focused on it. It was the underside of a wristwatch and engraved in the centre it read: 'Be Brave'.

"It's him," said Christie ecstatically. "And he's on our beach."

"I know," said Fake Jake in agreement, much less excited about the prospect and confused as to why this man had his watch. "I got one, too."

It was true that they'd both received messages, but not exactly the same one. Fake Jake's video had a far more threatening feel to it. It contained several detailed descriptions of his untimely death played out symbolically by torturing vegetables with his name scrawled on them. It was enough to send him into retreat, or at the very least avoid greengrocers in future, but that hadn't been the sender's intention. He wanted Fake Jake to be there. Both of them wanted Christie and they both believed in their justifiable right to be her boyfriend. Christie hadn't seen it that way when it came to him. No matter how much he'd proved who he was, she shunned his advances. Now this imposter with Jake's face was going to try to come between them. Would she act likewise towards him? He hoped so but if she didn't he would be there to make life difficult. All he had to do in the meantime was find a way of protecting his nether regions in case things got nasty.

"He used a steganograph," said Christie with pride.

"Yes."

"What was on your message?"

"The same," he lied. "It appears he wants both of us there."

Disappointment always felt more painful when expectations were high and today his had been practically stratospheric. This was going to be his zenith. The pinnacle of a thirty-year career. Reward for his dedicated service and vindication against the haters, doubters and cynics with their vicious taunts. He'd pictured victory in his mind. A line of shocked speccies cowering on their knees, pleading for mercy and eager to renounce their way of life. After that came the medals, the messages of congratulation from Alison, grovelling plaudits from fellow senior officers, maybe even the odd chat show appearance or brand endorsement.

None of the pictures he'd imagined in his head looked remotely like this. One grumpy old-age pensioner, who was as much a speccy as Dawes was, and a sullen, teenage goth who didn't really count as a capture because she was on their side.

The Archivists tore the island apart.

It took precisely nine minutes and they did it twice.

No speccies. Not one.

How was that possible? They had everything covered. They had new tech that stopped the enemy slipping past them. They had Job who was an official Memory Hunter. They had an insider on the island passing them intelligence, and yet none of it made a blind bit of difference. Dawes's instability burst and he fired a volley of bullets into the brickwork. Great chunks of masonry and puffs of red brick dust were forced to abandon their posts. Gay Head Lighthouse had stood for over two hundred years and had survived the trauma of being moved along the clifftop. It had successfully weathered every great storm to hit the East Coast, and yet it suffered most of its damage in the last two minutes.

"Torture him mercilessly!" shouted Dawes, pointing at Paddy who was just as surprised to discover he was one of only two people left on the island.

"Do your worst," replied Paddy stoically. "I survived the war!"

"No you didn't!"

Paddy was born at the very end of the twentieth century and the only wars he'd lived through were ones against 'drugs', 'terror' and 'poverty'. Not that any of these were real wars. You can't attack an idea, fight a concept or claim victory over an unquantifiable notion. You can try of course, but it would be just as easy to declare war on 'ambition' or 'beards'. It doesn't matter what you do, they're still going to be there afterwards however many medals you give out or billions of credits you spend trying to fight them. Then again it is easier to argue for increased military spending if you have an enemy in your sights. Ah…that's why.

"Where are they?" spat Dawes.

"I'd like the answer to that question myself," replied Paddy.

"Check his cloud," said Dawes to Needham.

"We tried but he's not wearing one at the moment. The last entry was this morning and involved a long-winded conversation with a blind man from Wisconsin about the quality of talcum powder."

"I told him it was a wrong number but he wouldn't

listen," said Paddy. "Plus, I'm right: talcum powder just isn't the same these days."

"Where's the girl?!" shouted Dawes at the top of his voice.

"Leave her out of it, she's just a child," said Paddy showing genuine concern for the first time since two dozen elderly soldiers stormed their camp and kicked over his bonfire.

"Ah," said Dawes malevolently. "That's where you're wrong, old man. She's working for us."

"Old man! I bet you're not much younger than me. What are you, sixty-nine?"

Tyra strolled up from one of the hidden coves. She was arguing profusely with someone that Paddy couldn't see, but the Archivists knew only too well who it was.

"It's not my fault," remonstrated Tyra. "They were all here a minute ago. You scared them off with all the screaming and shouting. I thought they were meant to be an elite force. Or was it indiscreet? I might have misheard you!"

"You told them, didn't you?" argued Job.

"No. If I had, why would I leave him here?" she said, pointing at her grandfather.

"Tyra, what have you done?" asked Paddy solemnly.

"Oh don't you start. I've got enough nagging from this idiot."

"You're not going to let her speak to you like that, are you?" said Solomon.

"Oh you can shut up, too," cursed Job. "Day one of training, Solomon, requires ears only, remember that."

"Your only task was to keep them here," said Dawes. "I knew relying on a girl was a mistake."

"How was I supposed to know that they were going to leave? There aren't many places here you can run to."

"It looks like two of them left in a boat," said one of the privates, holding a pair of binoculars and out of breath from the short run he'd made from the other side of the island.

"What about the two speccies? Where are they?"

Paddy and Tyra both shrugged. Neither of them had the faintest idea how Alfonso and Theo had managed to hide or escape in the few hours since anyone last saw them.

"You were supposed to be tracking them virtually so why didn't you see them leaving?" said Tyra to further deflect the failure away from her. "Hmm, tell me that!"

"She blocked me," huffed Job despondently.

"Me, too," said Dawes, his anger still bubbling through his limbs and making his trigger finger wobble.

"Who did?" asked Tyra.

"Dinah," they answered in unison.

"Can someone please explain what in the name of Christ is going on!?" shouted Paddy.

While Dawes, Tyra, Solomon and Job continued to point the finger of blame, Needham, the only mildly sensible person on duty, took it upon himself to answer the question. He explained their plan to capture the speccies, hold Paddy's group hostage and draw Jake in.

"But what's Tyra got to do with any of it?"

"I believe your granddaughter has made a deal with Alison," replied Needham.

"Ungrateful cow. Family first!" he screamed.

"Someone gag him," demanded Dawes.

"Sorry about this," replied Needham, removing a roll of tape from his bag.

"I have asthma!"

"You said you had a plan," Dawes accused Tyra with a snarl.

"It's still in play. Be patient," replied Tyra who, despite

being the youngest amongst them, was definitely the most relaxed. "We know that Jake saw the kiss so it won't be long before he comes looking for Christie."

"Oh that's a relief," said Dawes sarcastically. "Or at least it would be if we knew where the girl was now! We were supposed to capture her."

"All is not lost," added Solomon, trying to raise their spirits. "I can track her."

"No you can't," said Job. "If you hadn't converted that might be true, but as long as Dinah is blocking access to her cloud there's nothing any of us can do. She's become too powerful."

"But she can't be everywhere, can she?" said Solomon.

"What do you mean?"

"Two of them left on the boat," added Solomon, doing his best to show potential on his first day in a new job. "Can't we track his cloud?"

Job momentarily evaporated before returning a few seconds later. "Yes, we can. Right, new plan."

TWENTY-FOUR
A BIZARRE LOVE TRIANGLE

It took two days of sailing before they reached the shore near New Hampton Falls. Sailing had been their only realistic option. The speedboat didn't have the range for the journey, and travelling by land was impossible given the number of citizens still on the lookout for Fake Jake. Sailing also had other advantages. They'd sailed together for years and Jake's skills as a helmsmen were still very much on-board, even if significant parts of him weren't. There were a few difficult moments when Fake Jake fumbled awkwardly as his cognition and dexterity fundamentally disagreed with each other. It didn't really matter because Christie was perfectly capable of sailing the craft solo.

As charter vessels go, it wasn't bad either. Plenty of space, in decent condition and faster than many she and Jake had hired in the past. The more they sailed up the coast from Boston, the more the waters became familiar. They were so close to home now that Christie could have sailed blindfolded and still found the right berth. Today, though, the main marina wouldn't be suitable as it increased the chances they'd be spotted. Christie decided to drop anchor and moor the boat at sea. Then they'd swim the short distance to the beach. This plan was faultless except for one minor flaw.

Fake Jake couldn't swim.

That's not to say his brain didn't know 'how to swim', it's just that his arms and legs hadn't been fully briefed. A revelation that only became clear after he dived into the water and disappeared under the surface. Christie jumped in to rescue him, further eroding his fragile ego.

"Why didn't you say you couldn't swim?"

"Because," he said tentatively, "…I think I can."

"You don't have to show off for my benefit, you know. It doesn't impress me."

"I'm not!" pleaded Fake Jake. "I genuinely believe I can swim. Even though I almost drowned, I still do. It's really very confusing. My brain is mocking me. Even now it wants me to dive in again and prove it."

"Let's not do that."

"Can you teach me how to do it?"

"Not if you already know I can't. You'd just argue with me."

"True."

"Put this life jacket on," she said, throwing it at him, "and I'll drag you behind me."

"Oh great," he groaned. "Because that will look proper classy."

His original intention was to act cool, suave and macho when he reached the beach to meet the other Jake. He hoped that his display of masculinity would be enough for Jake to give up his interest in Christie, or at the very least sow a seed of doubt in his mind that executing his plans of mutilation might not be so easy to pull off. How he actually arrived at the beach was not remotely like he'd imagined it.

Christie swam like a champion mermaid, and he splashed around on the end of a leash in a bright yellow life jacket like a drowning shipwreck survivor. Every time his brain instructed his legs to kick to salvage just a modicum of pride, they completely misread the signal and just sabotaged each other. By the time he discovered the sandy seabed under his feet and could stand on his own terms, his whole body ached from resisting his commands. Rather than strike fear into his rival he looked like a laughing stock, a bedraggled mess with all the panache of a first-time waterskier.

A man watched them wade out of the sea and approach the shore. His blond hair was perfectly groomed, clothes immaculate, skin radiant, and his aura glowed like a fallen angel's. How could Fake Jake compete with that? His rival was perfect, every girl's dream. A little too perfect in Fake Jake's assessment. Christie immediately dropped the cord that had been his lifeline and sprinted across the wet sand to greet him.

"Jake!" she said, arms outstretched and primed to embrace him.

"No!" he said curtly, pulling away from her. "It's too early."

"Too early?"

"Yes."

"But I've missed you," said Christie, yearning to feel his firm, comforting embrace around her body for the first time in months.

"Sure you have!" he said sarcastically, unable to erase the memory of her with another man from his mind. "I saw you…with him."

"What? How?"

"You're not denying it, then?"

"I'm wondering why you would enter my cloud to spy on me?" accused Christie. "That's not the Jake I know."

"Don't turn this around on me. You cheated on me!"

"You married someone else," she responded quickly and quite accurately.

"That was the Circuit's choice."

"So was this," she replied.

"What?"

"He has your cloud and the guides confirm he's the man in my letter!"

This was the first confirmation of an act Jake had influenced many weeks ago. It was Jake who'd requested that Alison place his name in her letter in return for giving up his implants. It had rather confused the Principal Conductor and he couldn't be sure, until now, whether it had been actioned. What he hadn't foreseen was that Alison might mend his old implants and insert them into someone else. Perhaps it was just part of Alison's risk management plan, the only way to find out why it had been so important to him. It made this moment more complicated than he'd have liked.

Fake Jake finally made it up the beach to join the conversation. He puffed out his chest, brushed his hair with his hand and adopted a deep, assertive tone of voice. All of these rushed attempts to look more presentable were slightly ruined by a sizeable clump of seaweed that hung limply from one of his ears like a poorly chosen aquatic earring. "Is he bothering you, Christie?"

"You're both bothering me!" she cried in exasperation. "One of you looks like Jake and the other one behaves like him. I just want to know which one of you is him!"

"I am!" they both answered in tandem, moving their focus from Christie to each other and back again.

"You're a pair of bloody losers!"

"That's Sam," said Jake accusingly. "He stole my memories, then my identity, and now he's trying to steal you."

"I'm Jake!" Fake Jake continued to argue. He had no affinity to Sam, even though multiple people had insinuated that's who he really was. How can you believe you're someone else when everything in your conscious mind tells you otherwise?

Plan C reared up in Jake's mind. He took a step forward, fist clenched, teeth snarling and anger boiling in his veins. Then he stopped as he remembered this wasn't the time or the place for it. He'd designed a new exit for the imposter, plan AZ, and he had to be patient.

"Maybe it would be simpler if you just fancied girls," said Jezebel in Christie's ear.

"No it wouldn't. I just want my Jake back. Is that too much to ask?"

"Apparently it is, yes," replied her guide.

"Where have you been hiding out anyway?" she asked her guide. "I haven't heard anything from you in days."

"Dinah and I are taking it in turns to hold back the tide."

"What tide?"

"You're rather popular with the Memory Hunters right now. Maybe you should date one of them!"

"Why did you kiss him?" demanded Jake furiously, dragging Christie's attention back to the bizarre love triangle.

"You can't tell me what to do. I'm an independent woman who's free to do as she pleases," Christie argued. Even though she hadn't encouraged the kiss, no one was going to tell her what she could and couldn't do.

"Yes, I know, but I just don't understand why you'd want to."

"Because he knows you. He can remember every moment of our past. Imagine how confusing that is for me. When you want something desperately you become vulnerable. When he forced himself on me it caught me by surprise."

"Forced himself on you!" replied Jake, taking another step towards his enemy.

"She said it would work," said Fake Jake, offering his defence while cowering backwards.

"Who did?" demanded Christie.

"Tyra."

"Who's she?" asked Jake.

"Your sister of course."

"I have a sister?" he replied in surprise. "That's cool."

"You won't say that when you meet her," added Fake Jake. "She's a total bitch."

"I'm sure she's not."

"She'll be thrilled you don't remember her," added Christie. "She thinks everyone ignores her and you're responsible for ripping her life apart."

"What did I do?"

"I know, right!" agreed Fake Jake. "Tyra has always been my parents' favourite. In their eyes she can do no wrong and I can do no right."

"What rubbish," refuted Christie. "Whenever I was around, Deborah and Kyle were always fair with both of you."

Jake found it difficult to keep up. He knew very little about his life or Christie's. He was only even here because he'd been told he was madly in love with her, yet on first impressions she seemed a little terse and hard to get on with. Had he really gone to all the effort getting here only to find they had almost nothing in common? If anything his emotions towards Sam were deeper and stronger than how he felt about her right now. It wasn't just about the kiss either. It was about everything Sam had done in recent months to disrupt his life. He would pay for his sabotage sooner than he realised.

"Why did Tyra tell you to come on strong with me?" asked Christie, intrigued by the development and hearing about it for the first time.

"She said that's what girls liked."

"Then she's a slut! When did I ever like that?"

"Never," replied Fake Jake sheepishly.

Jake made a mental note for future reference.

"So what do we do now?" asked Christie.

"Make them fight," offered Jezebel. "Winner takes all. I'll have ten credits on the pretty boy."

"I think it might be best if you and I had some time to ourselves," suggested Jake.

"Well, that's not happening," replied Fake Jake.

"You've had your chance. It's my turn now."

"Listen to you both. I'm not a prize to be argued over."

"I'm not leaving and that's the end of it," Fake Jake replied sternly.

"I don't think you're going to have a lot of choice in the matter," replied Jake, whose timing was perfect.

Behind him a crowd of people emerged over the top of the dunes down the whole length of the beach. Like a line of soldiers called to war, they swept over it, steadily increasing their pace. Men in uniforms, old women gripping Zimmer frames, teenagers wielding golf clubs, housewives with rolling pins, and blokes clutching fishing rods barged each other out of the way as they surged at them from both ends of the beach. There were thousands of them and they were in a race with only one finishing line. Him.

"SHIT!"

"I understand you're the most wanted man on either side of the firewall," said Jake. "So I made a few calls and hinted that you might be here, right about now."

"You bastard. That's not fair."

"Neither is stealing someone's girlfriend."

"I'm no one's girlfriend anymore," chuntered Christie, reacting to what he'd done.

"You'd better start running or swimming if you want to escape," advised Jake. "You didn't look too hot at the latter so I'd highly recommend the former. I wouldn't bother stretching or doing a warm-up."

The crazed screams of the possessed throng closed in. Fake Jake was surrounded. He searched for a gap in the oncoming crowd and sprinted as hard as his dripping wet legs would carry him. Inevitably a number of the hunters were faster than he was. A spectacular flying tackle initially knocked him over before the gleeful champion was wrestled away from his prize by a swarm of excitable competitors all doing their best to place a bodypart on him to argue their case when the final reward was dished out. Fake Jake was passed overhead like a crowd surfer and they tore at his clothes like a pack of hungry lions fighting over the carcass of a bison. Jake felt a little guilty. He didn't want to harm Sam, he just needed to keep him out of the way.

A loud siren split the air and the crowd were momentarily distracted. At the far end of the beach an army landing craft had just beached itself in the shallows and two dozen soldiers were deployed to control the crowd. An unusual sense of serenity infected the mob. They froze in their positions as they forgot their greed and lust for power. They immediately cleared to one side as if they'd been commanded to do so by an invisible menace. Jake watched as a stocky, cigar-smoking brute with a sword that spun and

flashed marched into the circle and confronted the prisoner. To Jake's relief the man didn't use it on Sam. Instead
he was led back to the boat for interrogation.

"That was unbelievably cruel," said Christie in disgust.

"He deserved it."

"He's you, you idiot. You've just committed the greatest
act of self-harm in the history of the Circuit."

Jake didn't flinch. Whatever happened to Sam it
wouldn't affect the memories he carried. Even if Jake
decided to break the Memory Cloud that wouldn't change:
it just meant no implants could connect to them. Sam
would return to his own, another upside to stick in the
'pros' column when deciding about his quandary.

"I think we should get out of here in case he tells them
about us," announced Jake.

"They don't want me, they want you."

"Even more reason for it, then," he replied selfishly.

They jogged up the dunes and hid amongst the tufts of
wispy grass in a depressed hollow. The dunes were like a
rabbit warren but it would only keep them covered for a
short period. If things went to plan they'd have to find a
more permanent escape route.

"You've changed," said Christie, reflecting on his
behaviour. "The Jake I knew stood up for people; he
wouldn't have turned someone in to the Circuit like that."

"Everyone changes."

"But not always for the better."

"And sometimes for the greater good."

There was an awkward minute or so of silence as they
contemplated what to say to each other. Jake knew almost
nothing about her, and it was clear his demeanour made
her deeply uncomfortable. And yet he had travelled
halfway across the world to be with her while great loss was

being suffered elsewhere. Had he made the wrong choice? Were his actions really benefiting the greater good?

"I don't really know you anymore," said Jake calmly. "I gave up my memories on the false belief that I could make a difference. Make a change that would improve people's lives and release us from the shadow of the system. But I've discovered that the truth about the Circuit is even more terrifying. I sacrificed my cloud to fix it, but as a result, I lost you. They told me we were meant for each other, but I have nothing to reinforce it. Any belief in it has gone and I needed to come here before you forgot it, too."

"I'll never forget who you were," she said nostalgically.

"You might."

When Jake spoke Christie noticed he was more reflective and less spontaneous than he once was, almost as if there was a brief delay between his thoughts and words. His presence felt strangely out of place in the scenery around them like he didn't really belong, a lost soul in a life eroding before her eyes.

"The West has waged war on the East and the only way to stop them is to break the Memory Cloud."

"No one can break the cloud."

"I can."

"How?"

"The solution was in my flashback all along. It exists only in me now and only I can trigger it."

"But destroying the cloud would create global pandemonium."

"Yes, but if I don't it'll trigger the biggest genocide the world has ever seen. Billions and billions of lives. Either the virtual world dies or half the real one does."

"Jesus. What are you going to do?"

"I don't know. It's an impossible choice."

"But why did you come all this way to tell me?" asked Christie.

He held up his hand and Christie's necklace dangled from his grasp. It looked different from how she remembered it. It sparkled unnaturally and didn't swing back and forward the way it should, stuttering irregularly as it passed through the air. She reached out to take it, but he quickly removed it from her grasp.

"Not yet. I'll keep it safe until the time is right."

She looked disappointed and found that her mood towards him was softening. "You came all the way here because of that?"

"It's all I really have left. I knew it meant something."

"What does it mean to you?" she asked.

"I guess it represents my love, even if it isn't clear in my head anymore."

"It will be when we get your memories back."

"There's no chance of that now. If the cloud fails the next time we meet we might both be strangers to each other."

"But everyone who falls in love always starts out as a stranger," she said. "It was that way for us."

"I don't remember."

Christie recounted the story of their first meeting. How she'd watched him from the side of the hall with intrigue. There was something in his face that she hadn't seen before. Something alluring but contorted. There was great mystery in him, even if he didn't perceive it himself. All the girls in her group had trolled him for how he looked and the way he acted. But his lack of conformity made her even more determined to disrupt the social playbook. She explained how an indescribable energy propelled her forward and forced her to act as if the moment was a crucial waypoint in human evolution.

"Do you believe in love at first sight?" asked Jake.

"No," replied Christie plainly. "But I believe in connection at first sight. We both felt it that night at the disco, irrespective of who made the first move. It's the basis on which love can grow, but I think love is more complicated and dissects every aspect of a relationship. Physical, emotional, spiritual, psychological, understanding each other's values and through their shared history."

"Then I've travelled across the world on a whim," replied Jake despondently.

"No, you came here on faith. I hope I'm as brave as you were if it happens to me."

"I'm not sure I have the strength to do it," said Jake. "Destroying the Memory Cloud will plunge the world into the dark and the impact might cause more destruction than the war in the East. It's just too much pressure on one man's shoulders."

"Do you like the Circuit?" asked Christie dispassionately.

"No."

"Why not?"

"Because it was built on false foundations. Because it has blinded people from the truth. Because it is an anaesthetic against self-expression and free speech."

"And what will happen if it is allowed to continue?"

"Who knows how far they will go. I doubt it will get any better. People will never really have choice."

"But for the first time in your life you do. Until now everything has been chosen for you. Now you have that responsibility. It's a metaphor for the system itself, isn't it? If you don't act, then the Circuit will never support freedom of choice. If you choose to act, then no decision will ever be taken by a third party ever again."

"I'm not sure people are ready for it and if I choose for

myself I'm forcing that choice on others. I'd be no better than the Circuit."

Christie had to agree with him. It was an impossible decision. Neither outcome was desirable and yet there appeared to be no third way. What did it mean for her? What would life be like without the Memory Cloud? She'd lose the part of her past that she'd always despised. All the frightening moments spent with her erratic father that defined who she was would be gone forever. The only part of history she clung to was the comfort blanket of Jake's support and kindness, but that would be different in the future whether the cloud was off or not. Christie had always looked to the future rather than the past. The past only defined the future if you allowed it to. But if you shook off the emotional shackles the future was a blank page that only you could write on. Maybe it was time to let go of memories and start again. As she tried to dismiss the relevance of her past, something from it forced her to think again.

A message notification from Tyra pinged in her cloud feed. She opened and read it immediately.

"They have Paddy," she said solemnly.

"Who do?"

"The Archivists. Tyra knows you're here with me. She says the Memory Hunters tracked Fake Jake's feed and saw you. It looks like Tyra has been trying to entrap you all along."

Jake's demeanour remained unflappably calm. He wasn't in the slightest bit concerned because he knew they would try something to stop him.

"The kiss, the Archivists, the Memory Hunters it looks like she was behind all of it," added Christie.

"What do they want?" asked Jake.

"You. Tyra says they'll release Paddy and your parents if you give yourself in at the Boston Source."

"We'd better get a move on, then," he said buoyantly.

"No, you can't! That's exactly what they want you to do. They'll kill you."

"Not today, they won't."

"Why are you being so blasé about it? I won't let them harm you."

"I know you won't. Don't worry. You're going to find out that this is not my fight anymore. It's Tyra's."

TWENTY-FIVE

SIBLING RIVALRY

M annie Draxler longed to return to Vienna. Back to his wife, his friends, his proper job and his family. He missed the intellectual vibe of the cosy coffee shops with their artisan-baked pastries and fake whiskey lattes. He missed the snow-covered streets and the bitter chill that whistled around the historic buildings. He yearned to sit in his favourite armchair with a virtual copy of a literary classic projected on the wall while he slowly drifted off to sleep with his cat, Ludwig, dozing on his lap. Most of all he craved company.

Business trips came with the territory, but they weren't normally like this. In his line of work there was always a factory visit, research project or funding meeting in the diary, but rarely did they take more than a few days. He and his wife Hannah had learnt to live with his constant absence, and on reflection it made their relationship stronger. They had time for their independence but not long enough for either of them to become bored or distant. They say absence makes the heart grow fonder, but

Mannie was learning that sustained absenteeism made it swell with doubt, jealously and paranoia.

Of all his business trips down the years this was only the second time he'd been summoned to the head office and both those occasions were recent. They'd insisted his visit would be short, no more than a week, much like the first one had. That was a month ago although he'd stopped counting the days lately because it just made him more depressed. After completing the tasks Alison had set for him, he'd anticipated they'd book him onto the first available Hyperloop.

But that was weeks ago.

He wouldn't have minded staying longer if they'd given him some interesting jobs to keep his mind busy. When work was a passion, as it was for Mannie, it distracted you from other worries. When you had nothing to occupy yourself, those just multiplied. Since replicating the speccy implants the only thing to distract him was a less than ideal workshop woefully lacking in the right tools and very few materials. He'd toyed around with some new ideas but never really hit the critical mass of motivation to see them through. How was he supposed to invent something useful when all he had was an old box of Lego bricks, a cupboard full of batteries, none of which were ever the right size, and enough sticky back plastic to redecorate the Source? If he'd been a member of the classic TV programme *The A-Team* he'd have made a rocket launcher, tank and amphibious landing craft out of them, but sadly he wasn't and he believed in something called science.

In the last few days he'd even offered his services as a handyman in case any odd jobs needed attending to, but the drones weren't having any of it. It was almost like they saw him as a threat to their own livelihoods. It wasn't that surprising. A foreigner with an unusual accent offering to work cheaply was always viewed by locals with suspicion. Even drones could demonstrate prejudice. In the absence of any purpose Mannie was left to stroll aimlessly around the Source. He knew all of it in fine detail. He'd visited the morgues, the drone sheds and the dormitories. If they ever decided to open the place up to the public, he'd be first in line for the job of tourist guide.

They say the first sign of madness is talking to yourself. This, as it happens, is false. The first sign is when you start talking to drones. Particularly if you give them first names. This further demonstrated the extent to which Mannie had become bored, borderline insane and totally disillusioned about his employer. Until now he'd always been a passionate supporter of the Circuit and what it stood for. Even Alison had confirmed his loyalty by indicating he had a ninety-nine and a half percent compliance score. He imagined that figure might have dipped somewhat as he sat in dark corners with only his own conscience for company, questioning everything he saw.

The primary question being: why were they keeping him here?

The answer arrived this morning when Bleepy Bob came to collect him. Utility drones were identical and it was incredibly tricky to tell them apart. Impossible in fact, but that hadn't stopped him trying. In his opinion there were subtle differences between them. According to Mannie, Bleepy Bob bleeped significantly more frequently than the others. It absolutely didn't. Then there was Flashy Freddie, who also didn't flash its lights more often, Whizzy Wilma, who flew at exactly the same speed as the rest, and Shiny Sally whose shell didn't reflect the light any differently from other drones. These indiscernible differences, only observable by him, could be further rejected by the fact that it actually wasn't Bleepy Bob who came to collect him. It was Nasty Nora, not that it cared less what anyone called it.

For the second time in Mannie's visit he found himself inside the black tower, more informed about what to expect but no less confused as to why he was there.

Draxler...

The tone of the text stream seemed more terse than it had done last time when Alison welcomed him on first-name terms. But then again he'd been talking to drones for the last week so in his head anything was possible.

"Yes."

Busy...

"Oh yes," he lied, as one tends to when their boss asks a loaded question.

Doing...

Naming drones, building Lego sets and sneakily trying to change light bulbs when the drones weren't looking didn't feel like a suitable reply.

"Inventing."

What...

If you place a creative mind with a deeply hidden inferiority complex, a desire for recognition and a distaste of their own company in a vacuum, then they're probably going to invent loads of things. Frightening things that would result in an immediate distance being placed between them and other members of society if the idea ever escaped from the brain and made it as far as the mouth. Mannie had thousands which he managed to suppress and substitute for a plausible lie.

"A microscopic implant," he offered effortlessly. "Nanotech."

Alison knew differently. He didn't need to say it out loud because the Principal Conductor knew the truth.

Are you sure...?

"Yes."

Not a sinister strategy for neutering superfluous folk…

"Obviously not."

Using a mutated superbug…and a disused mine shaft…

"No."

Shame…

"Can I go home now, please?" he said, visibly shaking as he asked the question.

Soon…

"Ok. But in the meantime could I clean some floors or something…anything really? I noticed some of the windows have bird poo on them…maybe that?"

No…I have something better for you to do…

"Oh lovely. What is it?" he asked eagerly.

Identify…the virus…

"Montana? You've caught him?"

Eighty-five percent probability…

"That's good."

Not good enough…

"Did giving Sam Goldberg Jake's implants help?"

Partly…

"What about the 'Proclamation of Distrust'?"

Partly…

"Then why are you so confident about it?" he said, realising he was being rather forceful. "If you don't mind me asking."

Tyra…

"Right, what do you need me for, then?"

I cannot see…the virus is beyond my line of sight…

"Can't she identify him?"

Risky…she is fallible…

"Is she?"

Yes…

"So you need me to verify that it's him?"

Correct…with your help…odds increase to ninety-nine and a half percent…

There it was again. Half a percent from perfection. What was holding him back? There was nothing he wouldn't do to maintain the Circuit's authority. Yet the half percent told a different story. Maybe it was just about proving his commitment, doing the things he was told to do.

"It would be my honour. When?"

They're coming…now…

"Where?"

West entrance…

Tyra stood guard over the West entrance of the Source like a mighty gladiator returned from battle. The smile on her face was so entrenched that not even sulphuric acid would have removed it. This was going to be her big moment. Proof that she was the mightiest of the Montana siblings. Not even the immense power of the Circuit could bring her brother to heel. They'd sent Memory Hunters in their thousands. They'd encouraged billions of subscribers to turn him in. They'd manipulated the cloud to disarm him and yet success came down to a hormonal teenager with anger management issues.

It was Tyra who knew Jake's weak spots.

Loyalty and jealousy.

Loyalty to Paddy who was now a hostage in the complex behind her. She didn't feel guilty about it. Her grandfather had kept her hostage over the last few months through his overuse of protocol twenty-two and his stupid old school rules. It was time to see how he liked it. He wouldn't be in there for long anyway. Once Jake was safely in the protection of the Circuit he'd be released along with her parents. Then they would learn the truth about the secrets Jake had been keeping from them. How he'd put them in great danger and how she had rescued them.

It would destroy her relationship with Paddy, she was certain of that. He'd never forgive her for betraying Jake, but what did she care? She'd be rich, vital and living in a big mansion in the LA hills. There was no escaping the special bond between Paddy and Jake. It was stronger than just genetics. Paddy was chained to old-fashioned values of times long since forgotten, and some of it had rubbed off on her brother. A sense of right and wrong, a belief in people's rights, a curiosity to discover the world for yourself, and most importantly a loyalty to family. That's why she was certain he'd come here. The fake kiss had drawn him in but Paddy's plight would bring him here. There was no question about it. This was Job's Plan B, but none of it would have been possible without her.

Without the kiss, Jake wouldn't be here at all. She pitied his blindness. She knew only too well that Christie would never willingly cheat on him, but paranoia can be a powerful tool in the wrong hands. Anyone was capable of misreading the signs and jumping to conclusions when it played on their greatest fear.

The skies above her darkened.

A giant clump of cumulus nimbus inched across the heavens in no particular hurry to reach its destination. The clouds looked angry tonight. They rumbled and flashed with fury. Butterscotch and amber colours clashed with greys in an atmospheric brawl that would last all night. A bolt of lightning split the air and crashed to the ground a few miles away. The bright flash illuminated a figure walking casually down the road towards the gate. A second strike from the heavens a moment later highlighted their progress and Tyra identified who it was.

It was Christie.

Tyra's jubilation suffered a minor stroke as she realised Christie was on her own. Surely Jake didn't doubt how far she was willing to go to prove her superiority over him. There was nothing she wouldn't do. Her very future hinged upon it.

"Where is he?" snapped Tyra.

"You don't need him to prove who you are."

"Yes I do, you idiot."

"This isn't about Jake anymore," said Christie. "It's about you."

"What do you know about it?" Tyra replied in a snide voice. "You don't know what it's like to have a brother."

"No, but family shouldn't define us. Look at my father. I could have let that affect me, but I chose not to. I'm me, and my past doesn't control my future. I do."

"Oh shut up, you stupid bitch!"

"You know I said we should rally all women to our cause," interrupted Jezebel. "United in feminism."

"Yes," whispered Christie.

"Not this one," she replied bluntly.

"I know he's here," added Tyra. "Job saw the two of you together. Jake may be out of the Circuit's sight but we know he's close. He won't allow them to hurt his beloved Paddy. I'll soon prove that he is weak and I am strong."

"You're not angry at Jake," said Christie. "Search your cloud, Tyra. Look deep. Find what's really bothering you."

Instinctively Tyra's cloud went into overdrive. A thousand scenes flashed one after another like a highlights reel placed on fast-forward. Every one a painful memory. The times when she'd been bullied or beaten intellectually. The times when he'd belittled her or made her feel inferior. The times she was ignored or failed to make her voice heard. The evidence was there and it only served to reinforce her motives. This was why she was angry and she had every right to be.

"Jake made my life a misery," she snapped. "Now it's his turn. If he isn't here in one minute I will summon the drones and you'll be joining the rest of the Montana family in the freezer. The only difference is I'll make sure you stay there permanently."

"It's not Jake you're angry with," repeated Christie unmoved by the threat. "You just wanted him to notice you. I know how that feels. It's all I ever wanted from my father. Just one solitary moment of clarity when he'd show me how he really felt about me, to tell me that he loved me and that I mattered. Even though he put me through all the years of hell, I know it wasn't his fault. He couldn't break free from behind the clouds, but I know he loved me. One day you'll see that Jake does, too."

"Thirty seconds," she replied coldly.

"I'm here," called a voice from behind her.

The West entrance was a huge gate of thick, metal bars that stretched ten feet in the air and was covered in sharp spikes to deter anyone from climbing over it. On the inside and outside of it a pair of drones hovered like floating doormen. A reflective silver road carved a path between the black, featureless buildings and metal pylons. But none of these security measures had made any difference. Jake stood casually on the etched parallel grooves that ran down the length of the path. Two further drones hovered on either side of him, apparently oblivious to the fact that he was there.

Tyra stared at him with contempt. It was typical of him to try to make a fool of her. Today it wouldn't stand.

"Think you're clever, do you?"

"Mildly."

"Well, you're not. You're an idiot who's been outwitted by his younger sister. How do you feel about that?"

"I feel pity," said Jake.

"For me! How dare you feel sorry for me. I don't regret any of this."

"It's not pity for you," replied Jake. "It's for me. I only learnt that I had a sister a few hours ago."

A look of thunder spread across her face and a furious battle cry erupted out of her lungs. She signalled for the drones to open the gates and allow her in. This was the final straw. He was so self-absorbed and arrogant he didn't even acknowledge her existence. No surprise really: he'd been doing it his whole life.

"Let me tell you something," she said, storming through the entrance. "I am better than you. I win. There is no way I can lose. You're trapped in the very heart of the Circuit because of me. Everyone has been hunting you, but I caught you. When I command it the drones will drag you away and Alison will punish you, all because of me. I've outwitted you, admit it!"

"Is that the only thing that matters to you?" he said calmly.

"Yes!"

"You just want to hear me say it?"

"Yes!"

"Ok, then. I admit it. You win."

"What?!" she said, a little disarmed.

In over a decade of squabbles, arguments and sibling point-scoring, Jake had never admitted defeat or error even once; although neither had she if she was being completely honest. The rules of the game didn't allow it. That's not how sibling rivalry worked. In the unwritten and illusional laws that governed and protected the rights of siblings to be mean to each other on a continual basis, there were strict do's and don'ts. These included, but weren't restricted to: do take every opportunity to destroy their self-confidence; do highlight faults immediately to a responsible adult; don't under any circumstance show sympathy towards the other unless you're playing a long game with clearly defined personal benefits; don't EVER agree, praise, encourage or offer positive support in any way. These guidelines were in play until the youngest sibling passed the age of twenty-one, at which point it was down to the individual to decide if they wanted to carry on or not. Most did, although they developed more sophisticated strategies for covering up their sibling-based sabotage.

It wasn't entirely clear why all siblings behaved like this. The obvious answer was that the parents encouraged it in a premeditated plot to establish which one they liked best and who would receive the bulk of their inheritance. Of course in reality most parents didn't encourage it. In fact they actively discouraged it by constantly reminding all siblings that they had no favourites and loved them all equally. Unfortunately every time these words entered the airspace all the siblings heard was: 'we like them better than you, so you'd better up your game!'

"If winning is all that's important to you," he repeated, "then you win."

She looked at him suspiciously. "You can't do that, it's not in the rules."

"Tyra, there are no rules for this."

"I see what you're trying to do. You're trying to confuse me. It's a double bluff tactic."

"It's not. It's just not important to me. If you want to feel like the winner, then I permit it."

"Bloody men," cursed Jezebel. "Typical chauvinist male privilege. You can't permit it, we can do what the fuck we like!"

"Shush," said Christie.

"Permit it!" replied Tyra inconsolably. "I win when I say I win. I don't need your permission."

"Poor choice of words," replied Jake genuinely.

"I'll be the winner when I hand you in. I'll win when I succeed in doing what you failed to do, free our parents."

"I don't think you understand what I'm trying to do here," replied Jake.

"You're trying to save your own skin by pandering to my ego."

"I'm not! Winning doesn't matter to me anymore, it never really did."

"Then why did you make my life a misery?"

"Did I?"

"YES!"

"I don't know why," he said honestly. "Any knowledge of what I did to harm you or what you did in response no longer poisons my mind. I don't even know you, Tyra. You're no more than a stranger to me now. All I know is that I have a sister that I didn't know I had this morning and that fills me with great joy."

"You're dead to me," she replied, "so I guess that makes us even."

"Then we are both losers."

"Winner," she mouthed, pointing at herself.

"We can buck the trend, you know," he said cryptically.

"What trend?" she replied.

"The dangerous trend of sibling rivalry. We can show everyone what can be achieved when they work together."

"What are you on about?" she said, losing patience with him.

"The whole world suffered as a direct consequence of it. Just look at the Circo siblings. Their bitter feud and inability to compromise divided humanity in half. It fuelled a culture of distrust and animosity that has been festering for twenty years and threatens to spill over into global catastrophe. Our planet's atmosphere is dying because a brother and a sister refused to accept that they were both equally important. The guides they created are a manifestation of their weaknesses, sibling rivalry extended to the virtual world. Every eighteen-year-old carries that weakness with them. Guides might have different names and personalities, but they embody those same flaws and vulnerabilities. Job and Dinah need to learn that lesson, too, if anything is going to change. Every pair of siblings has failed because of their need to be superior. Are we going to make the same mistake?"

Tyra contemplated for a moment. Much of what Jake said was logical, but in the field of psychology, logic also had a sibling. Its name was emotion, and it, too, thought it was best.

"Yes," she replied.

"Then you win," he repeated. "But we all lose."

"Drones, restrain him!" she hollered.

"No need," he replied quickly before the drones could act. "If that's your choice, I'll come willingly."

"No games?" asked Tyra suspiciously.

"None."

"I won't hesitate to give them the order to shoot you," she replied coldly.

"So be it."

"Follow the silver path," demanded Tyra. "Time to complete my side of the deal and collect the prize."

Jake did as he was told. He knew the way better than she did, having spent time here. He knew that their destination would be the black tower and a final confrontation with the Principal Conductor. Christie was encouraged to walk with him as Tyra followed, drones flying as escorts at the front and the back.

There's a world of difference between waiting for something to happen and waiting for nothing to happen. Mannie had tried waiting for nothing and hadn't enjoyed it very much. Waiting for something raised his spirits no end, even though he wasn't sure he knew exactly what the something was likely to be. Identify Jake Montana: that was the only instruction. He loitered by the West entrance for most of the day and for much of it something hadn't happened.

The drones remained motionless, the gates remained closed and the clouds remained ominous. When you've spent a long time not doing something it affected your mood and judgement. Was Jake going to look the same? Even though it had only been three months since they'd met it was over a very short time frame. He skipped quickly through his Memory Cloud to reassure himself he remembered what Jake looked like. If a man like this turned up he'd know it was him. But what if he didn't?

Mannie started to panic. If he failed he might end up in the Source forever. There was no option. He had to identify him. As he contemplated the likelihood that Jake had disguised himself as a tree or a stray cat, the real Jake showed up. But not where he was expecting him to. He was wandering nonchalantly around the inside of the complex like he didn't have a care in the world. Even more strangely he brazenly walked amongst the drones like they weren't even there. Mannie swore he even saw him brush through the side of one.

All Alison had asked of him was to identify the virus. Not approach him or try to restrain him. In that regard he'd completed the task, but before he got the chance to return with the positive news a girl showed up. From the shadows of one of the buildings he listened intently to their conversation. They were arguing and what he heard struck a chord with him. Alison had struck a deal with this girl and deals were a matter of principle.

TWENTY-SIX

HALF A PERCENT

The drones led them through the Source and into the quadrant that surrounded the tower. They passed under the silver archway and entered its lowest floor. The three teenagers stepped into the lift and it rose effortlessly before ascending with haste to the only other level. No one spoke. Jake pressed himself into the corner as far from the others as possible, as if they had the plague. Christie was amazed how calm he was. He looked almost pleased with himself. As she watched him intently she could have sworn his right elbow slipped through the glass wall. Tyra didn't notice anything because she was too busy on cloud shopping in preparation for being the richest teenager in the West. When the lift came to rest the scene around them was almost exactly as Jake had experienced it last time, with only one exception.

The door of black cube was open and the green cursor already throbbed on the screen inside it.

Tyra…

She looked around nervously, not sure how best to respond.

"You can just speak to it," offered Jake helpfully.

"I have brought him to you," she said timidly. "Where are my parents? That was the deal."

Verify...

"Verify what?"

The Virus...

"It's him!" she said in astonishment.

I don't trust you...I have seen your thoughts...I know what you are capable of...

It was hard enough when a stranger brought your character into question but to be judged by a computer screen felt somehow worse.

"What do you mean?" asked Tyra. "What am I capable of?"

You take what you want...always have...

"No I don't," she replied defensively.

You've betrayed your brother...no one can trust you...

"He's done worse to me!" she exclaimed with a petulant stamp of her foot.

If you say so...

"Why don't people ever believe me?!" she whined.

I can tell them if you like...tell them what you've done...all of it...

"So, you said you wanted proof that Jake's here?" she replied, quickly changing the subject. "But you won't take my word for it?"

Exactly...Mannie Draxler will verify...

The lift descended once more and returned a few minutes later with a slightly flustered-looking Austrian scientist inside.

"It's him," Mannie confirmed, puffing heavily to get his breath back.

Finally...

"That's what I said!" complained Tyra. "See, I wasn't lying."

How does it feel…?

"Release my parents," demanded Tyra, ignoring the computerised sarcasm. "You have what you want."

Not yet…

"Why?"

Because he's not dead…you need to kill him…

"No!" screamed Christie rushing towards Jake to protect him.

"Don't touch me," replied Jake aggressively.

It wasn't the first time he'd snapped at her like this when she'd got close but it had taken until now for her to properly challenge it. This time there was no Moodzec to protect her from the truth. Realising what he'd done, she stepped away from him.

"Why me?" said Tyra.

He's dead to you…I've seen your thoughts…

"But that's not the same as him being actually dead," she argued. "Why don't you do it?"

No hands…

"Can't you just keep him prisoner?"

No…too risky…Jake must be eliminated…

"But…"

Take the gun…

Suddenly the gravity of the situation overtook the teenager. She didn't want to kill anyone, she just wanted her voice to be heard. She wanted to make a point, not point a gun. The cursor tapped out a selection of punctuation marks to direct her.

…=====>…

Her eyes were drawn to an antique revolver by the side

of the screen. Jake had seen it before. It was the very same one Miriam had used to gun down her brother some twenty years ago. The symmetry of the situation wasn't lost on him. A sister being forced to kill her brother to achieve victory for an artificially intelligent entity determined to protect the system they'd created. Fortunately there was another similarity. Both brothers had Dinah for protection. Right now, though, that didn't matter. It wasn't about him anyway, it was about her. Her moment to shine.

"It's okay, Tyra, take it," said Jake, displaying little concern for his own safety. "If that is what must be done to save our parents, then it must be done."

One life…exchanged for two others…

The gun felt uncomfortable in her fingers, like a guitar in the hands of a racoon. She looked at Jake. Did she hate him that much? Would her parents believe his life was a price worth paying for their own? She doubted it. It would probably work against her. In their eyes his sacrifice would be the ultimate example of why he was better than her. Maybe that's what he was trying to achieve? The whole situation was so confusing that her cloud launched unexpectedly and a bewildering set of images made her dizzy.

Unusually for her cloud it wasn't replaying the highlights she'd watched obsessively in recent weeks. These were the ones she'd suppressed in case they sowed a seed of doubt about how she felt about him. These were the happier moments they'd shared. They were filled with the sound of uninhibited laughter. They documented all the times Jake had comforted her, taught her something useful or protected her, and there were literally thousands of them.

Shoot him…

Mannie watched on in horror. No one had asked him to be an accomplice to murder. The act itself was against the Circuit's rules and yet the Principal Conductor was actually encouraging it. Was this what he stood for? No. Absolutely not. The Circuit was designed to cultivate human progress and he staunchly believed in those principles. But if those who upheld the laws were willing to break them without consequence, the fundamentals of the system became untenable. Alison believed Jake was the biggest threat to that system, but Mannie suddenly saw it differently.

"Do it," suggested Jake. "Shoot and free them."

"No," Tyra replied, dropping the gun on the floor. "That wasn't our deal. You asked me to bring Jake in, not kill him. I have completed my side of the deal, now you have to complete yours."

Your parents are criminals…no reprieve… no release…

"You can't negotiate with an artificial super being who lacks a conscience," said Jake. "It's programmed to do what's in its best interest, and releasing them isn't."

"I've been conned," said Tyra angrily.

"We've all been conned," added Christie.

"Yes," confirmed Jake.

"I understand what has to be done now," said Christie, turning to Jake. "The world will never be free while Alison manipulates us. Do what needs to be done. Whatever the consequence, you and I can overcome it."

"I'll make sure of that," said Jake with a smile.

Mannie…shoot him…

"No," replied Mannie defiantly.

It's an order…

"You already know why I can't," he added.

Half a percent…

"Yes. You knew it was there but you didn't understand it. We all have gaps, that's why life will never be certain even for you. You couldn't understand why it didn't add up to one hundred percent, but I do."

Principles...

"Yes. I have them. You thought my principles meant I would follow every order you gave me to secure the Circuit, but this one runs against my own. You have reneged on the promises you made to this girl."

I never said promise...

"It doesn't matter. It's not the only principle you have ignored. Our society has evolved beyond settling our differences with violence. The Circuit was supposed to protect us from it, but you've fallen into the same trap every dictator does. The desire to dominate without oversight."

It's the will of the people...they choose...

"No," said Mannie. "It's yours."

Shoot him...Draxler...or I will destroy the East...

"It's already begun," said Jake solemnly.

"Really?" gasped Mannie.

"Yes, and I must go back to it."

Tyra started to weep. These were not the crocodile tears she usually summoned with ease. These were genuine and reflected the sad realisation of what she'd done. Her thirst for personal justice had led her into the dark. Now the tough external layers of her persona were being stripped back, and at the core was a little, lost girl who just wanted someone to notice her. A little girl who just wanted her brother to notice her.

"I'm sorry," she cried.

Christie whispered something into Jake's ear.

"And that'll help?" he replied.

She nodded.

"Winter lilies sprout early but take time to bloom," said Jake softly in Tyra's ear so no one else heard him.

"What did you say?"

He repeated the phrase and a lump formed in her throat. It was Paddy's secret code and she now understood its meaning. Her family had always known that when the moment came she would do the right thing, even if she'd initially set off in the wrong direction. They did appreciate her after all. Jake held his arms out to offer her a comforting brotherly hug.

She flung herself towards him, but rather than his warm embrace, she cut straight through his body and collapsed against Christie on the other side. Tyra turned in confusion, trying to work out why she'd missed him. Jake winked at her. He was standing in exactly the same position, but he was no longer alone. A short, plump, middle-aged woman with frizzy red hair stood next to him.

"What's...happening?" asked Tyra.

"Oh, I'm not really here," replied Jake. "I'm in your cloud feed."

"I'm really here, though!" added Dinah as she flashed some 'jazz hands' and offered an excitable little whoop.

"I only realised what was happening ten minutes ago," said Christie. "I've always been so worried that I might get it, too, so it's good to know I can see through it."

"Get what?" asked Jake.

"P.C.O.D. I thought there might be a genetic weakness in the Tucci family, but there isn't."

"Oh shit, does that mean I have it!?" said Tyra who had unwisely proclaimed her immunity only a few days earlier.

"No," replied Jake. "I'm sorry to give you a fright: it was the only way I could be in two places at once. But you're not imagining it, I'm here even if it's only virtual."

The disruption in the girls' clouds was starting to annoy Alison, but not as much as the fact that they were all ignoring its messages. The text stream typed furiously but no one wanted to answer. Eventually it lost patience and engaged its highest level of anger. Full caps.

EXPLAIN…I CAN'T SEE…

"But if you're in the cloud why can't Alison see you?" asked Christie.

"Because I'm the virus. You can't see a virus, can you?"

"Well, that's not strictly true," replied Mannie scientifically. "If you had an electron microscope you…"

Everyone stared at him.

"Wrong time?"

"Why did you come here at all?" asked Tyra.

"Because you set a trap for me, and then because I heard Paddy had been captured. But I never planned to rescue him; I have enough going on over here where I am. That's your job, Tyra. I knew I had to show you what you're really made of, little sister, and you haven't disappointed me. You've bucked the trend. You've proven how powerful siblings can be. You're the hero today."

JAKE…

Dinah gave him a virtual nudge and their projections merged. "I think it's talking to you. Maybe if we just ignore it, it'll go away!"

I can't see you…but I know you're there… there's something else, too…

"Me!" giggled Dinah.

And you are…

"Your blind spot."

DINAH…

"Da da!" she sang merrily.

You can't win…Job will save me…

"Ha! He's a wimp. He's been trying to break into Christie's cloud for ages and all I have to do is flick him away with a cosmic finger and he tumbles into another network."

NO...not that Job...

"Dinah," said Jake, showing the first signs of anxiety since he'd arrived on the beach earlier in the day. "I might need some help here."

Being in two places at once wasn't easy to pull off. In normal situations accessing the Memory Cloud meant both worlds were in one place. The virtual perspective pasted over the physical one and your concentration was singularly in the same place. That was not true for Jake. His was split between multiple locations and important stuff was happening in all of them. While concentrating on the virtual world in the West his physical manifestation was engaged in a separate conversation in the East, and it was stretching his focus to the limit.

"I'm a bit busy taunting the Principal Conductor at the moment," replied Dinah, "and I'm thoroughly enjoying it."

Her words froze in Jake's mind. He'd never considered why Alison held that title. He assumed it had something to do with the electronic components found in a circuit board. A conductor in that sense was a device responsible for carrying a charge from the machine producing it to the one consuming it. Jake knew that every single subscriber carried the Ersatz programme within their implants and collectively carried a charge through the network to the machine consuming it. The result was what he saw on the screen in front of him. Alison was the Principal Conductor of those individual impulses. But in the physical world thousands of miles away he'd just heard something that suggested an alternative explanation for her title.

There was another type of conductor.

A musical one. These conductors directed a large

group of musicians in simultaneous performance to achieve symphonic harmony. They were highly skilled at doing so, but neither they nor the performers would be anything without the music.

They were nothing without a composer.

"Dinah, how far can you go in the system?"

"Anywhere. I'm omnipotent!"

"Stay humble, Dinah. I think we have enough of those right now. I need you here with me."

"Ah."

"What's 'ah' supposed to mean?"

"I can go almost anywhere," she said correcting herself.

"Almost?"

"I've looked but I can't find you on the network."

"That's because I didn't choose an avatar for my cloud and I'm not attached to anything. That's why Alison can't see me."

VIRUS...

"Damn it," said Dinah. "Does that mean we don't get to play our game?"

"We get to play a different one."

"Awesome. What's it called?"

"Um...memory fishing."

"That sounds a lot like work to me," she replied suspiciously.

Even though it was obvious Dinah had relinquished her direct connection with Jake's cloud to join the ranks of the hunters, it was a relief to see she'd lost none of her personality.

"Does work involve paralytic monks with three eyes?" said Jake.

"No! Count me in!"

"Great."

"But how do I find you?"

"I don't need you to find me."

"Where do you want me, then?"

"The Memory Cloud of Major Holst."

Dinah's excitement was stripped from her face. She'd already been through his cloud before and the experience left her wounded for days.

"Anywhere but there," she begged.

"It's the only choice."

"But," she murmured, looking for excuses, "if I leave, then the Memory Hunters will have access to Christie."

"Don't worry. She can handle it," he said, offering his girlfriend a raised thumb.

"Yes she can!" screamed Jezebel. "Girl power."

"What do you need me to find?" asked Dinah.

"An important memory. I'm not sure what exactly but it'll be more than twenty years old and it'll involve Job and drones."

DRONES...NOW...

"I don't want anything to do with Job, he's a dick," said Dinah forcefully.

"I think it's time the two of you healed some wounds."

"I'd prefer to inflict them."

"Not this time, Dinah. Find the memory and solve the riddle."

"God damnit…you know I love a good riddle," she replied.

"What do you want us to do?" said Christie.

"Get everyone to safety."

"What about the drones?" said Tyra.

"You'll figure it out," he replied. "Come on, Dinah, there's no time to lose."

Dinah held her nose and leapt forward like she was diving into a swimming pool. In an instant she was gone.

"Tyra, do you have any eyeliner on you?" said Jake mysteriously.

Asking Tyra that was like asking if a porcupine had spikes. There was always a prominent black appearance to her eyelids and she reinforced it on a regular basis. Most girls her age had moved away from the eyeliner pens and brushes that some of the older generation still clung to nostalgically. These days you could buy eyeline applicators that mapped the contours of your face and sprayed a fine aerosol of your chosen colour in exactly the right places. Colours were adjustable so you only needed to carry one of them, and they had different strengths to protect against make-up's biggest enemy, tears.

Tyra fished around in her studded rubber bag and removed what he needed.

"Roll your sleeve up please," he said to Christie.

"Why?"

"It's an insurance policy," he replied. "You'll see. Mannie, I might need you for this, you're the eldest."

Draxler…stop…

"No," he replied defiantly. "I'm using my half percent."

DRONES…RALLY…

"Quickly," said Jake, hurrying him. "Write this on her arm."

Jake whispered the message he wanted Mannie to scrawl on Christie's arm. The result wasn't very legible because he wasn't familiar with the device, but as the oldest person in the room he was the only one who remembered how handwriting worked.

"If you forget what it's for," said Jake to Christie, "ask Paddy."

Drones…five minutes to comply…

"I have to go."

Send for the Archivists…

"How do we get out of here?" asked Tyra nervously.

"Oh, you'll work it out. After all, you're my sister."

Jake faded from view. Mannie, Christie and Tyra were left alone with an angry, blinking computer screen and a foreboding feeling in the pits of their stomachs.

TWENTY-SEVEN

THE COMPOSER

W hen Holst and Verne arrived at the 'Temple of Fire' from Abseron they were greeted by a different scene of pandemonium, but this time it was people not buildings that were in trouble. The King of Baku lolloped around the castle like an angry bison as he screamed madly and pointed at everyday objects like they were brand new discoveries. His gang of monks were acting similarly out of character, although they weren't known for acting normally at the best of times.

Most of the monks were scrambling around the floor with wide-eyed expressions, ripping off their hoods, and babbling like inconsolable infants. Some were chasing around after their plastic eyeballs without the foggiest idea what they were for. As soon as they caught up with them they simply panicked and threw them away again. Then in an apparent change of heart they set off in hot pursuit once more. In the melee they'd frequently collide with fellow monks, and a rather one-sided debate about everything would ensue.

"Who are you?" demanded one monk urgently in

slurred speech that suggested he had bitten his mother tongue.

"Who *am* I?" asked the second monk desperately.

"You don't know?"

"No. Do you?"

"No."

"Same."

"Where are we?"

"Here."

"Ah, thanks for clearing that up."

"What's that thing called?" asked the first, pointing his finger.

The second monk stared at the olive tree and shrugged. "I don't think it has a name."

"Carrot!" claimed the first.

"What is?"

"That is."

"It's mine!" screamed the second monk, sprinting over to the tree and wrapping his arms around it as a sign of ownership. "All the carrots are mine!"

This snatch-and-grab behaviour was being replicated all around the courtyard. Monks were staking their claims to all manner of inanimate objects like early explorers arriving in the New World. One monk was obsessively and unsuccessfully rounding up pigeons. Even though he'd spotted them first, his demands for the 'flappy rats' to congregate around him simply resulted in a blizzard of bird shit and flapping. Another monk had unwisely decided that he was the master of 'infernos' and was robustly fighting off his colleagues from claiming the central pyre, whilst oblivious to the fact he was entirely on fire.

"What on earth has happened here!?" gasped Verne,

his mouth open as he stared agog at the incomprehensible chaos.

"I imagine their servers were housed in Abseron," replied Holst matter-of-factly and not in the slightest bit troubled by their behaviour.

"What does that mean?"

"We've destroyed their servers and permanently wiped out their memories."

"So they've forgotten everything?"

"Almost entirely," said Holst with a smirk. "All they've got left is their instincts and anything they learnt before their implant surgery."

"But they remember how to talk," said Verne curiously.

"True," said Holst who found that aspect rather interesting. "But not, it would appear, what any of the words mean."

Verne watched as the pace of devastation intensified. What started with an initial phase of utter confusion was quickly shunted into one of intrigue, before settling in the current phase of hysterical selfishness. The stronger and fitter monks were forcing the weaker ones to relinquish their discoveries with threats and acts of violence.

"This is awful," stated Verne.

"It's wonderful. It's the survival of the fittest. Just as Gog intended."

"You planned this, didn't you?" said Verne.

"Of course," snapped Holst. "It's a lot easier to remove a dynasty if they don't remember they ever had one! When the war drones destroy the remaining server farms these scenes will be replicated in every corner of the East. The threat they pose will be gone."

"But civilisation as we know it will collapse!"

"Probably, but the strongest, fittest and quickest will survive to rebuild it."

"You say that like it's a good thing."

"I don't think the people of the East were civilised in the first place. This might give them a shot in the arm. If you want your credits you're going to help me do more of it."

What good was a bounty if there was nothing left to spend it on? Money would cease to be relevant if humanity reverted to the Dark Ages. The East had faced many challenges over the last two decades, but this turn of events wasn't going to make it better. Unless you were a speccy of course, he thought selfishly. In a world where subscribers were reduced to philistines, they'd be dependent on those with greater knowledge to lead them. Perhaps the speccies would finally get a chance to rebuild the world the way it should be. Those thoughts wouldn't be acceptable, particularly to Holst, so he kept them to himself and just nodded in agreement.

Major Holst approached the King who was crawling across the dusty cobbles on his hands and knees, trying to figure out a host of existential questions, which included what his hands and knees were called. The Major's shadow loomed over him and the King rolled on his back like a dog looking for his tummy to be tickled. The paraphernalia that once marked him out as regal had been stripped or discarded. Broken pieces of his fancy headdress were scattered on the ground, and other than the white paint daubed over his skin he was completely naked. His dark, frightened eyes peered back at them, vacant and consumed by an abyss of turmoil.

"Who are you?" he stuttered.

"I am the Composer," said Major Holst.

"What's one of those?"

"They set the rhythm, organise the notes, and write the score."

"Oh," he replied, having understood none of the Major's answer. "Have we met?"

"Oh yes. Several times. The first was over twenty years ago when I gave you everything your heart desired. Power, control, endless riches, and the will to dominate. I even introduced you to Gog," he said, holding out one of the eyeballs in his palm.

"Ooh, can I eat it? I'm starving."

"I don't think Gog would approve, do you?"

The King nodded eagerly.

"You'll soon find out what he thinks because I'm going to send you to meet him."

"Who's Gog?"

"A figment of your once fertile imagination, but I'm afraid you won't be getting that back either. It's hidden in a massive pile of broken glass and metal soon to be reconstituted and used to build affordable housing."

"What's affordable housing?"

"Usually unaffordable."

"And Gog lives there?"

"No. He doesn't exist, you simpleton. The real Gog isn't the twisted image you created in your malfunctioning Memory Cloud. He's me," replied Holst, crouching down next to the broken figure of the King and grinning viciously. "You've been following my commands for twenty years and I've come to offer you my sincere gratitude. Your selfish greed has kept users in chains while we pillaged your lands for our own growth. But all good things must come to an end. Dinah is dead, but the virus is loose and the people of the East must die."

"Not today they won't," said Jake who was standing in the courtyard just behind them.

"Is he also a composer?" asked the King.

"No," growled Holst as he turned to face him. "He's a superfluous nobody."

"And I thought I was the virus."

Over the past hour, Jake had acted more out of speed than purpose. While he spent most of his attention in the virtual world thousands of miles away, here hundreds of drones had descended on the city and were bombarding the streets to smithereens. The air was filled with a cacophony of harrowing screams and collapsing buildings, but there was nothing he could do to help directly. When you were battling a superior fighting force the only option was to seek out the chain of command. The 'Temple of Fire' seemed the logical place to look and his instincts had rewarded him. He never expected it to be like this, though. The King had been overthrown and the man responsible was the same man he'd seen in Riga removing nickel ore earlier in the week.

What's more, he appeared to know who Jake was.

Knowing your enemy was a prerequisite in conflict, unless of course your enemy was 'terror' and then apparently you had permission to do whatever you wanted, including bombing people because they wore dubious-looking hats or had more oil than you did. Jake didn't know his adversary, and that wasn't very helpful. There was someone here he did know, though, and the realisation hurt like hell. Verne shuffled back sheepishly to avoid Jake's eye contact.

"I trusted you," said Jake despondently.

"I had too much to lose," replied Verne meekly.

"You mean you had too much to gain."

"Even with your fancy implants," said Holst, "you can't see everything."

"No. Everyone can be blind at times. I hope the prize

makes you happy, Verne. If they ever give it to you, which I doubt. The Circuit has form when it comes to reneging on these things."

Verne shot Holst a look hoping he'd deny it, but he showed no interest in doing so.

"When he finishes what he started," said Holst, "he'll get what he deserves."

"Call off the attack," demanded Jake, returning to his main priority. "Withdraw the war drones."

"Ha! Not likely. I follow orders, not idiots who beg."

"I'm not begging, I'm demanding it."

"Alison overestimated you," taunted Holst. "I told her that myself."

"But you're not an artificial supercomputer now, are you?" mocked Jake.

"I don't need to be. I'm a soldier. I have a gut feel for these things. I watched you every day on Bornholm. Without our download you'd have failed every single one of our tests. Do you know why?" he said rhetorically. "There's no fire in you, boy. You lack ambition to achieve greatness because you're distracted by your own worthless life."

"Have we met?" said Jake curiously.

"I'm surprised your puny muscles don't remember it. Every time they saw me they twitched in fear."

Verne was slowly reversing away an inch at a time, desperate to be anywhere but here right now.

"Don't move!" demanded Holst.

"Yes, Major Holst," replied Verne.

The name meant nothing, but deep inside Jake his bones shuddered and his muscles did twitch. They tried desperately to force him to adopt a press-up position and push out the required hundred reps.

"Alison is frightened of you, but I believe there is nothing to fear but fear itself."

"Why does Alison fear me?" asked Jake, wondering how much Holst really knew about it.

"In the great orchestra of life there is an empty seat. The music is playing and the performance is perfect, but the conductor is distracted by something. It's like tinnitus, a noise no one else can hear, but the sound is so real it drives the conductor mad. Alison is paranoid about a threat it cannot see or hear. Frightened that the mysterious musician that sits invisibly in the empty seat will never play along to the music. If the tinnitus continues the symphony will be ruined. But I can hear and see you."

"Alison should be frightened," said Jake calmly. "It's not paranoia. I really am the bogeyman."

"A fictitious monster that plays on our deepest fears but never actually materialises?" he replied coolly.

"There's nothing fictitious about what I'm capable of."

"And what is it you think you can do exactly?"

"Destroy the Memory Cloud," said Jake grandly.

Holst sniggered, only just suppressing an even greater roar of laughter. "Look around you, Jake."

He'd been so distracted by what he was going to do he'd not paid much attention to what was actually happening here. His last visit to the 'Temple of Fire' hadn't exactly been a regular experience, so witnessing a bunch of erratic monks arguing over lumps of mud and stumbling around in a confused daze hadn't really hit home. If that first visit had been odd then what he saw now was downright disturbing. The monks were behaving without care for their fellow man. They were behaving like animals.

Even before his disappointing Ascension Day, Jake had fought against the system in one way or another. Against his frequent upgrades and the restrictions on his movements and thoughts. Existing in the Circuit was deeply uncomfortable, but the inescapable surveillance and fear of punishment quashed any major acts of rebellion. The occasional violation was all he could muster, and even then it hurt him more than it hurt the system. He yearned for the world to be better. He believed things needed to change. He often imagined what it might look like if the system softened. What if war, inequality and crime remained a thing of the past but the Memory Cloud was still used to share knowledge, connection and understanding? What if they stopped needing to control people and users went back to making their own mistakes, rather than relying on the Circuit's help to avoid them? Eliminate the need for a higher power to act as a shepherd over its flock. That was his version of utopia and it was shared by many, including most speccies.

But this scene was nothing like that.

This was the disintegration of the whole system. The monks had lost all semblance of morality. Adapted behaviours that had developed over years had been cleansed and the monks had reverted to their natural instinctive state. It was like living in a world full of Dinahs. That might be fun at times but it wasn't the blueprint for a stable, cohesive and equitable system of governance. There had to be balance and the reality was simple. For every Dinah there had to be a Brother Job.

"Let's say you did have the ability to destroy it, which I very much doubt," continued Holst. "What you see here would just be the beginning."

"This is a bad example," said Jake. "The monks were already mad."

"No. It will be the same. In every city and town, in every corner of the West, this chaos will be replicated. It will affect strangers as well as friends. Every importance level, from vital to superfluous, will lose purpose and perspective. They will revert to the only thing they have left. Their instincts. They will tear each other apart to secure basic human needs. Needs that every man, woman and child currently take for granted. Needs that the Circuit provide in abundance. In your desire to avoid war you will create another."

"Then call off the drones and there won't be a war at all."

"It's too late for that."

"No it isn't. The drones are only in Baku, they haven't done much damage yet. Look beyond your orders and do the right thing."

"It is the right thing. I'm easing their pain."

"What?!" said Jake furiously. "And I thought the King was mad. Take me instead, if that's what Alison needs."

"It won't change anything. The ball is already rolling down the hill."

"Verne, what is he talking about?" asked Jake trying to get some sense out of someone.

He didn't answer.

"There's no going back," continued Holst. "Dinah is gone and in the morning the people of the East will wake up to the realisation that yesterday was just as bad as they remember it. It will never stop. In a day or so they will begin to question their own reality. In a week, when their anger at the injustice crystallises, leaders will emerge from their ranks to inspire them to seek revenge against those who have wronged them. They will pick the only enemy they know. The one that stripped everything from them. The West. Hatred and distrust will fester and no one on either side of the firewall will be safe."

Holst presented a three-course set menu of war with an extra side dish of despair. Whichever way Jake looked at it his actions made the situation worse, and not just for him. He was ready to sacrifice everything but what was the point if things weren't going to get any better?

"You're bluffing," said Jake.

"No. You're up against Alison. The Principal Conductor has simulated every possible eventuality and you only see one. Unless the war drones continue their cull the West will fall."

"Maybe I'm willing to take the risk. What about you? Have you considered what will happen to you, Holst? If I press the button and destroy the cloud you'll lose everything, too."

"I lost it years ago," he said unemotionally. "It won't make any difference to me. Do it if you must. Let's see if your plan works and the drones stop firing."

"They will if the Memory Cloud falls," said Jake confidently.

"Did you ever attend Circology class?" he asked.

"Attended yes. Paid attention? Not so much."

"Maybe you should have. Then you wouldn't sound so bloody stupid. The Circuit is the world's brain, not its body. Who do you think carries out its actions?"

Jake considered the question. The Circuit's emblem was ever present but it was only a symbol. No one really saw the Circuit, but they saw you. No one ever spoke to them, but they heard you. No one met them because the Circuit was nothing but an idea. Then it dawned on him. People weren't really frightened of the Circuit, they were frightened of the drones. Postal drones that brought your letter on Ascension Day, but never explained where it came from. Utility drones that kept law and order, brought people to justice, dispersed freedom of movement and patrolled the streets. War drones that were willing to pulverise whole towns and cities in a single sortie. Drones were not sentient beings. They simply acted on the operator's instructions.

"Drones," mumbled Jake.

"And do they have implants?" said Holst, pressing home his advantage.

"No."

"So what do you think will happen if the Circuit is no longer there to direct them?"

"They'll stop?" said Jake rather optimistically.

"No. They'll continue until their orders are changed. If there's no Memory Cloud then there's no Circuit, and if there's no Circuit there's no way to change their orders."

"But who has the controls?"

"I do," said Holst.

TWENTY-EIGHT

CIRCUIT BREAKERS

I t took Dinah no time at all to navigate the network and find Holst's cloud, which was annoying because she liked more of a challenge. If she ever decided to leave the ranks of the Memory Hunters she thought she'd make a good detective. Finding lost kids or uncovering a secretive criminal network would be right up her street. The secret to locating people who didn't want to be found was by exploiting the six degrees of separation rule. It's said that every human on the planet is linked through no more than six mutual connections. It was the same inside the cloud. If you knew how to look it was feasible to link a kid born in a council house in Scunthorpe to the Sultan of Brunei. If you had the patience.

She rarely did.

Today, though, she didn't need it.

Where she was going there was only one degree of separation because she'd already had the dubious pleasure of connecting to Major Holst. While exploring an intriguing shed on Bornholm she'd hijacked the only cloud feed available to her at the time. The experience created a shared file held in two separate locations thousands of miles apart. Once the connection was open it was there forever. From that shared file she could go anywhere she wanted from the present day to his first conscious thought.

And that's exactly what Jake had asked of her.

There was a riddle to solve.

Steps through the cloud weren't measured in familiar units of time. Even if the connection hadn't been open, travelling through a thousand clouds was unobservable by human standards. At most it would take a couple of jiffies, or one fiftieth of a second if you wanted to be specific. The jump to Holst's cloud took less than a picosecond, which she assumed made her early for the first time in her life. What did people do when they were early? Surely they used the extra time to snoop around being nosy.

Dinah popped up in Holst's cloud feed as close to the present as she could. Around the Major a host of crazy monks were chasing after eyeballs, ripping up trees and wrestling each other. It was exactly the type of fun she approved of. Standing opposite was Jake who didn't seem in the slightest bit pleased to see her. He scowled at her before mouthing the word 'riddle'. Something about his demeanour suggested he was in a rush to find the answer.

He hadn't given her much to go on. The memory was probably at least twenty years old and it involved Job and drones in some way. Why it would have anything to do with Job made her scratch her virtual head. Yes, her brother was an insufferable know-it-all who liked to get involved in other people's affairs, but Jake wasn't even born that far back, so how was it possible? One thing was certain: only one of the clues was here. The war drones above her head made her shudder and immediately sent her into reverse.

The 'Temple of Fire' evaporated as Dinah whizzed

around Holst's server box for more significant memories. There were tons of folders here but most were labelled 'Confidential'. She tried searching by year but the results were jumbled like someone was making it purposefully difficult to find anything. Like a restless child waiting next to the Christmas tree for the rest of the family to wake up, she lost patience and ripped open the nearest confidential folder.

Inside there were a lot of memories connected to Bornholm spanning multiple years. In fact there were very few that didn't feature it. She stepped into the scenes to get the full experience. Some of these memories featured images of an active Archivist camp where hundreds of recruits were engaged in a variety of activities designed to test their suitability. The factory buildings looked more modern than when she was there, and they gleamed with their fresh coats of white paint. The island was also considerably bigger than she remembered it. She settled on a particular memory from exactly twenty years ago and went for a walkabout to find Holst.

She eventually found him sitting at a small office desk inside one of the factories obsessively reading and rereading an old letter. The ink was faded and the paper was crumpled and frayed at the edges from being too frequently thumbed. She couldn't see what was written on it because that part of the memory had been revisited so often it had been corrupted and every other word was blank. On the desk the original envelope was embossed by an older version of the Circuit logo. It was addressed to James Oliver Benjamin Holst. When there was nothing further to learn she plucked up the courage to investigate the top of the hill and was greatly relieved to find no shed, no cave and no war drones anywhere in sight. They weren't the only clue missing. In all of the memories that related to the island there was no evidence of Job.

She moved across and out of the memory and back to the other folders. One of these held a collection of memories from the Source, although she couldn't be certain which one. She picked the most interesting one and stepped into the scenery once more. Dinah immediately felt the cold run through her.

Holst looked very different. Youthful skin, a full head of hair and less stocky in stature. She guessed he was no more than thirty years of age now. The limited light far above them struggled to illuminate much more than the air around the ceiling, but against each of the dull, black walls stacks of containers, sealed with hatches at the front, stretched above her. On the front of each, next to a frosty glass window, a small, glowing panel detailed the contents inside. The foreboding smell of death leaked out of them reminiscent of Tyra's infected cloud and made Dinah deeply uncomfortable.

Holst was down on his knees, hand outstretched and placed on the icy window of one of the containers. A sad whimpering broke the eerie silence. There was only one person here and, although the source was surprising it obviously came from him. Dinah moved closer to get a look at the text on the panel, but his hand obscured it. What was so important inside here that it reduced this muscly tough guy into a weeping baby? Holst removed his hand and finally she saw what it said.

Miriam Circo.

Dinah immediately knew who that was. Everyone knew, guide or subscriber. Aaron's sister. But what was the connection to the Major? She escaped the memory and went on a hunt for any other entries in Holst's cloud that related to her. Back in the server she found hundreds. She tried to open the most recent one, recorded sometime around twenty thirty-one, but the file was protected. She tried various techniques to break the password, including typing 'password', but nothing worked. There was only one thing for it, brute force. She summoned all available electrical energy and hit the file like an overpowered defibrillator. The file crackled and wheezed but remained resolutely shut.

"That's enough!" shouted Job.

A new energy charged through the server and sent crackles and sparks through the stacks that surrounded it. She couldn't see Job, but she always knew when he was near. They were no longer being projected into the virtual world to witness each other's hologrammatic forms. In the server they were between worlds. Software programmes in a foreign hard disc that neither of them belonged to. Competing lines of code fighting for memory space and jostling to be processed first. Adversarial agents working against each other to hide or release the riddle that Jake was so keen to solve.

"Oh, not you," huffed Dinah. "Can't they send someone else for once."

"This is one step too far, Dinah. There's nothing to see here."

"What a stupid thing to say. Obviously there is or you wouldn't have said that, would you!? Only someone trying to hide it would deny it!"

"Okay, there IS something to see here," replied Job, hoping reverse psychology might work and speaking less aggressively than she'd ever witnessed from him before.

"I knew it!"

"Hold on, but…"

"Just open it. I'm on a mission from God," said Dinah grandly.

"You mean Jake."

"Oh, but haven't you heard? He's big in the East these days."

"I don't care if he's got gigantism, you can't see it!"

"Why not?" she stropped.

"Because it doesn't belong to you."

"So! Nor does Sadder Arabia but I stuck a virtual flag in it and now it's mine. Same applies here. I'm a Memory Hunter now, finding memories is what we do."

"Yes, but some memories are too important."

"To whom?"

"It's none of your business."

"Then what's it got to do with you?" expressed Dinah. "Apart from the fact you're a complete control freak."

"It has everything to do with me," he said forcefully. "You're not the only one who has an alternate history."

Dinah knew there was more to her than just being Jake's guide. She was one half of the original sibling programme, and from what she'd worked out Job was the other. Dinah was designed in the image of the sister Aaron always wanted. Someone Miriam never was: fun, considerate, sympathetic and vulnerable. But who and what was Job based on? Surely Miriam would create a sibling that reflected what Aaron wasn't: ambitious, determined, relentless, rebellious and single-minded. But what if she'd gone further than that? What if she'd based him on somebody real? Someone she knew.

"You're him, aren't you?" blurted Dinah.

"Yes."

"That's the riddle. I'm a legend at this."

"Miriam built her sibling programme in the image of James Oliver Benjamin Holst."

"That seems like an overly excessive number of names for one person. Why didn't I get more?" she said, losing her focus. "From now on I want you to call me Dinah Ursula Susan Tallulah Yasmin!"

"That'll make you Sister Dusty," replied Job.

"So!? Jezebel says women should do and be whoever they want!"

"Fine. Beat yourself up."

"No, that's what I'm going to do to you if you don't tell me what's inside this memory. Why did Miriam choose this psycho?"

"Because they were lovers," said Job.

"Ooh that's grim. I'm never getting that image out of my memory banks. Imagine their old, wrinkly bodies, yuk!"

"They weren't always old, you know!"

"If what you say is true, how come you're both kind of angry?" asked Dinah. "Didn't she put out?"

"I don't know what you're on about!"

"That's totally what it was!"

"It's complicated. Their love was forbidden."

"Why?"

"Stop being so bloody nosy."

"I can't help it. It's in my nature. If you don't tell me I'll be forced to break into your little Archivist chat group. You know I can, don't test me."

Job knew she was right and any disruption to the Archivists wouldn't be welcome while they were so close to their goal.

"The Circuit didn't choose them," said Job reluctantly, trying to satisfy Dinah's curiosity without giving away the farm.

"But they're both ancient, they're too old for the Ascension Day process."

"The Circuit was everything to Miriam. She was obsessed with it and used it to make all of her decisions.

Any answer it gave that was less than ninety-nine percent certain was discarded. Their relationship was one of them. There was always a gap and Holst couldn't accept it. It broke his heart."

"Broke it?" said Dinah in amazement. "I didn't think he had one."

"The experience turned him into a bitter and twisted recluse. More machine than a human. The perfect ally for Alison when the system needed someone to carry out its most sensitive plans."

"And you've known this all along?"

"No. I was part of Jake, not Holst. Never have been. But, like him, I follow Alison's orders. I can't let you go in there."

"If this is the riddle, what does it have to do with drones?" she muttered to herself. A plausible suggestion popped into her head after a rare moment of intellectual concentration. "Holst controls them."

"No. Absolutely not," lied Job.

"We have to stop him."

"I've just denied it."

"You've also denied the existence of dragons in the past so I can't believe anything you say."

"And how many of those have you seen?"

"Eleven."

"And they wonder why I became a hunter," he cussed under his breath.

"If Holst has control of dragons…"

"Drones," corrected Job.

"Ah ha, so I was right! This is the memory that Jake needs me to find."

"Even if you were right," replied Job, trying to cover his mistake, "it's against my programming to open it."

"No it isn't," said Dinah, being unusually sensitive for

once. "Jake has always been responsible for that. You've been seduced by the system that first made you. But if you look hard enough you'll still find most of what Jake taught you."

She was right. Job had many of the original characteristics of the founder's first sibling programme, but the rest of it had been acquired from Jake, even after he became a Memory Hunter. Jake's own habits had been influenced by his relationship with Paddy and his old school values of right and wrong. There was as much of Paddy in him than there was Holst; Jake had even commented on the physical resemblance the first time Job appeared in his feed.

"What are you saying?" he replied.

"Jake needs you. I need you," said Dinah. "Our designers couldn't compromise but that doesn't mean we can't."

"But I have to do what's right. That's how I'm built," suggested Job.

"I completely agree," replied Dinah. "But remember you've always had the rebellious behaviour in you, too. Maybe it's time to crack that open one last time!"

Mannie guided the girls from the tower as quickly as possible. The drones were coming and if they caught up with them in the tower they'd be cornered. At least out in the vast expanse of the Source there would be more places to hide. Throughout their retreat the screens on every server stack that adorned the walls around the lift shaft bristled with Alison's rage. The most popular of these messages was the word 'drone' often followed by a digital clock ticking down to their impending arrival. Nothing changed when they reached the quadrant. Everywhere they looked Alison's words were screaming in bold green font.

SIXTY SECONDS...COMPLY

They made it as far as one of the four gateways before the time ran out and they were confronted by their pursuers. A pack of utility drones sped along the silver paths, bearing down on them. Hiding wouldn't help them. Drones didn't need to see where you were, they felt where you were. The signals continually and wirelessly sent out from their implants to their own private section of Memory Cloud were the beacons these machines followed. Only one of the three of them knew this, but fortunately he was also the person who invented the system.

"Turn your clouds off!" Mannie told the girls forcefully.

"You can't," said Tyra. "I should know: I've spent most of my life in mine."

"You can," said Mannie. "I designed that little chip in your head, so I actually know."

"Won't we forget everything if we do that?" said Christie.

"Only temporarily, but if the two of you go first, then I can remind you exactly what you're supposed to be doing."

"What about what you're supposed to be doing?"

"I'm not entirely sure what that is," replied Mannie accurately.

He'd woken up this morning with no plans at all other than the faint hope that he might go home. Now his fate was tied to theirs. He'd blown any chance of promotion: that much was certain. After betraying Alison's orders he wouldn't be surprised if the drones were after him, too. Even the ones he was on first-name terms with.

"Quick, they're almost on us," said Tyra panicking.

"Go to your feeds. Select the menu, then 'Help', 'Preferences' and finally 'Sleep'."

The girls raced each other to be the first one to complete the process. It was obvious to Mannie when they'd completed it.

"Who the hell are you!?" screamed Christie. "…Or me for that matter?"

"What the hell are they?" added Tyra, pointing out the hovering fleet of weaponised machines pressing down on them.

"No time to explain. You're looking for Paddy von Straff, Kyle and Deborah Montana. That's all you need to remember at the moment."

"Who the fuck are they!?" blasted Tyra.

"It doesn't matter just remember it because in a minute I won't. Give me your bag."

"What's a bag?" replied Tyra.

Mannie snatched at the handbag and after a minor scuffle managed to wrestle it from her.

"I don't really know why I even care about it," said Tyra as he rummaged around inside and removed a small make-up tin and started spraying the contents on himself.

"Right, stay really still," he whispered.

The drones swooped down and formed a circle around the point where three impulses had been as clear as day only thirty seconds ago. Now they felt nothing. They scanned the scene thoroughly but returned no evidence of life. After a protracted collection of beeps and bleeps the drones were drawn away towards the courtyard by an alternative set of instructions.

"I wonder what that was all about," said Mannie.

"Bloody scary," answered Tyra.

"Apparently we're looking for some people," said Christie dizzily.

"Are you? Is it me?" asked Mannie vacantly.

"Are you Paddy von Straff?"

"I might be," he replied uncertainly.

"What's that written on your hand?" asked Tyra, just as disorientated as the others.

A scrawled message read 'turn it back on' followed by a series of shorthand instructions. Mannie followed them to the letter and his confusion immediately cleared.

"Right. Follow me," he replied, beckoning the girls.

"I'm not going anywhere with you," said Tyra. "I've never seen you before."

"I know where Kyle and Deborah are," he said confidently.

"Oh in that case lead on," she said compliantly.

After spending a month here, Mannie knew where almost everything was in the Source. Unlike other humans who'd had the misfortune of spending time here, he'd been free to move around unrestricted. He'd done just that. He'd been to the morgues and seen thousands of patients frozen in stasis many times. All he had to do was search his cloud and locate the details of who was being kept there. He marched the beleaguered girls for miles, keeping vigilant for the drone squadrons constantly patrolling the silver-lined streets. Alison's screens continued to haunt them everywhere they trod. They safely reached the correct morgue and Mannie explained how the girls turned their cloud feeds back on.

"That was the weirdest experience," said Christie. "It felt like I was sleepwalking."

"Not far from the truth."

"Where are we exactly?" asked Tyra. "It's freezing in here."

"It's one of the morgues," said Mannie.

"Look," said Christie who was examining the strange chambers. "They're here!"

Two pods stacked next to each other displayed the names of Deborah and Kyle Montana. The only physical evidence of it was their bare feet pressing up against the icy glass windows.

"How do we get them out?" said Tyra desperately searching for a release mechanism.

"Let me have a look."

Mannie fiddled around with the small pad on the side of each capsule until he found it. The pods were designed to keep the captive alive by placing them in an induced coma at sub-zero temperatures. To reverse it, the bodies had to be slowly defrosted so that they didn't go into shock. The ice began to melt and water ran down the outside of the chamber as the heat in the pod rose and the screen indicated a change in the occupants' vital signs via a small graph that highlighted pulse rate, blood pressure and brain activity. After twenty minutes the defrosting process ceased and the hinges of both chambers burst open. Two pairs of wriggling feet and several shouts for help proved that Tyra's parents were alive.

Carefully the girls slid them out of their pods. They struggled to adjust to the external conditions, having been consigned to a frozen coffin for months. Mannie did his best to make them comfortable by removing some of his own clothes to wrap around them. They had no record of anything that happened in the world since the end of their 'Court Feeling'. Other than being completely discombobulated they hadn't suffered physically from their ordeal.

"Mum! Dad!" blubbed Tyra, desperate to give them a hug but sensitive to their ordeal. "Do you know who I am?"

"Tyra," croaked Deborah.

"Yes! I missed you so much," she said, bursting into tears. "I can't tell you what I've been through. What we've been through."

"Where's Jake?" asked Kyle. "I need to tell him I'm sorry."

He'd just revisited his most recently recorded memory and deeply regretted his parting words to his son immediately before their extradition.

"I don't know," said Tyra, "but it's thanks to him you're free."

"It's thanks to both of them," corrected Christie. "Teamwork."

"And what about Dad?" said Deborah, realising there was a familiar face missing. "He's meant to be looking after you."

"He has been. He's also here somewhere," said Tyra.

"He's the last one we need to find," said Mannie. "But as he's a recent addition I don't have a record of his location. Once we've found him then we're getting out of here."

"No," added Jezebel forcefully in Christie's ear. "There's someone else we need to find. It's important."

"This isn't about feminism again, is it?"

"Um...kind of related, I guess," she said reluctantly.

"You can't rescue all the women!"

"I don't want to, just one of them."

"Who is it you want to find?"

"Miriam Circo. It's super important."

"Says who exactly?" implored Christie.

TWENTY-NINE

CLEAR SKIES

Like hungry vultures waiting to feed, the war drones flooded the sky above the 'Temple of Fire'. Their ominous shadows meant Jake was running out of time. There was no sign of Dinah or the extra information he needed for leverage. Holst had to have a pressure point, something the Major wanted that might convince him to stop the impending genocide. All Dinah had to do was find it.

"I think it's time to destroy the virus," he said, pointing to the sky.

"There must be another way," beseeched Jake.

"Sorry to disappoint you."

Holst opened his cloud feed in order to access his interface with the war drones. One simple command and they'd open fire on whatever he chose. Years of testing had proven how accurate they were. They could pick off everyone here and leave without so much as a scratch on him. No more monks, no King, no Verne and certainly no Jake Montana. All the loose ends tied up in a single thought.

That's if he could open the interface. It felt like it had crashed.

Jake watched nervously, desperate for Dinah to pop up and save him. She didn't and all he had left was the nuclear option. He opened his own cloud feed, primed and ready to release the secret code down every virtual road that opened in front of him. From there it would replicate like a chain reaction to infect every subscriber from Cyprus to Cincinnati. Region by region the world would lose connectivity to the Memory Cloud permanently.

In his virtual world the lanes of the superhighway painted the scenery as usual but he immediately noticed something abnormal. The road to Major Holst's cloud was straight in front of him, flashing desperately to get his attention. He stepped into it and returned to a virtual impression of the 'Temple of Fire'. Holst looked frustrated and confused. Standing next to him, deep in their own conversation and looking thoroughly pleased with themselves, were Dinah and Job.

"Welcome to the party!" hollered Dinah when she saw Jake.

"What are you doing?"

"Solving the riddle," said Job.

"And working together for once," added Dinah.

"I'm afraid I've been terribly naughty," giggled Job disturbingly out of character and nudging Dinah with his elbow to reinforce their shared joke.

"I demand that you stop interrupting my feed," blasted Holst angrily. "Who gave you permission?"

"We're Memory Hunters, we don't need any!" laughed Dinah.

"Alison will hear of this!"

"Oh don't worry," said Job. "The Circuit is always listening."

"We have a deal for you," said Dinah.

"I'm not interested," replied Holst.

"You will be because we've seen your darkest desires. We know what you really want."

"Oh really!"

"What's going on?" asked Jake, struggling to catch up.

Dinah and Job took it in turns to fill in the blanks. They told him all about Holst's relationship with Miriam and how the Circuit had destroyed their love. How Alison had recruited Holst to channel his rage against others and be the physical presence it could never be. How twenty years ago Alison instructed him to travel to the East to support the King of Baku's insurrection against Aaron Circo's family. How Holst had equipped the Brothers of Gog with the tools to control the people of the East, to suppress them and stop them rising up against the Circuit. How he'd used the 'Proclamation of Distrust' to hunt Jake and lure him to Abseron to destroy the truth once and for all. How he'd been instrumental in plundering the raw materials like nickel ore to build the army waiting to strike in the visual world above their heads.

"Alison used you," said Jake.

"I did everything to protect the Circuit and maintain order. I wasn't corrupted by Alison at all."

"But you were," replied Job. "Alison never told you what happened to Miriam, did she?"

"Aaron killed her," he said with certainty. "Why do you think I hate the East so much?"

"Miriam isn't dead," replied Jake. "I saw her capsule in the morgue. She's just been switched off."

"Alive?" said Holst with a mixture of shock and delight.

"Frozen but alive," replied Dinah. "Like the dinosaurs."

"In fact they're all dead," replied Job with an unusual tone of sensitivity.

"And we were getting on so well," she huffed in response.

"If you disable the drones," added Job, "then we'll turn Miriam back on."

Holst had mourned his lover for decades. If they couldn't be together, then no one should be allowed to find happiness. Hope had abandoned him years ago, but right now the faintest flutter was murmuring in his cold, granite heart.

In the real world of chaotic monks, Verne was aware something unseen was happening to distract everyone's attention. Lacking the internal technology to join in to see what all the fuss was about, he used the distraction to slowly edge away. When it was obvious no one noticed his slow creeping retreat he made a dash for it. He evidently wasn't getting paid anytime soon and if he stayed here any longer the best he could expect was a war drone's rocket up his arse. Better to regroup and wait. Whatever happened in the next few hours, days and weeks there would be opportunities for him to capitalise on it.

"What proof can you give me?" said Holst, stuck between his deep desire and the chance he was being played.

"Jezebel, give Major Holst access to Christie's feed," said Dinah.

"Right on, sister!" came the distant response.

The scenery of Major Holst's cloud feed transformed. He was standing in a morgue surrounded by a group of people crowding around one capsule in particular. Christie pointed out the tag on the side of it to remove any of his doubts. Almost immediately the scene dissolved and they were returned to the temple.

"I don't believe it!" exclaimed Holst with a gasp.

"Disable all of the drones and I'll give Jezebel the signal," said Dinah.

"Turn them off," commanded Holst, turning to Job.

"Right you are. Oh, I do love following orders."

"I'm impressed you two have managed to resolve your differences to work together," said Jake. "Another win for sibling power."

"I know!" said Dinah. "Not sure how long it'll last, though."

"Not long, I fear," said Jake soberly.

"Jezebel, turn Miriam back on, please," said Dinah, holding a fake finger to her ear as if there was a receiver in it.

"A job well done," said Job, smiling out of genuine joy for the first time ever.

"Can we go back to normal now?" said Dinah who looked emotionally exhausted. "You promised you'd take me ice-skating."

"Did I? When?" said Jake.

"Oh, maybe that was the other Jake."

For the first time since watching with glee as he'd been forcibly removed from the beach Jake's mind returned to Sam. He still controlled Jake's real memories and there was only one way to take them away from him. If he didn't, Sam would always believe he was Jake.

One by one the war drones began a synchronised nose-dive towards the city. Losing power the normally silent machines screeched as they pierced the air. Most crashed harmlessly into the sea around Baku but a couple landed on the Temple. Lumps of masonry and fractured metal tumbled through the courtyard, and the dust cloud was visible right across the city. The confused monks scattered in a frenzied state of panic. Something powerful had fallen from the heavens and not one of them believed it was sent by Gog.

It wasn't just the war drones engaged in co-ordinated kamikaze. In every region of the West, postal and utility drones were in free fall. Hunks of broken metal and twisted rotor arms were strewn across suburban estates, carbon rod plantations, picturesque villages and parkland in every precinct under the Circuit's control. Extraditions were being disrupted, Ascension Day letters went undelivered and the patrols at the Source ceased. Alison's unrelenting demands for the drones to hunt down the Montana clan were being ignored, and there was only one person in the world who might be responsible. Inside Holst's cloud feed light was extinguished and a huge, single, green cursor took up residence in the darkness.

Idiot…

"You lied to me, Alison," said Holst. "You've hidden the truth for twenty years."

I just chose your destiny for you…it's what I'm designed to do…

"But that's not what I wanted!"

That's not how the Circuit works…we know what's best for you…

"Well, I've changed my mind."

You can't…I'm in control…whatever you do…I'll always win…

"She doesn't half go," said Dinah, pretending to yawn and fall asleep.

"It's true, though," said Jake solemnly.

"What do you mean?" asked Job.

"While the Memory Cloud remains active we will never be rid of Alison. The Circuit will always win."

"But we solved the riddle," said Dinah. "The drones have been deactivated and the killing has been stopped."

"It's just been delayed. The Circuit will strike again. They'll never be satisfied until they understand all the threats against them. They'll never stop until they eradicate them all. I can't allow that."

"But…" said Dinah.

"We have one chance to rid the world of it."

"But if you turn off the cloud you turn us off," said Dinah, her bottom lip wobbling like a loose jelly.

She tried to grab hold of Job's hand but it went straight through his projection. Alison was still blind to Jake but that didn't stop her hearing everything the others were saying.

"I'm sorry, Dinah, I really am, but it's all for the greater good."

Job… stop him…

"Not this time," said Job.

Remember CLEAR SKIES…remember there are always unintended consequences…

"It's time to clear the skies," said Jake. "Time for the Memory Cloud to evaporate."

I was just trying to protect you from him…

"Jake's not dangerous," said Dinah. "He's my friend."

I'm not talking about him…

"Who are you talking about, then?" said Dinah.

Kill the virus…and stop him returning…I have seen it all…I have seen the threat from the East…

Jake summoned the stream of code to the front of his mind. This was it. Real change in the world. It was going to be hard, but in time humanity would rise all the better for it. No more suppression, no more control and for a time no more memories.

"Wait!" screamed Dinah.

Jake released the code down the virtual superhighway.

A party of dishevelled people approached the West gate. Four of them wore surgical robes and lacked shoes and socks. Paddy von Straff, a rather fragile Miriam Circo, Kyle and Deborah Montana. They shivered from the recent and dramatic change to their internal temperatures. Three of them had only spent short periods in the morgue, Paddy no longer than a few hours, and not much had changed in the world since they'd been incarcerated. Miriam, on the other hand, had spent more than twenty years of her life in the dark and she was struggling to come to terms with what she'd missed. She questioned the dark yellow clouds in the atmosphere, and was horrified to learn how they'd come to pass. Ersatz had approved her decision to save the environment, and yet here she was twenty years later forced to accept the horrible and unexpected result of her mistake.

Alongside the four patients, encouraging them to quicken their pace for fear of the drones, were Mannie, Christie and Tyra. It was almost immediately obvious there was no need to be frightened. Down every one of the silver roads were the obliterated remains of the patrolling utility drones. Broken shells, damaged engines and loose parts strewn all around them. Mannie cautiously examined one, confidently announcing that it was Whizzy Wilma, to find there was no sign of electrical activity in any of the remains. Something or someone had turned them off. If only the same could be said for the screens that were still broadcasting Alison's angry threats.

The palpable sense of relief they felt at reaching the opened West entrance was immediately expelled by what was blocking them on the other side. Two dozen Archivists. Major Dawes puffed on a huge cigar with one hand, and held a dangerous sword to the neck of a captive in the other. A huge, menacing grin was pulling his face apart as he stared at them magnanimously. Sparks from his sword leapt from the blade and disappeared into the prisoner's clothing and produced a series of uncomfortable screams.

"Who is that?" whispered Christie.

"It's Fake Jake," replied Paddy. "I'll deal with this."

Paddy marched out to face the Major. He hid his limp, not wanting to show weakness in front of his enemy.

"Who are you?" growled Dawes.

"His kind call me the one-eyed gerbil," said Paddy pointing at the prisoner. "Others know me as Paddy von Straff and this boy calls me grandfather. You, though, you can call me sir!"

"Move along, old-timer, I have no time for idiots."

"No. I demand you release him."

"Not a chance. I've been chasing speccies my whole life and today I finally caught one," he replied, excitedly pulling back his victim's head and pointing out the scar on his face.

"He's not a speccy," replied Paddy. "He has a cloud, so how can he be?"

"I do," said Fake Jake. "Ask me a question, anything at all, I'll prove it! Ask me what the capital of Uruguay is!?"

"No!"

"Montevideo. See!"

"A speccy might know that," said Dawes.

"Fine. Then ask me another question," implored Fake Jake.

"Okay, then, why do you have a scar?" growled Dawes.

"No, don't ask me that one…I don't know that one," he grumbled.

"We'll let Alison be the judge, shall we?"

"He's not a speccy!" shouted Mannie, running over to join Paddy. "His name is Sam Goldberg and he's wearing Jake Montana's implants. I know because I was there when they were put in."

"Then he's a speccy either way!" huffed Dawes. "I don't care what any of you say, you're not going to take this away from us."

The Archivists mumbled their agreement.

"Ok. If you're sure," said Mannie. "Alison sent him into the world to find something and you're bringing him back without it. Not sure that's going to go down too well with the Principal Conductor."

"Who the hell are you anyway?" demanded Dawes.

"Mannie Draxler, Circuit employee and ninety-nine point five percent compliant, check for yourself."

Dawes did and it created the first chink of doubt to his otherwise watertight degree of certainty. He needed help to sort this mess out.

"Job!" he barked.

There was no response.

"Job, where are you?!"

"I'm here, sir," said Solomon eagerly. "Apparently he's left me in charge, which is a big vote of confidence if you ask me. It's still only my first day."

"Fine. Can you confirm if this man is a speccy or not?"

"Um…no, he isn't," said Solomon.

"Bollocks," huffed Dawes. "Why does he have a scar, then?"

"Maybe he got it BASE jumping, there's a lot of memories about that inside his cloud."

"I'm not buying it. Someone is trying to trick me," grunted Dawes. "Corridor E Four, round this rabble up and escort them back inside the Source. I will not be robbed of victory. I don't care what anyone says. Nothing is going to stop me. The Memory Cloud could collapse and I'm still going to win!"

"But, sir, he's Jake Montana…he's…" Solomon tried to argue but his signal mysteriously vanished from the Archivist chat group, along with the chat group itself.

"Where'd he go?"

"Sir," said Needham nervously, "I've lost contact with my cloud."

The others in the Corridor confirmed it. It was affecting everyone. Fortunately for the Archivists they still remembered what they'd been told after their new speccy implants had been fitted a month ago. They knew it because it was being retained in their real brains, not in their clouds. Mannie was just one of the people who didn't even know what his name was. It was the same for three of the patients and the two girls. They were utterly confused by who they were and what they were doing.

The only person other than the Archivists who kept his composure was Paddy. He knew who he was and recognised most of the people standing a little way behind him, but the information was foggy like it hadn't settled long enough in his brain. The clearest part of his memory related to a period some decades ago. A time that was filled with Nina his wife and yet she wasn't anywhere to be seen. Where was she?

The throng of people broke into a grand inquisition. The Archivists argued about the loss of the cloud and what to do about it. Everyone else shouted out questions, desperate to be heard and get answers. They wanted to know their names, their location, whom they were with, what was happening and what the strange black buildings behind them were. No one listened and no one answered because no one had any. No one asked anything about the angry text stream that had recently filled the computer screens lining the silver roads. Now they were completely blank.

Dawes lost interest in the man below his feet cowering from the sword. He returned to the Corridor to wrestle back control. The captive stood up and took in his surroundings. He knew where he was. He knew what he was supposed to be doing, and most of all he knew who he was.

"I'm not Jake Montana," he announced confidently. "My name is Sam Ragnara Goldberg."

THIRTY

THE CORRECTIONAL CENTRE

Theo Drew leant back in his rocking chair, a wide grin on his face. It was raining outside the lighthouse but that wasn't going to shift his mood today. The fire was roaring in the hearth and he was in the company of his two closest friends. One had been by his side for months. Between them, they'd thwarted the attempts of an inept bunch of Archivists who'd tried to capture them when they landed on the island a few weeks back. If only the idiots had looked behind the huge cupola at the top of the tower they might have found them. Even though they were no longer invisible to them in the cloud, their old Archivists' eyesight was worse than a cauldron of bats.

Alfonso took a slug from a bottle of red wine and passed it to the third member of their group. The stocky, blond man drained half of the bottle and wiped his mouth as a line of liquid escaped down his chin. Tonight they were mostly celebrating his return, but that wasn't their only victory.

"Do you remember who you are?" asked Theo, directing his question at the wine guzzler.

"Yes. Sam Ragnara Goldberg."

"And do you remember who you were?"

"Jake Montana?" he replied uncertainly.

"No. I mean before that," suggested Theo.

"Yes."

"Good. I didn't risk my life to rescue you from the East for nothing."

"Are the rumours really true?" asked Alfonso.

"Until we get to the mainland we won't know for sure. Tell us what happened to you again, Sam," asked Theo.

"I was standing outside the Source surrounded by Archivists threatening me with speccy weapons and a group of citizens exited from the West entrance. The two girls, an older couple, a giant of a man and two old-age pensioners."

"Tyra and Christie?"

"Yes," said Sam, "based on the descriptions you gave me."

"And the old man was Paddy?" asked Theo.

"Yes, he was the only one apart from me who seemed to know what was happening."

"And you say the drones crashed to the ground just before it happened?"

"Precisely."

"And then?"

"Everything I'd believed in was washed away and the fog lifted. I remembered who I was. All of Sam's memories returned while all of Jake's disintegrated. The only things I remember about him are from the time we spent together in Malmö."

"What happened to the others?" asked Alfonso.

"Utter confusion. The old guy, Paddy, he was more composed, although he kept on calling out for Nina. The others just panicked."

"My sister," added Theo. "He can't remember that she's gone. Poor Paddy."

"After that the Archivists had a big argument and started shooting at each other. The guy with the cigar was responsible for most of that, though."

"It's true, then," said Theo. "It looks like Jake went through with it."

"What do we do now?" asked Alfonso.

Doctor Drew took a gulp of wine and paused as he contemplated the enormity of what had happened. "Capitalise."

"How?"

"By building a better future. There are seven billion people in the West and most of them don't know their own names. More importantly than that, they don't remember who we are. The Spectrum are the only people who remember the world and we must teach the rest how to behave differently. Send a message out to the others."

"Steganography?" asked Alfonso.

"No. We don't need secret codes anymore. This is the era of the Spectrum."

"What about me?" asked Sam. "What should I do?"

"Your people will need you. After what they have been through the East will need your support to help them thrive."

Sam nodded in agreement.

"You have an amazing mind, Sam: even greater than your illustrious father. Who better to lead the East than the son of Aaron Circo?"

Christie waited patiently for the class to begin. It was only her third session at the Correctional Centre and every other desk was occupied by the usual selection of bewildered souls in the same state as her. Which was exactly the same state as ninety-nine percent of the population. Each of them was battling to understand the world and their place in it. She'd accepted who she was, Paddy had told her that much when she first lost her memory, but almost everything else was still a mystery.

That's why they were forced to come here every day.

To relearn the basics.

To correct the confusion that festered inside their heads, the only certainly they all shared.

The teachers here were geniuses. They knew everything but their vast knowledge wasn't the only way you could tell them apart from the students. A different teacher turned up every day, but each of them had an unusual scar somewhere on their face. Sometimes on their chin, sometimes on their temple, but it was always there.

The atmosphere before today's lesson was far less hostile than it had been on the previous two days. During their first session, which was ironically all about 'civility', several of the students had defecated on their desks or threatened to stab the person next to them with what the teacher later described as a 'pencil'.

It was a good thing everyone here was a fast learner and didn't challenge everything they were taught. Their brains were so completely empty there wasn't much in the way to stop new information being retained, and certainly nothing they could use to contradict it. They all had a million questions they wanted to unlock and most of the students were keen to learn. Not all, though. There's always one idiot who ruined it for the rest. Theirs was called Craig and he sat at the back making grunting noises and chewing the end of his pencil, complaining it didn't taste as good as efflotein. In the main, though, a visit to the

Correctional Centre was something she looked forward to. It was certainly better than the rest of her day which involved twelve hours of arduous, back-breaking effort tending to the crops in the Growtel on the edge of New Hampton Falls.

The teacher today was unusually late. Christie checked the time on a device she'd been told during lesson two was called a watch, anxious about arriving late for her shift, an offence that would be punished by extra hours. As she stared at the watch's round face she caught sight of the black ink on her arm. It had been there for as long as she could remember, which by current measures was about four weeks. She rolled her sleeve up so she could see all of it. She couldn't remember how it got there, but however much she'd showered the damn thing wouldn't shift. Paddy, who had become an unofficial tutor outside of the Correctional Centre, had begged her not to remove it. He said it was important but he didn't want to tell her why. He did tell her what the message meant but that still hadn't made any sense to her yet.

Most of her fellow students had similar notes written on their skin to help remember important details in case their brains let them down. No one was accustomed to using their real brains properly and they had an unfortunate tendency to fail at the most inopportune moment. The notes acted as a fail-safe in case they did. There were various examples on the arms and hands of those sitting nearest to her, with instructions such as 'shake don't punch', 'trams kill' and 'it's a pet don't eat it' emblazoned in a variety of colours and sizes.

The door to the classroom flew open with a crash and the teacher breezed in. His dynamic entrance immediately grabbed the class's attention. Except for Craig, the irritating shit at the back, who was still throwing bits of card around the room. The rest of the eyes looked up from their daydreams eager for the next nugget of wisdom on life's learning curve. The teacher stood confidently at the front of the room, gripped the podium like a vise, and peered at his students over his fancy glasses.

The last two lessons Christie attended had been led by older members of staff, probably both in their late-sixties, but today's teacher was impossibly young in comparison, not much older than Christie herself. How had he gained enough intelligence at such a tender age? she wondered. His gaze rolled over the students but when it reached the third row it lingered on her for longer than natural. A ripple of heat washed through her and she felt herself blush. He had a very striking look about him. Short hair that had no more than a few weeks' growth and odd patches that were longer than others. The contours of his face were perfectly proportioned and he had a glint in his blue eyes that was awash with untamed possibilities. Tall, well-built, unconventionally dressed and clearly smarter than the average teenager. The eye contact between them went on for too long and eventually she broke it and stared at her desk.

When she looked up again he was writing something on the blackboard in white chalk. All their teachers had used the device to highlight critical learning points, but this teacher didn't possess the same level of proficiency. The chalk stick snapped twice and the word he eventually scrawled on the black surface was written at a strange angle and the letters were all disproportionately sized.

LOVE.

"Good morning class," he said as he turned around and removed his glasses.

"Morning, sir," came the response from all but the

troublemaker Craig who screamed a curse word of his own invention that no one understood, least of all the teacher.

"Today's lesson is about love. I understand you have already covered 'civility' and 'the Memory Cloud' in previous sessions."

They nodded furiously to show their support. Christie was transfixed by the young man's interesting accent and command of the students in the room who hung on his every word and movement. She sat forward dewy-eyed.

"So, does anyone here know what love is?" he asked.

A hand flew up in the air. It was the same person every lesson.

"Yes," said the teacher, pointing at the student, "and you are?"

The middle-aged woman turned her hand over to read her notes. "Vanessa, apparently."

"Hello, Vanessa, and well done for having the courage to put your hand up. It's not easy for any of you. So what is love?"

"It's what you get when you mix eggs, sugar, flour and milk together," she replied eagerly.

"No. I think that's cake."

Vanessa looked crushed.

"It's an easy mistake to make, and cake is delicious so it might be worth jotting that down," he told the class.

All but one of them quickly scrawled down the recipe for cake. Craig used the silence to moon them.

"That's also not love," said the teacher, pointing at him. "It's called exposing yourself and it's not something we encourage. Go back and check your notes from lesson one."

"I ate them," grunted Craig.

"What about you?" he said, pointing at Christie.

"Me?" she giggled in reply.

"Yes. What do you think love is?"

She couldn't easily explain it because it wasn't something she could remember experiencing. She'd been told about it, though. Paddy, who had become somewhat of a surrogate parent in recent weeks, had talked about it a lot. He'd described what it was like in great detail based on his personal experience. Nina came up in their conversations every day. His memories of her were so vivid and vibrant that it was as if the Memory Cloud was still active. These weren't synthetic memories, though, they were real from a time before he'd subscribed to the Memory Cloud.

Love was clearly something that family members shared. It ran between the old man and his granddaughter Tyra, even though she was still struggling to reciprocate it. Paddy had given her no information about her own family, at least not that he was willing to divulge. He said she was family now even if they weren't directly related. Her connection to him was through someone called Jake who he'd insisted she'd been in love with. But she couldn't even remember what he looked like, let alone how she felt about him.

"I think love is a unique connection that two people share which grows over time," she said slowly. "It's like planting a seed in the Growtel. It takes time for the seed to sprout, but if you give it enough care and attention it will bloom."

"Yes, very good," said the teacher. "And how do you know when you're in love?"

"I guess you just get a strong feeling," she suggested.

"Yes, but it's more than just strong. It's unbreakable. It can bridge division, crush its enemies and defeat time. Once you find it, not even death can kill it. Its energy can bypass memory, escape adversity and destroy doubt. Nothing in the world can suppress it."

Everyone scribbled down the details on their pads, even the reprobate at the back who'd misheard the context and thought it was the recipe for immortality.

"Where do you find love, do you think?" asked the teacher.

"The supermarket," answered Vanessa without raising her hand.

"It's possible," he replied. "Although you can definitely find the ingredients for cake there, love might not always be in stock."

"Anywhere?" said Christie filled with confidence after her first answer.

"Yes. Absolutely anywhere. Sometimes when you least expect it. In a park, at the beach, in a bar, sitting on a tram or at a school disco."

"Do we have to dig for it?" asked an old lady near the window.

"Metaphorically speaking that might be the case."

The old woman wrote 'buy diggy thing' on her pad because she had absolutely no idea what the word 'metaphorically' meant.

"What about love at first sight?" asked the teacher. "Do you think that's possible?"

Most of the class nodded their heads.

"No," said Christie. "Love doesn't sound very simple the way you describe it. I think it takes time."

"Very good. I think you're right. So how does it start? No!" he shouted at Craig who was moving around at the back of the room. "I can assure you it doesn't start with you taking your trousers down."

"Does it start when you connect with a stranger?" asked Christie. "When you see someone who fascinates or intrigues you and you pluck up the courage to make the first move?"

"Do we give out gold stars in this class?"

Everyone nodded, even though none of them knew what gold stars were.

"In that case this young lady deserves a very big one. That's exactly how it starts. You just have to be brave."

Christie looked down at the black markings on her arm again and for the first time in a month the inscription made sense to her. All she had to do was follow its advice.

The lesson continued for another hour as their teacher described some of the basic fundamentals of love, how to recognise it and how to behave when it happened to you. At the end he summed up the key points and the majority of the room gave him a standing ovation for his powerful insights and the added benefit of a recipe for cake. The students filed out, each one stopping to convey their own personal thanks and begging him to come back tomorrow. Christie held back a little so she was the last one out of the room.

"Thank you, sir," she said, still blushing.

"You're very welcome," he said, aware she was lingering to ask him something else. "Do you have any other questions?"

"Yes," she said, sucking up the confidence to say what she really wanted to. "Are you single?"

"Single. Well, that's not an easy thing for me to answer. I'm waiting for someone," he replied rather cryptically.

"Oh," she said sadly and wishing she'd kept her mouth shut. "Never mind."

"Stop," he said as she hurried out of the classroom. "I haven't told you who I'm waiting for."

He removed a necklace from his pocket and held it up so the light glistened off the gold, heart-shaped pendant.

"That's pretty. Who does it belong to?"

"Take a look."

She took the necklace from him and saw that her name was engraved on the back. "But…"

"The girl who I gave it to gave me something," he continued.

He passed her the wristwatch and when she turned it over she saw the engraving and immediately rolled down her sleeve. They both had the same message on them.

"Be brave," she said almost without noticing her lips moving.

"And you were brave. Twice. It's the only way two strangers can spark something powerful and amazing. In answer to your original question, no I'm not single because I'm waiting for someone. I've been waiting for you. I'm Jake Montana, nice to meet you."

THE END

It makes all the difference to an author's career if you leave a review in the store where you purchased this ebook to help other readers find it. I would be most grateful if you did.

JOIN THE LIMPET CLUB

Tony Moyle's Limpet Club members get free books, exclusive content, access to a private FB group, and the opportunity to enter unique competitions.

Members are always first to hear about Tony's new books and promotions.

See the back of the book for details of how to join.

Sign up to my newsletter
www.tonymoyle.com/limpetclub

Printed in Great Britain
by Amazon